SABABA

A NOVEL BY

YAMIN LEVY

BERWICK COURT PUBLISHING
CHICAGO, IL

Most of the characters, scenes and dialogue in *Sababa* are the complete creation of the author and entirely fictional. Certain historically significant people and events were used as inspiration for the story, but it is a work of fiction.

Berwick Court Publishing Company
Chicago, Illinois
http://www.berwickcourt.com

Publisher's Cataloging-In-Publication Data
(Prepared by The Donohue Group, Inc.)

Names: Levy, Yamin.
Title: Sababa : a novel / by Yamin Levy.
Description: Chicago, IL : Berwick Court Publishing, [2016]
Identifiers: LCCN 2016950053 | ISBN 978-1-944376-07-9 |
   ISBN 978-1-944376-06-2 (ebook)
Subjects: LCSH: Soldiers--Israel--History--21st century--Fiction. |
   Kidnapping--Israel--History--21st century--Fiction. | Alexander, the
   Great, 356-323 B.C.--Fiction. | Rape victims--Jerusalem--History--
   To 1500--Fiction. | Maccabees--History--To 1500--Fiction. | Jewish
   fiction. | LCGFT: Historical fiction.
Classification: LCC PS3612.E99 S33 2016 (print) | LCC PS3612.E99
   (ebook) | DDC 813/.6--dc23

Prologue

Dimona, Israel
December 25, 2005
Eighth Day of Hanukkah

HANUKKAH IS ALWAYS FESTIVE IN Israel. Leon and Maya Samet, along with their two children, celebrate the holiday as a cultural, historical event that hails Jewish pride and patriotism. It being the last of the ancient historical holidays, they feel it has relevance to their lives in Israel and their nation's struggle for peace. The Samets pride themselves in not celebrating Hanukkah like everyone else. They have their own traditions. Most other families light candles every night for eight nights. The Samets only light their Hanukkah menorah on the eighth night. They also celebrate the holiday alone. No extended family. No guests. Just the four of them.

This year is special. Lior, their eldest son, has just finished his basic training in the elite Givati Brigade of the Israeli Defense Forces. The IDF gave him two days off for the holiday. He left his base early in the morning and arrived at Kiryat Gat bus station around 10 a.m. Shortly after, he found a ride to the southern city of Dimona.

Maya sees him approaching from her kitchen window, walking

toward their home, carrying his packed military duffle bag, his M16 and a bottle of water. Even from a distance he looks exhausted but strong. His neatly rolled sleeves and wristband draw attention to his thin but muscular forearms and accentuate his Middle Eastern December tan. *How unflattering his narrow shoulders make his uniform look*, she thinks, *but then again, they all look beautiful in their uniforms.*

Noa, Maya's 16-year-old daughter, separates her right ear from the headphone and yells, "Ima, have you heard from Lior?"

"Yes, he is down the street. I am looking at him right now." Maya always waits for her kids to enter the house before greeting them, a tradition she adopted from her grandmother. A tradition Noa wants nothing to do with. She bursts out of her bedroom, opens the front door, runs out onto the walkway and leaps into Lior's arms. Maya is amazed by how he keeps his balance and is able to carry his bag, weapon and Noa through the front door.

"Welcome home."

"Shalom, Ima," he says, followed by a kiss. Lior drops his bag on the kitchen floor and crashes on the couch in the living room.

Lior's last thoughts before he enters into a dream state are mostly about Moran. *Should I call her? Probably not—she's busy with school and with her family. She probably doesn't want to hear from me.*

His father wakes him up just in time to light the Hanukkah menorah. Waking up is one of the least pleasant parts of basic training. Even a father's loving voice can startle a soldier into a flash of anxiety. He realizes where he is, spots his M16 leaning against the wall, and takes a deep breath. There is so much he would like to share but can't. His parents are loving but a bit distant. If it weren't for Noa, there would be no drama in their home.

Someone must have taken off his boots while he slept—something he truly appreciates. He has no sense of how long he was on the couch. The last time he looked at his watch was 10 a.m., when he jumped into the car. It was now close to 5 p.m. Dinner smells great, but he smells like hell. He is grateful for his family. He is happy to be home.

Maya selects colorful candles for the occasion. She places the gifts for Lior and Noa on the table right next to the gift Leon has for her. Leon, with a warm smile on his face, says, "Lior, can you give us the honor of lighting the candles for the family?" As Lior does with most requests, he complies.

Leon hands him a lit candle and a prayer book. He looks at his parents, at Noa, and reads:

> For the miracles, the mighty deeds, wonders and saving acts You, God, wrought for our ancestors and for us today—we thank You.

> In the days of Matityahu, ben Yochanan, the High Priest from the town of Chashmona, and his sons the Maccabees, when the wicked Hellenic government rose up against Your people, Israel, to make them forget their Torah and violate Your Mitzvoth—You in Your abundant love stood by them in time of their distress. You waged their battle, defended their rights. You delivered the mighty into the hands of the weak, the many into the hands of the few, the wicked into the hands of the righteous, those who observe Your Torah. You brought about a great deliverance for Your people and Israel then and today.

> Your children purified Your temple, kindled the Menorah and instituted these eight days of Hanukkah to give thanks and praise to Your great name.

"Happy Holiday, Abba, Ima, Noa," he says, giving each of them a kiss. Noa gives him a big hug.

After his shower, dinner and the opening of the presents, Lior goes back to the short prayer he had read. It speaks about miracles then and today. It describes warriors of old called Maccabees and their leader, the Priest Matityahu, who fought the mighty Greek empire and prevailed. He could not help but think of his people's struggle for national security, the pursuit of peace and the damn uniform he has to wear.

1

Jerusalem
Outside the Walled City
332 BCE

YAEL PICKS THE GRAPE BLOSSOMS one by one—pink, lilac, yellow, green—making room for them between her fingers like a small girl gathering a bouquet for her mother. However, Yael is not a small girl. The last thing she wants to do is give a gift to her mother. Yael is almost 15 now and, though she loves both of her parents, she feels as if they hold a rope around her neck, leading her and restraining her as if she is no more than a goat. They might be keeping her for the milk she will provide one day or, she thinks with a flush of rage, taking her to the slaughter. Her mother, in particular, makes her feel as if she has been pulled, pushed and crammed into a tight space. Since Yael was 12 and her monthly cycle began, her mother has kept her very close, not to cuddle as when she was younger (which Yael sometimes, in spite of herself, still yearns for), but to watch her carefully, wanting to know everything—where Yael has been, what she has done, with whom she has spent time. Lately the world has grown more confusing and complicated to Yael. It seems that her mother has become less playful, that her eyes have narrowed with constant worry

4

or suspicion. *What have I done to earn such distrust?*

Today, thank the Almighty above, Yael has managed to break free, at least for a few hours. She has come to the farthest part of the vineyard outside the walls, where she has been forbidden to go, and she feels like she has retreated to a tiny slice of heaven. Alone among the arbors, she is free. For an instant she imagines herself beautiful, her long, dark braid hinting at auburn in the bright sun. The air is pungent with grapes. Unable to resist, Yael puts down her little arrangement of flowers so she can reach out to pick a handful of the enticing globes. Eagerly she bites down, separating the fruit with her teeth and tongue, spitting the seeds out onto the ground. She knows she shouldn't be pulling off grapes that are not meant to be harvested. This is a fallow year and this field must be left to replenish the soil. Nonetheless, she doesn't hesitate; she feels a wave of pleasure at her small sin, savoring the purple juice in her mouth, remembering to wipe her lips with her hands, to suck every last bit of purple stain from her fingers so no one will know.

Today is a special day—Yael is sure of it. Something amazing will happen. Maybe it already has. Yael feels graceful in a way she doesn't remember feeling since she was a young child: her arms outstretched, spinning and swirling around and around her admiring relatives. That was so long ago, when she had the confidence of a smaller beloved child. In the years that followed, she'd felt awkward and ungainly like a camel, all knobs and patches. But now, today, she marvels at the miracles of her body. She is almost a woman. A new life will begin for her soon. After all, Yael is a *Kohen-et* on both sides. Both her parents are descendants of priestly families. She has always lived in the Priestly Quarters, but it has never been as important to her as it is now. When she is presented for marriage, she will have great value, and now, today, for the first time, she feels truly worthy. Like her mother, she will marry a Kohen as well. The priestly dynasty will continue through their offspring. God has plans for her, and she has dreams for herself. She is an important part of her people's history.

Until recently, she had only one remarkable feature: her large, unwavering eyes, dark brown, long-lashed, intense. Everyone comments on them, the way they hold their focus in a tight grip, pupils large and bottomless. Her father once said that Yael could stare down a lion. But now her eyes are not her only noticeable feature. Her body has filled out, her hips are padded with soft curves, her breasts have rounded out under the keen awareness of her nipples. She slides her hands inside her dress to stroke one breast. The mound has risen like warm dough, the way her mother's stomach rose before the birth of Penina, Yael's youngest sister. *Where does this extra flesh come from?* She loves her breasts, loves seeing how they draw the eyes of village boys who peek at them and quickly look away with both longing and shame. Even the men avert their eyes to avoid temptation. She used to blame herself, some mistake she made. Now she knows better.

For a long moment in the ripe vineyard, Yael is lost in reverie, oblivious to her surroundings except for the bright sun. A flash of dark, an unexpected shadow to her right, brings her to quick attention. Yael turns to her right, but nothing is there. *It must be my eyes playing tricks*, she thinks, *after all this time in the hot sun.* Nonetheless, she is a bit unsettled, the shadow a smudge on her otherwise idyllic afternoon. *It could have been an animal, if it were anything at all.* Now there is a rustle in the underbrush. Though she scans the brambles with her ferocious eyes, it's hard to focus in the density of tangles. Turning back, she muses, *Anyway, I should be getting back.* The thought provides a modicum of comfort. *Go home. Be a dutiful daughter.*

Suddenly another shadow in the periphery of her right vision, this time it is unmistakable. A very brief blockage of full light but too high up to be an animal. This time she doesn't have a chance to look around. Someone grabs her from behind, strong arms across her chest, one leg wrapped hard around her calves. Her fear is less a shrill cry than an abrupt yelp of sharp surprise. Before she makes another sound, the shadow she had seen emerges from the right: a man, a foreigner, it appears from his garb, a soldier.

To her dismay, she watches not one, but two men approach. She feels a wave of nausea, part fear and part revulsion.

Such unclean men, so alien, she thinks. One edges closer to her—his hair unwashed, his tunic gray with grime. His dirty teeth clinched in intense focus. He holds a sharp knife in his hand, more statement than threat. He does not menace her, but his lips are thin and grim with determination. As he draws near, Yael sees him stash his dagger into a small sheath on his belt, apparently feeling it is unnecessary for the task at hand. She is, after all, an unarmed girl already tightly held against her will. She now stares at the eagle on his shield, its beady, unforgiving eyes. *What does it mean, this symbol of predation? Who is the predator? Who is the prey? Why has God created either one?*

The shining brass plate of his armor nearly blinds her, throwing glints like unexpected sparks directly at her eyes. The soldier clamps a hand over her mouth and with his other hand begins to wrap her in wide swaths of cloth. Her whole body trembles now. Her legs feel numb. The fabric scratches her tender skin. As she is wrapped, the man behind her loosens his hold and winds a rope around the cloth, binding her. Yael cannot move or speak or see but recognizes she is not in pain. Oddly, the men are not too rough with her, just very firm, almost parental. She feels she is an animal they've come to tame, not kill. Yet, she also has some vaguely apprehensive understanding of what taming entails for young virgins.

Yael's nose is the only part of her face exposed. Through it, she takes the world in as she can: the heavy, rancid perspiration of the men; a foreign spice that permeates the cloth they've wrapped her in; the presence of a horse. Through the cloth, she hears the horse stamp down the earth nearby. Her captives lift her, not exactly gently, but with care, laying her across the horse's broad back. To be deposited so abruptly on her stomach takes the wind out of her. She gasps for air as they tie her down. Suddenly it hits her. *They're taking me away!* she thinks. Her trembling increases. Terror plunges down her throat like a stone she's swallowed whole. She's crying now, the cloth sticking to her dampening eyes.

One of the men speaks. Though Yael cannot understand his language, she thinks he sounds pleased with himself. The other man seems to agree. She assumes they are talking about her. She surmises they feel they have done a good job in capturing her. *But what do they want with me? A ransom from my father? I wonder how much I am worth to them, to anybody. Where are they taking me? What were they doing in the vineyard? Did they plan this or did they just see me and decide to take me with them?* She curses at the way this will confirm all of her mother's unspoken anxieties and fears.

In fact, the conversation between her two captors is about her. One of the soldiers smiles at the other with satisfaction.

"Ho Megas," *the Great One,* was the way they refer to their general, Alexander the Great. "He will be very pleased with us. Not only will we bring him news he wants to hear, but we will bring him an unexpected tro-phy—a pretty young virgin with sparkling eyes to do with as he pleases." He pauses and breathes deeply in satisfaction. "The gods favored us today. There will be rewards for us in this."

His friend smiles back. "We have done well. Your idea was a fine one. We will be heroes when we return."

Yael feels sick thinking of how she was admiring her own body. *Is that what they want?* She longs to tell them that she isn't really beautiful.

"There are lovelier girls in the capital, especially Tamar, so much more voluptuous than me," Yael mumbles to herself with quivering lips. Immediately she feels guilty. Offering up her girlfriend as a sacrifice. Imagine!

Did I make this happen? I never really wanted to go far, to leave my parents, to be alone. Is the Master of the Universe punishing me for the un-clean thoughts?

As the horse begins to move and her body bounces, her mind stut-ters out a prayer: *Forgive me for disobeying my parents. Forgive me for being vain. Forgive me for eating the grapes. Forgive me for stroking my breast. Please, please forgive me.*

I don't know what I'm thinking, she thinks apologetically, *I don't know what I'm thinking.*

Kerem Shalom, Israel
Border Patrol
June 2006

LIOR ENJOYS AN UNUSUAL MOMENT of stillness. A sense of peace comes over him. He breathes it in and lets it out, pure gratitude. He awakens from a surprisingly satisfying sleep, especially considering his position: slumped over, being jostled in a moving armored vehicle with very little shock absorption. It must be near dawn by now. He doesn't know what brought about this sense of almost euphoric tranquility, but wherever it came from, he recognizes it for the gift it is. He feels it roll deep in his bones, along the sinews of his thighs, around the tendons of his arms, his neck. He feels it ease the complex convolutions of his brain. Even his blood flows smoothly, every corpuscle in sync, streaming along his being to some unseen ocean, maybe God. Vaguely, distantly, he wonders at the strangeness of this last thought. How odd that he, a confirmed nonbeliever, should imagine God in this miserable and dusty desert, but he lets the word pass through him undisturbed. *Who knows where thoughts come from anyway?*

Lior doesn't look at his watch, but much later he remembers this peaceful moment as having occurred only minutes before the incident. The contrast between his sense of calm and the things that came next somehow made each sensation more graphic.

He rides in the Alpha AV, lulled by the latest Kobi Peretz song on the radio, feeling in tune with the hum of the motor, the bounce of the seats and the nearness of his buddies. Omri, with one booted leg extended as he drives; Shalti, as always, snoring as he sleeps; even Dudu, that pain in the ass, tolerable when, at rare times like this, he's quiet. Lior knows enough to appreciate such moments of peace, how rare and short-lived they always are. As his grandmother used to tell him, "Enjoy peace when it comes to you—it won't stay long until you're dead."

Each time she said it, he felt both thrilled and fearful at the implications. Even as a young child, Lior knew what she was talking about. "Hush!" his mother would scold her mother-in-law. "You're scaring the boy." But he relished the slightly forbidden words. He knew he was being told an important secret.

Remembering his grandmother's caution now, he wonders how long this sweet sensation will last. Even as he wonders, he feels it slipping away. Anxiety, his unwelcome companion for most of his time in the Israeli Army, is back. He cannot ignore or dismiss it. The best he can do is pretend it is a worried friend he is trying to calm. His mind becomes a maze of voices and perspectives, some urging caution while others preach peace.

Still, bumping along, Lior reminds himself that they *are* protected (after all, they are trained soldiers, armed with the most sophisticated weaponry an army can buy). Lulled back into a kind of reverie by the rumble of the motor, he remembers something he hasn't thought of in years—an early memory? A dream? Whatever it was, Lior visualized a scene late one night as his family was returning home from *Yam HaMelach,* the Dead Sea. Lior was a young boy sitting in the back seat of his parents' Skoda Octavia. It too could have used some work on its shocks. As tonight, he was safely enclosed, watching lights and shadows sliding past the open window frame. He remembers the hot breeze brushing along his cheeks, against his forehead, and through his hair. Although it wasn't allowed, he'd snuck his hand outside the window, felt the wind push knowingly against his palm—or was he holding back the wind? In any case, the sense of oneness with the wind, and subsequently the power of the universe, was undeniable. The murmur of his parents' voices in the front seat blurred into the music to which some tiny portion of his body swayed. No longer belted to the car, no longer tied to family, not even tethered to his body, he felt himself let loose above the earth, way up among the migrant species of the stars.

He had since struggled to replicate the sensation, often drifting off to sleep while trying to escape the borders of his bed, even the boundaries of his bedroom. It became an almost nightly ritual. How could he have forgotten? If he concentrated and let himself go, sometimes he could experience that same amazing freedom he had felt in his parents' car. At times, he was able to feel himself float up off the bed; once he'd even floated out the bedroom window. He dubbed it *la'uf*, flying away, and it became a part of his childhood repertoire—private, magical, embarrassing. He never told anyone.

How strange to remember all this now. Here, bumping across this forlorn piece of desert near the Gaza Strip in an AV with other soldiers, serving time in an army whose ideals he doesn't embrace. Many of his peers feel similarly disillusioned, though most of them *look* a bit less prone to naivety.

At 19, Lior still has a baby face, still looks the way he did in middle school, except for his elongated arms and legs. His father calls him long and lean, to put a positive slant on his skinny build, but Lior knows the truth. In the mirror he sees a stereotypical scholarly Jewish boy: dark, bookish, with deep-set eyes that correctly intimate his docile demeanor. The demeanor that destined him to be one of Chagall's floating grooms—slender, pale, almost amorphous.

Enlisting in the Army stirred plenty of ambivalence in Lior. In the end, he'd felt there was no choice. Enlisting is what patriotic and decent Israelis do. Being the grandson of Avigdor Cohen, one of Israel's national military heroes, pretty much sealed his fate. Truth is, he never relished the thought of leaving his parents, wearing a bulky uniform, or carrying a weapon. Particularly, he never wanted to leave Moran, the girl of his dreams.

Now fear sneaks back in, a tiny rustle of discomfort like a mouse rustling in the pantry of his mind. Why should he have to be here? He, the good boy, the good student, the good son! At least the decent son. What has he done to deserve being put in harm's way? What if he never gets home? Why have his parents, who always taught him to be kind, to be non-combative, let this happen to him? What if Grandma's words prove prophetic and the next peace he knows turns out to be death?

A sudden stop of the vehicle almost alarms him.

"What the hell. Why are we stopping?"

Omri answers him matter-of-factly, "Dudu has to take a leak."

"No surprise there," says Shalti. "He must've guzzled a gallon of water last night."

With these words—could they be more mundane, innocuous?—the world explodes.

Terror.

A noise so huge it is unbearable; Lior's eardrums vibrate as if about to burst and then, for minutes, he cannot hear at all. Maybe they shattered. A flash of fire in a ball of smoke, metal fragments rummaging the air for targets. No, not the air, the black soot that has now become the atmosphere. The enemy are golems, black and faceless, shouting words that must be curses, not ordinary curses but demon curses, the kind with power to cast awful spells.

Lior is outside the Jeep now, being pulled hard, so hard he thinks his shoulder socket has been yanked apart. *Is that the right terminology? No. Out of socket*, he thinks. But that phrasing seems too organized and fixable to describe what he now feels. The pain possesses him. Sound returns. A scream he cannot bear to hear comes like a siren from some vocal apparatus he never knew he had. *Was it a gunshot near his head?* He thinks his brains have been pulverized, can feel them splash, disgusting bloody innards on his face, his chest. But those are not his brains. They are the brains of Dudu, whose head is now a mass of blotched red meat. As Dudu falls to the ground, a quick illumination shows his bottom half, pathetically intact, his fly still open for that fateful piss.

He sees his weapon, the loaded M16 at arm's length. He remains paralyzed, unable to reach for it.

Lior tries to look around for Shalti, for Omri, but only sees a fire burning in the blackness. He hears a moaning, almost like the bleating of an anguished sheep at slaughter, but cannot tell the direction from which it comes. For all he knows, it may be coming from him. Beyond the blinding tearing agony of his shoulder, he feels other pains, in his calf, on his side, as if nails have been hammered deep into his flesh. He thinks these may be shards of glass but finds out later that they are pieces of shrapnel, propelled into his flesh by the force of the explosion.

Absurdly, Lior remembers a doctor once asking him after a sports injury to rate his pain on a scale of one to ten. What would he say to that doctor now? In his delirium, Lior envisions a balance scale piled high with weightlifting discs, the scale collapsing under the pounds of metal bulk. There are no words or numbers to describe this pain; it is immeasurable. Lior feels the weight compress him to the ground. He is aware that it is not only the pain that has knocked him to the ground. Someone or something is pulling at his hair as if preparing him for scalping; another force has lifted his feet off the ground. Vaguely, he is aware he is being carried by black marauders. A part of him surrenders; the child inside him momentarily believes that they are taking him to medical assistance. In a tremor of hope, he yields. His body relaxed for a split second, Lior fades quickly into oblivion. His captors wonder if he has died or simply passed out.

When he wakes up, he is enclosed and unable to move. He is trapped in blinding, deafening, cataclysmic pain. And the smell is horrific. The stench of excrement and blood, and now, as he grows sickened, vomit too. He gags and spits. Beyond the vomit, mucus and blood, he feels harsh grains of sand coating his mouth. *Did they force me to eat sand?* He shudders, then shivers, not sure if he is chilled with terror or burning with fever. Probably both. It occurs to him that they put sand in his mouth to stop him from screaming. He thinks he remembers being hit across the back of the neck and being told to "shut up!" (this much Arabic he knows). With this memory, other pains come calling—anguish on his scalp, his neck, the inside of his mouth.

He is confined, that much is clear. Inside a container, legs bent at the knees. He wonders if they have buried him alive. Before his terror is reactivated, an instant of coherence fills him with rage. *The fucking no-good sons of bitching bastards! They could have had the decency to kill me first!* The wave of anger uses up what little consciousness he has and he is out again. This time, there is no one with him to even wonder if he has died or passed out.

At some point, he comes to his senses again. The pain is still there in all its force. It is all encompassing. Lior is now also aware of motion. With a sinking heart, he realizes he must be in a moving vehicle, locked in the trunk. In some strange way this seems even more awful than if he'd been buried alive. Now he is still in their power. At least underground the torture would be finite. He has no way of anticipating just what horrors await him once the car stops, once he is retrieved as their trophy and outlet for hatred. *The golems must be Hamas. How did they get there without being observed?* He, Shalti, Omri and Dudu always took turns being lookouts. Say what you will about Dudu, whose turn it was tonight (or was it last night?), he is as alert as a panther.

Not anymore, Lior remembers, realizing Dudu's brains and blood are still on his shirt. The thought makes him retch again. Then he feels a strange wave of jealousy for Dudu. This is over for him now. He feels nothing. If only the pain would stop or just slow down. If only he could stretch out his legs. If only he could get some of this stench off. As the car bounces over some poorly maintained surface, it doesn't seem to Lior that any of these things will ever happen again.

Like gophers, he thinks, *they must have tunneled through to catch us by surprise. But why did they take me? Where are Omri and Shalti? Are they dead too? Will they come after me? Would I go after them? What will these people do with me? Why didn't they kill me? What use am I to them?* The questions make him dizzy. *Use up too much energy? Too much air?* This last thought makes no sense, he knows, since he is not asking the questions aloud. Yet somehow he feels there is only enough air in this space to breathe carefully.

Don't think, he thinks, *don't think.*

3

Tel Aviv, Israel
Israel Defense Forces Command General Headquarters
Directorate of Military Intelligence (Aman)
June 25, 2006
6:25am

"GET THE SHABAK ON THE phone immediately," Major General Moti Rachmani screams over the pandemonium that flared up that morning.

Shabak is a Hebrew acronym for *Sherut HaBitachon HaKlali*, the Israeli Internal Security Agency. Rachmani, the head of Aman Military Intelligence, wants as much information as possible on his desk before the briefing with the prime minister. The Internet is already buzzing with news of an ambush on Israeli soldiers near the Gaza border. What does this mean for relations between Israel and Gaza? How might Israeli leaders respond? It is a bonanza for newsmen and aficionados of international intrigue.

"The fact that a soldier is missing means nothing until he is found—dead or alive. The possibility of a soldier kidnapped will not be considered until we have factual confirmation," Moti asserts to the two security attaches standing in front of his desk.

This confirmation is more than a mere formality. It will prove essential to whatever steps are to be taken. The IDF has a stated code of honor that no soldier is ever left behind. If soldiers defend Israel, everything possible will be done to bring each and every one of them back. Rachmani needs to know how his resources are going to be allocated, what sort of operations he needs to plan for.

The IDF classifies soldiers as MIA if they are, or might still be, alive. This is distinct from those who died in battle but whose burial place is unknown. The latter are given the designation, PBU, an acronym that is at once both optimistic and pessimistic: **P**lace of **B**urial **U**nknown. The military's label presumes burial at least, when, in many of these instances, soldiers' bodies are treated much less respectfully. Rachmani has always viewed that label—PBU—as a bit too euphemistic.

Buried in a place that is unknown. "More like cut up and passed around like some sort of trophy for those barbaric shits. Whatever. PBU is the label. Fight the fights you can win," Rachmani mutters to himself.

Israel is the only country in the world where a PBU designation has religious connotations. As a result, the only person authorized to determine the status of a PBU is the chief rabbi of the IDF. He makes his determination based on evidence presented to him by fellow soldiers who fought on the battlefield. The rabbi's verdict certainly has emotional implications for grieving families. But it has many practical implications as well. It determines the *agunah* status of the woman married to the PBU.

An *agunah* in Judaism may never remarry unless the rabbi asserts that her husband is dead, for fear that said beloved may reappear to find his wife remarried and adulterous. Since 1948, the IDF has listed only fifty-eight soldiers as PBU on the battlefield and the sixty-nine crewmen of the submarine Dakar that disappeared at sea in 1968. After years of bureaucratic messes, the IDF now has a special department that handles MIAs. After the Yom Kippur War, more than 1,200 men were initially listed as MIA. The special MIA agency, in concert with the Army rabbis and some of Israel's top professionals, worked countless hours reviewing POW charts, visiting hospitals, and conducting innumerable inquiries and reconnaissance missions behind enemy lines. After all that effort, they brought the number down to nineteen. The chief rabbi ruled that all nineteen had fallen in action and each one was reclassified as PBU.

Similarly, at the end of Operation Peace for Galilee, forty-three soldiers were classified as MIA. After much work and research, the IDF could not confirm the whereabouts of seven men. Those names were designated PBU. Their widows were given freedom to both grieve and re-marry.

"Make sure the IDF gets to the homes of the soldiers before the next news report. No mother or father should find out the fate of their child from those lecherous newscasters. Leeches with microphones..." Rachmani calls out as the men begin to leave his office.

"Rivkin is on the phone, sir," Rachmani's secretary, Nicole, announces through the intercom on his desk.

Who the fuck is Rivkin? Rachmani wonders as he races through the catalogue of people who could get in touch with him so easily. Five departments run through his mind, he remembers that Rivkin was the new head of Shabak.

"Rivkin, Shabak?" he calls to his secretary.

"Yes, sir."

That damn place is a revolving door, he thinks as he picks up the receiver.

"Rivkin, what do you know about the ambush this morning?"

"Well, sir. We have two dead soldiers, one critically injured and one missing in action," Rivkin responds.

"Missing for sure? There is no room for error here."

"Yes, I am in communication with ground troops as we speak."

"Who's taking responsibility?"

"Hamas." Rivkin mutters the name Rachmani very much expected to hear. It is nonetheless an eternal disappointment. This group of ragtag sons of bitches is like a thorn in your foot that never goes away.

"How the hell did they get through?"

"The tunnels, sir—the tunnels inside the Palestinian homes."

"Rivkin! We've known about those tunnels for over six months. They must be over 600 meters long. Why the hell have they not been blown up yet?"

"I don't have a good answer to that question," came the honest response.

"Fuck, Rivkin—do your damn job or go back to picking flowers on the kibbutz—shit! We've known about those tunnels for a hell of a long time. It's a lot harder to explain how the enemy found success when their methods are plastered all over fucking YouTube. They are advertising this shit, Rivkin. And you can't do anything about them? All of you are supposed to be certified tough men, right?"

"Getting to them is not easy, sir."

"The prime minister is on line two, sir," came the secretary's voice, this time from the other room not the intercom.

Rachmani picks up the other phone and hangs up on Rivkin.

"Good morning, Mr. Prime Minister. I expect to be in your office within two hours."

"Give me something now, Rachmani. What happened?"

"We have two dead soldiers, one in critical condition and one is missing."

"The missing one, the missing soldier... kidnapped?" The prime minister skips straight to the question that is going to involve the most political fallout. Israel is in a constant state of readiness. A couple of dead soldiers in a skirmish is not going to cause a huge problem. Neither will the news of an injured one. But a kidnapped soldier on videotape for all to see in a digital world... talk about a PR nightmare.

"Very possible he was kidnapped. Yes, sir."

"Shit! Have the families been notified?"

"I believe so."

"Get over here immediately. And no media on your end until we figure out what our lines are going to be on this." Rachmani hears the prime minister's voice drift away from the telephone, calling out, "Get me Goldwasser right away." The phone line goes dead.

As Rachmani makes his way to the prime minister's residence, the 7 a.m. news radio reporter states what he calls "the facts as we have them now":

"This morning, at 5:20 a.m., in the course of an infiltration and attack by terrorists from Hamas in the area of Kibbutz Kerem Shalom, an IDF officer and soldier were killed, a soldier was wounded, and a fourth soldier has been presumably abducted by the terrorists. The soldiers killed have been identified as Private David Dudu Halprin and Cpl. F.C. Shaltiel Shlomi; the wounded soldier's name is Cpl. Omri Barlev. Cpl. Lior Samet is missing in action."

Seldom did so many reporters and newscasters appear so early in the morning. The prime minister stood behind the podium flanked by two Israeli flags and his press secretary, and began:

> The State of Israel considers the Palestinian Authority and the Hamas government to be fully responsible for the Kerem Shalom attack that took place early this morning and for the fate of abducted soldier Cpl. Lior Samet. Palestinian Authority Chairman Mahmoud Abbas has all the necessary resources to ensure Cpl. Samet's release and safe return to Israel. I call on him to act immediately to resolve this crisis and to avoid any unnecessary escalation of this conflict. We expect an unconditional release of Cpl. Lior Samet. Israel will not negotiate with terrorists.
>
> I call on the international community to use its influence, vis-à-vis Chairman Abbas, to obtain the release of Cpl. Samet and to make clear to the Palestinian Authority the grave consequences of its failure to release him safe and sound. At this time, I have nothing more to add.

With that, the prime minister stepped away from the podium and the communications team took over.

"Excuse me, Mr. Prime Minister, before you leave," Michael Knafo, Knesset reporter for Channel 2, called out. "Just one question." The prime minister stopped and turned around. "How do you see this conflict resolved?"

"Abbas, Abu Mazen, is the only hope in resolving this conflict successfully," the prime minister responded and went on his way.

Mahmoud Abbas, also known as Abu Mazen, became president of the Palestinian National Authority in January of 2005. Abbas was born in the mystical city of Safed in the Northern Galilee region of Israel prior to the declaration of the State of Israel. In 1948, he and his family fled to Syria. Unlike his predecessor, Yasser Arafat, Abbas called for an end to violence and publicly stated on Arab television that "The use of arms has been damaging and should end."

Abbas became the darling of Western media when he fired his own security forces after Palestinians attacked a Jewish settlement in February of 2006. Now, less than five months later, comes another attack by Palestinian jihadists. The difference is that this time, they are holding an Israeli soldier. The prime minister knew Abbas was watching and he hoped that Abbas would respond the same way he did in February and immediately return the abducted soldier.

In his office, the prime minister wants answers. Very few are making sense. One layer of this crisis should have been clear to him from the beginning. But… it was a common name. After issuing his statement, as he reclines in his leather wingback chair, he mutters absently to his secret service deputy, "What's the deal with this kidnapped soldier? What do we know about him?"

"Well, as his name suggests and most important to our purposes, he's Avigdor Cohen's grandson."

"Holy shit!" says the prime minister. "How did I not put that together?"

"Sorry, sir. I should have made sure. I just figured someone had told you, or that you reasoned it out," the deputy replies.

"Get Avigdor on the phone immediately!"

4

Lower Galilee
333 BCE

THE SUN IS GENTLY SETTING in the western desert sky. As the shadows of his men, his tents, and his horses lengthen, Alexander becomes increasingly impatient. *Where can they be?* He taps his palm against his thigh, almost as if in rhythm to the sound of music only he can hear, a habit picked up recently that both soothes and excites him, as if he is tapping out the rhythm of his march to destiny. He knows he is already a great leader, a warrior, a hero, the conqueror of most of the Persian Empire, a god in the eyes of his subjects. His teacher had focused a great deal on gods and half-gods, those weaker deities, as they were depicted in the poems of Homer. Destiny has reserved for him something special, this much he knows. He is fated to become a true god, to attain the cosmic proportions of Zeus come down to earth. He also knows what his teacher repeated countless times, that gods and mortals never mix happily.

He stretches his muscled arms, rolls his neck on its axis and tightens his calf muscles. He is prepared for battle. No, he is prepared for anything.

"What is taking them so long? They have already been gone for many days," he says out loud while walking around his field tent. If he is to move forward, he needs the information they were sent to bring back. "Do they think they are on a break from their duties?" No one responds.

Though the cities on the western shore of the Sea of the Galilee have been plundered successfully, the bounty of meat and wine taken is only enough to nourish his army, 13,000 strong, for ten days. He knows he must move forward quickly to succeed. *War feeds my desires and it also feeds my men,* he thinks. The unadulterated craving to conquer Egypt burns in him like a rage, but before he can unleash it, he knows he must first vanquish Jerusalem, the walled city.

His teacher, Aristotle, taught him so many things: medicine, philosophy, morals, religion, logic and art. But the thing he thinks of most is the enjoinder to always plan before taking action. This is why he sent his scouts—to make sure, before leading his enormous army forward, he has taken every precaution. There is no time for miscalculations or mistakes. But there is always time to plan. His soldiers are to bring him information about Jerusalem. How fortified are the walls around the city? Are there many archers guarding them? How well are the Judean soldiers trained? What kind of weaponry are they armed with?

Watching the shadow of his own horse slinking toward him, he taps his thigh again. *How long can it possibly take to assess the situation?* He'd expected them earlier that day. He gets so anxious that he leaves the cooler, more relaxing confines of his tent. But walking out to watch for them brings their news along no quicker. *Where can those fools be?* This time he taps harder, almost slaps, but he quickly subsides, does not let anger overcome him. Alexander is a man of control. He was raised to be a warrior, but he has also been taught to think carefully. He is not a brute; he is a strategist.

His men respect him because he respects himself. It had always been so.

From birth, his parents knew of his immense promise. His mother, Olympias, had told him how he was conceived through the power of a thunderbolt—a jolt from the gods straight to her womb. He knows he was an astonishing child: handsome, strong, highly intelligent, bold and brave beyond his years. The countless stories of his feats of strength and words of precocious wisdom, he can never hear enough. He remembers the events themselves because they have been told to him over and over, but there is only one story he remembers vividly, not just remembers, but actually sees in his mind's eye.

He was 12 years old. It was an overcast day, the clouds above, like dust, swept evenly across the Macedonian sky. He remembers standing beside his father, King Philip the Great Warrior. Every boy looks up to his father; Alexander was not just any boy. His mother would prod him with the refrain: "You will be greater than your father." When Alexander looked up at Philip, he always saw beyond, knowing in his heart that one day he would indeed overtake his patriarch. Even so, he worshipped his father, the man he planned to surpass.

That day, as young Alexander watched and listened, Philip was offered a horse for sale for a large sum. Alexander recalls the exact amount: 13 talents of gold. The horse was magnificent, with an almost perfect white star on its forehead. The boy, along with everyone else in the palace, came out to the field to see the stallion.

Young Alexander was immediately enraptured by its stature, the sheen of its muscled body, the way it whinnied and reared above their heads, its mouth frothing, its shadow doing a ferocious dance on the ground beside them. Seeing how wild the horse was, how even the most experienced horsemen could not control it, Philip refused to make the purchase. It looked the part, but 13 talents of gold was a lot to spend on an unpredictable project. Even as his father rejected the deal, Alexander knew this creature was fated to be his. As he watched the stallion stomp and blow, he clearly felt that his life was supposed to be intertwined with this amazingly powerful animal. *If I am to be great, then I need this horse, for it is the greatest I've ever seen.*

He first asked his mother to lobby for him, but she instructed her young son to be quiet and trust Philip.

"That is a dangerous animal—your father's most trained horsemen have been injured trying to tame that wild beast," she scolded. "I will find you a nice horse in your father's stable for you to ride."

This was not the answer Alexander wanted or expected. This was not about having any horse. He wanted this horse! He redirected, turning his entreaties directly to his father. "Please, buy him. Buy him for me!"

At first Philip rebuffed his son, "He is a handsome steed, son. But handsome will not charge into battle with you. Handsome will not turn on a dime to avoid a deadly lance. You want a horse with a level head. Not this beast."

Alexander had nothing of it. He insisted he wanted the horse. "I'll tame him myself," he offered. "And if I can't tame him, I will work to pay you back for the price."

Amused but intrigued, Philip relented. "Have it your way. But if my personal horsemen can't get a handle on him, I don't know why you think you can."

Olympias was furious. She raged at Philip. "How dare you offer the animal to the boy without consulting me?" She knew that the right kind of kick from an angry and fearful horse could be the end of her hopes, the shattering of any prophecies of greatness, the unthinkable death of her only child.

"The child must learn," the father insisted.

"But the animal can injure the child, even kill him. He's too young," Olympias argued.

"It is the gods that destine this child's fate, not I and certainly not you. Maybe he will not surpass his father's glory," Philip said.

Olympias studied her husband's eyes as he said this. She perceived some element of hubris and misplaced jealousy in Philip's sarcasm. But she could not tell him what to do. The horse was purchased. On that very same afternoon, Philip gathered his advisors and servants, along with Olympias, to watch young Alexander come face to face with the wild animal. Under the watchful eyes of his father and those gathered, and to the sounds of his mother screaming threats at her husband, Alexander walked toward the animal. He vividly remembers the sense of strength and calm that came over him as he observed the horse. Introductions were in order. Alexander took the lead and placed his face inches from the horse's.

"Bucephalus will be your name." Alexander smirked as he said the words. "Because your head is so massive, it looks like an ox's head."

Alexander laughed at himself and at his horse as he repeated the word. "Bucephalus, Bucephalus," he groaned louder and louder.

Laughter turned to concern as the horse stomped its feet, then reared up on its hind legs. Alexander held tightly to the lead and wondered who was more terrified at that moment—himself or the horse? The noise, commotion, heat and setting sun all made for an unsettling moment. He searched frantically for a solution, thought back through the things he'd seen tried with this massive animal, the things that had failed.

Alexander's voice became soft yet firm, cajoling yet authoritative. He spoke soothingly, waiting for Bucephalus to begin to trust his voice. Always an acute observer, Alexander had noticed that others tried to restrain the horse by pulling at the ropes from various angles. Instead of restraining the animal, these efforts kept it in a state of frenzy and confusion. He also recognized that, as the others pulled Bucephalus in different directions, the horse would see its own shadow rearing up as if in attack. Through the horse's eyes, that shadow transformed into a savage beast. Alexander was always taught to lead. *I must lead the horse—identify its fears and use them to my advantage.*

Alexander looked up at the setting sun and gently positioned Bucephalus in a way that faced the sun. Once Bucephalus felt the heat on his muzzle and was unable to see his taunting shadow, he became much calmer. The horse's shadow was not distracting the animal. No longer did he fear a rival stallion whose motions tracked his own. The sun was blinding. The sun's rays, Alexander learned in weapons training, can offer an opponent an advantage. *Once you've got that advantage, you must work to exploit it.* Alexander used this moment of calm to communicate with the beast.

Alexander continued to speak to him gently, seemingly in a language only he and the horse understood. Exhausted by his attempts to rebel and escape Alexander's charge, Bucephalus surrendered, perhaps perceiving in the boy a genuine concern for its well-being. Before too long, Alexander was able to stroke his horse's mane, to pat his neck, eventually even to stroke his velvet nose. With each tender touch, the horse relaxed just a bit more. Within a few minutes, his breathing slowed and he appeared to enter some form of relaxation.

The crowd was amazed. It was as if Alexander had performed a miracle. To be sure, he had done something many men twice his age had been unable to accomplish. Generals slapped him on the back approvingly. The women looked at him with some different sort of glint in their eyes. His mother finally calmed down. He made his way through the throngs of supporters to his father. He expected to feel his father's pride. He thought to himself, *Finally father will pull me close, accept me and love me in the way I have always wanted to be loved.*

Instead, impressed, but swelling more with admiration than affection, Philip told him, "Get out and find yourself a kingdom worthy of your spirit; Macedonia is too little for you."

Surely his father had meant these words as praise, but after all these years, Alexander still feels a sting of pain as he remembers them. The words that ring the loudest in his ears still today are "Na vgei," or "Get out!" When they were first uttered, his face burned and stomach sank. His mind becomes a maze of pain and hurt when they are replayed in his mind. He'd accomplished what others could not. He'd done the work that good men could not do. He'd stepped outside of his mother's protective hand, and his father did not regard him.

For the remainder of his life, Bucephalus responded to Alexander as his master and trusted friend. He'd lost a childhood but gained a horse. His father never spoke with him again.

The memory torments him. Alexander has always associated his father's insistence that he go to battle at an early age with the horse incident on that humid evening.

"He is not even decorated with a man's body hair," Olympias had insisted in her strong-willed manner, ardent that Alexander first finish his education before going out into the world to play the role of a soldier.

"Mother, I do not fear battle," he pathetically interjected. Truthfully, he was eager for it. But the squabble between his parents, he interpreted as his father wanting him dead. What had he done to create this mysterious anger? Like a blind man, he stumbled toward any possible solution.

"Should I pay father the 13 talents of gold for the horse?" he asked his mother, confused at the absolute lack of praise Philip had shown him, at the silence to which he'd been treated since breaking Bucephalus.

"Hush, you silly child," his mother responded. "Your father does not need your money. That won't fix anything."

She did not tell Alexander the answer to the unspoken question. She did not volunteer any explanation for the lack of spoken affection between father and son.

Alexander asked questions, as well, of his teacher. Aristotle, the son of Nicomachus, the personal physician of King Amyntas of Macedon, had worked as Alexander's private tutor since the boy was nine. They'd known each other's faces before the teacher-student dynamic was initiated.

Aristotle had been recognized as a precocious young man. He had earned the approving glances of royalty, as he roamed the palace halls, from a young age. Aristotle spent his teenage years under the tutelage of the then famous Plato, the great wrestler who'd long ago earned the reputation of the finest teacher in the Greek empire. Now Aristotle carried that banner. Olympias liked to say she hired the finest teacher for the finest student. Aristotle taught Alexander well and taught him everything: physics, philosophy, mathematics, the laws of the natural world, and ethics. But when asked by Alexander about Philip's silence, Aristotle himself grew quiet. There were some people you did not cross.

Alexander nonetheless believed that, at that young age, he was better prepared to lead than his father had ever been. His successes would soon prove those suppositions correct. He forded great rivers and crossed daunting deserts. He commanded the respect of everyone, except for the one person from whom he most desired it.

5

Gaza City, Gaza Strip
June 2006

L IOR IS LYING IN THE trunk of a car, that much he knows. It's violently rocking from side to side, up and down. He feels every turn and
bump on the road until, finally, the speeding vehicle abruptly stops. The
ear-piercing sound of the motor, which seems to be right below his head,
is replaced with the deafening sound of a mob. At first he is not sure if the
people are screaming or singing. Later, he realizes, it is a combination of
yelling, banging, screaming, singing—all sprinkled by gunshots and what
could have been fireworks.

Lior wonders to himself, *Why are people banging on the car? If they
break the car, how will I possibly get home?* The thought, absurd as it may
be, is real and a source of deep anxiety. Shortly after, the car stops for a
third time. The trunk opens. Lior stays still. Maybe he is in shock. After
hours in the complete dark of the trunk, the Gazan sun blinds him. Adjusting to the sunlight, he sees the blue sedan that transported him to this
hellish location.

They open the trunk to reveal their prize to the swarms of people surrounding the car while Lior continues to lie in a fetal position. People are crowded together, pushing one another. Men are dancing frenziedly on the streets, rooftops, flatbeds and on the hoods of cars. Terror turns into paralysis, his nervous system completely shutting down. Lior is hovering somewhere between a state of shock and oblivion.

His captors take a long moment to relish their victory. In the meantime, Lior lies cooking in the midday sun, his vomit seeping more deeply into his clothing and bare skin. *How long have I been laying here marinating in barf, shit and the guts of at least one of my friends?* Despite his discomfort, he does not dare move. His eyes glance from side to side while his body lies still. *Will they publically execute me? Will they cut me up and rip my heart out? Will they send my body parts to various sides of the Israeli borders? Death has to be better than this. Hopefully it will be quick.*

If it weren't for the five or six masked, armed men, who are both holding him steady and acting as a shield, Lior would have been ripped to pieces by the mob of men, women and children. Their eyes flash and their yelling and screaming penetrate. Lior remembers a line he'd heard in some now distant memory: "Individuals are more compassionate than groups." *Who'd said that? Who cares? This is sure as hell a mob, and they want nothing more than my blood. What individuals might save me now?* The men who pull him out of that car—one on each appendage—cover their noses with scarves. *Is it in order to protect their identity or to protect themselves from the foul smell emanating from my cramped figure?* They bring him into a building that appears, from the façade he sees overhead as they pass through, to be a hospital. Instead of seeing men and women in white medical coats, however, Lior finds this non-hospital to be filled with men in military fatigue, carrying weapons and screaming orders.

In a room tiled with white ceramic, he is stripped and hosed down with cold water. No one speaks with him. They toss him a towel and a green jumpsuit to wear. He is immediately taken out the back door and escorted into a big black SUV. Once inside, one of the men put a hood over his head. No one says a word. The silence screams in his ears, in some ways worse than the din of the mob. The drive is bumpy but comfortable. Lior does not dare to speak. The car stops; the engine is turned off, and one of the men holds Lior's arm to escort him out of the car for a walk.

The grip this stranger has on his bicep is tight. It reminds Lior of times from his childhood, when he would get in trouble, how his father would grab his arm and escort him somewhere private to chastise him. Despite the firm grip of his captor, Lior nonetheless stumbles over stones and rubbish. The escort doesn't seem too intent on helping him further. He can't see anything, but suddenly the ground under his feet is smooth, like he'd come inside. Once inside, Lior keeps stumbling. He feels like he might have been drugged, but he can't remember. He does, however, remember the pain of his stubbed toe. "Upstairs," his escort says in pigeon Hebrew. Finally, they come to a halt. Then his hood is removed.

"Sit down," comes the command from the same voice behind him. Lior obliges immediately and sits on a small wooden chair. He is facing a small boarded-up window. The door clicks behind him. Lior slowly looks back at it. He is alone. *How much time has elapsed since the explosion?* He leans his head back in fatigue and breathes deeply.

He stands and walks back toward the door. He can't stop shaking. *Is it fear or some sort of sickness?* His head is pounding. The quiet is welcome. There is no window on the door, so he leans in and places his ear above the knob. He hears distant murmuring but no distinct words. He turns back to further examine his surroundings. In the corner, a small bed nestled on the wall, the frame made of laminate intended to look like oak. Lior thinks to himself ever so briefly, *I saw this exact bed a few months ago while shopping. They probably bought the bed at Ikea in Netanya. How odd.*

The light blue concrete walls are bare, though small holes indicate that someone in the room's previous life had seen it fit to hang pictures. The floor is a cheap laminate tile, like one would see in many buildings throughout Israel. There is a doorway on the side of the room opposite the bed that leads into a closet-size bathroom. The bathroom has a stainless steel toilet, simple sink and shower. He notices that there is a small bar of soap, some shampoo, a little toothbrush and an electric shaver near the sink. *This isn't much of a prison.* The strangeness disorients him. *What next?* Lior has no idea. Even thinking about escaping seems too tiring. Lior doesn't even try opening the door. Screaming for help might get him killed, or worse, beaten.

The injuries, Lior can clearly identify, are relatively minor; there is a slight cut from shrapnel in the back of his ear, and his left arm could use a stitch or two. The blood has clotted though. He just needs to make sure he keeps it clean enough. Lior sits down on the bed and runs his smooth hands through his hair. He leans over and stretches out on the mattress. It is firm but livable. He lies there in a maze of fear for no more than a few seconds before drifting into a fitful sleep. When he awakes, it is with a startle. *Shit. It wasn't all a dream.*

6

Lower Galilee
323 BCE

F INALLY!
Alexander, in spite of his annoyance at the delay, cannot help but smile at the sight of his two scouts as they appear, a single dusty silhouette in the distance. He knows they are skilled warriors, well disciplined, but even so, he has been slightly anxious. *What if they had been captured? What if they had been led astray?* The Judeans are known to be ruthless. But he is not surprised. The moon is half full, a good omen.

His men are a bit dirtier than when they left but clearly alert and uninjured. Over one of the horses lies a body, not limp enough to be dead. *Apparently, they have taken a prisoner—but for what purpose? Why travel with that extra weight?* As they get closer, he sees that the captive is a female. Taking strides nearer, he realizes that she is quite young. Presuming this young virgin is meant for him, he licks his lower lip in anticipation. *They are good soldiers, thoughtful. I should never have doubted them.*

As they draw near the campsite, he motions for them to approach. Dismounting, they bow to their leader, hoping he will be pleased with their news.

"What did you find out about the walled city?" Alexander asks. "Is it well fortified?"

The higher-ranking scout responds, "Jerusalem is not a fortress, Great One. That wall of stone is nothing but an enclosure, no more able to keep us out than a fence to pen livestock."

Briefly, his eyes meet those of his companion; both almost laugh but restrain their gaiety out of respect. Alexander is squinting in the distance, processing what they are telling him and thinking of the implications.

The first scout continues: "There will be no impediment to your conquest. The Judeans will not struggle against us. Compared to the taking of the North cities, this will be child's play."

Alexander frowns and looks perplexed. He had studied the history of the Jews with Aristotle, who spoke of an austere nation that is ruthless and cruel in combat, known for amazing conquests, and for their god who aids them in battle.

Their leader barks out, "Have none of you ever heard of King David's military conquests? It has been said that 1,000 men were no challenge for him. It was he who slew the great Goliath. Have you not heard of the time these religious warriors walked around the great city of Jericho and brought the walls down with only the force of their lungs?"

The men stand dumbfounded. They have no response.

"You must be mistaken. How can it be as you describe?" Alexander presses.

"Respectfully, Great One," a voice speaks from the back of the tent, "David was not, you must recall, a pure Israelite. He was born illegitimately to a Moabite woman. His own son, Solomon, pursued commerce over war. David was by no means typical of the Israelites."

"Is not Jerusalem a city of great resources?" Alexander asks.

The second scout speaks for the first time, confidently proffering, "We will be able to walk through its fields and pick it clean—its fruits, its meat, even its beautiful women."

With this last statement, he points to the girl slung across his horse. Even in disarray under the clinging fabric of her skirt, her young body looks supple and appealing.

Hephaestion is convinced that what the scouts reported was indeed correct. He always feels as if Alexander inflates the abilities of his enemy in order to glorify his victories. And he often thinks that Alexander can be too cautious and obsessed with preparation. *Had they not the most impressive army in the world? What was there to fear?* But, so as to not contradict his master, he says, "These people are masters of many disciplines. They know warfare, but they are primarily people of commerce. They love their land, but they love their law even more. They hold their generals in high esteem, but their wise men are adored."

It is this sort of non-answer response, which straddles both worlds and accommodates all opinions, that makes him such a politically savvy advisor. To the scouts, it sounds like he'd said everything and nothing at the same time. But the person who matters most nods in agreement.

"Indeed," Alexander declares. "I insist we be prepared for a ruthless battle. Advise the generals that, with the rise of the second sun from tonight, we will engage the city of Jerusalem in war."

"Yes, sir," Hephaestion agrees.

"For now," Alexander continues his orders, "feed the men the reddest of meat—I want blood in their souls. Bring me that lovely flower you picked for me from the garden of Jerusalem. And don't worry, you will be rewarded when the time is right."

A tinge of jealousy streams through Hephaestion's blood. It is he who is Alexander's lover on the battlefield.

Alexander, his advisors and soldiers are not the first to struggle with the mystery of that place. "What is Jerusalem?" Alexander murmurs. "Is it a city of peace or a hub of warriors?" Though the news from the scouts is reassuring, Alexander remains a bit uneasy. *If they are indeed feared warriors, will my men fair well against them? And if they are but pathetic civilians, what glory can there be in defeating an enemy who is inferior?*

"Egypt is the prize and nothing will get in my way," he announces abruptly and to no one in particular.

His men wonder what he had just said: *Egypt? That was where they were going, for sure. But this morning, Jerusalem awaits.* They were eager to get on with it.

Alexander moves on in his mind's eye and marches to the kingdom of the mighty Pharaohs; in the desert, he can taste the waters of the Nile. *Egypt.* The very word is a source of energy and excitement. It is the last hurdle to his infinite glory. Egypt, the land of riches and gods, is awaiting the magnificence of his conquest, the glory of himself.

If I am to be a god, I must rule the empire by the Nile. Only then will I have fulfilled my destiny. As he comes to this conclusion, Alexander looks around the tent and eyes what he wants. He reaches for an open scroll, a recent communication from his mother. He touches her seal and whispers to the insignia of letters, "Mother, I am already greater than he ever was. I knew I would be. He too knew I was destined for greatness, but why could he not love me? Why did he hate me?"

The entourage was watching with concern until Alexander came back to his senses and announced, "Bring me meat, bread, cheese and wine. I have an appetite for conquest tonight."

With the mention of conquest, Alexander reaches for the young girl who fearlessly looks up at him. Trembling, as he expected, yet her posture is almost defiant. And those eyes! Her black eyes appear to be all pupil as she raises them to meet his. Her olive skin is as smooth as the skin of the fruit itself. He sees that she is young, perhaps only 14 years old. He notices that her body is just beginning to find form. Her breasts, although not large, are full; the nipples are taut under her garment. *Ripe for the picking*, he thinks, already hardening under his tunic.

As he approaches her, he is surprised to feel something other than pure lust for this girl. She reminds him of someone; he can't think of whom. She is clearly feminine; yet, there is strength about her like that of a boy coming into his manhood. The defiance belies her gender as well. Then, with a jolt, he realizes that she reminds him of Peleus, his devoted male companion of youth. Not Peleus now, but Peleus when he and Alexander first met. There is a tough gentleness about her, as there was in Peleus when the two first found pleasure in each other. This girl, this Judean flower, will have no choice but to be taken by him. Yet, he feels the urge to woo her and not conquer her as he will her people. He is too great to be a tyrant. Tyranny, his teachers taught him, is weakness in disguise. True power, he remembers them saying, is achieved through influence and inspiration. He will seduce her as he seduced countless other lovers. He will seduce her like a god, the god he will soon become.

"Come," he says roughly, leading her into his darkened tent, lit only by three oil lamps hanging from hooks on the center pole. "What is your name?"

She looks blankly into his eyes, not knowing what he is saying. She searches for some signs of decency and earnest goodness. He draws close to her and strokes her arm. As his finger traces the inside of her elbow, she withdraws but does not cringe. Alexander takes this to be encouraging. He sees that she is wary, not afraid. He feels a fraternal pride, as if she is a younger relative whose bravery he admires. He imagines being this girl, kidnapped and away from home, only a bit older than Alexander himself was when his father first threatened to send him off to war. *What must she be thinking?*

He pauses and goes to the flap of his tent.

"Drakon!" he calls out to an advisor who had spent time in the Jewish country and speaks the language.

"Yes, your excellency?" replies Drakon, hustling to answer Alexander's summons.

"Ask her for her name."

"Yes, sir."

Drakon comes through the flap of the tent held open by Alexander. He walks closely to the girl and speaks the foreign tongue,

"*Mah Ha'shem sheLakh?*"

The young virgin raises her shoulders a bit at the question. It is almost like she is reminded, by hearing her native tongue, of some hidden strength in her lineage.

"Yael."

"Yael." When Alexander hears it, he finds it to be a fitting label: "A beautiful sound for a beautiful maiden."

"Drakon, you are dismissed."

As Drakon leaves, Alexander watches Yael for what feels to her like hours. *She must be full of fear, yet she is poised as if prepared for whatever will befall her.*

Yael feels the focus course through her veins. It feels like her eyes are blinking less frequently than usual. She is absolutely and totally aware of every smell in the tent, of the way the jagged gravel under her feet presses into her sole. She will not look away. She is being held against her will, but she will not show weakness.

Alexander, as Yael stares him down, has the feeling she can see right through him with those deep eyes, as if she knows something about him he is not ready to reveal.

Does she know who I am? he thinks. *Does she know my importance? Does she understand the privilege destiny has afforded her in the act we are about to commit?*

He waves to her to sit beside him. She does not respond. He gets up and walks over to the table, grabbing two goblets and a casket of wine. He pours both of the goblets until they overflow, and offers her one. She refuses. Alexander fills his mouth with wine, puts both cups down, and forcefully reaches out for her. He presses his mouth against hers and fills it with the wine in his mouth. When he pulls away, her lips are red, dripping with the juice of the grapes and saliva. She looks at him, disgusted, still not blinking, and does not wipe her face. The droplets glisten unexpectedly in the lamplight flickering against the tent's fabric.

Again he pulls her close to him. This time he uses brute force. He can feel her heart beating against his own.

Nuzzling into her neck, he breathes in her aroma, a smell he hasn't inhaled in some time. His right hand reaches across her back and presses her even more firmly against him. Now he is ready. He slides his hand down over her buttocks, cupping her flesh to press them together.

He removes her dress. She is helpless, knowing that he is much bigger and stronger than she is, but does not protest. She moves her arm to cover her naked upper body. The gesture of modesty touches him, yet is highly erotic. He grabs her arm and bares her breasts. She tries to resist his touch. She pushes him away, but his strength dominates. He bends to put his mouth over her nipple. She pulls back but has nowhere to go. Her body is his for the taking. She gives up and whimpers.

In his delusional mind, Alexander questions whether she is desirous or merely compliant.

Yael is defeated. She does not want to yield to this dominating captor, but what choice does she have? Does she even want to have a choice? She feels guilty that his touch feels good, but how can she be guilty? She is incapable of resisting. There is no question that he will do whatever he wants with her.

What does she want him to do? She should want him to stop; she should want to defend her honor at all costs; but he moves slowly, carefully, as if asking permission for each caress. Small noises come from her. Is she whimpering with fear? Or is it desire? Or regret? His tongue slides down her neck while his hand firmly slithers down her stomach, closer and closer to the secret entrance to her body. "No, may God forgive me," she mutters in Hebrew. He hears her tone. He interprets her noises to mean that she does not want him to stop.

He is about to turn her over, as he has with Peleus and Hephaestion, but just then she spreads her legs to allow him access to the center of her being. Her pubic curls entice him. He puts his face between her thighs and licks. The lance between his legs frees itself from his tunic; he begins to penetrate. She cries out in anguish, but he thinks he hears delight. Then he turns her over and pushes into her as if to break the fortress of her innocence, determined, unrelenting. She pulls away, or at least she tries. With a shudder and a grunt, he finishes. She sobs against him, holding onto him. For several minutes, she does not move. He strokes her hair, her cheek, her shoulder, soothingly, as if to calm a child.

"All right, all right, no harm will come to you," he says kindly.

There were rules in Alexander's military culture. Female virgin captives are always brought to him first. Once he is satisfied, she is shared among his top commanders and deserving soldiers. The captive is then sold into slavery, often for good coin.

"Tonight is going to be different." He knows she does not know what he is saying, but as he tells her this, he tries to use gestures and tone to give her some solace from the physical pain and the profound sense of guilt. As Alexander strokes her neck, he has a sudden memory of when he first mounted Bucephalus, the wild horse. He remembers stroking the animal's long neck, its flank, and feeling that the horse could somehow understand the meaning of his touch. He feels that now he is communicating with Yael the same way, his arms and hands soothing her like a balm. He feels the reassurance flowing from his body into hers, a power as great as any he has ever felt in battle. Perhaps this is the power of being a god, not strength but overwhelming tenderness.

He removes the leather strap with a silver eagle from around his neck and places it around her neck. For him, it is a promise that she remains alive and only his—for now.

She looks down at it and touches it with her hand. Her mind, too, wanders to another place and time. Strangely, Alexander's touch reminds her of her father's when she was a little girl. She'd tripped over a stone and fallen hard; her leg was bleeding, sand pressed deep inside the cut. What she remembers most is not the pain but the sweet touch of her father holding her against him, as if his touch alone could heal the wound.

This man, this warrior, this stranger, holds me against my will, she thinks. *Why am I thinking of father's touch? Do I really think this brute will protect me?* She feels soreness down below, but it is more an ache than a pain. She feels so open and so vulnerable. She pushes him off her body and closes her legs but continues to cling on to his shoulders. She doesn't let go of him. *Will he provide safety for me tonight? Can I expect some sort of restoration?* She sighs. *Is this what being a woman feels like?*

7

**Dimona, Israel
June 2006**

TRANQUIL MORNINGS IN THE INDUSTRIAL city of Dimona are nonexistent. Maya hears the cats fighting over some garbage outside her bedroom window. The noise of daily traffic rumbles up and down their narrow side street, which is often used as a convenient shortcut for drivers who know the neighborhood. Leon, her husband of twenty-three years, lies in bed next to her, stirring in a state between slumber and consciousness. The clock on her end table strikes 7 a.m. Maya gently pulls the cotton sheets off her waist and steps onto the warm floor. She stands by the open window for a moment, hoping to feel a cool morning breeze as a relief from the summer heat of southern Israel. As she walks past the full-length mirror on her way to the bathroom, she thinks about how good her middle-aged body looks and feels. Sitting on the toilet, she ignores the magazines sprawled on the floor in front of her. She can hear Noa getting out of bed. Her thoughts are with Lior. Ever since he enlisted, she has been uneasy. Her Lior was never "military material." While the boys his age played soccer, lifted weights, wrestled and played tough, he listened to music and played video games. Her father, Avigdor Cohen, one of Israel's

40

most decorated soldiers, tried in his brutish way to toughen Lior up. Instead Lior always felt tortured and unloved by his grandfather.

She has always struggled with her upbringing. Growing up in a home that glamorized the military made her uncomfortable. From her childhood, she came to the conclusion that war is an unavoidable evil. She married a man who reluctantly wore a uniform and raised a son completely unmoved by patriotic Zionism. As far as she is concerned, she loves her country and is proud that Israel is a true democracy in a region of monarchs, despots, tyrants and terrorist regimes. She is proud of her father's military heroics, but his post-military life was far from glamorous. Shame might be too harsh a word—she is tired of her father's sense of self-pity and bitterness at his failed attempts at national politics. She tries to avoid over analyzing her own complex feelings about her parents' divorce, her life in Israel, her distaste for religion, and her own shattered dreams. And yet, the sight of the Israeli flag always brings tears to her eyes. She was very proud of Lior when he successfully finished basic training.

She steps out of the bathroom and heads to the kitchen to prepare two espressos. She and Leon have a habit of starting the day off with a strong shot. *How strange*, she thinks when she sees from the kitchen window two young men dressed in military service uniform, without ties, coming out of a red four-door Toyota Camry. They jump out of the front seats, with their purple berets neatly tucked over their left shoulders, and stand alongside the car for a moment. Then they begin to walk.

She wonders where they could possibly be going at 7 o'clock in the morning.

She stops what she is doing—her body freezes as she watches the two men walk toward her modest home. They stand still at her front door for what seems like an eternity. Confused, she continues to watch one of the men pause to ring her doorbell.

Is this the moment I have always dreaded? she thinks. *Are we about to enter our most feared nightmare?*

"Leon!" she yells. "Leon, Leon get up right now."

The doorbell rings. Leon is in his shorts. "What is it? Who is it?" Leon's face is contorted with confusion. He loses all coloration as he opens the door.

"Mr. Samet?" The men wait for confirmation.

"Yes."

"Can we come in for a moment?"

"Yes, of course. This is my wife." He gestures at Maya. Maya cannot move. The men let themselves into the kitchen. Noa hears commotion and enters the kitchen.

The older of the two soldiers says in an assertive but compassionate voice: "We are here on behalf of the IDF. Early this morning, Lior's unit was ambushed. Lior was abducted by infiltrators and taken to an unknown location." Maya takes a loud deep breath. Her hand shakes as she places it over her mouth. Noa curls up next to her mother. They both stare into space, tears filling up their eyes. Leon's knees begin to feel weak; he stumbles, almost falling to the ground.

"The Army has dispatched a team of professionals who will help you through this process. ZaHaL will do everything in its power to bring Lior home safely," the young man says, using the Hebrew acronym for *Zeva HaGanah LeYisrael*, the Israel Defense Forces.

Maya sits on a chair close by. She is out of breath. Two more soldiers let themselves in. The first introduces himself as Lt. General Michael Edry; the second introduces himself as Commander Boaz Gafni. "Mr. Samet, please have a seat," the Lt. General says. Two more women in uniform let themselves in and close the door behind them. One of them carries a medical bag. Edry barks commands in quick short phrases, "I don't want any reporters near this home. Bring them water. I want a log of every phone call in and out of this house. Take Mrs. Samet's blood pressure. She looks faint."

Edry turns to Leon, "Mr. Samet, two hours ago, Lior's unit was on patrol duty and was ambushed. The boys were very courageous. We know Lior was taken alive. We dispatched immediately so that you and your wife would not hear about this from any media source. I am here to give you as much information as I have and enlist your help in securing Lior's safe return. Please get dressed, and ask your wife to do the same, because we need to sit and talk."

"Talk to me now," Leon says, stressed and eager.

"Please freshen up; I am not going anywhere," Lt. Edry replies.

Leon looks at him, annoyed, and says, "I need to call my father-in-law, General Avigdor Cohen."

"Your father-in-law is on his way here—he has already been contacted. Mr. Samet, we are a number of steps ahead of you. Please get dressed and come back as soon as possible."

Leon glances over at Maya; it pains him to see how distraught she is. Her eyes swell while her unadulterated morning look turns into a disheveled, ghostly, pale appearance. The phone rings, and the young sergeant answers politely and assertively that Leon and Maya are not available at the moment. "Everything will be back to normal in a few hours," he says. "Mrs. Samet—we need you to be strong and patient." The young female nurse walks Maya to her bedroom. She helps brush her hair and pins it into a neat ponytail. She changes Maya's clothes, making sure she feels somewhat refreshed.

Both Maya and Leon are escorted into the living room and seated. Michael Edry inspires confidence. He sits right in front of the Samets and says, "Look at me; look into my eyes. This entire experience is much more difficult for you than it is for Lior. We know for a fact that he was not injured. We also know his abductors are not interested in hurting him. Do you understand? Both of you have served in the IDF and both of you know that our military is committed to bringing each and every one of our soldiers home. We need you to work closely with us to achieve the results we all want. Please show me you are listening and understand everything I am telling you." Both Maya and Leon nod their heads.

"Right now," Edry continues, "we are protecting you from curious visitors and from those who have political agendas, professionals who sell gossip and news at the expense of your son and your lives. Journalists are already beginning to line up outside your home. They are shameless. They do not care about bringing Lior home. They want to sell newspapers and magazines. I need to know that you understand this." Again Maya and Leon nod their heads. "The people who have your son want attention, they want news media to be covering this story. They thrive on media attention. If you give it to them, they will *not* release your son."

"Under no circumstances should either of you speak to the media. Do you understand what I am saying? If you want your son to come home safe and sound, this story must be silenced. The only way Lior will be brought home is through political and military channels."

"When did this happen? How is this possible? Yesterday Lior was at his base." Leon pleads for some information.

"I will tell you exactly what we know," Edry says. "Lior and four of his fellow soldiers were on guard duty this morning when their armored vehicle was ambushed. Lior was taken alive. We have video of the armored vehicle showing Lior being taken alive."

"Can we see that video?" they ask.

"Absolutely not. That is classified material. Under no circumstance are you to reveal to the press, or anyone else, that we have such a video. Show me that you understand what I am saying." Both Maya and Leon nod.

It is already 9 a.m., and the commotion outside their modest home is beginning to take on a life of its own. The street fills with the expected media, concerned neighbors and friends, as well as curios thrill-seekers. Maya and Leon have always shunned the limelight. They cannot believe what is happening to them.

Lt. Edry insists the home has to remain a controlled environment until further notice. "Who would you like us to allow into the house? It should be people who will lend you emotional support. We don't need heroes right now," Edry insists.

"Where are my parents?" Maya asks. "Where are my mother and father?"

Edry comforts her, "Your mother is on her way."

"Where is my father? Why isn't he here?"

"Your father is being briefed by the military. He will be here in a few hours."

Some of Maya's close friends are allowed in. Her mother can be heard at the door promising not to be hysterical and emotional. The moment she is allowed in, she begins to sob and yell. She curses the military, the government and her ex-husband.

There is a sense of absolute helplessness. Time stands still. The IDF Special Division is successful in holding people back and controlling the environment for longer than they thought possible.

The initial news reports are brutal. Contradicting reports by varying stations, and even reporters from the same station, make listening miserable.

A military social worker is assigned to the Samet home. Maya and

Leon are told that all they can do, and should do, is wait.

8

Tel Aviv, Israel
Shin Bet Headquarters
June 2006

IN THE THROES OF WAR, it is the ability to be bold, adaptable and creative—and, at times, ignore the rules—that wins battles and makes heroes.

The Israel Defense Forces' culture is averse to heroes. Heroes are considered hotheads, unpredictable, and usually put themselves and others in danger. Military professionals prefer managing outcomes based on carefully planned and executed strategies. Heroes are always a last resort. As far as the military elite is concerned, Avigdor Cohen is a national hero and a reckless soldier.

Shin Bet identifies all of Lior's relatives and relevant friends within minutes of the abduction. The list is sent to military special services that are responsible to send a team to the Samet home. Avigdor Cohen's name is immediately tagged as requiring special attention. Cohen is gifted and courageous, but he has a tendency to overestimate himself and take unnecessary risks. It is the combination of these characteristics that Aman, the Directorate of Military Intelligence, know well and the reason they send a special team to see him personally. Two senior officers are dispatched to inform Avigdor Cohen of his eldest grandson's kidnapping.

9

Caesarea, Israel
June 2006

AVIGDOR COHEN'S MORNING ROUTINE IS never the same. Despite his long military career, the culture of discipline is something he has never bought into. This morning, he is startled from his slumber by a measured banging on the front door of his modest home in the upscale coastline town of Caesarea. Annoyed, Cohen responds with a loud: "*Mi zeh*? Who is it?" He looks at Michal, his live-in partner for the last three years, who is sound asleep. He rolls out of bed, glances at his clock on the end table and begins processing as he walks to the door.

"It's 7:30 a.m. Who the hell is banging on my door? *Mi zeh*?"

"We are from the office of Lieutenant General Rav Aluf. We are looking for Brigadier General Avigdor Cohen."

The Lieutenant General's office? What could they possibly want? The two young men are dressed in their finest khakis. What Cohen does not know is that they have been instructed to hold him at his residence for at least two hours. Aman, along with the prime minister's office, do not want Cohen taking matters into his own hands.

In his illustrious military career, he has achieved an almost mythic

48

status. He received the Medal of Distinguished Service after the Six-Day War of '67, in which he was seriously wounded when his Centurion tank was hit by enemy fire.

The 1967 Six-Day War recast the entire map of the Middle East. The surprise, multi-directional attack was an utter rout of the combined Arab armies at the hands of the IDF. It left Israel with vast chunks of new territory, including the Sinai Peninsula, the Golan Heights and the entire Gaza Strip and West Bank, as well as the entirety of Eastern Jerusalem, which included the Old City and Silwan Valley. That conflict had also established the IDF as the undisputed military power in the Middle East.

In battle, Cohen's division had seized great chunks of the Sinai Peninsula. Cohen's tank was struck by mortar fire, but he'd pressed on, even while wounded, to help seize the ever-important Suez Canal. Pictures of Cohen, blood staining his shoulder and thigh, a bloody bandage wrapped around his forehead, walking out to the canal with his tank in the background, had become a symbol of Jewish power after centuries of impotence. Following his hospital stay, Cohen had been invited on to talk shows and news programs for weeks after the war.

For Israel, and for Jews around the world, this victory was interpreted in messianic terms. A sense of national pride and religious fervor entered the psyche of a previously vulnerable nation.

For the Arab powers, the defeat was a huge embarrassment. It did not take long for Israel's enemies to begin planning the next war. With massive logistical support and Soviet military advice, the Egyptian and Syrian armies re-armed themselves with the latest Russian weapon systems and rebuilt their shattered forces and egos.

Israeli strategic and intelligence officers, on the other hand, committed the cardinal sin of warfare: underestimating the enemy's ability and resolve. They assumed all future conflicts would be a replay of their great success. The hubris of its foes had been the IDF's greatest advantage in the '67 war. Following their brief honeymoon with success, that same sense of hubris hobbled Israel's forces as well. The fact that the IDF had sufficient advance warning, to mobilize and deploy its troops to conduct preemptive offensive attacks, was taken for granted.

They ignored clear indicators; Israeli intelligence refused to believe that their Arab neighbors would launch a full-scale invasion, until, of course, the morning of October 6, 1973—the holiest day of the Jewish calendar, Yom Kippur—when that invasion began.

The Egyptians launched the first attack in the south. They stormed across the Suez Canal, overwhelmed the thin Israeli forces, and entrenched themselves deep in the Sinai. Once they'd gained a preliminary foothold, they set up strong defenses.

In the north, on that fateful Yom Kippur afternoon, the Syrian army attacked with three mechanized armored divisions and the elite brigade-size Assad Republican Guard in reserve. More than 900 Soviet T-54 and 55s, supported by 140 artillery batteries and another 600 Soviet T-62 tanks, advanced toward Israel beneath an umbrella of SAM batteries. The hour-long artillery barrage was apocalyptic. It decimated the less than 150 obsolete British-made Centurion tanks manned by the IDF.

Less than six years after the Six-Day War, Cohen found himself in the midst of the action once again. He could have easily asked for a job away from the frontlines. He still walked with a limp due to his wounds from the previous experience. But he'd insisted on maintaining an active role in field forces and served in the 77th armored battalion, famously known as Oz 77. (Oz is Hebrew for strength.)

Oz 77 consisted of forty operational tanks. This battalion was charged with holding the northeastern line of Israel. If they failed, the Syrians would have an easy waltz through the Galilee region, divide Israel in two, and overtake Haifa in the north and Tel Aviv and Jerusalem in the heartland. Many of his men thought that Cohen had been promoted to his leadership role more for his moment of heroism than actual military and tactical skill. Whatever their perception of him, when the Arab armies launched their multi-directional attack, Cohen's Oz 77 was the only hope standing between possible annihilation and 500 Soviet-built tanks and armored vehicles equipped with night vision and sophisticated equipment. That math merits repeating: forty tanks to 500. Like a modern-day David and Goliath.

The Syrians hit Cohen's positions with a withering barrage of artillery and rocket fire. Cohen was ordered to pull back as the Syrians closed in rapidly and reached a point of no return. Cohen defied orders and charged forward into smoke and dust, firing at point-blank and taking out T-62s like they were toys. Legend has it that in just a few minutes of ferocious fighting, Oz 77, with just seven operational tanks left, decimated two battalions of the Assad Republican Guard.

That battle proved to be the turning point of that front in the war. Had he given up his position and retreated, the Syrian forces would have cut the state into two and marched on to Tel Aviv and Haifa.

Cohen, a Medal of Valor recipient, wasn't just a hero. Given the numerical impossibility of his victory, he was regarded as a walking miracle, even to the non-believers.

After the war, the valley where the battle took place was littered with the remains of hundreds of burned Syrian Tanks. The only explanation experts could come up with was that Cohen had created such confusion with precise but random-seeming hits of enemy tanks that the Syrian tanks started firing at one other.

Given all that destruction, the valley was renamed *Emek HaBacha*—the Valley of Tears—after the war.

"Brigadier General, we need a word with you." Cohen opens the door. He looks disheveled, clearly surprised by the visit. He feels somewhat insecure. His mind always races at a pace that requires catching up to. He has already considered two scenarios as to why the Lieutenant General would dispatch two men in the early morning to see him. Either he is being invited to a top security briefing or being arrested for something.

"Your grandson, Lior Samet, was abducted this morning at 0555 hours. We have evidence that he was taken alive. Your daughter and son-in-law are being notified as we speak. We have a number of questions for you."

"You have questions for me? What the… I need to call my daughter right now." Cohen gets agitated. The news is so abrupt, so unexpected. His mind races.

"General, you and your immediate family are on black-out until noon today. Please understand the military has to take all precautions."

Cohen darts for the phone. The young officers ask for him to please cooperate. "Have a seat. Here is what we know."

Cohen listens intently and asks questions. At 8:30 a.m., the home telephone rings. The young soldier picks up the receiver, listens for a moment and hands the phone to Cohen.

It is with full awareness that Brigadier General Avigdor Cohen may very well be responsible for the continued existence of the State of Israel that the Prime Minister begins his phone call.

"Avigdor, this is Ehud," he begins.

"Yes, Mr. Prime Minister, Ehud," his voice shakes. "It is kind of you to call. Do you have any information on my grandson?"

"I'll let you know personally as soon as we know something more. In the interim, Avigdor, you should know we will do everything in our power to bring Lior home."

Avigdor is silent. What runs through his head at that moment is the State of Israel's long-standing position to never negotiate with terrorists. He can't help but think of the four Israeli soldiers missing in action who have not been heard from for years. Images of the remains of Ron Arad, the IAF pilot, being returned in a little black box filled his mind. These facts were well known to all who read the papers. Precedent did not support the prime minister's promise.

"Avi, are you there?" asks the prime minister.

Unwilling to participate in the charade of niceties and empty promises, the war hero purses his lips and pauses. "I'm here. Thank you for the call, Mr. Prime Minister."

As he abruptly hangs up the phone, one of the few people in the world who could do such a thing, Cohen knows that something much greater than himself has just been put into motion. No amount of *protectsia*, slang in Hebrew for "connections," will bring Lior back. For the first time in his entire life, he feels completely helpless. Avigdor throws on some clothes, races to his car and heads out to Dimona.

10

Jerusalem
Summer 323 BCE

JERUSALEM IS A CITY OF stone. The streets are made of stone, the courtyards are made of stone and the homes are all made of stone. Tonight it is as if every stone in the city braces itself for pending doom. The dark is amplified by the hysterical shrieks of the city's inhabitants, all of whom are thrust into a sense of dread and anxiety. The entire capital is in a state of panic. Confirmed information reaches the city by mounted couriers: Alexander the Great and his army of thousands of trained and armed soldiers are just hours away from attacking the walled city.

The horrors of Alexander's cruelty reach Jerusalem from the many refugees who fled the northern cities that were decimated by the Greek army. People are worried based on what they have heard, but the panic is also fueled by a sense of helplessness. There is nowhere to go. There is no refuge outside the walls. The Judean Desert only offers Bedouin raiders and bandits, in addition to miles and miles without water. Most seek to hide their wares and barricade their children. Those who have some coins hire young men with weapons to protect their families. The pious pray and the rest just cry.

Word of Yael's disappearance is immediately linked with the impending attack. "She was taken," is the word on the street. Rachel and Samuel, her young parents, are devastated. They plead with night watchmen not to close the city gates in the hope that Yael returns before nightfall. While Samuel desperately calls out Yael's name, asking, begging any and all passersby for possible information of her whereabouts, Rachel and her sisters implore the counsel of Kohanim, the priests, to send out a search party into the vineyards and fields. Under normal circumstances, that would be the standard practice. Many children fall asleep on a hilltop or in the wheat fields, only to be found and returned. Some slip on the rocky slopes and break an ankle but are fine when they are returned home and splinted up. Tonight is not normal. Tonight, the threat of an impending attack by Greek forces makes a search and rescue operation out of the question.

"She is a child, a good girl. She cannot be far. Please," Rachel begs. "I will go myself—I will not endanger anyone else."

The response is definitive: "No one leaves Jerusalem tonight."

While a mother and father worry about their lost daughter, an emergency meeting of the Sanhedrin is called into session. The Sanhedrin is the newly formed governing body that replaced the governance of the Great Assembly and is now considered the supreme court of Judea. It is made up of young scholars and political activists, many of them trained in rabbinic academies influenced by Greek culture. These young scholars feel that the old-school scholars are not addressing the needs of the emerging youth. They complain that the old teachings and policies are no longer relevant in their world. Worse, those teachings promote a fear of the new and an uncritical reverence for the past.

The lack of leadership led to political turmoil and a rocky transition of power.

This occurred under Simon the High Priest's watch. He was the head of the Great Assembly, and it seemed like he could get nothing right. His impeachment was painful and, as much as he tried not to take it personally, he had a hard time focusing on his spiritual duties.

Under his leadership, the Great Assembly had made some decisions that led to distrust from the people. In the fallout that occurred after this power struggle, Simon was persuaded to focus his attention on the temple service for which he was responsible. He'd relinquished all political and legal influence to the Sanhedrin, doubtful though he was that they could handle said influence in a manner consistent with Jewish principles.

In their formation, the Sanhedrin took a Greek name as a sign of the times. The conceived purpose was to guide the future of the Jewish people and Jewish law, but also to appeal to a young generation. Antignos of Socho, the Sanhedrin's first president and chief judge, cleverly presented a precedent for such a governing body from the biblical narrative of Moses.

When Moses, the first leader of the Jewish people, expressed frustration with those he was empowered to lead, the Bible tells that he turned to God and said:

"Why have You dealt ill with Your servant, and why have You not shown me kindness that You have placed the burden of these people upon me? Did I conceive them or bear them that You, God, should say to me, 'Carry them in your bosom as a nurse carries an infant'?"

In response to Moses' complaint, God advised him to select seventy elders of the people who would govern along with him. Antignos, in a stroke of genius, likened his leadership to that of Moses. "We too shall select seventy elders. Those wise men and I will make seventy-one. Together we will govern and legislate for the people."

As a courtesy to Simon's long-standing service, Antignos gave him a non-voting seat on the Sanhedrin. Simon's role would be limited to an advisory and spiritual capacity.

On the evening before the mighty army of Alexander arrived, Antignos called the session of seventy-one scholars to order.

"Scribe, record the date as the evening of the twenty-fourth day of Tevet in the 3397th year since the creation of the world," Antignos said as he looked out to the elders and scholars sitting in front of him. "We have a crisis on our hands. I, along with members of this chamber, have cross-examined the witnesses. Each of them has independently reported that Alexander, the son of Philip the Great, is on his way to Jerusalem with an army of 13,000 foot soldiers. His intentions are clear. He wants to destroy the city, as he has done in the north, plunder our resources and take our children as slaves. My colleagues, time is of the essence and we need a plan. The people of Jerusalem and Judaea are in a panic. We face absolute anarchy. It is our duty to lead. So I open the floor for suggestions."

"Arm the young men and let us fight!" Akiva said.

"Yes! The God of our forefather wins our battles for us."

Another agreed, "If we are to perish, let us perish as warriors fighting God's war."

One of the older members stood to disagree. "We have no time nor weapons with which to arm our boys. Even if we did, we would be sending them to the slaughterhouse. Let us appeal to his compassion, send a delegation immediately and beg for mercy."

The younger members rebuked such an idea.

"Never. We will not reduce ourselves to be beggars. And if we do, we will have to pay a huge price. Who is willing to give their sons and daughters to those savages to let them be raped and abused? Not I!"

Another scholar stood and offered a third option. "Gentlemen, please let us immediately begin an escape out of the city. The women and children will go first. Let us take them south to the Negev villages."

He was quickly shouted down. "Fool! Alexander's army is headed south. He is merciless and will catch up with any refugee and do as he wishes with them. But he may just be more frustrated if we all flee."

Yosseh, son of Yo'ezer, raised his hand and asked for permission to speak. Antignos granted the young, charismatic scholar the floor and motioned to the others that his words would be heard.

"These circumstances have occurred once before. It is our duty to learn from our sacred past." The room listened in silence to this young man who rooted his answer in history. "Ours is the story of Jacob, the son of Isaac, in the book of Bereshit."

"How so?" Avraham called out.

"When Jacob was returning to the land of Canaan," Yosseh continued, "to see his parents, he was traveling with his wives and children and all his possessions. He was told that Esav, his brother, was coming toward him with 400 men to avenge the theft of his birthright and fulfill his promise of killing Jacob. Was he not?"

All the heads in the room nodded.

"Jacob faced the same existential threat we face tonight—the enemy is headed in our direction. Our enemy is armed and trained in the discipline of killing, while we, like Jacob of old, are people of the tent. All we know is the law. We have no reason to believe we could possibly defeat Alexander in battle."

"Where are you going with this?" came a voice from the back. "We have no time for biblical lessons."

"This, like every lesson in the Bible, is also a lesson in life. How did Jacob respond to his threat? He did three things. First, he prepared for war; second, he prayed; lastly, he sent gifts to his enemy. It was his three-pronged preparations that saved his life and spared his family. This is what I suggest."

No one spoke for a second as he paused. Then Yosseh continued, "If war is our destiny, then we shall fight as King David did against Goliath. It is not chariots and horses that win our wars, it is the Lord of heaven and earth. Second, we shall dispatch all elderly men and children to houses of worship for prayer and fasting to beseech our God in heaven to have mercy upon his people. They should beseech him that he not allow his great name to be desecrated by the sword of the uncircumcised. Third, I suggest we send a delegation at sunrise with gifts to meet the men of war and reason with Alexander. Not to offer our children as sacrifices, but if it is meat and wine he wants, we will oblige."

The nodding led to stamping of feet, banging on tables, and clapping of hands.

"Silence in the room, I insist!" Antignos shouted.

"He speaks wisely," Avraham said.

Antignos called the room to attention. He immediately dispatched five elders to begin enlisting as many young men as possible to prepare for war with whatever weapons they can get their hands on. "Remind them to have faith in God of Israel." He then selected five of the most pious elders and commanded them, "Gather those who are not of military age, young and old, in prayer. Urge all to fast and repent in order to find favor in God's eyes." The elders dashed out of the hall.

Antignos then looked out into the chamber and asked for a volunteer to go and meet the Great Alexander. There was silence.

"He will never even speak with us," some lamented.

"Going out of Jerusalem is certain death, like that poor child who was taken. Only God knows what they did with her," Asher whispered.

"These men are savages, we all know that," Barak added.

"They are not men, they are not human—they are more like animals than they are human," Benyamin protested. "They do not possess the image of God."

Other than the murmurs of doubt, silence lingered.

Antignos exhorted the others, "We need a volunteer. Speaking with Alexander is our only chance to survive. We need someone who is fluent in their language."

There was no shortage of members who knew Greek. In fact, in order to qualify to sit on the Sanhedrin, one had to be fluent in at least six languages.

A few members of the group wondered why Antignos, himself fluent in Greek language, culture and philosophy, was not volunteering for the task he was soliciting. The silence lingered until Simon the High Priest, the man who'd received a pity-seat in the room and who'd lost so much political and spiritual influence over the last few years, raised his hand and said, "I will go see the man. If I am to be our people's sacrificial lamb, let it be so. I have sacrificed many animals on the alter—now it is my turn to be sacrificed."

To Simon's surprise, no one objected.

"It will be so," Antignos announced. "At daylight, the gates of Jerusalem will open and the fate of our people is in the hands of God Almighty, creator of heaven and earth. If we are to survive the morrow, we will make this day a feast of praise and thanksgiving to the Lord."

The gallant words could not avert the unasked question: Why had this chamber agreed to send an old man to his death instead of its young leader?

11

Jerusalem, Israel
Office of the Prime Minister
June 2006

THE FEMALE GUARDS AT THE main gate of the prime minister's office cannot hide their delicate features behind their drab gray uniform blouses. Their bodies slim, tall, tan and athletic. Their faces are made less fierce by the tint of eyeliner and touch of lipstick. Their movements are young and lithe as they walk around the vehicles to inspect them. Their job is to check each driver's identification card and examine passengers with their trained smiles. One wonders what these young girls would be doing in another context. A country with a military requirement following high school is a country with a much more diverse military force. Israeli beauties, who might have been wandering college campuses or lounging under the shade of an oak tree, walk around vehicles with mirrors looking for bombs planted on the bottom of cars. Scholarly looking boys, who otherwise would have been buried in obscure books of study, carry out patrols at checkpoints.

Kiryat HaMemshala, also known as Kiryat Ben-Gurion, is a series of government buildings opposite the famous Israel Museum in the Givat

Ram neighborhood of Jerusalem. The well-camouflaged razor-wire fences and high-tech security equipment is backed up by constant patrols courtesy of the most elite infantry. Those infantry members are often outfitted in such poorly chosen civilian clothing, it can feel like their attempts at operating undercover are carried out with a wink and a smile. *Sure. Everything is normal here. Nothing to see.* Kiryat Ben-Gurion houses the three branches of government: the Knesset, the Supreme Court of Israel, and the Office of the Prime Minister.

From the outside, this house of government looks modest and retro. The buildings are mostly white stone. There are no grand columns, and few of the exterior trappings one would associate with a national house of governance. But humble aesthetics are hardly an adequate representation of power. The independent circular structure of stone, glass and steel has a built-in means of descent to a much larger underground complex in the bowels of the Kiryah. It is built in such a way that, if the enemy showered the state of Israel with conventional, nuclear or biological warheads, it would not impede the conduct of the government nor prevent the shattering acts of retaliation that would emerge from those bunkers of safety.

There are no shortcuts in or out of the prime minister's office. Every vehicle enters through a main gate, which is protected by underground hydraulic steel teeth that could thrust from the ground at the push of a button, stopping even the hardiest of field tanks. In the back seat, Rachmani is on his cell phone gathering as much information as possible. He knows full well that in a few minutes he will be the target of piercing questions. As he talks frantically to his subordinates of various departments, he watches the inspections occur outside his window. Rachmani's experienced eye always assesses soldiers' ranks, not by the stripes on their shoulders, but by the weapons they carry in their holsters. The two young women at the gate are not carrying the standard-issue pistol, which means that each of them, not quite 20 years old, has earned the right to select their own weapon. Such a right is earned by showing prowess and proficiency in the art of close-range killing. They might look like sweet college girls, but they obviously carry a punch that belies those looks. Rachmani's bulletproof, fully equipped gray Range Rover SUV—even with the black IDF plates—goes through the same inspection as any other vehicle. In Israel, rank does not preclude precaution.

One of the young female officers approaches Rachmani's window. She knocks on it and requests that he roll it down. It is both strange and appropriate that they are just as rigorous, even though they have every reason to believe the person in this car is one of the most powerful people in the entire country. As he responds to her demands, he looks above her pistol to her stripes, which rank her as a sergeant. She is not especially tall, but she certainly gives off a sense of abundant confidence. Her cool black hair is pulled back into a ponytail. She looks into the back seat while the thumb of her left hand is hooked into her green Sam Brown belt. Her right hand tickles the butt of a glistening Jericho 9mm handgun.

"Boker Tov." Rachmani puts his cell phone down and flashes his Aman ID card to the guard.

He is treated to a perfunctory smile as her eyes glance at his ID and face in a flicker. The car is immediately waved through. The driver circles the round building, and Rachmani steps out, takes a deep breath and visually absorbs the maze of clashing architecture.

The prime minister's quarters, unlike the residences of other heads of state, are not a private enclave. Instead, it is a suite of modern boardrooms and secure meeting places used by various cabinet members, defense ministers and intelligence personnel. On the upper floor, behind glass doors, is the prime minister's office. To that floor and office, Rachmani heads. He strides purposefully down the hall; his short legs pump with purpose. He has always been a fit man, since his days in the service. He associates fitness of body with fitness of mind and feels a sting of regret at the pains in his lungs from the quick pace. Running a country—dealing with the various shit Iran, Syria, Hezbollah and the thugs out of Gaza pull on a weekly basis—leaves little time for the treadmill or weight room. When the president of the United States is due on the phone a half hour after meetings with the Turkish prime minister, time is better spent prepping for those conversations. *I've got to get back in the gym,* he thinks as he makes his way up the stairs.

The people he sees that morning use the somber greeting, "A'lan," and then lower their gaze in silence and move along. This is not the time for social niceties or small talk. The prime minister has made it clear that he wants everyone there immediately, so his cabinet ministers and military assistants will have to chug their coffee and smoke their cigarettes a bit earlier this morning.

They meet in the boardroom. To improve the room's ambiance, there are no plants. There are no paintings of scenic idylls. The only décor in the room is four towering Israeli flags, one in each corner. In the middle of the room is a large oak table with eighteen leather chairs, nine on each side. A nineteenth chair is placed at the head of the table reserved for the prime minister. When he enters the room, the expected cast takes every seat. No media and no interns. Everyone is on a cell phone or scrolling through the news on laptops, with the exception of three military leaders whispering in hushed conversation. This room is perhaps the only collection of individuals in the country that does not stand to acknowledge Rachmani's arrival. He actually prefers it that way. They have business to attend to. They want to leave the formality and pomp to countries that don't have the dogs of war breathing readily at every border.

Yehudit Goldwasser is sitting cross-legged at the far corner of the conference table. She holds her phone to her ear with one hand and motions with the other for Rachmani to sit next to her.

"Email me the latest information every three minutes," she says into her phone and puts it down on the table. "I'm holding this seat for you," she says to Rachmani. Of all the people in the room, a close relationship with Rachmani serves her best. Fortunate for her, Rachmani is not good at discriminating when it comes to pretty women.

Yehudit is the prime minister's communications director and chief of staff. Access to Rachmani and the information he is privy to is critical to her success.

"*Toda*, thank you," Rachmani responds.

"He is in a shitty mood today," she whispers. "I tried to convince him that this abduction, unfortunate as it is may very well be, is a blessing in disguise for him—an excellent diversion from the media's obsession with his travel expenses and his fucking ice cream fetish." Yehudit is referring to the prime minister's lavish winter vacation and his habit of ordering 60 shekels' worth of gourmet ice cream—weekly—for his wife with taxpayer money.

Uri Rivkin strolls in like he owns the room. He doesn't even look around to notice who else is there. He has the rank and role to feel confident. Rivkin is a career officer recently appointed to head the Israeli Security

Services, or Shabak. Shabak is one of three arms of Israeli intelligence. The branch motto is, "Defender that shall not be seen," or "The unseen shield." This differentiates it from Aman, which deals mostly with military intelligence, and Mossad, which is Israel's foreign intelligence service. The spies.

Like the United States' FBI or Germany's BFV, Shabak is essentially responsible for domestic counterintelligence. Being that Israel is a country whose borders and citizens are under constant threat from enemy states and terrorism, Shabak's role in protecting citizens, heads of state, air and seaports is of massive importance.

As Rivkin bulldozes his way into the room, he glances at Rachmani and says cryptically, "All is taken care of."

Rachmani has no clue what Rivkin is talking about. Rivkin goes over and sits next to his colleague, the head of Mossad. Next to them sits the minister of defense, the IDF general and his secretary, the foreign minister and certain cabinet members tagged for this meeting. They all make their way toward their seats a couple of minutes before the prime minister is set to arrive.

As the prime minister enters, the room goes silent. His forte is running productive meetings. He detests wasted time and nonsense. In no way does he resemble the image of a diplomatic, personable world leader. He doesn't say "hello" to these men and women who have gathered to give him counsel. He doesn't greet them "good morning."

Instead, he strides purposefully to his chair, gives a quick glance at those who have gathered, and announces, *Bli chochmot*," a Hebrew expression that approximately means "no bullshit." It is his standard opening address. It actually explains why everyone gets so quiet when he arrives. They do not trifle with his time.

"Major General, can we please have a detailed briefing of what transpired this morning?"

All eyes turn to Rachmani, a subtle shift in the room's focus that only makes things worse for him. Rachmani never succumbs to the cherished perks of his position. He always maintains a defiant simplicity to his lifestyle, choosing falafel and ful over expensive restaurants. He is fearless on the battlefield; as a soldier and a commander, he can stare down the barrel of a tank and not blink. He runs Aman like he ran his division in the military, with discipline and authority. He is fierce with those who make mistakes and loyal to his soldiers. He dreads social gatherings and tends to hide in his work. When it comes to speaking in public, he begins to tremble. The feeling of anxiety begins in his belly and works its way down to his knees, a progression that, when he is standing, makes him feel like he might fall over at any moment. It is not just a physical feeling. It is a physiological change that is accompanied by a fear of complete incompetence. Within seconds of being called upon to talk in front of others, Rachmani goes from a fearless general to a nauseous and claustrophobic ball of anxiety. The fact that there is no air ventilating the room that morning did not help him.

"Mr. Prime Minister," he starts quietly.

"Speak up!" he is ordered from the other side of the table.

"Mizta'er, I'm Sorry," he mumbles.

"Ladies and gentlemen, at 5:43 a.m. our southern military headquarters received a code red distress signal. Ground and air backup was dispatched immediately. At this time the following is what we know took place: After entering into Israeli territory northeast of Kerem Shalom, seven terrorists split into three squads. One group headed north toward our military's tank outpost, one group headed west toward an active armored personnel carrier, and one group headed southwest toward the Telem Matmon Armor Post. At around 0540 two terrorists near Telem Matmon opened fire at the outpost. IDF soldiers returned fire, killing both terrorists. The terrorists were found bearing numerous explosives that could have caused significant damage. The three terrorists that headed north toward our tank outpost in the region fired an anti-tank rocket that struck an empty tank. At around 0550 a four-man AV on guard-duty in the Kerem Shalom region of the Negev was ambushed. The attack left two soldiers dead, one severely injured, and the fourth was abducted. This attack was carefully planned. There was a getaway vehicle waiting for them. They then escaped back into the Gaza Strip.

Hamas is claiming responsibility for the attack.

As far as we can tell, this attack was unprovoked. It involved seven terrorists armed with explosives, anti-tank missiles, light arms and grenades."

"How the hell did these weapons get into Israel?" A question came from the back of the room.

"These weapons were brought into Israel through a tunnel that spans the Israel-Gaza border." Rachmani responds assertively without looking up at the questioner.

"Those damn tunnels," the prime minister mutters. "Go on" the Prime Minister barks.

Rachmani pauses to catch his breath. His forehead is sweating and his collar is soaked. He raises his head from his notebook and looks around at his colleagues. Most are furiously taking notes. Others, who are more aware of the situation, spend their time typing up emails as they listen absently.

"What do we know about the AV ambush? Do you have names?" The Prime Minister asks.

"As I just said, at 0550 two terrorists, headed west, fired an anti-tank missile at our Alpha AV, catching our four soldiers by surprise. The terrorists then approached the armored vehicle, wielding light arms and grenades. The AV driver, Omri Younker, and gunner, David Bitton, were killed in the initial blasts. The radio engineer, Staff Sergeant Shealtiel Shlomi, was severely injured and left for dead, and Cpl. Lior Samet was kidnapped and taken into the Gaza Strip."

"Do we know where, precisely?" the prime minister was sounding frustrated.

"No, sir. They escaped through a network of dirt roads and were met by a large number of cars that scattered in various directions. There was no way for our intelligence to track where every car went. We do not know where he was taken."

"Okay. Go on." The Prime Minister nodded.

"At 0630, IDF forces reached Telem Matmon and joined the forces there. At some point, between 0630 and 0650, an explosive charge was detonated, wounding three IDF soldiers. A total of two Israeli soldiers were killed, five were wounded and one was kidnapped. Two Hamas terrorists were killed and five escaped."

"Just another day at the office," Prime Minister Ehud Olmert says grimly. "Except for the damn kidnapping. How did that happen? Did we know about those particular tunnels?"

"Yes, sir," Rivkin interjects in a self-deprecating voice. "The timing was unfortunate, Mr. Prime Minister. We knew about the tunnels. They were on a long list of security measures that had to be taken care of."

At that moment, Rachmani begins to understand what Rivkin meant when he said, "It's taken care of." He doesn't know why Rivkin had fallen on this particular sword, but he is sure he'd owe something for it later.

"Now is not the time for a mea culpa," the prime minister replies. "What's next? Where do we go from here?"

At that question, the minister of foreign policy sees his opportunity. "Mahmoud Abbas has to be personally accountable for the safe return of this young man," he shouts and starts pounding his fist on the table. "If he is the darling of the world, as the media wants to portray him, he must release the soldier immediately."

"Minister Lalush, with all due respect, get off your damn high horse," Yehudit blurts out. "We all know Abbas is powerless. The sooner we deal with actual realities in this discussion, the more productive we can be."

Rachmani agrees with her, "Let's not get this kid killed over dumb rhetoric and unrealistic ideologies."

Yehudit nods. "So let's start with a practical request that might get answered. I suggest we immediately call for the International Red Cross to examine the boy and provide him with whatever medical care is necessary. We insist publicly on a full report of the young man's condition."

"Thank you, Yehudit. At least that looks like we are doing something," the prime minister agrees.

Rivkin clears his throat. "If we stand a chance at getting this kid home, we need to do it within the next forty-eight hours. Let's reach out to our contacts in Egypt and Jordan, offer them whatever incentives we can so that they help bring him back."

The prime minister smirks just a bit. "Looks like some time on the phone for me today. I'll call Egypt and Jordan. To that list, I'd add the White House and Downing." The prime minister feels a surge of energy. "Reach out to each of the families. I want to meet the Samet family this evening in Dimona. I want all of us to be consistent with the language we use in the media. The young man was abducted. He is not a prisoner of war—he was taken on Israeli territory and this attack was unprovoked. We need to make clear to Hamas, we will not negotiate with terrorists."

Everyone around the table nods robotically.

The prime minister turns to his right. "Avner, open lines of negotiation immediately—keep it classified. Make contact with Abbas through our back-door channels. Tell him he has our support and we understand he is in a difficult situation—let's get as much information from him as possible."

Everyone begins to gather their papers together and head to their next task, but they are stopped short as the prime minister continues, "One more thing—let's do what it takes to get this kid home. We, as a government, have a commitment to working in a coordinated manner and using all instruments of national power to safely recover hostages. This is not just about us—this is a human rights issue." The prime minister stands up and continues, "I want to starve this story of any fucking media attention. I don't want to give these *mamzerim*, these bastards, a platform to spew their hatred on our dime. Is this clear? No CNN, no BBC shit, no international news here. Starve them!"

Yehudit concurs, "We don't want an Israeli version of Daniel Pearl."

"Thank you, Yehudit. You know what has to get done, so let's get on it!"

"Yes, Mr. Prime Minister."

"I'm done here—where's my coffee?" As he leaves the room, the prime minister can be heard grumbling to his assistant, "I need to see today's daily briefing."

After the prime minister steps out, the entire room turns quiet for a few seconds. Then participants scatter in various directions. Yehudit looks over to Rachmani and says quietly, "To be honest with you, there are many more pressing issues right now. No one is going to give this a second look. The top man has already forgotten about it. Shall we grab a coffee before we head out?"

12

Jerusalem
Inside the Walled City
323 BCE

"WHAT WILL BECOME OF US?" Simon's wife asks.

Simon sits quietly and withstands the onslaught of her anger. He knows that it comes from a place of both love and fear. He has some of the very same sentiments reverberating around his head any moment he sits still. *How can this end well?*

Malka, Simon's wife, continues, "What will become of our children, our neighbors, everyone we love and everything we hold sacred? How can you possibly believe that Alexander is anything but a monster? These people are not human."

"How could I possibly know what he is? All of God's creations have a divine spark in them," Simon says in a voice that is both calm and defeated. "I've certainly never met the man. And I know from personal experience that rumors aren't always true."

"It is well known the entire world over, Simon!" she says. "Little kids who wander the streets below the Temple Mount know that Alexander has

68

an appetite for infinite conquest. His very arrival on our doorsteps is proof. He wants to take over the world—Jerusalem is but a tiny pebble on his road to victory. He will crush us under his enormous boot. And you have volunteered to go out to welcome him on his way into our city."

Simon wants very much to soothe his wife. For one, he hates to see her so afraid. She is a good mother and a dutiful wife. She is not someone who frets constantly. More practically, he needs to keep her frenzy from infecting him. If he panics, all is lost. He must be cool-headed, even as people are losing their minds all around him.

As his wife screams in panic, and his servants, children and grandchildren gather in secluded places with as many supplies as possible around the Old City, Rabbi Yosseh's plan is quickly being implemented. Simon takes a short walk from his residence to see the events unfolding. All around the temple, men gather for prayer. Priests find refuge in the sanctuary and holy places. One after another, and with the highest degree of reverence, sacrifices are offered to the Holy One above. Meanwhile, young men gather anything that might serve as a weapon in case they are called upon to defend their city.

At the change of the third watch, Simon returns back home. Once there, he mentions to his wife that he needs to be alone. She looks at him with an expression of exasperation, turns and walks out. He then calls out to Tobi, his trusted servant, "Yes, here I am."

"Tobi, bring me the priestly garments from the safe."

At first, Tobi just looks at him blankly.

Simon repeats the request, "Tobi, I need you to retrieve the priestly garments for me, please."

"But, your honor…" Tobi stops himself before he goes too far. He is not one to disagree. In fact, he has always prided himself on knowing his proper place. If he does his job the right way, he's hardly there. He can support the priest and help him achieve his duties best by quietly anticipating what is needed and doing it. Nonetheless, in response to this order, Tobi can't bring himself to move.

Looking at his frozen but speechless servant, Simon asks him, "Yes, Tobi. What is it?"

"It's just… your excellency, those garments are special."

"I know that, Tobi. That is why I need them."

"But, my master. I mean… they are special and reserved for the one day, the great day of the year, Yom Kippur, when, you, the high priest, after days of preparation, enter into the Holy of Holies, the most sacred place on this earth."

"I am very aware of that, Tobi."

"Well, why do you need them now? To meet this godless heathen?"

"Tobi, I am not asking for your permission. I understand that this is not ordinary. That said, if you do not procure them, then I will do it myself."

Tobi stomps toward the doors of Simon's chambers, mumbling, "What is Simon thinking? How dare anyone, even the high priest, desecrate the holy garments?" The moment Tobi scuttles down the corridor, he recognizes the urgency of the moment, even if he does not agree with Simon's approach to it.

Simon is emphatic. He doesn't quite know why he feels the need to don the priestly garments for this appointment with death. *Maybe, if there is to be a miracle, the merit of the Holy Service will bring it upon us.*

Simon considers just how differently he views the garments today compared to how he had twenty years earlier. Then, he would read the prophetic passages about them. He knew the stories of Aaron the High Priest. He knew that Moses had been commanded to make his brother special garments so that he might minister to others. He knew that they conferred a great spiritual power. He'd heard tales of their beauty and mystical essence from his parents and grandparents from the time he could remember. His predecessor, Akiva the High Priest, once told him: "While we are clothed in the priestly garments, we are clothed in the priesthood. But when we are not wearing the garments, the priesthood is not upon us."

For some reason, that teaching seems to resonate tonight for the first time. Up until now, the garments were simply an essential prerequisite for temple work. But tonight, the secrecy and mystery surrounding them is titillating. *What will it feel like to wear them when it's not Yom Kippur?* he'd thought over and over. *Will I feel more divine? Will they give me the inner wisdom, courage and strength I will need to save our people from doom?*

As a young priest, he'd had so many moments of arrogance when thinking about the clothes that Tobi fetches. He remembers thinking, "God forgive me that Akiva the High Priest is the only thing that stands between me and the priestly garments." That old priest seemed like he would live forever. "Maybe the garments confer some taste of immortality." How little he'd known!

Others had whispered to him from the time he was 30 years old that he'd make a fine "High Priest." He'd eventually grown to believe those whispers.

Akiva the High Priest was very pious and famous for his humility. Even clothed in all of his power, Akiva had lived a simple life. He passed away in the middle of the month of Elul, which meant that the choice and election for the next high priest needed to happen quickly. Simon heard the news from one of his trusted advisors. He was on the short list, that much he knew. But he was also aware that others were vying for the title. "Whoever is chosen," Simon remembers telling his young family at the time, "will be representing our people in fewer than twenty days. This is not a small task, ministering before the God of Gods, deliverer of the Jewish nation from the bondage in Egypt, the God of Samuel, Elijah, Elisha, Isaiah, Amos, Jeremiah and Ezekiel."

When the sages and elders came to his home on that fateful night to announce the passing of Akiva, the Saintly Priest, Simon knew they came to his home for more than just reporting news. He knew they came to induct him as the next high priest. Despite his youthful ambitions, Simon experienced a healthy degree of youthful ambivalence. He knew enough to recognize that the "blessing" of the high priesthood came with a life of immense stress and responsibility. He was well aware of the political turmoil fermenting in the religious and social community. It was part and parcel of the mantle; it would be his responsibility to deal with it. Despite these points of concern, as the elder sage finished his thought, Simon recited a blessing declaring absolute submission to the righteous decrees of God for the sad news of Akiva's death. In the same breath, he recited the blessing of gratitude and bounty for the news of his election to the position of high priest.

For a man with ambition, there was plenty to be happy about. At the time of his election, high priest was the most powerful religious and political position in the state. The high priest was expected to be judge, legislator, governor and ambassador. Simon had many years of experience on the legislative governing body called the Great Assembly, but nothing could prepare him for the challenges he faced as high priest. As soon as he took the job, he realized just how much he'd underestimated Akiva's grace and capacity. With each new demand and each new stressful moment, he saw more and more clearly how much his predecessor had shouldered.

Yet he'd made it through. He'd successfully survived a quasi-coup attempt by the younger members of the Sanhedrin. He'd been unable to stop them completely, but he'd wrestled as much control as he could from them. He'd felt during those months a bit like Jacob of the Bible.

So Jacob was left alone, and a man wrestled with him till day-break. When the man saw that he could not overpower him, he touched the socket of Jacob's hip so that his hip was wrenched as he wrestled with the man. Then the man said, "Let me go, for it is daybreak."

But Jacob replied, "I will not let you go unless you bless me."

Jacob walked with a limp after that fated wrestling match with the divine. Simon too feels crippled by the political discord. But here he is, 50 years old. He has been serving as high priest for almost fourteen years. And he is going to be the sacrificial offering of his people to Alexander. It is a task both great and humbling. He will go in the finest attire his people can provide. He doesn't know of any time in history when these garments were used the way he is about to use them.

Ever since he has been wearing the priestly garments, they have made him feel different. On numerous occasions, Simon physically experienced what others had described. The garments infuse him with a sense of awe. They make him feel simultaneously more connected to the God of Gods and tinier in God's presence. They give Simon a sense of gravity that he only feels when wearing them. But now that he is years into his service, and after all the problems with the Sanhedrin, Simon also knows that the garments do not give him magical powers. He is just relying on the inability of this great Alexander to recognize that same fact.

Simon sits on the cot in his room. Ever since he could think outside his own mind, Simon perceives the world in numbers, shapes and patterns. Everything has a numerical value, and everything of worth needs to be counted. The number three has special significance. It holds the key to all shapes. Three is both finite and infinite. He does not know where the knowledge comes from, but he always knew that if you multiply the diameter of a circle by three, you get the circumference.

The prayer Simon teaches is always addressed to the God of Abraham, the God of Isaac and the God of Jacob. The one irreducible God is beyond names. But, if one has to try, this trinity of names is better than any single choice.

In addition to his great erudition, Simon is famous for his extreme piety and charitable work. He is also an expert in law, astronomy and logic—a polymath if there ever was one. He has learned, over the years in his role, that intelligence is not nearly as valuable for success as piety and wisdom. He sits quietly on his cot, trying to summon up some forms of wisdom from the old stories. There is the tale of Abraham and Isaac. *Maybe this time, God is just testing his people. Maybe God is testing me,* Simon thinks. *Maybe once I walk out to meet Alexander, the hand of the Almighty will provide some metaphorical lamb as an alternative for sacrifice. There are plenty of stories of miraculous military exploits. Perhaps some intervention from above will save me and my people this morning.*

"Master, I have the garments," Tobi announces, breaking Simon out of his meditations.

The gold-plated chest that Tobi wheels into the room is a national treasure. Its contents have been worn by generations of high priests. The First Temple was ransacked and destroyed by Nebuchadnezzar, the Babylonian, and his soldiers in the year 3174, counted from the time of creation. It was absolutely terrible. But it was not as bad as it could have been. Immediately prior to the Babylonian attack, the priests wisely hid the chest, and many other treasures and vessels, that dated back to the time of King Solomon. They knew that they were not a worthy opponent for the mighty Babylonian armies. But they also had complete faith in the words of Jeremiah the Prophet that some portion of their people would survive and, when the winds changed, they would return to Jerusalem. They knew it as surely as they knew their own names. It was the promise. So they prepared for destruction by protecting that which should never be destroyed. When the priests returned some seventy years later, the chest was still whole and untouched.

How had they done it? The hiding place was preserved in an encoded sequence of letters and words in the third book of the Torah, the Book of Leviticus, also known as the Torah of the Priests. The Book of Leviticus was written as a guide for the temple service. But it is more than that. It is written in code, filled with patterns and sequences of letters and words known only by a select group. The secret messages encoded within the Hebrew text have been passed on from priests to priests. Just like the priestly foods that cannot be shared with a non-priest, the priestly secrets cannot be shared with non-priests. This method of communication and ancient coding ensured that these garments were here for Simon today.

Tobi removes one item at a time and places each one on the table. Silently, Simon steps out of his chambers. To the right, alongside the stone walls of the courtyard, is a small pool of purifying waters. The water, used for ritual cleansing, has to be "living water," fresh flowing water, and not water lifted from a cistern. Jerusalem is amply supplied with water that originates in the Hebron Mountains north of the city. The water is collected in Bet Lechem in the three pools built by the great King Solomon. From those pools, the water gradually slopes its way toward the Temple Mount, the Priestly Quarters and Jerusalem. Two tunnels supply Jerusalem with water. The higher tunnel is called the Spring of Eitam. It runs directly into the Priestly Quarters and cuts right through the foot of the mountain along the southern end of the Western Wall. The waters of the lower tunnel supply the commoners and enable the cleansing of the sacrificial blood that drains from the temple.

Because the Mikveh has to be flowing water, it is located at the lowest point in the Priestly Quarters. Simon squirrels his way through the narrow stone streets and stairs. The men present at the Mikveh turn to see him approach. They wordlessly defer to Simon and let him go ahead of them. He disrobes, recites his blessing and dips into the welcoming cold waters. The chill of the flowing spring water, even in the heat of the desert summer, takes his breath away.

He dunks his head in the water and instinctively meditates on the prayer he recites every Yom Kippur:

May it be Your will,
Adonai, Lord our God,
God of our Fathers,
That this year that is coming upon us,
And upon Your entire people Israel,
Be a year in which no woman shall lose
The offspring of her womb.

And that the trees in the field
Give forth their produce…

Simon jumps out of the water, looks up to the heavens and calls out, "Dear God, save your people tonight!"

Those who have been waiting to cleanse themselves are silent. Some of the men realize, for the very first time, just how much weight is on the shoulders of the high priest. Others grimace as they imagine themselves walking out to confront Alexander the Great. They do not envy Simon's task.

He begins the return to his chambers. The walk up is always harder than the walk down. He takes it slow. He is hardly eager to proceed. When he reaches his quarters, Tobi, his faithful helper, greets him. Tobi reaches out with a towel for his master. Simon starts drying his arms. He then leans over and grunts a bit as he dries off his legs. Finally, he reaches up to dry his face and hair. Tobi watches wordlessly, waiting for Simon to hand him the towel upon finishing. Once Simon dries his face, he holds the towel by his side. Tobi notices his tears. Simon purses his lips, hands the towel to Tobi, and says:

Let us begin:
For the sake of His Unified Name, I fulfill the commandment of wearing the holy garments of priesthood.

Tobi immediately begins helping Simon put on the priestly undergarments, the pants of linen, the sacred tunic and robe. Once the undergarments are on, Tobi walks over to retrieve the outer pieces hanging from the hook by the door. The outer robe is embroidered with red and blue threads and has beautiful shiny gold bells and scarlet wool pomegranate-shaped knots hanging from its hem. As those bells ring, Simon smiles to himself, thinking about the old explanation: The bells are purportedly necessary because the sound of the bells are evidence that the high priest is still alive while doing his service in the Holy of Holies. It is a well-known fact that even one mistake or one irreverent thought during the performance of the service in the Holy of Holies can bring the priest's certain death. The Torah records the death of Aaron's two sons, Nadav and Avihu, who both perished during the dedication service in the temple. It is told that a fire from heaven consumed their innards and they died instantly. Others who approached the holy place without proper preparation have also been met with death.

Every Yom Kippur Eve, Simon would be surrounded by the elders and sages, his relatives and close friends, and was asked to publicly vow numerous times that he would not change any part of the service he was trained to perform. He often felt offended that they would even suspect his being a heretic. He learned over the years that what lay in the deep recesses of a man's heart was always suspect. Why would he change anything? It was his life on the line, after all. Simon had every intention of following the rules as accurately as he could possibly follow them. That didn't stop the eldest sage from warning him, "Heed before whom you are entering."

Others reminded him, "You enter into a place of fire and burning flames… the congregation of Israel is depending on you… and through you, will come our pardon."

Simon had heard some variation of those words immediately prior to his entering the Holy of Holies every Yom Kippur for the last fourteen years.

No one is here to remind him tonight of his sacred task. As the hour grows imminent, no sages or scribes are here to demand that he follow in the old traditions. No one is here to worry with him. No one, but Tobi.

"It may not say so on the calendar… but tomorrow," Simon whispers to Tobi, "is our people's Yom Kippur—I will enter into the burning furnace."

"Yes, your excellency." Tobi nods gently. He turns his attention to wrapping the apron around Simon's chest.

"Ephod," Simon mutters the ancient word for "apron." *Everything has its value. Everything its number.*

The Ephod is an apron worn backward so that it covers the back of the priest from above his waist down to his ankles, and overlaps his shoulders in the front. It is embroidered with gold, blue, purple and scarlet threads. It is tied and secured with a golden sash across the priest's chest. Two brilliant onyx stones are fastened on each shoulder. The stones have the names of the tribes of Israel engraved on them, six on one stone and six on the other:

> *Judah » Issachar » Zebulun » Reuben » Simeon » Gad*
>
> *Ephraim » Manasseh » Benjamin » Dan » Asher » Naphtali*

Simon runs his hand along each of the names. It reminds him of those who came before him and of the lineage of his people. They were all unique. They were all chosen. Would the ancient promise that links them all be kept when he walks out of the city in a few moments to confront the most powerful man on earth?

The sacred language of the Torah is Hebrew. There are no numbers in the Hebrew language, just letters. All students of the Torah know that Hebrew is unlike any other language. His teachers, who in turn were taught by their teachers, taught Simon that Hebrew is the language of God. Hebrew is the "matter" with which God created the world.

When an Israelite child is taught the opening chapter of Genesis, the creation of the world, the teacher recites the words "And God **said** let there be light." God creates with words and through the power of language. The child is also taught that the combination of letters and numbers are, indeed, the creative force that brought the world into existence. They are not just letters and words. They are God's intentionality in the fate of humanity written across the universe.

Each letter possesses a numerical value. Aleph has the numerical value of 1, Bet has the numerical value of 2, Gimmel 3, and so on until Yod, which is equivalent to 10. The next ten letters work differently, but in a similar orderly fashion. From Chaf until Zadi, the incremental numerical value is 10. Chaf is 20, Lamed is 30, Mem is 40, and so on until Kof, which has the numerical value of 100. Then the value changes again. Resh is 200, Shin 300, and Taf 400.

In Hebrew, therefore, combinations of letters represent numbers. The interrelationship between words and their numeric value is a doctrine through which Simon and the Jewish mystics perceive the world. Uncovering the numerical value of words leads to profound insights into the nature of the object or concept the word describes. That is why Simon thinks so frequently of the meaning of words and their numerical values.

If two words have an equivalent numerical value, it is not chalked up to coincidence. Rather, it is believed that the numerical value of the words reveals an internal connection between the creative potentials of each word.

Simon always felt ambivalent about the fact that the Greek thinkers and philosophers adopted Hebrew numerology. He loved the intellectual exercises and the ways they led to symbolic value. But he also worried about pretty much any connection to the Hellenistic values that were creeping into every facet of his people's belief systems. When Socrates's student Plato claimed that the essential force of a thing's name is to be found in its numerical value, the Jewish sages recognized where that concept was taken from. When Greece adopts Jewish ideas, the sages wonder: Is this good or bad for the Jewish people?

The *Ephod*, the apron, is being wrapped around Simon's chest as his mind wanders:

Ephod is spelled: אפוד

א = 1
פ = 80
ו = 6
ד = 4

Total numerical value of the word Ephod is 91.

The significance of the number is found in a corresponding concept, a popular word in the Jewish story:

Malach, angel, is spelled מלאך

מ = 40
ל = 30
א = 1
ך = 20

For a total numerical value of 91, the same numerical value of Ephod.

It hits Simon for the first time. Ephod shares something mystical with Malach, with the word for angel. *This is not a coincidence… if only God would send a guardian angel tonight. An angel like the one that appeared to Joshua of old, strapped in armor, ready to fight the Jewish people's wars.* Maybe the garments he wears tonight will be his armor as he faces the warrior?

The Jews are not a warring people, Simon reminds himself. *The last wars we fought were long ago. The mysteries by which they were won are buried in the myths of time.* Simon is still as thinks about these esoteric associations.

Tobi once again helps him come back to the present. "Please hurry, your honor," Tobi insists. "Sunrise is in a few minutes. You must be out of the gate before Alexander's armies charge the city!"

Tobi places the *Choshen*, the breastplate, over Simon's shoulder. The breastplate is woven of the same materials as the Ephod. It is decorated with rare precious jewels in gold settings, each brilliant in its own color. Like the stones on the Ephod, each of its precious jewels also represents a tribe of Israel. Judah was the red sardius, while the Tribe of Reuben was the green emerald. Gad had the most brilliant diamond, Simeon the deep blue sapphire. Zebulun's red carbuncle and Issachar's shiny green topaz were both marvelous to behold. Each of the Choshen's stones combined to a create a whole that was infinitely more stunning than the sum of its parts. *There is no garment like this in the world and there will never be such a garment*, Simon thought.

The tradition that has been passed down from priest to priest teaches that, through the breastplate, God revealed his divine will to his chosen people. If only Simon can unlock the oracle tonight—to know what God wills of him and his people today. The breastplate is unfortunately not complete. Missing are the two precious stones, the Urim VeTumim. These stones have not been seen since the destruction of Solomon's Temple. Maybe it is their absence that has weakened the power of the oracle. Maybe the concept of a lost people was an essential component of the story.

The turban and the tzitz are left in place. The turban is a high-standing blue and white hat. The tzitz is a gold plate affixed on the forehead of the high priest on the exterior of the hat. Tobi walks behind Simon, steps up on the stool and begins to wrap the golden tzitz around his master's forehead. Simon reaches for the tzitz, feels the engraving of God's name, and kisses his fingers. It seems like the tzitz is especially sparkling tonight in the dim light of the burning candles. Simon is fully clothed in the history of his people, in their symbolic glory. He finally remarks to Tobi, "I shall now go. My fate and the fate of our people is in the hands of God. May he have mercy upon us and save us from destruction."

13

Dimona, Israel
June 2006

AT THE BUS STOP OUTSIDE of Dimona's secular public high school, the usual crowd gathers, standing around smoking, gawking and watching.

"Can you believe it? Lior a prisoner of war?" Arik smirks, standing in his dirty beige hip-hugging khaki pants, black military boots and Jim Morrison T-shirt.

"Shut up, you idiot," Yossi responds, looking the other way to show just how little regard he has for Arik's ignorance. "He was abducted, kidnapped. He is not a POW, asshole."

"You indoctrinated Zionists don't know what the hell you're talking about," Arik fires back.

"What does indoctrination have to do with it, Arik?"

"He is not kidnapped, and you are brainwashed. Get with the program, man."

"Can someone please explain to me the difference. The poor boy has been taken against his will. Kidnapped or prisoner, who cares?" one of the girls ask.

"Huge difference," Yossi shoots back.

Arik starts yelling, "The difference is, kidnapped victims don't do anything to instigate the nabbing. Think… little-girl, street-corner, bad-man shit. High drama, crappy cable TV."

"And Lior is different from that description because?" Yossi prods.

"Because Lior was out on a damn patrol as part of our defense efforts. Because we are at war."

"He was patrolling our borders," Yossi argues. "That doesn't mean we are at war. We are entitled to protect our citizens and our borders, and that is not war. Anyway, this military-industrial complex you rage about is going to welcome its newest member, Arik Melamed, just as soon as you finish school. You don't have a choice, man. You just got your physical like everybody else, Mr. Revolution. And I doubt that anyone would believe you need to be excused from the military for religious reasons. You burned that bridge long ago."

Arik shakes his head in disagreement. "I am never putting on a uniform. I went to the military physical so that I can have that cute nurse feel my balls. I will never fight for this Zionist, racist nation. It's pathetic what happened to Lior and he's a prisoner of war! The sooner you all admit that we are at war, the more clearly you'll understand shit around you. I'm going to class," Arik blurts out as he storms off.

As Arik leaves in a huff, Yossi looks at his friends, soaks in victory and follows him to the front entrance of the school. Cigarettes are thrown down and stamped out as people start to make their way from the bus stop to class. They avoid walking onto campus as much as possible. The bus stop is a safe haven for the students, a place where they can speak and teachers can't tell them what to do.

Two young women who'd been listening to the dispute glance wordlessly at each other, then follow their classmates. Ruti turns to her friend Moran to seek her opinion. "Who cares if he's POW or kidnapped? Lior is missing. What's worse? Being dead, wounded or missing?"

"Shit. I don't know. It certainly feels like being dead would be the worst. But who the hell knows what he's going through? There are surely some things worse than death. And if anyone is capable of those things, it is bound to be Hamas."

"True," Ruti agrees. "Hey. I love that blouse."

"Thanks," Moran replies absently, torn by appreciation for the compliment and guilt that they'd so quickly changed the subject.

Moran takes compliments like a greedy child anxious for that next sweet. She doesn't love her figure and makes every effort to find clothes that accentuate the positives. She is short, and when she wears the wrong jeans, her legs look like twin stumps of old olive trees. Not gnarly so much as stubby, and more firmly rooted to the ground than reaching to the sky. She wears iron horn-rimmed glasses in an attempt to suggest she doesn't care. But that is a lie. A poorly disguised lie at best. If she would wear the right blouse and a pair of pants that hang just so, she could spark the reaction all teenage girls long for.

Moran is set to graduate in two weeks from Dimona High School. She did well on her Bagrut, the standardized high school exit exams. Not that it matters all that much. University is unlikely for her, mainly because of questions about money. Who would pay? And with what? Maybe during the next three long years, as she wears the olive greens of Israel's military for her required service, she will figure out some funding options. She likes learning. She wants to keep at it. Her affection for reading began when she was young, when her grandmother read to her from the old Agnon stories. She'd loved the smells of that old corduroy couch; she had even liked the scratchy afghan they pulled over themselves in the cooler months. She can still hear that expressive voice, can picture herself reaching up to turn the pages. It was hard to imagine that little girl serving in the army and walking around with a semi-automatic rifle.

All of a sudden, she snaps out of her thoughts once again. *Poor Lior!* Moran thinks. *He had never seemed like he was into being a soldier or fighting for the army. He wasn't like Arik though. He was normal. Arik is really messed up.* She can't follow his arguments about POWs or kidnappings, but she thinks that he was pretty critical of the government and their homeland. *Is he a traitor?*

Moran's feelings about Lior are a mixture of empathy and guilt. She knows –she'd heard through the usual word of mouth—that Lior liked her. When he was in the twelfth grade and she was in eleventh, he'd asked her to a Friday night party. It was a rather subtle move on his part, a kind of unofficial and unassuming date. They'd just ride to the party together, really. Despite the harmless nature of the request and her lack of other

invitations, she'd said no. *How had I said no?* She ruminated. No expla-
nations or words of kindness. Just, "No thanks." Going to a party with
Lior didn't fit with the persona she wanted to project. She always imagined
herself with a different crowd, a tougher-looking guy. Lior looked more
like a gangly preteen. He had a baby face, big ears, and not enough stubble
to justify a regular shave. He wore his hair short, had a high forehead, and
wasn't even tall enough to stand out in a crowd. He was nobody's definition
of dreamy.

Moran excuses her cold shoulder internally, *He's just not my type.
He's just…* she trailed off. *He's not like Moshiko. Moshiko is my type. He's
tall and dark and funny, a great soccer player, has hair on his chest, and that
smile, but he never takes a second look at me.*

"Hey, Moran!" Ruti calls out to break up the daydream.

Moran looks up to see that she'd walked right past their turn.

"Sorry."

"What are you thinking about?" Ruti asks.

"Nothing. Just… a quiz I've got in History."

"OK, Ms. Studious," Michal says, "catch you later."

Before they part, they notice a sign that reads, "ASSEMBLY IN AU-
DITORIUM 3RD PERIOD."

"I'm going to try and sit next to Moshiko," Ruti whispers to Moran.
"During the speeches, I'll put my hands in his hair."

"That's not fair," Moran fantasizes out loud. "Moshiko is mine!"

"Yours?" Ruti asks playfully. "Moran!"

Third period comes around uneventfully.

Every student is gathered in the auditorium, everyone except Arik
who went out to smoke. The principal strides to the stage and raises his
hand to silence the rowdy teenagers.

"Quiet, kids!" he shouts.

The side conversations slow and the room quiets down some.

The students shift in their seats. Today's gathering will be about
Lior's abduction. Just a few weeks ago, they'd devoted an assembly to an-
other alumnus, Yumi, who'd been hurt somehow on a raid in Gaza. Now,
with Lior missing in action and rumors about where he had been taken by
Hamas, the tone of the discussion feels a bit different. As the principal says
Lior's name, eyes glaze over in a different way. Lior had been one of them a

little over a year ago. They too could have been taken.

The talks themselves are pretty worthless. The counselor, who everyone mocks on a regular basis, talks to them about resources available throughout the school. One of the teachers, who'd been Lior's advisor, stands and speaks about some of the discussions she'd had with him. To these speeches, Moran doesn't listen much. She hears them vaguely, as if the volume is turned down, catches words like "stress" and "abduction" and "bravery," but ignores the details. She doesn't have the energy to listen empathetically to all of their words. It all feels so burdensome. Of course she feels bad for Lior.

But what can we do anyway? This assembly sure isn't helping. Shit… we live in a war zone. How is any of this going to help?

For some reason, when the principal stands up to address the students once again, Moran snaps back to reality.

"I want you all to listen closely to me for a second," he starts. Before he continues, he rubs his hand over his mustache in a gesture Moran interprets as stress relief. "Reporters will be coming to your homes, stopping you on the streets, probably calling you if they can find your cell numbers. They'll be doing whatever they can to ask you questions about Lior and about Lior's family. Some of you may have already experienced this."

As he says this, a couple of students around Moran glance knowingly at each other. Apparently it has already started.

The principal continues, "You'll be tempted to answer them. I'd like to urge you not to. I know that you all usually regard stuff adults tell you as worthless. But listen to me on this. The right thing to do is to ignore the reporters. Things are difficult enough for the Samet family. They should not have to worry that personal information about Lior is leaking to the press."

He pauses; the auditorium that had just minutes earlier been a din of teenage conversation becomes eerily quiet.

"If you talk to the media, they are going to come back for more. You'll quickly get sick of it. Meanwhile, Lior's poor parents are going to wonder who the hell is telling all of these stories about their son. God forbid… imagine if it was you!"

Those last words scare Moran. *Poor Lior. He's been kidnapped. Shit, that's pretty bad.*

"I want the entire twelfth grade class to stay for a few extra minutes.

The rest of you are dismissed."

Dismissal ordinarily is a raucous occasion. Ninth grade boys would chase one another around the room in childish games of tag. Girls would giggle together and avert their eyes from boys. Kids would laugh and chat as they made their way to the next class. Not today. Today, dismissal is somber and orderly.

Dimona High School isn't huge—it is home to about 600 students. Dimona is not a large city. It has a population of about 35,000, not much of a town in many European countries. Yet, that modest number still made Dimona the largest city in the Negev region of Israel. The reputation of the place outstrips its size. It is best known for being home to Israel's nuclear reactors. Dimona's well-known secret went fully public in 1986. That year, a disgruntled employee named Mordechai Vanunu took pictures of top-secret sections of the reactor and left the country with the roll of film. Vanunu had served in the military but later grew disenfranchised with nuclear weapons and became involved with radical leftists at Ben-Gurion University.

In a classic honey trap, a Mossad agent lured Vanunu to Rome, where he was arrested brought back to Israel for trial. He was found guilty of treason and sentenced to eighteen years in prison. Dimona was at the center of the story. Public perception of Dimona around Israel was shaded by that event. It was a place laced with controversy but also a place that, if the mullahs in Iran grew itchy, was perhaps Israel's greatest defense.

The demographics of the city are pretty much reflected in the high school. About 15 percent of the city is middle to upper class, with scientists, university professors, government officials and families that live somehow outside of their means—probably old money. About 5 percent of the student body is made up of black Hebrews from Ethiopia who years ago made Dimona their home in Israel. The other 80 percent are lower-income working people, taxi drivers, factory workers, and falafel stand owners.

Once all the underclassmen have filed out of the room, about 150 twelfth-graders are scattered around the auditorium. Wondering where all of his peers are and why class isn't beginning, Arik walks in as the principal asks everyone to come forward and sit in the front rows. Moran notices a seat next to Moshiko that is open and quickly makes her way next to him. She looks back at Ruti, whose wide eyes and open mouth make Moran laugh.

"A psychologist from the IDF is here this morning to talk to you about the abduction of Lior Samet," announces the principal.

Arik, who refuses to sit down and is leaning against the wall with one leg propped up, calls out from the side, "Who needs a psycho in a clown uniform?"

Some kids sitting near Arik laugh. No one else does. The principal gives him a death glare and says quietly, "Arik, please meet me in my office after this assembly."

Moshiko looks at Moran and she returns his gaze. He seems so serious and upset, and whispers, "That son of a bitch, Arik. He's sick—let him go live in Amsterdam and grow pot all day. We don't need people like that."

Moran nods in agreement. Some part of her shares a bit of Arik's disdain, though she would never agree out loud. But she certainly doesn't want to argue with this gorgeous boy sitting next to her. Another part of her thinks that Arik is too young to know as much as he thinks he does. Moshiko knows where he stands. He leans over and brushes Moran's shoulder. She thinks about his subtle touch as he whispers, "We should be doing something."

"What do you mean?" she asks.

"About Lior. That could be me. It could be you. We have to do something!"

Maybe Moshiko awakens something in Moran. Maybe she is so eager to be involved with him that she readily agrees to anything he suggests. Either way, she feels her mind turn a bit. Gone is any trace of apathy. It has been replaced with a mixture of outrage and motivation.

This could have been my own little brother. This is one of our boys.

"I'm in," Moran replies.

14

Jerusalem
Outside the Walled City
323 BCE

AS SIMON GOES THROUGH THE ritual of dressing, Alexander is deep in thought in the dark of night. He is eager to take care of business and move on toward Egypt, the land of beauty and everlasting glory. The only thing standing between him and his destiny is the conquest of Jerusalem. A young bull had just been killed hours earlier, spilling its blood into dark bronze bowls. It went to its death quietly—a good omen. Alexander had watched the sacrifice, eager for a sign that things would go well for him and his men. He'd smiled when the bull faced its fate bravely.

The strategy of choice had been tried and tested on the battlefield. His armies will make a frontal attack from the west at sunrise. The sun will rise behind Alexander's armies, blind the enemy and give him an advantage for at least two hours of battle. As he discussed his plans with his advisors the previous night, over wine and a meal of freshly killed beef, Alexander frequently reminded those generals of his old tutor's adage: "Use everything to your advantage."

"Perhaps we should attack at night, sir," they urge him. "We could use the element of surprise."

He brushes off the bad suggestion. "Do you not think they are expecting us?" Alexander asks. "Do you think anyone is sleeping peacefully tonight in that old city?"

"They surely know we are near," his advisors had to concede.

"And if we attack at night," Alexander continues, "we perhaps surprise them briefly. But who knows the streets better? Who could operate in the dark in that place with more familiarity? We'd have the advantage for a short period of time. They would have it for the remainder of the night."

These sessions with his advisors are sometimes fruitful. But they usually just result in Alexander explaining to his advisors why their ideas are wrongheaded. He is open to good ideas. But, like the day he tamed Bucephalus, he usually sees the nature of problems more accurately than others.

Once his men leave him alone in his tent, Alexander stands in front of his shiny armor and looks at himself in the flickering light of the candles. What would his mother say if she saw him now? She'd probably say something to make him feel braver.

"My son, he has the face of a lion," she would often announce as she sweetly caressed the side of his face. Was it his unruly blond curls or his droopy eyes that made her say such things? Either way, he still has both traits. His teeth are long and narrow like those of a dog. His neck is thick and his shoulders broad.

Why is he thinking of his mother at a time like this? Better her than his father. The night before a battle, he usually thinks of his father. It was only normal for him to do so, given Philip's prowess on the battlefield. He was a magnificent warrior. As a child, Alexander had been so proud of his father. He'd wondered if there would be lands for him to conquer after his father finished.

There were plenty of lands. There will always be more lands. But there was only one Egypt. And that was still left for his son. Even if Philip had wanted to press on across the Arabian deserts, over the Red Sea, his assassination by two of his more trusted guards had kept him from doing so.

Should I have known what they were thinking? Could I have saved him? Wouldn't I have been more able to protect him had he not cast me out and treated me with silence for all those years?

Mother. Back to mother! Alexander thinks. He doesn't want to worry about what Philip thought as he prepares to march against the Israelites. He prefers to imagine what his mother would say to him now. *She'd say I was a lion. Indeed, I am a lion. I will rule the world.*

At this thought, Alexander remembers his tutor once asking what favors he would receive once Alexander took the throne of Macedonia. It was a strange question for Aristotle to ask. Alexander had never known him to worry about material things. So he thought for a second before he answered. Finally, Alexander responded with a belligerent tone in his voice, "How dare you ask a question about the future we do not know. As I have no assurance about the morrow, I can only say that, when that day comes, I will answer it."

"Well said!" said Aristotle. "Well said, Alexander." The flattery immediately melted the belligerence away, and Alexander smiled as the teacher continued, "I believe that one day you will indeed rule the world. But wise rulers take nothing for granted. My belief in you should not relieve you of your utmost duty. Be prudent, assume nothing, make choices on facts and strategy, not emotions and intuition."

"Gather the troops," Alexander shouts as he steps out of his tent in full armor and regalia. At that command, the camp becomes a frenzy of activity. The soldiers, who had previously dressed quietly and struggled to shake off fatigue from a short night, feel an electric surge of adrenaline. Alexander's generals begin shouting orders. Alexander steps on the back of his footman and saddles his horse. He rides from one legion to another, exhorting them, "In the morning, we take that which stands in our way to glory. Jerusalem is ours to be had! Our army always attacks! The day on which we put ourselves in the defensive, we will see ourselves lost."

Alexander is a practical man. He needs to plunder Jerusalem in order to have supplies for his army's journey to Egypt. They love him. They fear him. But both love and fear run out quickly in the face of hunger. They need success. He seeks more than just a material victory. He cannot help but think of finding a few more virgins like the girl he ravaged the day before. There was something about her that both intrigued Alexander and caused him to fear. He rides out toward Jerusalem a bit ahead of the troops that are gathering into formation. He hops off his horse and gathers a bit of the dust under his feet. He picks it up and runs his fingers through his palm to feel the texture of the earth as it escapes out of his hand. He looks west, where his destiny lies. He can only dream of extinguishing the rage that burns within him. He considers the future. And in doing so, Alexander allows himself a short daydream of Yael.

Though not exactly beautiful—she is nothing like the Greek goddesses from home—her soft strength is unlike anything I've ever been with. Her fragrance is absolutely intoxicating, like a vineyard in blossom. There is something special about her. There was something strange about our encounter. Something… beyond this world. Maybe the word to describe it is "mystical." Those moments with her were pleasurable. But I've never before felt such a need to reciprocate. I wanted to make her feel what I felt. Why her? She is such a tender little foal. So tender and innocent, yet it had seemed like she knew so much more than her years would suggest. Why? I would like to bring her joy for years to come, he thinks. *I would like to make her feel the way I felt when we embraced.*

Suddenly the thoughts are gone. They must wait. Now the troops are gathered behind him. They are eager to get moving.

"What happened in the city of Tyre will not happen again," Alexander yells out to his men. "You may be hungry and eager for the flesh of women. You may have no regard for this people. But we will kill them like soldiers, not like barbarians. Do you understand me?"

The shouts of his men in military formation echo over the empty, sandy land; they cannot yet be heard in the Old City, but scouts a few miles between city and army hear them loud and clear. Destruction is on its way to the people of Israel, led by a lion of a man called Alexander.

15

Dimona, Israel
June 2006

"SHALOM, IMA!" MORAN YELLS OUT as she charges through the front door of their third-floor walk-up apartment building in Shikun Dalet. Along her daily route home, Moran finds nothing unusual. She notices the regular crowd at this time of day, kids with knapsacks on their backs and falafel in their hands on their way home or to the library or the playground.

Though it is midafternoon and school has just let out, Moran's father is glued to the big flat-screen television that assumes a regal share of their tiny living room. He just woke up and has not yet departed for his night shift at Magen David Adom, the government-financed Israeli national ambulatory service. Her mom hasn't yet left for her afternoon shift at the local Mashbir. Her dad mumbles "Shalom" to his daughter as she flurries into the room. "I'm watching the latest on Lior. *Ma nishma*, how are you?"

"Fine," Moran answers. "We had an assembly about him at school."

"Oh yeah?" asks her dad. "What did they talk about?"

"They told us that there are people to talk to if we get upset. They also told us to expect the media to come after us looking for quotes."

"The media, huh?" her father turns and asks. He looks at the television in a brief moment of reflection—he is the audience for this 24-hour news cycle. He feels a tinge of guilt but then leans back into the couch, more motivated by his desire to relax than some sort of internal set of virtuous consumer choices.

Moran turns to look at her mom dutifully preparing dinner for each member of the family to eat on their own time, her hand framed on her aproned hips as she too glances at the TV. Moran immediately notices her red, baggy eyes. She notices that her mom's mascara, always perfect, is smudged.

"Mom? You don't look ready to go to work."

Her mother, always eager to see her daughter for this brief window of time before work takes her away from home—so much so that she pleaded with Moran to avoid after-school activities—and a woman who usually verged on loquacious, says nothing. Instead she stares at the television through damp eyes.

"What's going on with Mom?" Moran asks as she sits uneasily next to her father on the couch.

"Huh?"

"She's been crying and won't answer me. What's up?"

"Oh. The news of poor Lior is bringing back memories for your mother—she'll be OK."

Moran gets up and goes to hug her mother. "Sorry, Mom."

The touch of her daughter snaps her out of it. "Huh? Oh, I'll be fine," she says. "I'm going to work now. Pull the casserole out of the oven at 5. Shelly might bring the kids over tonight. She has teachers' conferences and asked if you would mind babysitting."

As Moran's mother hangs her apron near the stove and heads for the door, Moran thinks back to the event that caused such dazed, sad memories. She can't remember specifics. She was too young to really have even registered specifics. But eight years earlier, Moran's uncle—her mother's elder brother—had been killed in Gaza. The entire universe, from a young girl's perspective, mourned his death. Why wouldn't it? Her uncle, Dod Yitzik, was funny and cheerful. He smoked like a chimney and loved to show off his muscles and very hairy chest.

They hadn't seen him often, but Moran loved her uncle. He'd joke with her, acting as if he'd lost his thumb when his fierce niece pulled it off. Other than his rare pranking at holidays, she rarely saw him. Yet when the news arrived that he died, everything changed.

Once her mother has left, Moran hesitantly sits next to her father in front of the television. She hears the words coming out of the screen, but they seem somehow foreign and unintelligible. Words like "reparations" and "international relations," descriptions of treaties signed long ago, lists of factions and religious sects, all seem so odd and disconnected from the boy in the upper right-hand corner of the news feed.

It isn't the most flattering picture of him, Moran thinks. Lior is not the most glamorous man on earth, but he certainly looks better in person than in that picture. The last time Moran saw Lior, he had much more hair on his head. The short haircut causes problems. It somehow makes his ears more pronounced. He has this strange smirk on his face. *What an odd image. It doesn't even look like Lior. If his name wasn't up on that screen, I wouldn't have known it was him.* But, of course, it was.

"The Israeli military has not released an official statement. But we have no reason to think that they'd deviate from their long-standing policy of refusing to negotiate with terrorists," the announcer summarizes. "For those who know and love Lior Samet, these may be a long couple of months."

At that conclusion, Moran gets up from the couch and walks to her room. *This is some serious shit.* She'd known Lior in a variety of contexts. She'd been in the same level math as he was, so they'd had geometry and algebra together. They'd seen each other on the weekends of their childhood, at the scouts program in which they both participated. Lior was always quiet. He never wanted to lead anything. He was just there. He'd taken the step of running for student council last year. Since Moran was on the council for juniors, she served with him. But it seemed that Lior had expended all of his initiative in running his campaign. Once in the meetings, he never initiated any activities or volunteered his ideas verbally. Whenever there was a midnight bonfire scheduled on the beach or hikes or bike rides, he was always there, but only as a participant.

He was quiet. Over the years, he'd made his affection for Moran known in subtle ways beyond friendship. In their early teen years, he'd written her the cheesy letters full of trite nothings and clichés. As they grew older, he asked her to accompany him to movies or out to ice cream. She always ignored those invitations. She even tried to steer away from accepting social invitations where she knew there would be lots of mutual friends. She just didn't want to give the wrong impression.

How odd to see his face all over the television.

Moran's cell phone rings.

"Hi, Mimi, *ma nishma*?"

"*Sababa*, what are you doing?"

"I just got home from school. I need to go get dinner out of the oven soon. Generally, just thinking about this stuff with Lior Samet. It's awful."

"I guess it is. I overheard my father tell my mom that Lior doesn't stand a chance. If they haven't killed him yet, they will make crazy demands, like some sort of prisoner exchange."

"That's awful. Did you say prisoner exchange? They never exchange prisoners, especially when those Hamas people demand them. Please don't talk that way. I'm sure Lior is fine and he will be found somewhere soon. Shit, it must be horrible for Lior. Who knows what they're doing to him?" Moran asks.

"No, you idiot!" Mimi says sarcastically. "They need to keep him alive and healthy so that they can negotiate—*hu oseh hayyim*—I bet he's having a blast."

"Mimi, I love you. But you sound crazy. Lior's been kidnapped, taken, abducted. His parents must be devastated. Lior must be terrified. He may be getting tortured. I have no idea what they are doing to him."

"I doubt it," Mimi argues. "Besides, they're trained for this shit."

"I guess. But I doubt Lior was trained for much of anything. He was just in school with us last year. How much could he have changed between then and now?"

"Whatever. Let's stop talking about it. It is bringing me down. I just bought the most amazing color nail polish. You need to come over and check it out."

"Sababa. Tomorrow. Bye bye."

Over dinner, Moran asks her father about Dovi, her older brother.

"Have you heard from Dovi recently?"

Dovi is in his second year in the Israel Defense Forces in an elite combat unit called Golani. Everyone was pretty proud of him when he made it into the Golani unit.

"Yes. He called yesterday when you were still at school. Woke me up! He's good. Sounds like he is busy, but good."

"Nothing else?"

"No. He still can't talk much about what he is doing. I can't wait for him to be done with those years of service."

We celebrate and hate the army at the same time, Moran thinks to herself.

And with that, Moran and her father sit quietly and eat their food, the silence punctuated by the sound of flatware clanking on ceramic plates. Sitting with her father has always been awkward and weird. It seems like he has nothing to say to her and little interest in knowing anything about her. He must find it mystifying to have a teenage daughter.

If someone asked Dad something about me, she thinks, *he would have no idea what to answer, even about the most practical stuff. I wonder if he knows what grade I'm in.*

He is not a particularly educated man, but he keeps up with politics on the news and is passionate about wildlife. He could sit and watch National Geographic for hours on end. He isn't much of a religious man, but he nonetheless enjoys going to synagogue every Saturday morning. His synagogue of choice is half a block down the street, a small building that is relatively well kept by volunteers. Moran always thinks of her father's synagogue fixation as an appropriate escape with his male friends away from home. The whole thing is a kind of alternative to a more traditional boys' night out, something her strict mother would never tolerate. No one else in the family ever steps foot into that synagogue, or any other synagogue for that matter. The last time Moran was in synagogue was for Dovi's bar mitzvah. The entire experience was irreverent and strange. Women sat behind a wall while the men led the service. No one prayed—people were just talking and laughing and gossiping.

Dovi could barely read his Torah portion. When he finished, the women threw candy, the men drank, and Dovi became a man. It was the last time Moran wore a skirt. Her mother had insisted that, as a sign of respect for the sacred place, they both dress modestly. But, that "sacred" place felt more like a circus than a holy shrine, and Moran swore to herself as she left that event, "never again."

"Abba," Moran asks her father, "what would you do if it was Dovi who was kidnapped?"

"Don't be ridiculous, Moran."

"Abba, I'm serious. It could be anyone. What if it was Dovi? How would you react? What would we be doing right now?"

He doesn't even want to contemplate the hypothetical question she posed. "Our family has made enough sacrifices for this country." Moran imagines her father referencing the death of her uncle Yitzik, her mother's brother. She thinks it is a bit of a cop-out. What other sacrifices have they made for this country? Her dad doesn't even like spending time with mom's family. But he claims that event relieved him of patriotic obligation?

"What if we needed to make more sacrifices? What if it was one of your children? What if it was me?" Moran persists.

"God forbid such a thing!" He grows angrier. "These kinds of words should not even come out of your mouth."

Her father continues speaking while staring blankly at his newspaper, almost to himself, "They are all our children. I do not know what I would do. Your mother… your mother could never handle such a thing. She is devastated over Lior. God forbid it was Dovi. My heart breaks for that family."

Moran sits quietly at this uncharacteristically emotional ramble from her father. She replies in tacit agreement, "I'm thinking of going over there tonight to offer my help."

"No," her father responds, "let them be—they want to be alone."

Moran doesn't know much about the political and military matters discussed on the news. But she knows when it comes to interpersonal stuff, her father is clueless.

"Abba, I'm going over there. Lior is a friend—I'm sure there is something I can do."

"There is nothing to do. Let's pray the boy is alive."

"How did Dod Yitzik die?" Moran asks.

"Like a shmuck—it wasn't even a hero's death—I don't want to think about it. Please let me read my newspaper."

Moran goes back to her vegetables and chicken casserole. Once dinner has come to an uneventful end, she quietly heads to her room. She leaves the dishes for her father.

16

Jerusalem
Outside the Walled City
Summer 323 BCE

I F LIGHT MADE NOISE, THIS morning's sunrise would be the gong of heaven, a clang loud enough to reverberate inside the heart of every man, woman and child. As the shimmering gold disk begins to cast its fiery, bright beams behind Alexander's army, the walled city slowly becomes illuminated. To Alexander's surprise, there is no army, no soldiers readying for war. He turns to his men. They look eager to fight. Not a hint of fear in their eyes.

"We attack the front gate and enter the city. Our scouts are certain that no ambush is awaiting us," Parmenion says. "Even if they have prepared something our scouts missed, no ambush can stop us, your excellency."

Parmenion sits on the horse to Alexander's right. He has offered several messages such as this, trying to prompt his leader into signaling the first legion to make a frontal charge on the city's western gate. Alexander has seemed to him to be in a hesitant mood all morning. He is not nearly as demonstrative and aggressive on the approach as normal. Parmenion thinks of what he could say next, what other combination of words he might proffer to stir Alexander into action. He looks toward the gleaming sandstone walls, the combinations of yellows and oranges and grays just growing to clarity. An unusually bright morning, Parmenion notices.

All of a sudden, the gates of the city begin to open. Alexander is about to shout the orders, but instead he calls out to his men, "Wait!" His shout is accompanied by a hand in a closed fist, their signal to hold.

His men, who have been leaning forward in their saddles and ready to spring, relax their shoulders ever so slightly and return to rest.

Alexander does not relax. His every muscle is charged with adrenaline. He can taste the victory and smell the spoils. Every cell in his body is ready to charge forward. But his mind says something different. The sight of the opening gates intrigues him.

The sound of charioteers corralling their horses behind him is deafening.

"WHOA!" they scream. "STEADY!"

The horses have been snorting and stamping their feet in anticipation. They know as well as the men, perhaps better, the patterns of adrenaline that foreshadow the order to attack. They have come to know Alexander's voice and expect him to send them forward. Restraining them is no meager task.

Ignoring the din behind him, Alexander rubs his eyes, not sure what he is seeing. An apparition is walking out of the city unarmed and alone. It looks like a ghost—no, maybe an angel—a brilliant colorful image with shining rays going up to the heavens from its head, colorful stars circling its body and yellow rays harnessing it to the ground.

"What is that?" screams Parmenion.

"What indeed?" asks Alexander. *How fascinating!* He never saw such a thing before. There is something mysterious about it that intrigues him.

"Whatever it is, your excellency, let us attack. The gate is open. The city is ripe for the taking. We can be finished before the sun positions itself overhead."

"No!" shouts Alexander. He is relieved that he is not the only one seeing this apparition of color and luminous rays now walking methodically toward them. He does not want to attack until he knows more about it.

As Alexander restrains his men, Simon orders the gatekeepers not to close the gate behind him. If Alexander charges, the flimsy wood gate will not hold. If it is left open, it may be interpreted as an act of peace.

Simon steps out of the walled city through the western gate and begins walking toward Alexander's army. He feels the rays of the sun shining on his golden headband with God's name on it, and the colorful precious stones on his breastplate. The little bells, meant to signal his continued survival, are sounding the music of heaven. *He hasn't died yet!* And they are not charging. He cannot help but marvel at how especially blinding the sun is this morning.

If I am to be sacrificed for my people, so be it. Death is the destiny of all men, he thinks to himself. *If my people are to be plowed over, they will sprout again. This is the promise given by God. It will not be broken. If we are to be plowed over, let me be the first.*

As Simon begins to slowly walk down the hill from the gates of the city, Alexander kicks his horse to move forward. He looks as if he is lost in some daze. This apparition coming forward mesmerizes him.

"Where are you going, your excellency?" Parmenion asks nervously. "This is not normal. It is quite strange indeed. Very strange."

Alexander does not turn to answer the question. He just hollers back, "No one moves without my order."

As Parmenion and the men sit anxiously, Alexander begins to ride Bucephalus to the angelic figure walking toward all of them.

"Shall we follow, great one?" Parmenion shouts.

"No!" Alexander turns briefly, "I go alone—no one moves without my order. Or you will pay dearly."

As Simon continues his long walk, the image of him from a distance does not get clearer. It just gets brighter and brighter. The men are discomfited. They do not like what they do not know. And this, they do not know at all. They feel particularly anxious about their great leader heading out toward a strange vision—all alone.

Within twenty handbreadths, Alexander jumps off his horse and continues by foot. The sound of his armies becomes a more distant echo with each step. Soon he can no longer hear the rattles and creaks of the chariots. The sound of armed men shifting in their stance fades. He can now hear his own footfalls as he walks steadily toward his greeter. Despite his explicit instructions, Parmenion sends a few footmen to follow their leader. They keep their distance and Alexander does not turn around to see their disobedience.

Simon walks with a sense of poise and assurance. He has relinquished control over his fate to higher powers. He has the confidence of a man who no longer fears death. Once Alexander can see that look of fearlessness on Simon, he grows a bit more uncertain about what will come next. The differences show in their pace. Alexander shortens his stride a bit, slows his gait. Simon maintains his steady pace. In fact, when he hits a bit of a decline, he speeds up.

After what feels endless to the armies behind Alexander, the two men come together in the middle of the potential battlefield.

Simon stops and looks intently at the great conqueror before him. Both men wait to speak. They know that speaking first is a sign of weakness. After a few seconds, Alexander can no longer stand it.

"Who are you?" he asks.

"What brings you to our city?" Simon replies in perfect Greek.

Alexander shakes his head subtly in disbelief. He is not used to people ignoring his questions.

"Who are you? I insist you answer my question," Alexander says in a firm voice that those close to him would have recognized as strained. "Are you the king of this city? I demand an answer."

"My name is Simon, son of Elazar. I reside in the walled city of Jerusalem. I am not a king nor the general of an army. I am a simple citizen of the world who seeks to live in peace. I worship the one God of heaven and earth," Simon says calmly in familiar Greek.

Alexander thinks he sounds a bit like Aristotle. *So sure of himself, so ready to ask questions.*

"Tell me, what brings you in our midst?" Simon asks his question again, though he knows well the answer.

Alexander stammers for a second, "I… I want to know more about the one God of heaven and earth."

Alexander cannot quite make sense of what is happening. *Am I talking to a man or an angel? Is this actually taking place or is this a dream or hallucination?* Simon's garments do not lose their majesty up close. The jewels of Israel shine even more vividly. Alexander has conquered much of his known world. He has rarely encountered that which could withstand his will. But he has never seen anything like Simon in the morning light.

He wonders for a second if his mind is somehow altered. He was once given an herb to eat by a lover. He saw all kinds of things and images, beheld colors both real and unreal, only to wake up to the reality of his life. *Is that what this is? Am I standing before a fiction of my own creation?* He looks into Simon's eyes. They do not look anything like fiction.

Alexander says, "I want to know more about the one God who resides within those walls."

"No, my son," Simon answers paternally. Alexander cringes ever so slightly at the word "son," but it also holds some sort of mysterious power over him. He'd craved to hear it for so long. Simon feels Alexander somehow ceding ground, and continues, "The one God fills the universe with his presence. The one God has no walls—walls are for men, not for God."

"So, this God defies the rules of the universe? That is not possible."

Simon places his hand on Alexander's shoulder and says knowingly, "My son, the one God of heaven and earth is a God of peace, love and compassion. The rules of the universe are his law."

The moment Simon reaches for Alexander's shoulder, the footmen reach for their weapons. The entire army briefly lurches forward. Alexander hears and turns to respond, "No! Stay back."

Simon's hand has a soothing effect on the great warrior. Alexander draws closer. He can sense his soldiers' unease. Simon looks at him with compassion, "Great king, your reputation precedes you. We do not want war. We worship a God of love and compassion."

"No," Alexander interjects. "This is not what I have been told. You are a deceitful and vicious nation of war and conquest—my teacher, Aristotle, told me about David the King Warrior, about the conqueror Joshua."

Simon nods at the names. But he knows very well that those great warrior kings are not behind Jerusalem's walls. "That was in the past," Simon replies in a whisper, "my son."

He watches as he carefully enunciates those last words and thinks that he sees a flicker in Alexander's bright blue eyes at the title. Indeed, every time Simon uses the word "my son," Alexander feels weak in his knees. He wants to kneel before this man who is both human and godly—like the father he never had.

"What brings you here, my son?" Simon asks again.

Alexander looks back at his men, their horses ready to charge the city. It is pretty obvious what they are here for. Nonetheless, he shrugs his shoulders. "I do not know anymore—I thought I came to conquer."

Alexander removes his bronze helmet that is tightly held on his head by the thickness of his hair. He is especially proud of the mane on the helmet, carefully dyed blue and red by his craftsmen.

"You have already conquered this nation," Simon assures him. "This city is yours already. There is no need to spill her blood."

Alexander cringes at the thought. His men are fighters who know only the language of force. He likes this man who calls him "son." But he is on a quest to fulfill a destiny. What will help him do so? He can hear the men behind him, who were once anxious, now grow frustrated. They want blood.

"Your face is the face of a lion and yours is the strength of the lion," Simon says. Alexander turns away just slightly, unable to hide the crimson developing on his pale cheeks. He feels as if all the wind has been knocked out of him. Simon continues, "Be strong like the lion, and take your army away from here."

"My mother used to call me her lion."

"Then be the lion you were destined to be!" Simon almost orders Alexander. He feels the stress of doing something that, by all conventional wisdom, he should not be doing.

"What are you talking about?" Alexander asks, puzzled. "A lion is strength—the king of all beasts. The lion rules the animal kingdom with fear of his proven might."

"Yes, indeed… the lion is king," says Simon. "And he is the fiercest of all animals. But he is also the only great beast that lives with other cats in peace. The lion, as you know, lives in a pride. All other big animals of its kind live alone because they do not know what peace is."

Alexander has never thought of this. His teachers never taught him this lesson. Can he live peacefully with others? Must he rule through fear, even among his own?

Simon continues, "The lion's strength lies within. The lion's true strength is its ability not to kill, even when it knows it can—your mother was right, you are a lion. Your true strength, just like that of the lion, is within, not without."

Alexander's eyes are unfocused, his mouth gaping slightly by the man's wisdom and knowledge. "Tell me more about your God!" he almost pleads.

"The one God creator of heaven and earth will also protect you. We refer to our God as the one—the one and only, the one that is unique—unlike anything we can possibly know."

This sounds so mysterious and vague to Alexander. Yet he is intrigued.

"I have a gift for you," Simon whispers. "Listen to me very carefully. Alexander, I know you are a wise man. The Hebrew word for 'one' is *echad*. Its numerical value is thirteen; Aleph is 1, Chet is 8, Dalet is 4. You are one, and I too am one. Together, our numerical value is twenty-six. The numerical value twenty-six is also the number that represents the one God, *Yehova*. Yod is 10, Heh 5, Vav 6, and Heh 5. From here on, thirteen will be your number and thirteen will be my number. Together we will bring the one God to this world."

Alexander is mesmerized.

"Thirteen is your number. It will protect you and watch over you. Make thirteen stars and place them over the eagle on your shield, and you will have *echad*, the one, at the forefront of your might."

Alexander remains speechless and confused. He feels as if he has truly been given a gift, yet he does not fully understand it. He wants to spend more time with this man, desires for Simon to travel with him and teach him like Aristotle once did. Yet he simultaneously respects and fears him too much to make such a request.

"Are there no warriors in your city to fight? How do you protect yourself?" As Alexander says it, he regrets it. Here is this man telling him the secret of numbers and names. And he asks about warriors.

But Simon smiles knowingly. "Good question, great king! We live by three principles—in fact, it is these three principles upon which the entire universe is sustained: the study of God's law, service to our God, and compassion to fellow men. If you want to know who we are, this is it."

These vague virtues sound appealing to Alexander. They sound like something that Aristotle would have appreciated.

Simon looks over Alexander's shoulder at the armies in front of him and asks with a wry air of critique, "My son, is this who you are?"

Alexander feels the hairs on his neck rise just a bit. "That is who I am. I was destined for this, I was promised greatness and glory… Old man, do not accuse me."

"Calm, calm," Simon replies, "I do not accuse anyone, my son. We all have a purpose in this world."

Alexander's life flashes before his eyes—his father, his mother, his tutor, all the blood that has been spilled. *Was it necessary?*

Simon breaks the silence. "I ask just one thing of you, my son: give me the girl!"

Alexander is confused. How dare this man ask of him anything at all, let alone that, which is rightfully his? A conquered people belong to the conqueror. He has not yet decided to spare this people. And here he is requested to do a favor? He is not yet done with the girl. Alexander can't help but notice that she shares some of the same irrational confidence with this man standing before him. He struggles with the possibility of relinquishing her. And yet he does not dare turn down Simon's request. This man is attired like a god. He speaks like a sage. He is unlike anyone Alexander has ever met.

"You give me the one God for protection and success, and I spare the city and give you the girl?"

"Yes," Simon responds with poise and confidence.

As much as he hates the arrangement, Alexander concedes. He needs food for his men and horses, but he can spare the city. He also knows very well that, as much as he desires her beauty, Yael will not last long with Alexander. She will be given to his generals and their subordinates, and eventually sold to a brothel in the alleys of Ashur, the capital of Assyria.

"She will be brought to you. I need supplies for my men."

"Bring her now," Simon instructs, "I will wait."

This man has the lives of his entire people in his hands. Yet he thinks of one life in this way. Alexander recalls a story Aristotle once told him about a shepherd who worries about the life of one lamb rather than the flock. This richly attired apparition in front of Alexander reminds him of the Messiah in his teacher's story.

Alexander turns around and yells, "Bring me the Hebrew girl."

One of the soldiers that has been sent—against his orders—to follow behind Alexander, rides his horse back to the main army to fetch her.

Parmenion, when he hears the request, is dumbfounded. "What in the name of Zeus is he doing?"

"I don't know. But he says he wants the Hebrew girl. Do you want to disagree?"

"Not at all," Parmenion mumbles confusedly. He sends a soldier for her.

Yael is near the front lines. She has been ordered, kept there by Alexander, to see her people decimated. Slaves learn through submission and suffering. There is no better way to subject a slave than to have her watch as her people are destroyed. It teaches them who is in charge, the futility of resistance. Yael watches over the shoulders of Alexander's men as the high priest emerges from the gates. She feels the soldiers around her grow restless. She perceives the strangeness of the encounter occurring out in the middle of the field. She knows, perhaps better than the soldiers surrounding her, just how futile opposition will be for the meek citizens inside the walls. She knows they have no chance. So it is with great surprise that she finds herself being escorted up to the front lines.

Simon greets the young girl as she arrives at the two men.

"You will be coming with me," he says in Hebrew.

To this news, Yael looks at him in confusion. *Why is he wearing the garments of Yom Kippur? Is that allowed?* She does not know if she is being brought forward as some sacrifice or offering. No, it appears that she is being returned.

She looks at Alexander, who stares off in the distance. Part of her, dare she say it, is torn. She is being ordered back into the city of her youth. To a city where her mother would most certainly scold her, "I told you not to be off on your own!"

She remains silent.

Yael releases herself from the hold of the armed Greek soldiers and runs toward the high priest, while Alexander stands on a rocky stretch of land framing the holy city. He feels a sense of equanimity. It is so unfamiliar. He is no longer sure of who he is. Yet he feels a surge of rebirth, an awareness of renewal.

Again Simon puts his hand on Alexander's shoulder. No one has ever dared to touch him this way.

"Thank you, my son. You have my word that the one God of heaven and earth will always protect you. Like the great city of Jerusalem you spared today, a great city by the Nile will be named after you, and you will be immortalized forever. You will always have a home in Jerusalem."

Alexander does not respond. His mind is spinning. *A great city named after me?* He looks longingly at Yael for a moment. He wonders whether he could have grown to love her. Then he jumps on his horse and returns to the front lines with his men.

As Alexander rides back, Simon reaches over and embraces Yael. "Come, my child. Do not turn back. The God of our people has graced us with a great deliverance today. May we not enrage that army more than they are already going to be."

As they walk back toward the city, those who have been watching from atop the wall grow increasingly confused. Before Yael and Simon reach the city, those with the best view can see the army begin to break battle formation. It appears that the city will be spared.

When he reaches the gates, Simon's job is not yet done.

"Prepare a feast the likes of which we have never prepared. Give them wine and entertainment. Deplete the stores of food by one half. We will feed this army until they forget they ever wanted to kill us!"

"What happened out there, your excellency?" people ask Simon.

Songs have been written about the encounter between the warrior and the priest, the angel and lion. Poems have been composed that praised the glories of the one God who saved his people once again from destruction. But to those questions about what exactly took place out on the battlefield, Simon never spoke a word.

17

Dimona, Israel
August 2006

I T'S BEEN TWO MONTHS SINCE Lior's abduction. Avigdor Cohen is experiencing something that is completely unfamiliar to him. He feels helpless. Shula suggests something else completely unfamiliar to Cohen - prayer.

The reason Avigdor Cohen cannot remember ever praying is because he never prayed. There were many opportunities on the battlefield, such as in June 1967, in the Sinai Desert:

It happened without warning. The tank rocked. The explosion was deafening. He felt a sharp pain, like a knife plunged into his back. His body shuddered. Cohen went blank for a moment and then fell back into the tank. He was jarred by fierce pain. It took a while until he understood his tank had been hit. His two crewmen were instantly killed in the blast. The turret was immediately enveloped in flames. He tried with all his strength to push his body to the hatch overhead. He could not—he fell back into the belly of the tank.

For a moment, Cohen lost his senses. He felt like a newborn baby, all pain and confusion. A minute later, he snapped back to adult consciousness.

He howled to himself over the tumult outside the metal death box he was trapped in, *Don't cry. Don't panic. You are a commander of men. Live up to your training. Live up to your oaths.*

The option of prayer did not even enter his mind.

Stench and slime filled the tank. Cohen and the two mangled corpses were in a furnace.

He tried again to reach up for the ladder that might lead him out of the tank. The turret was cracked open. He could see the light from the noonday sun calling him, inviting him to live. He pulled one leg toward the ladder, tried to gain some leverage and help his arms. But he couldn't even get his hand up to the second rung.

This is it, he thought to himself, *my moment of death has come.*

Cohen thought of food, of falafel sandwiches drenched in tahini. There was one place right off Damascus Avenue... *What the hell did they put in that stuff?* He thought of sitting right off Dizengoff Square, drinking wine with Asaf. He thought of watching the girls on warm nights as the sun set over the Old City behind them. He thought of his parents, of what they'd think of having sacrificed a second son for the cause.

I don't want to be a martyr. I don't want to...

Yet he was fading. A smaller explosion shook near the front. *They are still shooting at me? They are still shooting? Those shits!*

Perhaps it was the combination of affectionate memories and anger that catalyzed some biological response, but suddenly Cohen tasted the metallic tinge of adrenaline in the back of his mouth. He was up on his knees, reaching in determined anger, straining every muscle upward toward the hatch. His feet reached the ladder. He lifted one toward the next step and gripped it with surety. The next lodged itself with a sense of firmness as well. Suddenly, his head pushed the partially ajar hatch door fully open. He emerged into the light like some more purely distilled version of humanity, all confusion and ferocity and will to live.

Finally, his body was out on the tank. But the exterior of the tank was burning hot. And with the introduction of oxygen into the mixture of oil and heat, Cohen was a burning vision of olive-green uniform and flame. He was a human torch. In a flash of insight, he knew that he needed to roll. He stumbled down the front of the tank and leaped into the sand of the Sinai Desert. That very desert, the biblical Sinai, has seen its share of human history. But never before had that sand been so welcomed as it was in that moment.

Cohen rolled frantically in the sand, burying himself like a beach crab. Within seconds, his whole body was enveloped in sand. Only his head was exposed.

In the old tale, when Jonah was spit out by the great fish, he landed on dry land. From that place of safety, the reluctant prophet went on to do what he'd been told. Cohen had not refused any prophetic orders. And when he came up into the world again, he was not greeted with safety. He was greeted instead with an end-of-days-type din of destruction. Shells fell everywhere. Tanks from the company scrambled in every which way, their commanders unsure which direction might lead to safety. Cohen looked at his battalion's movements, looked to both sides at the enemy surrounding them, and realized that he'd navigated his men into an ambush. His heart dropped. *Shit. What have I done? How could I not have seen this?*

While he lay in the sand cursing his ignorance, he looked to the left to see one of his own tanks lurching toward him. *That thing... they don't see me!* Again that bitter taste entered his mouth. Again he summoned the strength to move. Cohen burst into motion on foot once again. When he emerged from the sand, people would later say that he looked like an "overgrown newborn baby." The fire on his uniform and his frantic rolling to get the flames out had caused his clothes to disintegrate. So, as Cohen ran toward one of the still-operable tanks, he did so completely naked aside from his boots.

The battalion's second in command recognized him from atop his tank, leaned out past the turret, and yelled amid all the noise, "Commander!"

Cohen was headed in the other direction and responded over his shoulder, "Enemy tanks all around! Get back in the fight."

The second in command watched in confusion as Cohen continued to run, skin dangling from the various parts of his body. *What the hell is he doing?*

Cohen didn't know what he was doing. But he knew what he was thinking.

My tank was hit. I abandoned my soldiers. I am about to die. I have failed.

Lt. Ilan Maoz saw Cohen running. He navigated his tank alongside

Cohen and stopped next to him briefly. "Sir, climb on!"

Cohen jumped on the hull and climbed into the radioman's position in the turret.

"Turn this thing around!" he shouted.

The sight of their commander upset Ilan's men. He barely looked human. Up close, they could see the bubbled skin, the blisters already developing, the sub-layers of human flesh that were never supposed to meet the air.

The sound of the tank tracks screeched as Ilan worked hard to turn the tank around to head back into the action.

"Don't break the chain," Cohen whispered. Even during those desperate moments, he was alert and mentally able to respond like a commander.

"Sir," the radioman said to Cohen, "your boots."

"What about them?"

"They are smoldering. They are still on fire."

"Oh," Cohen replied absently.

When the guns grew too hot for touch, the radioman reached into his vest and pulled out a set of leather gloves. He reached down and pulled off the commander's boots as gently as he could while they rode full-speed into battle and through gunfire on a tank. As the boots came off, so did his skin and toenails. The radioman, an experienced combat soldier, fainted.

At that moment, a recon jeep pulled up beside the tank. Both slowed as their respective drivers shouted, "It's Cohen, platoon commander. Get him to the back lines to a medic!"

Both tank and jeep stopped briefly as Cohen was helped down off the turret and into the passenger seat.

"To the hospital tent!" Lt. Maoz commanded the jeep's driver.

"Yes, sir!"

Cohen absently clutched the jeep's handlebars on the dashboard to keep from being launched out of the moving vehicle. As they drove past the last column of tanks, where reinforcements were waiting to engage the enemy, Cohen could recognize almost all the crewmen. He saw their faces cringe and felt terribly guilty—he knew his was not the sight you want to show young men immediately before a battle.

The last thing Cohen heard when he reached the armor infantry company field hospital were the words, "Give this man morphine." The last thing he remembers was the sweet relief when the pain stopped, right before he passed out. He woke just a few minutes later but didn't feel like he was fully conscious.

There comes a time in a man's life when his existence is suspended between heaven and earth while given over to the mercies of those around him. No one asked him anything. It was clear to the medical team that there was no point in asking those expected questions like: How do you feel? Where does it hurt? What happened?

Cohen, incapacitated as he was, yearned to share something with someone. He wanted reassurances of the humblest sort. *If I die, will they know who I am? Will they know how I died? Will they know how to notify my family?*

He had so many questions swirling around in his clouded brain. He had plenty of thoughts. He had ample reasons to pray. But he never did.

The will to live and to survive is a soldier's most critical motivation in battle. The soldiers who fight for the IDF know they will never be abandoned in the battlefield. They know that, if they are wounded, they will be given the finest medical care as efficiently as possible. But the will to live is inextricably linked to survival. And nothing undermines the belief that life is possible more than the sunken and scared faces of visitors.

The first time Cohen saw his father cry was when he came to the hospital the day after his arrival from the battlefield. Tears flowed down his cheeks; he turned away and walked out of the room. Cohen had known that the prognosis was very bad, but that vague idea didn't convey the dread and doom written on his father's tearful face. Dr. Irwin Kaplan, head of the plastic surgery department for IDF field forces, later told Cohen's father what he already knew: chances of survival were slim to none. There just was not enough skin left for grafts. There was no hope of preventing the infections sure to come.

Other visitors meant well. Solemn and emotional, they came and went. Friends from high school. Aunts and uncles who'd made the long drive from the northern parts of the country. Some brought flowers, others cookies and chocolate. Few understood what Cohen was going through. Some said silly things like, "I know you will get through this."

Isn't it easy, he always thought, *to profess belief when you are standing and healthy? When you still have skin on your body?*

The most welcomed visitors were those who offered to listen if he was in the mood for talking. On better days, Cohen found it very therapeutic to retell the details of the moments of his injury. It made the experience real and helped him process the trauma during the daytime as opposed to reliving it in nightmares. It gave his listeners nightmares, but so what? They could bear some of this sacrifice as well. Night was the most terrible time of all. Gaping into the dark, staring at the ceiling, lying motionless for hours on end, thoughts running wild. If he'd thought it would have helped, he might have offered up his thoughts to God.

He just wasn't a man of faith.

18

Jerusalem
Nine Months later
Spring 322 BCE

T HE SMALL ROOM IS DISTINCT. It smells like sweat and blood and wet earth. Once the pushing begins in earnest, it also smells like piss and shit, and the amniotic fluid adds an odor of rancid peppermint oil. Somehow all of these smells combine to make a new odor that is not altogether horrible. Shifra, the assistant midwife, has begun to associate that particular mélange with optimism and promise. It doesn't bother her. She hopes that one day she might be on the producing side of it.

"The baby's head is too big," the midwife screams, knocking Shifra out of her meditation.

"Too big?" she asks. She hasn't been doing this long enough to know what those words imply.

"Yes. It is not going to fit through the passage. She could push for hours and all we'd get is two dead bodies. We are going to have to cut through her uterus if we are to save at least one life."

Shifra winces and looks at Yael. *If this expectant mother understands the implications of that statement, if she knows that her life would be the one sacrificed, she doesn't wear it on her face.* Yael instead wears an expression that is both calm and determined. It is in a sense almost serene. Her eyes glow as if she has just been promised something magnificent. Like the world has granted her a higher purpose, the purpose of survival and creation, a divine act conceded to a mere human.

"What do you need from me?" Shifra asks.

"I need you to grab three cloths. With two of them, tie down her arms to the legs of the table."

Shifra does as she is told. With the first knot, the midwife chastises her. "Tie her down tightly. The point is to keep her from moving. It isn't to keep her comfortable."

Yael looks to Shifra almost sympathetically as she tightens the knots and takes out the slack in the first rag. She moves around the table to tie down the left arm. Once that is done, she asks the midwife, "What do you want me to do with this other rag?"

"Put it in her mouth. It will help her to have something to bite down on."

Shifra has never seen a mother die. The knowledge of what is coming almost causes her to freeze. *Maybe if we don't cut, maybe if she just pushes a bit longer...*

Yael speaks soothingly to her, even as her body rocks in contractions, "Here, give me the rag. Let's get this baby out."

"What now?" Shifra turns to the midwife.

"Come and lie on her body. Lie down and hold her tight right on her thighs. When I cut, her instinct will be to thrash. You have to hold her body steady. Otherwise, my knife tip could slip. You must hold her as still as you can."

"OK." Shifra lays her body horizontally across Yael's.

"Try to be still, Yael," the midwife says right before she starts cutting.

As the blood spurts with the initial plunge of the sharpened old blade, Shifra grows lightheaded. She looks down, only to see her arms covered in the darkening red. Yael takes it all bravely. She bites instead of screams. Takes what the world has given her with resolve rather than protest. The baby's screams lift Shifra's heart for a brief moment. The midwife deftly pulls the squirming baby out, trims the cord, and places him in the crook of Yael's left arm. The new mother looks lovingly at her child,

"Hello, great one," she slurs, the last word softer than the first. The midwife puts her hands under the child as Yael's right hand unclenches. A small silver eagle drops to the floor as one life ends and another begins. From her angle, Shifra sees the eagle fall. She rolls off Yael, stoops, and quietly places the talisman in her tunic pocket. When the community of Jerusalem hears of Yael's passing, the great stone walls of the city nearly shake in sorrow. Family members rend their clothes. Despite the cold shoulders and nasty rumors that swirl around, Yael's passing is a sad blow to the ancient city's citizens. Everyone grieves her loss. No one more than the beleaguered Simon the High Priest.

Simon is a man of many secrets—some of significant consequence. Not long after their return to Jerusalem and their hero's welcome for saving the city from sure destruction, Yael became an outcast. Rumors of her being desecrated spread throughout the city. A daughter of priests, Kohanim, who'd been raped and tarnished would never find a suitor for marriage. She'd known enough to refrain from telling anyone of the events. But one look at her beauty and even the vaguest understanding of a military man such as Alexander, and it wasn't hard to imagine what had happened that night she was away.

The women in the city adopted their typical catty criticisms. "She went out into the fields without permission. She asked for it."

Men unemotionally lamented the loss of such a promising bride for a lucky Jewish boy. "It is a shame. She would have made someone very happy."

Three weeks after their return, Yael comes to see Simon. She is unsure as to why she trusts him so explicitly. Maybe it is because they alone had met the great Alexander. Maybe because they'd walked back into the city together or because she'd been asked so many times to describe what Simon had done out there on the battlefield dressed in the priestly garments.

"I need to speak privately, Your Honor," she says.

She looks at Tobi as she says this.

Simon looks in the direction of her gaze and replies, "Tobi is my trusted servant. I cannot be with you alone in a room, young lady—you know that."

Tears appear in the corners of her eyes. She scrunches up her face in an expression that is incredibly endearing. She summons her strength to disagree with the high priest.

"Please, for just a moment" she pleads.

Noticing her desperation, Simon motions Tobi to leave the room. "Stand outside, Tobi."

As the door shuts behind him, Yael motions somewhat frantically to her stomach. "I am with child in my belly."

"Are you sure?"

"Yes. I have missed my cycle. I never miss my cycle. And I've been waking in the morning, sick to my stomach. I do not want to eat. When my mother was pregnant with my brother, she too threw up."

"Have you shared this with anyone else?" asks Simon. "Even your mother?"

"That beast of a man, the warrior, defiled me—he wanted to kill me."

"Have you told anyone?" Simon asks again.

"No one, not even my mother. I want to die—for what is my life worth?"

"Calm, child."

"No one looks at me. My mother and father do not touch me, and all they know is what they suspect. This baby will confirm it for everyone. I cannot live with people looking at me this way. And now God of heaven and earth has destined that I bring a bastard child into the world!"

Simon cannot help but agree with her. This is a damning development almost any way you spin it. She will be ostracized, a sexual leper among her own people. But he cannot help but think about that meeting with Alexander. He'd felt some strange calm and purpose surge through every bone in his body during that meeting. It had confirmed for him the chosen-ness of his people and the legitimacy of his own stature among them. For Simon, this child is living evidence of God's great salvation. At this very moment, the young lady impregnated with Alexander the Great's child shares a profound connection with Simon. All of this has meaning—it is destined to be through this child's existence.

His mind spins. He has saved Yael physically. He thinks frantically of how he might save her spiritually. *One who begins an act of service must complete it.*

Simon has never been a man who makes impulsive decisions—this is how he reached his stature. Today will be a first.

"Tobi," Simon calls through the door.

"Yes, sir." His servant appears instantly.

"Prepare a wedding feast—I take myself a new wife tonight."

Yael is shocked.

"Excuse me, sir?"

"A feast. Tell the cooks. Tell the servants. Send out the word. Tonight I will be married to the most beautiful woman in all of Jerusalem!"

As he says these words, he cannot believe they are coming out of his mouth.

Yael's cheeks are scarlet red.

He imagines this is how Joshua of old must have sounded when he announced he would be marrying Rahab, the prostitute of Jericho. Of course, Yael was no prostitute. Then again, Simon was no Joshua either.

Joshua, the great biblical conqueror, married the prostitute of the walled city Jericho shortly after the Israelites conquest of that fabled city. His choice of a wife was intentional. She'd betrayed her people because they had betrayed her, abused her and sold her into prostitution. Why had they sold her into depravity? Because she was destitute, and her own society, instead of providing shelter, took advantage of her weakness. When two Israelite spies entered the walled city of Jericho, she felt no regret in making an alliance with them. She'd been drawn to these Jewish men because she knew of their people's storied code of ethics. The God of the Jewish people hears the cries of the widow, orphan and stranger. Theirs was a society that promised to care for the weak. She was weak. And the people of Jericho had not just abandoned her, they had taken advantage of her in the cover of night, and in the light of day criticized her for it.

After saving the two spies, Rahab the whore never really believed their promise. But they kept their word—the Israelites destroyed the city. Every man, woman, child, cattle and possession was burned to the ground. The soldiers left her residence intact and she was invited to live among the Israelite nation. But they did not welcome her. The men looked at her with lust and the women with disgust.

They too spoke of her as "The Whore of Jericho." At times, she wished she had perished in the destruction of the city rather than live among a people who would not even look at her. When she came to Joshua and asked him to take her life, she finally found an Israelite who lived out the ethics of their books. He married her instead. He married her to set an example, to teach a lesson. This is a society that cares for its weakest members. No one is rejected, no one is abandoned.

There is my precedent, Simon says to himself. *Yael will live under my protection. No one needs to know she is with child from another man.*

Yael immediately understands the depth of the act, the self-sacrifice and risk being offered to her by the most powerful man in Jerusalem. She is grateful. She tries not to look desperate in that gratitude.

"I will marry her tonight!" announces Simon.

"Yes, sir!" Tobi replies, bustling quickly out of the room in something of a huff.

Simon is not a young man—according to some counts, he has reached his sixtieth year. Yael will be his third wife. Yocheved, his first, died years earlier. Malka, his second wife, had been dutiful and attentive for years. He'd married Malka while still married to Yocheved for a practical reason: a high priest must be married in order to maintain his post. The possibility of one wife dying during the service was a risk the sages would not accept, and so the tradition was always to have two wives. Though he'd married Malka as something of a formality, he'd grown quite fond of her. Since Yocheved's death, Simon never remarried out of respect for his second wife. And the sages never pressed him on the issue. No one will object when he marries the young Yael, daughter of a distinguished Kohen family.

Jerusalem, for its historical greatness, is still a small city. Word spreads quickly. The entire city is in attendance as the aged Simon and the resplendent, beautiful, young Yael are wed under a full moon. Rumors of her being impure end in that moment. She is now beyond reproach, beyond questioning. Simon has indeed saved her.

She nonetheless has her doubts as they make their way into the wedding chambers. It isn't like she feels like fulfilling any wifely duties. Her feelings of affection and gratitude toward this high priest do not equate to desire. Her body feels nothing like it felt when she was alone with Alexander. In no way does she want Simon to ravish her.

In the wedding chambers, they lie side by side but do not touch. Neither speaks nor sleeps very much. In the morning, Simon asks her for her foot. She laughs and asks, "My foot. Whatever for?"

"This will hurt just a little," he doesn't explain as he takes a small needle and draws blood from her ankle. He uses the bed sheet to clean it.

That morning, Yael has no idea how, but the word spreads throughout the city. He must have shown the sheet to some proper authority on these odd matters. Regardless, news spreads that Simon had married a virgin and their wedding was properly consummated. The bed sheet is evidence proudly kept in the home of Yael's parents, displayed to anyone who might dare doubt their daughter's chastity.

Yael lives with her parents during the pregnancy. Her mother has suddenly started speaking with her again. Her father can once again smile upon his beloved child with pride. She barely sees Simon, and that is OK with her. Her thoughts are with Alexander. Every time the baby kicks, she wonders where her warrior might be. Will he come back for her and their child? Does he even know that, within the walled old city, he will have a son? She prays for a strong and healthy son.

There are moments when Yael feels gripped with fear: *Will Simon love the child as his own? Will I ever be found out?* She takes long walks in the orchards outside Jerusalem. Later in her pregnancy, those walks take place mostly in her mind. She barely leaves her home. But in the depths of her mind, she seeks solace in those lines of swollen grapes from which she had been taken. Her mind goes again and again to that day she was abducted. Did she somehow earn this fate?

She isn't much help around the house either. She doesn't get out of bed much. She doesn't help with the dishes or chores. Her siblings mutter about "waiting on Yael," but she doesn't care. She spends countless hours looking at the silver eagle Alexander gave her and reliving her ordeal. She feels powerless. While the baby grows in her belly, she loses her sense of self. It is as if she is being replaced by something else, some other identity that she has had little part in forging.

Her father, every evening, lovingly places his hands on his daughter's growing stomach to feel the baby kicking. "My little grandson, the future high priest of Israel," he declares. He glows with pride as the strength of the movements increase.

Meanwhile, the Yael that once existed is no more. She feels as if she was once a glamorous young girl with the world before her. Now she is simply a vessel for this new life yet to appear. She is a vault of secrets that can never be told to anyone. She is the harbor of the seed of a supposed deity.

Yael gives way to Simon's third child and his first son.

On the day before the baby's circumcision, the child's mother is buried outside the walls of the city, alongside the vineyard she knew so well. Simon grieves her loss. As he returns from her eternal resting place, he thinks about her lost innocence, his own choices and the awesome charge she left behind. Simon names the baby Yochanan. It is a name thoughtfully chosen. In Hebrew, the name means "God have mercy." In Greek, the name means "divine." Only time will tell whether or not this boy will be the beneficiary of such divine grace.

On a quiet afternoon, a week after the mourning period, Shifra, the young assistant midwife, comes to see Simon. "Your excellency, this was in your wife's hand as she left the world of the living. A treasure she must have brought back from the heathen's camp. I think you should have it." Shifra's conjecture could have been interpreted as condescending. When Simon sees the silver eagle dangling on a thin leather strap, he loses his breath. He feels the blood stream out from his face into the innards of his stomach. He reaches for the silver eagle and places it in his palm.

"Thank you, dear child. Thank you."

19

Dimona, Israel
June 2007

MORAN FEELS A SURGE OF energy, inspired as she puts on her sneakers and runs to the Samet house. Ever since she was young, she has relished running. When she was 10 and 11, her lungs were elastic; her legs could go for days. Now that she is sneaking the occasional teenage cigarette, her lungs feel a bit more limited. But her legs still yearn to stretch as much as they had seven years ago. Her mother, too, had been a runner in high school. She'd competed on a national level in track and field competitions. There are days when Moran wonders what it might be like to feel that energy spike whenever she laces up her shoes. She quickly pushes that thought out of her mind; the track team practices during the only time of day she sees her Mom. *Whatever the rush, it wouldn't be worth it.* She has a carefully cultivated air of indifference to maintain. To run or jog in public is too much of a commitment even for something she loves.

The energy and high are swiftly extinguished when she reaches the end of her jog. The Samets live in a more upscale neighborhood on a street of attached two-story homes with cute little gardens. It is hard to get to their home. The street is closed off and clogged with people, cars, trucks,

121

men and women in uniform and what appears to be reporters. Some local military personnel direct cars at intersections. Closer to the home, guards stand still and watch into the distance.

"Maybe father is right," she thinks. "Maybe not."

Moran makes her way through the maze of people holding cell-phones, looking serious. Somehow she reaches the front doorstep, but before she goes any further, she realizes it is futile. Every light is lit. She cannot make out what people are saying through the windows, but the fear and anxiety and energy emanating from the commotion inside is palpable. She hangs around a little longer, looking for a familiar face. *How odd,* Moran thinks, *not one person I know.* It is weird to have known Lior fairly well, and to arrive at his home and feel like a total stranger. Her father's words, "They want to be alone," ring in her mind as wrong. They are far from alone. Mimi's words, "They're trained for this shit," sound less callous than credible at this moment. *I've made a mistake. I should not be here.*

No one notices as Moran creeps away from the doorway, back down the driveway, and toward the street. Whereas she'd jogged over to the house, she walks home conscious of every step she takes. Her feet feel heavy. First, she thinks of her uncle. She remembers how they'd gone to his home when he was killed, how the whole place had been bustling with cousins and long-lost aunts and uncles. She wonders if there had been friends of her uncle, *friends that actually knew him,* who'd felt as unwelcome as she'd felt to share in grief. Then, her thoughts grow broader.

With each step, the realization of her own selfish ignorance strikes deeper: *Why have I never thought about this stuff before? It is in the news every day. But it always felt somehow foreign. This is where I live?* War always seems imminent. As inevitable as it feels, it also seems like something others do. When the news reports come on each morning to announce the newest barrage of rockets that have landed in Sderot or Be'er Sheva, she brushes it off like she'd been taught, *Hell, that's life here in Israel. The constant threat from outsiders is why we need a great army. It's why we all have to serve.* The sight of Lior's family gives her a new sense of doubt about the inevitability and accuracy of those clichés. *What is it all for?* She always feels as if Arik's opinions are scary. *But shit, maybe he's right. Maybe we are fighting someone else's war?*

"Moran!" She hears her name over the soft purr of a motorcycle, turns around, and sees Moshiko behind her. He wears a sleek black helmet that hardly contains his brown curls. He crouches toward her from the seat of his silver moped.

"Oh hey, Moshiko."

"Where are you coming from?"

"The Samets."

"Huh," he purses his lips. "And where are you going?"

"I don't know—home, I guess."

"Well, get on. I'll take you."

"OK," Moran answers anxiously.

She feels flustered and overwhelmed as she sits behind Moshiko. He takes her hands and wraps them around his waist. It feels like his hands linger over hers for just a second longer than is necessary. The ride seems longer than it actually is. But, she wishes as they pull up in front of her building that it could last longer. When they arrive, Moshiko turns off the moped and hops off. He turns to help Moran.

She is about to thank him for the ride, when Moshiko asks her, "What were you doing at the Samet home?"

"Well," she starts, "I knew Lior…"

"Of course you did. We all did. But that wasn't my question."

"I know…" She can't get her thoughts straight. She looks toward the stars for some clarity, but none is forthcoming.

"Why did I go there?" she says absently to herself before breaking down in a flood of emotions, "I don't know, I thought maybe there was something I could do—I feel so bad about Lior. I just wanted to do something for his mother."

Moshiko gently places his hand on her shoulder to calm her down.

"Take a breath, Moran," he says in a soothing tone.

She breathes in deeply as he continues, "I feel the same way. There must be something we can do."

"Is it true that soldiers are trained for this?"

"Well, I guess that depends on what you mean by this," he says, "and, whether Lior is going through the normal things that happen in these cases. I'm sure they are given some training for what to do if taken. But how much good could that stuff actually do? He wasn't some sort of highly trained expert. I was sitting next to him eight months ago in calculus, you know?"

"I know, it's a silly question but– Mimi started talking about—forget it. It just feels like no one gets it. Or no one cares enough."

"I disagree, Moran. We definitely have some dumb and self-absorbed classmates. But for the most part, people get it. Israel is not like other countries. We really care about our soldiers. I'm sure the army will do whatever it can to get him back. The problem is what those Hamas shits are going to ask for. They will demand the moon and stars. And I don't know that Lior will be worth it to the military."

"What can we do?"

"I'm not sure. What if we make a huge sign and hang it at school tomorrow and wake this town up?"

"Moshiko! Yes, let's do it. I have some poster paper at home."

"No," he startles her and looks at the streetlight shining across the block, "I'm thinking something massive."

"Like what?"

"I can grab a big white bed sheet from my house—we'll need paint…"

"Perfect. I can probably get paint from the art room at school." Moran volunteers. "I'm in there all the time and the teacher likes me. I think she'll be supportive of what we're planning on doing."

"Great," Moshiko answers. "Let's meet at 8 a.m. in the art room. I'll bring the sheet."

"OK! I'll see you then." Moran feels a spring in her step return as Moshiko drives off. She is not sure what she is feeling, but whatever it is, it feels right.

The minute she gets into her bedroom, she calls Mimi. "Guess who took me for a ride on his motorcycle?"

"Who?"

"Moshiko."

"No way, I don't believe you!" Mimi yells. As soon as they start giggling to each other, Moran feels a subtle but unmistakable trace of guilt creep up from her gut and into her throat.

"Yep. Just wanted you to know. Gotta go!" she cuts the conversation short.

"I want details," Mimi prods.

"Can't now. We'll talk tomorrow!" It feels like she is betraying

Moshiko, Lior, and some part of herself with this call to Mimi. *What is wrong with me?*

"Bye."

Moran doesn't sleep much that night. She tosses and turns, worried about Lior. She berates herself for being awkward with boys she finds attractive, and berates herself once again for thinking about that kind of thing while one of her friends is being kept against his will and probably tortured by Hamas. She can't stop herself from obsessing over Moshiko, yet she knows how shallow that sort of obsession seems in the face of what really matters. She has seen the pain on the faces of Lior's family through those windows. It is a pain that makes her conversations with Mimi feel worse than shallow.

When she rolls groggily out of bed to the sound of her alarm clock the next morning, she looks awful. She didn't plan time for her early rendezvous with Moshiko. She wraps a scarf around her hair to hide the fact that it is frizzy. She even neglects her makeup. It is all worth it when she arrives in the art room and finds Moshiko there waiting for her.

"Hey!" He lights up. He doesn't seem the least bit worried that she is less made up. He looks almost through her, like he is searching for some inner traits that matter most.

"Hey, Moshiko," She shrinks under the heat of his amber gaze. "You got the sheet?"

"I've got it!"

"Did you steal this off your bed?" she jokes.

"No… but I would have. We have a couple extra sets. Hoping my mom doesn't notice it's missing, or at least doesn't figure out it was me that raided her linen closet."

"It's for a good cause, anyway," Moran assures him. "I wouldn't be too worried. She'd probably be proud."

They debate for a while on what to write on their blank canvas. The resulting phrase, painted in massive blue letters across the center of the sheet, is short and simple:

The simplicity of their slogan alone would certainly have received some attention. But when they talk the third floor Biology teacher into letting them hang it outside of his window, they achieve instant and visible success. The spot is visible to community members walking past the school, and to all students and teachers entering the building. The impromptu testament of solidarity is an instantaneous success. Everyone cannot help but cheer it on. In school, the word spreads like wildfire. Moran and Moshiko are instant heroes. It seems like everybody wants to get in on the action. Everyone agrees that the Israeli government should do all in its power to bring Lior home. No one really considers anything other than that. For the teenagers, the campaign is one of solidarity, not of politics. They want everyone to know that Lior will not be forgotten.

Moran finds herself very quickly in a role that is unfamiliar. She and Moshiko become the sort of impromptu leaders of a protest, an advocacy movement. She is the person in her grade who, on occasion, decides where the Friday night parties will be—a sort of unofficial social chair. But she has never really been seen as a leader of any other sort. The sheet changes all that. Teachers congratulate them on getting the school motivated and caring enough to do something. The principal now knows her name, and has offered to help. People she has never spoken to before greet her in the halls. Over lunch the next day, she and Moshiko sit to chat. "Well, it seems like we've woken them up!" she says eagerly.

"Yep. Now we need to channel this energy into more action," Moshiko agrees.

"Let's have a lunch meeting tomorrow for people interested in doing more. I can make an announcement over the speakers in homeroom."

As Moshiko nods in agreement and they head to their respective classes, Moran takes a step back for a second and thinks about how strange this feels. She has never cared much about the world outside her own. Now, within the span of a week, here she is exhorting others to do so as well. What is it her dad sometimes says? "No zealot like a convert."

She makes the announcement and can hardly sit through morning classes before lunch. The only thing that gets her through is all the people whispering to her—between classes and in them—that they will be there. They didn't lie. The seminar room doesn't come close to accommodating everyone. They all head to an outdoor gated area where walls can't constrain their numbers. Moshiko stands up on a table and raises his arms to quiet everyone.

"We are glad that you are all with us. We want to do more to spread our message. We need your help and ideas."

From the crowd of high school students comes shouted suggestions:

"Let's plaster the city with flyers!"

"We need a website!"

"What about a Facebook page?"

"Deal. And we need a picture of Lior. A better one than those news organizations are using. Who can get us one of those?"

Moshiko is in his element. He nods at the recommendations and instructs Moran to take down notes for who is doing what. Mimi stands off to the side and watches in amazement. She does not volunteer to help much, and Moran wonders if she is jealous of all the attention.

Signs and banners spring up throughout Dimona. It all started with a late-night conversation with Moshiko. Now, three days later, it feels like everyone is involved. The printers in town do not charge for the services, school administrators are lax with students who skip class to work on the Free Lior Campaign. In technology class, students work on the website that will take donations for the family and serve as a central hub for volunteers to lobby the government officials. When she tells her mom about things after school, she feels like some of the pain in her mother's eyes recedes a bit to make room for pride in her daughter's passion.

Moran has never felt like this before. She has never felt the thrill of working on something bigger than herself, doing something for the good of others. It feels wonderful. The day after the recruiting meeting, Moran gets out of bed flying high. She hasn't slept much, but this time it is due to excitement rather than guilt and confusion. By working to raise awareness for Lior, it feels like life has taken on a new meaning. There is purpose in where she is going, what she is thinking and what she is doing. And her partner is Moshiko to boot!

She goes to her first class and zones out as her teacher talks about some sort of math formulas. *Whatever. I'll figure that stuff out later.* As she walks from calculus to history class, she receives a text, "I'm on my way to pick up the fliers now. I've got an off period.—M."

As she texts Moshiko back, she keeps walking down the stairs. Suddenly, her right foot misses the last step of the staircase and she tumbles to the landing.

POP!

She registers the pain before she figures out that it went along with the noise that echoed around the stairwell.

"Shit!" Moran screams.

Her entourage of friends and bystanders do not know whether to laugh or worry. But as soon as she rolls over from her stomach to her back, they see her face. The pain etched into every bit of it gives clear instructions.

"Oh my God. Moran, are you OK?"

"Let me help you up."

"I can't get up," she mutters as she hopes the excruciating pain in her ankle will subside. It doesn't.

"What happened, Moran?" Mimi says as she comes up the stairs to find her friend helpless and in pain.

"I fell."

A couple of students help her up. She hobbles over to the bench near the stairwell and takes off her shoe and sock. Mimi watches Moran's face and sees that she is unable to hide the pain.

"Shit, shit," Moran mutters as she looks at the swollen ankle, already changing to a shade of dark blue.

"It's broken," one of her helpers guesses. "It's definitely broken. You need to see the nurse."

The visit to the nurse leads to an immediate trip to the *Kupat Cholim*, the local medical clinic, where X-rays are taken and a diagnosis made. Moran has severed a few ligaments. She is given painkillers and a plastic boot with black Velcro straps. She is as bitter as she has ever been in her life. She finally found something that made her want to get up in the morning. Now she is unable to stand.

She spends two days curled up in bed, unable to put any weight on her foot. When she takes her foot down from an inclined position, it throbs mercilessly. Her mom takes the time off from work to wait on her patient. Her mom greets Moshiko when he comes by to visit.

"Moran," she announces with something of a playful tone in her voice, "you have a visitor!"

Moshiko is sympathetic, but Moran can tell that he is busy and wants to be out working on their campaign.

"This thing is blowing up!" he says, "On to Tel Aviv and Haifa after Dimona!"

"That's great," Moran smiles.

"And there is a Facebook badge now. Everyone in school has it. It appears that almost everyone in Israel—at least who has Facebook—has it too."

"Wow!"

When Moshiko leaves, and after her mom has lightheartedly interrogated her about this handsome young boy, Moran lays in bed, thrilled and slightly bitter. She has no idea what Moshiko thinks of her and if he cares for her as she cares for him. She knows Lior liked her but she never thought of him that way.

As she closes her eyes, she thinks to herself: *I wish Moshiko would give me a sign, a hint, so that I don't embarrass myself. Crazy, Lior has gone from a nobody to a celebrity. I hope I never embarrassed Lior.*

20

Gaza City, Gaza Strip
September 2006

I F IT WEREN'T FOR LIOR'S ability to *la'uf*, mentally fly away and dis-
appear into his imagination, he would have lost hope a long time ago.
Of course, even the expression a "long time ago" is relative. He is not sure
how much time has actually elapsed since his abduction. If not for Faisal,
the guard who brings him food twice a day, he would spend his entire time
sleeping and dreaming.

Lior's mind takes him to all sorts of places. He never realized how
vivid the places in his mind could be until now. In the past, he never had
the luxury to la'uf for extended periods of time because there were always
interruptions. Here in the bowels of Gaza, in this small room with no one
to interrupt him, he flies into the world of his imagination for hours on
end. And he could not be more content. At times, he goes back to memories of home and school or the army. Most of the time, however, he goes to
places that only exist in his mind.

Not all those places are pleasant. He sometimes imagines the horror
of his mother or father being dragged through the streets of Gaza. Or his
little sister stepping on a mine planted by terrorists in their neighborhood

in Dimona.

Lior tries hard to keep the places positive. His favorite places are in the sky. When he is able to just fly into the air over the ocean and feel the wind blowing his hair back. The sky and the sea create a palette of beautiful colors.

Does anybody miss me, he wonders, *or even know I am missing? Does Moran think of me often? Or am I just kidding myself?*

The memories of family and friends, when pleasant, are like wine for his lonely soul. They can lift his spirits, if only for a little while.

As much as he tries to forget the horrors of the event, they keep playing back in his mind like an old black-and-white movie. If not for the trembling they bring, he can tolerate them.

He can't keep track of time. Still, he is pretty sure it has been more than a week since anyone spoke to him. Those initial days, Lior didn't do much of anything. Twice each day, once after sunrise and once right before, a buxom elderly woman, covered from head to toe, opened his door gingerly and passed him a glass of water and a plate of food. The food varied. It was sometimes cold, sometimes hot, but always generous. He didn't eat at first. He was too worried they might try to poison him. But hunger erases that fear quickly. Now he looks forward to those meals.

The same woman who leaves him food opens his door and walks to the bathroom with a bucket full of spray bottles and rags. She cleans his bathroom thoroughly and leaves without looking in his direction. *Food. A place to sleep. A woman to clean my toilet*, he thinks.

During the day, activity outside picks up. He can hear the belch of trucks driving, an occasional car horn, and some voices from the building in which he is being held. But his tiny window doesn't enable him to see anything other than the dusty abandoned alley below. Not even a cat comes by. Lior naps so much during the day that he doesn't sleep well at night, and eventually both start to meld together into one long, fitful slumber broken only by the arrival of food.

The IDF prepares their young recruits on what to expect and how to respond in case of abduction. Lior is amazed at how accurate they were. There are no interrogations, no torture. In fact, Lior is surprised at how ignored he feels by his captives.

Restless nights lead to drowsy days, and pretty soon Lior isn't getting up much anymore. He has been taking showers every morning as a bit of a routine. That stops too. Lior doesn't even stand to greet the woman at the door. He pulls himself out of his slumber to drink a bit of the water, and then to relieve himself when necessary. Otherwise, he is paralyzed in fear and doubt and a lack of motivation. *Am I a forgotten man?* The landlady looks at him for a long while when she notices he is looking a bit despondent. A day later, Faisal appears.

"Hello, dear guest. I am Faisal. You are my guest. I hear that you are not moving around much. You must eat!"

This man, the first person to speak to Lior since his abduction, acts as if they have known each other for years.

"Hmmm," is all Lior can mutter. It is like his vocal cords don't even work anymore.

"Too much sleep is not good for you, my dear guest. Work the brain, work your body, do something."

"Ugggh."

"Here, get up, soldier!" He pulls at Lior's shoulder ineffectually. He speaks in the kind of Hebrew one would expect from an Arab living in Gaza. It is sloppy but understandable. Lior looks from his prostrate position up to Faisal's kindly face, at the well-groomed mustache, the dust of gray hair just settling on his sideburns. *He must be in his late 30s.*

Faisal motions to a plate he had placed on the table by the door,

"There. I've brought you a special treat to get you eating again."

Faisal grabs the plate filled with pita, dates, a cucumber, and falafel and waves it just in front of Lior's nose. The falafel gets Lior up. It smells freshly fried.

He eats quietly and quickly at first, but loses his momentum after about half of the food. Once Lior pushes the plate away to gesture that he is finished, Faisal speaks to him again in something of a frantic tone, "Come, get up soldier. Let's jog in one place for a few minutes."

"I can't."

"Yes, you can. You are young and fit. Come on!"

Lior reluctantly complies. Faisal grins stupidly and jumps up and down, waving his arms like a helicopter. Lior lifts one foot, then the other, until he is actually jogging in place. Slogging in place is probably a more appropriate term, actually. It is exhausting but feels good.

When he sits back on his bed, out of breath, Lior looks to Faisal.

"Where am I? What am I doing here? What's the date?"

"You are in Faisal's care! Otherwise, I cannot answer any of those questions, my guest. But no worries. No one will hurt you here."

"Please take me home. My family will give you more money than you can imagine. Just get me out of here please."

"Money will not help either of us. Your government knows what it has to do in order to bring you home," Faisal replies in a tone much sharper than he'd used with Lior thus far. He turns and heads for the door.

"Don't leave!" Lior begs of him, "Stay here. Talk with me."

"For a bit, then," Faisal turns back towards Lior, takes a step to the left, and sits in a small wooden chair facing the bed.

"Faisal, can I get a note to my family? Can I call them for just a moment to tell them I'm fine? I have a mother. She must be worried sick about me. It would make her feel so much better to know that you are treating me OK, feeding me."

"Do not worry, my guest. Your family knows you are well. Soon enough, you will communicate with them."

"How do they know? I haven't spoken to anyone in weeks."

"They know. Our people are communicating with your people."

"So I am to sit here and rot until your people agree that I should be returned?"

"Unfortunately, my guest… that is pretty much the case. In the meantime, exercise your brain by reciting songs or poems. If you do not use it, you will lose it. You know how that saying goes."

Lior nods quietly, unsatisfied but nonetheless impressed with Faisal's advice. That is exactly what the military advised. Use your brain—exercise your body. He cannot remember her name, but the military psychologist must have said it a hundred times: "Exercise the brain, keep it working." At the time, her warnings seemed so insane. Neither Lior nor anyone in his unit could fathom being taken alive. They were invincible, as teenagers always are. He wishes, at that moment, that he'd listened more carefully.

"Faisal, I don't know any poems and I don't know any songs by heart."

Lior cannot think of one song he knows by heart; he cannot think of one poem he memorized. Mrs. Herzberg knows every one of those poems they'd read in class by heart, Agnon, Bacher, Carmi. *How she begged us to memorize them and we just joked around.*

"How about the Torah, your scriptures? I'm sure you know that by heart," Faisal says as he stands up once again, ready to leave.

"Please don't leave me alone. I'm going crazy."

"Do not speak this way, my dear guest. I must be a good host. In our tradition, bringing a guest into your home is a huge responsibility. I would risk my life in order to protect a guest in my home. There is nothing to make you crazy. Nothing to fear. You will be fine. I will return this afternoon and I will be a better host." With that, Faisal stands up, walks to the door and calmly leaves the room.

This moment of human contact awakens in Lior a deep sense of empathy about what those who care about him must be thinking. Of course he misses his parents. He wonders how worried they must be. But mostly he just feels sorry for himself. Not until now does he fully understand how random these events are. If he is in the twilight zone, surely they are as well. He cannot help but think what his Saba, his grandfather Cohen, is going through. *Is he disappointed? Why didn't I fight back? I didn't even shoot one bullet. My grandfather is a war hero—like someone straight out of the stories of old, a modern-day Maccabee—and I'm a fucking war loser! I never wanted to be enlisted. Fuck! Get me out of here. I've got to get out of here.*

As he awaits Faisal's return, Lior tries his hardest to remember other things from the military training session on abductions. He vaguely remembers other memory tricks they had recommended. Practicing multiplication tables. Making mental lists of all the people you know. *Who do I know? I don't really know so many people. Funny how that's what they had suggested we think about. I guess they knew none of us memorized any poetry.*

Lior refuses to lie down on the bed again. *I might not be able to remember anything, but I can do the physical bit.* He walks around the room. *Who do I know?* He counts twenty names before it starts to become difficult to remember whether he has named each person yet. At times he debates internally just how well he needs to "know" someone before he can count them. *What the fuck—I don't know anybody—no, wait, did I count Ellie and Lily? I really don't know them.* His mind is scattered. The walking gets tiring. The thought of yelling seems futile. He lays back in bed in a curled up position. His mind first goes blank and then transports him to a blissful place.

21

La'uf
Lior's Mind

Memory: The Beautiful Envelope

The envelope arrived from Lishkat HaGius, the IDF draft office. It actually was a beautiful envelope. The shiny, crisp white envelope with an olive and sword logo on the top left corner, presumably symbolizing strength and peace, had a window in the middle with the name "Lior Samet" on a letter inside. I knew that letter was most certainly my Tzav Gius, induction notice. I opened it very carefully. I intended on saving it. The only important information was the date in the middle of the page.

Mom and dad were pretty sober about the whole thing. Not grandfather.

"Now you are a man!" Saba bellowed while he sat at the head of our Friday night Shabbat dinner. His once-a-month visit from Tel Aviv, when Savta was not with us, was never without drama. Ten years after their divorce, Saba could not be in the same room as Savta. It was hard for Saba to be in the same room with anybody who didn't share his views on politics, religion, arts and life. Ima was patient. He was her father and she loved him.

"This army, Tzva HaGanah LeIsra'el, is the greatest miracle of all time, young man. What an honor to serve. After 2,000 years of persecution and humiliation, we can wear the Star of David with pride, defending our women, our children, our land and our people. Your great grandparents would have given everything for a Jewish Army as they watched their entire family burn in the gas chambers of the Holocaust." Father sat silently, as did everyone else at the table. Experience had taught the family not to debate grandfather's patriotism and not to interrupt his military bellicosity. It was best to let him finish and hopefully fizzle out.

Mother's look said it all. She was miserable; she knew her husband was fuming. She knew, as did Abba, that I just didn't share that enthusiasm about the military, and I certainly did not feel a part of the militaristic culture that was so pervasive around us. Grandfather was not finished. "We serve our country or we face extinction!"

"Saba, it's not black or white. Not everything is going to be resolved by war."

Boy, did I regret saying that.

Grandfather saw red. Blood filled the veins around his neck. He was about to respond when Michal, his latest live-in, and mother got up and announced the next course for dinner.

"No more army talk tonight. Let's talk about something else."

22

Jerusalem
Winter 314 BCE

THE RABBIS HAVE BEEN COMPLAINING to Simon for years. They began with requests for help or advice. He understands how bad the situation must be in order for them to continue complaining to him, their spiritual superior. Yochanan will not sit still for his lessons. He distracts the others. He refuses to memorize his prayers. But lately, the tenor and frequency of their entreaties have reached new heights.

"The boy is just too wild, your excellency. We cannot keep him in the school any longer!" Rabbi Joseph the Melamed, the teacher of the children in the Priestly Quarters, says emphatically.

Despite his rank, Simon flinches a bit at the implicit threat and critique of his parenting. "He can't stay here? I don't know where you are suggesting he go, Rabbi Joseph. I will speak with the child this afternoon and you, you will give him another chance. We are all doing our best. But you know he doesn't have a mother."

When he rebukes Rabbi Joseph, he moves closer to him so as to accentuate the difference in their height. Simon's physical build defies his age. He is tall and slender. If not for his thick white hair and soft white beard, he could hide the years he has lived. Those years have not yet taken a toll on his posture.

It is a good thing too. And not just because Simon can use his physical size to convey a metaphorical strength. It also provides cover. The boy's height is the only feature attributable to Simon. Yochanan stands a full head taller than all of his 8-year-old friends. People easily associate that size with his presumed father, the high priest.

Though the height confirms his lineage, his blond locks and big blue eyes prompt attempts to recall whether Simon had blond hair. No one dares ask him, so the discussions stay in the realm of vague guesses.

"Of course he did," argues one of the local merchants.

"No. The hair of his family was dark," says another, "and we can see easily enough the eyes don't match either."

Underlying these discussions is a suspicion the gossip-lovers of Jerusalem endlessly enjoy. Everyone remembers Yael's abduction. They all remember the abrupt and unexpected wedding. They remember that Yael had given birth *just a bit* early. No one dares voice the presumptions poorly hidden in their questions about Yochanan's appearance.

"No one remembers Simon's hair because he covers his hair with a turban all the time. His hair was blond and his head was full of curls!"

Among the most trusting of the citizenry, the blue eyes and square jawbone shared by almost no one else in Jerusalem is chalked up to the random nature of biology and mysteries of God.

When Yochanan arrives home that afternoon following the morning complaints by Rabbi Joseph, he darts straight to the food on the table. He rolls figs and dates in a big round sheet of bread. He dips the tip in a round bowl of freshly squeezed olive oil. Before he bites into it, Simon reminds him, "Do not forget to bless the one above. Whoever partakes in this world without blessing steals from the creator!"

"Yes, Father," Yochanan answers. He dutifully offers his thanks and then digs into his afternoon snack with the relish of youth.

The servants comment frequently about how much food this boy consumes. Simon watches him with pleasure and amazement. *What to make of this great hunger? How will it manifest years from now? Will food be enough to satiate such an appetite?*

Simon waits patiently while the boy fills his stomach. As he waits, he looks to the table on which Yochanan has dropped his daily possessions. Among them are several round and glowing stones. "Where did you get all those lovely colorful pebbles?" Simon asks the child.

"I won them playing dice against other boys."

"Won them? Rabbi Joseph tells me you stole them from the older boys."

Yochanan looks up and responds in a tone fraught with honesty and hurt at the accusation, "Father, that is not true. I won these pebbles in a fair way playing with my friends. I also played with some of the older boys, but the older boys come and take what does not belong to them. They take the pebbles of my friends and even of the girls. So today I took and returned the pebbles that were taken from us unjustly."

"Well, that is a bit different than winning them playing dice. I also heard you hit one of the boys."

"It is true, Father. But were you also told that they hit me first?"

"How many older boys were there?"

"Three of them."

"You are not scratched up after fighting three older boys?" Simon asks almost despite himself.

"No, Father. But they are."

This fierce and strange boy, who always seems so similar to Simon and yet so far away from his understanding, does not brag as he tells of his victory. He is unassuming and practical. "I am not scratched, but they are. All of them." Somewhere deep inside, Simon feels a touch of satisfaction from Yochanan's strength. He does not reveal that satisfaction to the boy.

"Yochanan, we never ever hit other children—there is always a peaceful solution."

"Not this time. There wasn't a peaceful solution. Those boys started it before I knew what they were doing."

"We are the descendants of Aaron the High Priest. Our way is the way of loving peace, pursuing peace, loving every human being and bringing Torah to the world. Ours is not the way of violence."

"What if violence seeks you out?"

"Promise me there will be no more fighting, my son."

"I promise." After a short pause Yochanan mutters, "Father, I don't want to lie to you. Sometimes I will use my strength. Rabbi Baruch said sometimes we have to fight for God!"

Simon is shocked and angry, "What did Rabbi Baruch teach you?"

"That, at times in our history, we have not been strong enough. That we should prepare to be strong in the future."

"He did?" Simon is angry but not entirely surprised. Rabbi Baruch is a young activist in the Priestly Quarters who teaches at the school. He has a misplaced passion that Simon finds disturbing. Simon is sure that Baruch finds the high priest's approach equally unsavory.

"He told us," the boy continues, "that Pinchas, the son of Aaron the High Priest, killed Jews who rebelled against God. This story is in the Torah and God rewarded him for his actions." As he nears the end of his explanation, the 8-year-old boy's tone changes from calm disagreement to angry defiance, until finally he is yelling in a high-pitched voice as his face turns red with rage. "We too must defend God and our country and our honor with our strength."

Simon is taken aback. "Yes, Rabbi Baruch is right. The Torah does tell the story of Pinchas the priest. Those were extenuating circumstances."

Simon is surprised that he cannot come up with a better response, and Yochanan looks anything but satisfied. The Torah indeed describes Pinchas, the grandson of Aaron the High Priest, who zealously took justice into his own hands. In so doing, he defied the legal system established by Moses and by God in order to avenge the honor of none other than God. And yes, the Torah does teach us that God rewarded him. Simon has always glossed over the story, so incongruent was it with his overarching ethos and belief system.

"We will discuss Pinchas tomorrow," he says, stalling for time in hopes the boy will forget about it. "Now get yourself ready for bed."

"Yes, Father."

Later that evening, as the last of the candles flicker, Simon begins his nightly routine of chanting the Book of David's Psalms,

"O, how I love Your teaching! It is my study all day long. Your commandments make me wiser than my enemies."

A high-pitched voice comes from the other room and chants, "They always stand by me."

Simon continues, "I have gained more insight than all my teachers."

The young voice calls out, "For your decrees are my study."

Simon sings, "I have gained more understanding than my elders."

Yochanan finishes the verse, "For I observe your precepts."

"I have avoided every evil way," Simon sings.

"So that I may keep your word," Yochanan responds.

"I have not departed from your rules."

"For you have instructed me."

"How pleasing is your word to my palate?"

"Sweeter than honey," Yochanan calls back. He always liked that part.

"I ponder your precepts."

"Therefore, I hate every false way."

As they sing the last verse, Simon feels the same tinge of guilt he always feels when the Bible admonishes the sin of falsehood. In the eight wonderful years of raising this precious and precocious boy, the high priest has struggled to navigate the tension between living a lie and doing what he feels is right. He is not sure if he has always chosen correctly. But he certainly set a course in the early days that he would have a hard time changing now.

"Go to sleep, my sweet child," Simon blesses the young boy. "May God always protect you. Tomorrow, we prepare ourselves for the Yom Kippur service."

"Father, when will I be old enough to serve in the temple?"

Simon does not answer the child. That question hurts the most. In answering it, through his actions, Simon will either demonstrate his own piety or undermine it. The boy was born of a Jewish mother. In that fact, Simon takes great solace. But it isn't enough to answer that question. He caresses the boy's forehead and heads to the ritual bath to bathe before sunset. "Go to sleep, beloved boy. Let us worry about that tomorrow."

As Simon holds his breath, he closes his eyes and thinks, *What have I done?*

In the cold chill of the still but living water, his mind is a flowing stream of various random associations. *I did the right thing. That poor girl was being ostracized.*

What next for this child?

Is he one of us or is he not?

He is like King David, who was born to a Moabite woman…

The son of a Greek warrior?

This child cannot serve in the temple.

Why can't he?

The purity of the line of Kohanim must be preserved.

Why?

We are descendants of Aharon, The Kohen Gadol…

Aharon was the older brother of Moses. It is his legacy we preserve; the boy had a Jewish mother but his paternal seed is foreign; no one must ever know this. What do I do next?

The problem is complicated. The boy is not the only one asking these questions. Others are waiting for him to start his training. Others wonder why Simon has been so slow to bring his pride and joy into the inner circle of heavenly service.

If I am here, then he is here, and there is no explaining it. Maybe we can't stay in Jerusalem. But my purpose is here.

With that last thought, he bursts out of the Mikveh. He quietly and somberly gets dressed and starts the walk back up to his residence. Simon is tired. He is tired of everything. His heart hurts with worry for Yochanan. His pride, that creeping temptation he works so hard to squelch when it rears its ugly head, shudders at the idea of leaving the temple. *What is there to do?*

On one hand, leaving will be something of a relief. The many changes that continue to rack Judea feel more overwhelming. One cannot deny the influence of Greek culture that is taking root in every aspect of life in Jerusalem. Even the sacred temple service absorbs traces of Greek influence. Prosperity is everywhere, but it tears their heritage apart. He tries to chart a course that is progressive but also preserves their sacred traditions. He navigates the Greek influences without inflaming their proponents, but he does not give in on the issues that matter most. After years of serving the will of his people and God, with this extra weight of Yochanan, Simon is tired. He is tired too of waiting.

We pray for the Messiah. Where is he? Why has the Lord not sent him yet?

No Messiah has appeared. In the meantime, Simon is tormented by the thought of the boy even doing menial work in the temple. Simon has told no one about the father of this child, but there are no secrets before

God. It would be a damnable offense.

When he returns to his quarters, Simon closes the door behind him, sits defeated on his bed, and gathers his thoughts. *No Messiah. Yochanan cannot work in the temple. There is no other way.*

"Tobi," he calls out to his trusted servant.

"Yes, sir," the door opens.

"Tobi. Tomorrow morning, summon Antignos here to see me. Tell him it is important. I also want you to ask my brother, Yonathan, to come and see me as well."

"Should I tell them what this concerns?" Tobi asks innocently. For Tobi, one of the greatest perks of serving a man of such stature is being in the know before anyone else. Tobi's loyalty to Simon prevents him from ever betraying his master.

"No. Just tell them to come to me."

That night, Simon lies in bed and struggles to sleep. *Can I really do this? It has never been done. Leave Jerusalem? Step down from my position of high priest? My grandparents returned with the exiles from Babylon. Jerusalem is the soul of our nation. God's Shekhina, his divine shadow, rests upon this holy city. Ezekiel the Prophet referred to Jerusalem as the center of the earth. This is the holiest place in the universe. It is, indeed, the dwelling place of the divine presence. On this hilltop, Adam brought a sacrifice to God on the first day of his creation. Abraham presented his son Isaac as a sacrifice to God.*

His thoughts torment him. He knows this city like no one else. Situated on a low hill, its steep east, south and western sides make it a formidable natural fortress that needs to be defended only from the north. The valleys to the south are broad and fertile enough to produce provisions for its inhabitants.

He muses to himself how his mother, when putting him to bed at night, would tell him that God gave the world ten portions of beauty. Jerusalem took nine and the rest of the world took one.

Simon considers how David, the son of a herdsman, was anointed king by the great prophet Samuel 700 years earlier. Despite his tainted lineage of Moabite blood, he proved himself worthy on the battlefield as he defended the borders of Israel. To centralize his power, he chose a neutral location as his capital. Jerusalem was not yet captured by any of the tribes, but its sanctity was well known by all. King David challenged his best soldiers to capture the city from the Jebusites, who were confident that their city was impenetrable. Simon knows the story well: Two of David's finest soldiers crawled through a tunnel that runs down along the eastern bedrock of the city. Once inside, they made their way to the gates of the city and opened them for David's army to conquer.

The Holy Temple that adorned the highest point in Jerusalem was built by King Solomon, the son David had with Bat Sheva. God did not allow David to build the temple because he was a man of war. It would be David's son who earned the right to build the temple.

Hezekiah, the direct descendant of David and Solomon who reigned some 250 years after them, expanded Jerusalem dramatically. When the pillaging Assyrian Empire was extending its reach, Hezekiah undertook various fortification of the hallowed city. He built a new wall on the western ridge and then dug a tunnel under the city in order to divert water to the western side. To expedite the project, Hezekiah had his engineers dig simultaneously from both sides of the tunnel. They zigzagged under the mountain an S shape, neither side ever backtracking. From above, the miners met at 500 cubits from each side deep under the mountain. This feat seemed undeniably a miracle in the ancient world. The diggers immortalized that moment by etching their jubilation on the stone where they met.

Though the Assyrian king failed to invade Jerusalem, the Babylonian tyrant Nebuchadnezzar managed to destroy the city and the temple. But the exiled Jews returned to Jerusalem under the rule of Cyrus, the great king of Persia. The temple was rebuilt, and here is Simon.

And here I am—exiling myself from this holy city. Leaving seems outrageous. Living away from this city is an affront to the promise that the Messiah is near. It will be a daily source of doubt for the Jewish faith, as Jerusalem is the religious epicenter, particularly for the priestly family. When the Jewish people returned from exile, it was like they'd once again found favor in God's eyes. And yet Simon is considering leaving it voluntarily.

When Simon finally drifts into a fitful sleep, his dreams take him to unusual places: He is a young child. His parents take him to a well and place him in the bucket that is attached to a long rope. They start lowering him down the well. The child in him thinks it is fun at first. But with each feeling of descent, the darkness grows thicker. He calls up to them frantically to bring him back up, but he keeps going down and down. *Please,* he yells out to them, *bring me back up.* Yet he keeps going deeper into the darkness. The adult Simon watches this child version of himself and feels two types of fear. It is as if Abraham has sent him to the alter, and instead of God coming to free him of his task, the knife blade keeps easing closer and closer to Isaac's neck. No lamb is provided as an alternative. The darkness worsens. When Simon wakes the next morning, he is sweating. He is more tired than he was before he slept. He is hardly more ready to do what he needs to do.

To Simon's chagrin, Antignos, the president of the Sanhedrin and his most exceptional student will not need to be convinced. He will seize the opportunity to administer the future of the Jewish state without being held back by the old guard.

A brilliant scholar of law and scripture, as well as a powerful orator who dabbles in Greek philosophy and sciences, Antignos is either loved or despised by his fellow colleagues. Is he the harbinger of a strong Jewish future or a traitor? Simon chooses to see his student in a positive light.

"The Bible of Moses, the word of God, answers one question and only one question," Antignos preaches to his friends and foes alike. "What does God require of me?" Antignos has little patience for those who preach what he calls "a narcissistic religion."

"Do not use the word of God to seek comfort," he cautions, "or security or even edification. There is no substitute for faith and no surrogate for commitment. Those who teach self-reliance and call it faith, shrewdness and call it wisdom, inner security and call it religion, those people fool themselves and mislead the youth."

On other occasions, he exhorts, "Stop asking 'What will I get out of life?' Instead ask, 'What will life get out of me?'"

Antignos has been a predominant force in the daily fight to prevent Greek values from making their mark on the youth in Judea.

"Satisfying one's needs," he preaches, "is looked upon in Greek culture as the ultimate act of human existence. Human desires are the gods of the Greeks and they toil and spare no effort to gratify them. The suppression of a desire is considered a sacrilege and viewed by many as some mental disorder. The Greeks worship the pantheon of material goods and have created a world that looks upon moral and spiritual norms as nothing but personal desires in disguise."

Simon always listens to Antignos' description of this mindset, so accurate in its depiction of Hellenistic values, and fears for the message of Judaism. Compared to this insistence on worldly pleasures, the spiritual life required of good Jews is a tough sell.

The ultimate purpose and human response to the sacred teachings of the Bible, according to Antignos, is for man to declare, "Here I am, and I expect nothing in return!"

Man's service of God has to be absolute and unconditional. It needs to be the highest form of love and awe. These conservative and altruistic teachings rattle many and are the source of a radical split in the educational circles. None of this bothers Simon on this morning or causes him to pause in his choice. Antignos is the undisputed leader and scholar. As head of the Sanhedrin, he will be the first to be informed that Simon is leaving Jerusalem.

Antignos is dressed in distinguished clothing that combines traditional Judean style with contemporary Greek fashion. Tobi leads him into the study, where he finds Simon looking haggard and ill-rested.

"Good morning, Antignos."

"And to you, high priest. You look well."

"That isn't true, Antignos, and you know it."

"Why have you summoned me?"

"Thank you for being here, my trusted friend and colleague. What I am about to tell you has nothing to do with anything that has transpired between us or between my office and the Great Sanhedrin. I have complete and absolute trust in the Sages of Israel. Antignos, I am tired and I am weary," Simon explains. "I have thought a great deal about the decision I have made and I plead for your full understanding. I will take my family to the Northern town of Chashmona, outside of Modi'in. Yonathan, my younger brother, will serve as high priest in Jerusalem. The time has come for me to depart from this holy city."

Simon's announcement is greeted with a long and uncomfortable silence. Antignos is a man who prides himself in seeing the less obvious, but here he cannot understand. He makes some perfunctory efforts to dissuade Simon, which fail. He knows Simon's leadership faced numerous challenges, but it is not like the high priest to walk away from what he considers his life's purpose. Antignos thinks to himself, and cannot recall any moment when something like this has happened before.

"What of the boy's training?"

"Precisely," Simon says almost too quickly. He turns and walks away from Antignos as he finishes his answer to hide any hints on his face. "The boy needs to flourish in a different environment. The walled city is too small for him."

"But if he is not trained…"

Simon interrupts Antignos' protestations quietly. "Please do not take affront to my desire. Let me go peacefully," he begs.

With that last line, Simon stands up, not sure of which direction to go. He turns around and walks in a circle around the room. Antignos watches in disbelief.

Without saying a word, Simon slowly walks backward out of the room. At the doorway, he turns around and speeds down the narrow streets of the old city.

23

Gaza City, Gaza Strip
September 2006

66 GOOD AFTERNOON, MY DEAR GUEST. Have some chai with nana. Very good and very healthy," Faisal says, breezing into the room like he has only just left.

"OK." Lior sits up in his bed, rubbing the sleep out of his eyes. He is happy to have a break from the monotony of lying there all alone, in the purgatory between sleep and wakefulness. Lior has made no progress in his efforts at self-improvement and recovery in the twenty-four hours since he has last seen his host.

Other than the loaded AK-47 tightly secured over his shoulder, the strap wrapped around his left arm, Faisal looks the part of a nonthreatening host. Like something out of a British caricature, he carries a stainless steel teapot and two glasses into the room and sits down. "Here, my guest. Drink up."

Lior looks at Faisal with caution and amusement in his eyes.

"Don't worry, my friend. It is not poison!"

Lior lowers his shoulders slightly in a sign of relaxation. He lifts the cup off its dainty saucer and drinks slowly.

"So, what did you do all day? Please do not tell me you slept again." Faisal chides Lior, playfully raising his hands in an exaggerated manner.

"I guess I did," Lior concedes. "What else should I be doing?"

"Well, we talked about this yesterday. I suggested you recite verses of your holy Bible, the Torah. It is a beautiful book—I am sure you know it by heart. Belt it out. You are alone. Entertain yourself, my guest!"

Lior has no clue what he is talking about. *Why would I possibly know the Torah or any part of the Bible by heart?* He can't remember ever even opening a Bible...well, at least since suffering through bar mitzvah lessons with the old man from the little synagogue. Those long and drawn-out hours slaving away at some obscure passage about dietary restrictions is the extent of his knowledge of Torah.

"I don't know the Torah by heart," Lior says.

Faisal looks at him in total surprise. "How is this possible, my dear guest? My 7-year-old son has already memorized the entire Koran. We celebrated his accomplishment just last week with all kinds of delicacies."

"When I was 7, I was playing video games and watching cartoons," Lior replies, "not reading any scriptures."

"No scriptures?" Faisal holds his hands up in dismay.

"Sorry."

"Well," Faisal searches for another option, "maybe you know some poetry… Yes! How about some poetry? In Arabic we say 'Verse' or 'Ash-shi-ru.' You must know some beautiful romantic or patriotic Hebrew poems!"

"No, not particularly," Lior mumbles in a defeated tone.

Faisal doesn't hear him. He starts in on a recitation in Arabic. His intonation is dramatic. He waves his fist in the air as he reaches the climax of whatever he is saying.

"I don't know anything like that," Lior almost apologizes.

"Well, my guest. In what are you educated?"

"Faisal, why am I here? Please, why don't you all just let me go home? What have I done to deserve this?"

At that question, Faisal stands up in a gentle manner. He leans over Lior in a mixture of confidence and subtle frustration. "Your Zionist forefathers have taken our land. Your Zionist leaders kill our children and rape our daughters, and you ask me why you are here?"

"Faisal… I haven't…"

"Your prisons are full of my brothers and sisters who are innocent. I treat you like my guest while your government tortures them and rapes them on a daily basis, and you ask me why you are here?"

Lior doesn't answer. He knows not to argue with someone this angry.

"I don't blame you, but if your family wants you back, then your government will have to do the right thing," Faisal says.

"What thing is that?"

Faisal is too busy lecturing to hear the questions. "We have not taken your land or your farms or your homes, but your Zionist imperialist leaders have taken what is ours and we will not and cannot stand by and not respond."

Faisal walks over to the window and leans against the sill. He taps his fingers on the window sill as he thinks. Then he turns and, with something of a pained expression, raises his voice. "I want my children to grow up as free people in their ancestral homeland."

The last thing Lior wants to do is piss Faisal off. His zeal on this topic is scary, especially compared to how soft-spoken and congenial he'd been earlier. Faisal sits down and takes a deep breath. "Do you know why they do not teach you your own Bible?"

"I don't know what you are talking about, Faisal."

"I'm talking about your own Torah, the scripture of your people."

"Not everyone in Israel reads the scriptures, Faisal."

"That is my point! Your own government does not want you to study your own scripture. If they did, they could not perpetuate the greatest lie of humanity, the greatest lie that history has endured."

"It's an old book, Faisal." Lior tries to back away from any argument, insisting that he doesn't have a dog in this fight.

Faisal isn't buying it. He continues, "The greatest lie of all! Your Zionist Western leaders like to claim things about the Bible that just aren't true. They claim that it states that Allah, Allahu Akbar, gave this land to the Jewish people."

Of this much, Lior, even in his youthful ignorance, is educated. He nods in agreement. Everyone knows that much, even the non-observant.

"That is what they tell you. But, my dear guest, this land was given by Allah, Allahu Akbar, to Abraham and his descendants," Faisal shouts. "His descendants! This is what YOUR Torah states. Abraham was not a

Jew—this, my guest, is the greatest lie ever perpetrated in humanity."

At that line, Lior unintentionally screws his face up in an expression of confusion. *Abraham, not a Jew?* It is a crazy thought. *What about menorahs and challah?*

Faisal notices Lior's expression and keeps arguing, "Abraham, Isaac and Jacob were Semites, not Jews! The Europeans are Jews. Judaism began in Europe! We are the true Semites!"

Faisal is inching closer to Lior with each word. But to Lior's fearful eyes, Faisal's hand is also moving closer to his gun. At this point, Faisal starts screaming, and his tanned face grows beet red. "We are the descendants of Ibrahim!"

Lior sits quietly, trying not to betray the abject fear he feels. He doesn't really understand what Faisal is talking about. But he knows enough to know that he is guilty by association. He is trapped behind the enemy lines of a group that most certainly shares Faisal's frustrations. Lior looks down at his knees, hoping that this can end.

When he looks at his guest, Faisal snaps out of his anger and back into his role as a host. "I don't mean to scare you. How is the chai? Do you like the nana?"

"It is all very good. Thank you."

"I am sorry I got so angry. It is not your fault, my guest. You have been fed and raised with these lies."

"I'm not interested in these things, Faisal. I just want to go home."

"Home is a complicated word, my friend. Tomorrow is an important day. We bring a camera in this room and you will say some nice words to your government."

"What sort of nice words? How will I know what to say?"

"You will find out soon enough, my guest. Between you and me, though, it would be wise to cooperate fully with the men who will come see you tomorrow. I have come to like you and I do not want any harm to come your way. Please cooperate tomorrow. If you cooperate, I will bring you a nice gift."

"OK."

"Good night."

As Faisal leaves the room, Lior sheepishly mutters, "Thank you."

Even as he says it, he hates himself. *Thank you? I am thanking you for coming in here and ranting about political nonsense to a kidnapped victim? Thank you? For keeping me locked in this room? What is there to thank him for?* Even as he feels this flash of anger, Lior also feels completely defenseless in the face of his arguments. Faisal seems to know so much more about this stuff than he does.

Shit. I graduated high school and did relatively well on my Bagrut, and I know nothing, nothing at all. Fucking Faisal is either really smart or a very effective liar. There is no way we rape our prisoners, torture them. Well, maybe. But only so we can get information that saves lives. Torture... maybe. But fuck, we don't rape them. And for what? Whose land is this anyways? It doesn't make sense. My grandparents on both sides are Europeans. We came here because of the Holocaust. That's why we came back to our homeland. That is what I have to tell Faisal.

At that, Lior lies down on his bed, closes his eyes and transports his body to a better, quieter place. Funny enough, it isn't home.

24

Dimona, Israel
September 2006

AVIGDOR DOESN'T SLEEP MUCH. WHEN he drags himself out of bed, an unfamiliar feeling comes over him. Growing up, he believed that real men don't know fear. He sought it out every chance he got, with the mission of vanquishing it for good. He later learned and preached that real men learn how to control fear. This morning, after spending days with Maya and her family, and coming to terms with the fact that Lior is missing in action, he realizes for the first time in his life that there is no escape from fear. And he is totally paralyzed by it.

As he admits defeat to this primal foe, he slumps over his now luke-warm coffee and sobs into the table. This surge of emotion is completely new to Michal. All she can do is put her arm over his rounded shoulders.

They sit like this for a while. Michal pats him as he tries to get some control over his emotions. He never cries, but this morning he cannot find any strength within. The tears just flow. After a few minutes, he rolls his shoulders back and stands abruptly. He makes his way to the hooks beside the back door and grabs his windbreaker.

"Where are you going?" Michal asks.

"Out," Cohen responds. Even though he doesn't know where he is going, he knows he needs air.

Cohen wanders the streets of Dimona. He sees the bakeries and newsstands opening their storefronts for the day's business. Coffee shops are already humming with activity and young professionals are coming in for their first espresso of the day. He keeps walking, past this activity, and somehow ends up, for the first time in what feels like a lifetime, in front of a synagogue.

As he ducks into the unfamiliar place, he thinks of his father. He hasn't been a particularly religious man, but he has taken great pride in his religious heritage. His father's love of Israel was deeply connected to the Jewish people's 3,500-year-old spiritual culture and 2,000-year-old yearning to return to the land of their ancestors. Both of his parents were Holocaust survivors. His father was from Lithuania and spent years as a prisoner of war before he jumped on a boat to Palestine. His mother came from a town called Oleszyce in Poland. She escaped from a death train and also made her way to Palestine in the early '40s. They met at a dance at a local Kibbutz to the soundtrack of traditional Polish music. She was dancing. He was standing awkwardly off to the side until she approached him. They married shortly after they met, and in the spring of 1944, Avigdor was born. Avigdor was a child of Zionism—a new kind of Jew.

"Never again will we be led into gas chambers like sheep," his father would yell out during meetings and gatherings at their cigarette-smoke-filled apartment in Tel Aviv.

His mother professed similar sentiments, albeit more quietly. She would whisper as she'd put him to bed at night, "The world is a dark place. We have to take care of ourselves. We have to take care of each other. Bad men will come after you for no reason other than your lineage. You must be strong, Avigdor."

Both of them would sit at night, his father's arm over his mother's shoulder as they listened to their idol and leader, Menachem Begin, speak. Avigdor was taught during those evenings that Ben-Gurion was a great leader, but that Begin had the right approach for Israel's future. His words were passionate:

I wish to declare that the Government of Israel will not ask any nation, be it near or far, mighty or small, to recognize our right to exist. The right to exist? It would not enter the mind of any Briton or Frenchman, Belgian or Dutchman, Hungarian or Bulgarian, Russian or American, to request for his people recognition of its right to exist. Their existence per se is their right to exist. The same holds true for Israel. We were granted our right to exist by the God of our fathers, at the glimmer of the dawn of human civilization, nearly 4,000 years ago. For that right, which has been sanctified in Jewish blood from generation to generation, we have paid a price unexampled in the annals of the nations."

As he hesitantly steps into the small synagogue, Avigdor wonders what Menachem Begin would do about Lior.

The small synagogue is packed with men, young and old, wrapping their arms with black leather straps, covering themselves in their prayer shawls. He sits in the back of the small chapel, unsure why he is even there. His mind wanders from one thing to the next. He thinks about his children and grandchildren, his failed marriage, and his failed professional career.

After receiving the medal of valor for his combat in the '73 Yom Kippur War, Avigdor Cohen became a national hero. News reports ascribed supernatural powers to him. His fellow soldiers embellished his bravery. He met his first wife and, after twenty-five unhappy years, he divorced her, or she divorced him. He used his new-found celebrity status to pursue politics. It was something he'd been interested in since listening to those Begin speeches with his parents. He even founded his own party on a conservative platform. But a national reputation for war-heroics was no guarantee for votes, especially in a place like Israel where so much of the population had served in combat operations. His undertaking never panned out. In the 1999 elections, he could not even muster enough votes to cross the electoral threshold for a seat in the Knesset.

Even his attempt at writing an autobiography, which he believed would be a national bestseller, failed miserably. The stories hadn't leapt off the pages like he'd wanted. No matter how many edits and rewrites he tried, he couldn't quite capture the subtleties of his story, the smells of battle. He was a divorcee, a failed politician, someone scraping by on the poorly told stories of his past. Now Lior is missing in action. The list of failures haunt Cohen. Not that anyone knows it. The military gives him an office and a secretary. He spends his time visiting soldiers and delivering what he hopes are inspirational talks. The world assumes he is successful, self-confident and impenetrable.

In reality, he walks into the synagogue that morning a broken soldier, fearful for his grandson.

Unfamiliar with the morning prayer service, Avigdor is surprised by how much of the liturgy he recognizes. When the group that is assembled chants "*Shema Yisrael*," he finishes the verse, "*Adonai Eloheinu Adonai Echad.*" He doesn't cover his eyes like everyone else does, but he recites the words nonetheless. His high school teacher Mar Rabinovitch was a strict scholar of German descent who hated religion and anything religious. He often mocked those very words in class with his students, challenging them to defend to him a faith whose people had suffered so terribly.

"These words mean nothing," he would say with a sly smirk on his face, "and it is these words that the great religion of Judaism makes such a big deal about. There is no syntax and there is no logical meaning to the phrase."

"What do you mean?" the students would prod.

"Shema Israel, Listen O Israel—who is talking to whom?—who is asking to listen or be listened too?" Rabinovitch would pontificate. "Adonai Eloheinu Adonai Echad. Adonai is our God, Adonai is One—what does this mean?" he would yell in frustration.

That frustration would evolve into mocking everything that was sacred in the Jewish religion. As a young man, these sessions of Judaism bashing were very influential in Avigdor's life. Growing up among secular, socialist academics left him hating religious Jews and religion. The frustration was only exacerbated by the fact that the religious wielded too much political control and would not allow their youth to enlist in the army. Those who guarded the borders and defended the interests of Israel with their very flesh and blood, surely those Israelis were more patriotic than the orthodox chained to their traditions.

The men next to him in the small synagogue stand in silence, swaying their bodies back and forth, their lips moving but no sound emanating from their mouths. Some close their eyes. Others read out of their prayer books. Cohen just stands. The young rabbi walks over to Cohen and places a Tallit, a prayer shawl, over his shoulders. Cohen shudders a bit at the touch. He is startled when the rabbi leans over his shoulder and gently whispers, "It is time for the priestly blessing. Go and bless the community."

Avigdor is not really surprised by the young rabbi recognizing him. He has grown used to strangers approaching him as if he is an old friend. Yet he is embarrassed to be asked to stand before those assembled to recite a blessing he has no business leading. "I am not a religious man. I cannot possibly bless anyone," Avigdor replies meekly.

"Your faith is not on trial today," responds the rabbi. "It is your privilege to recite the blessing. It is a Mitzvah."

"Rabbi, I eat pork on Yom Kippur. You don't get it. I am not worthy of standing before anyone here."

The rabbi looks Avigdor in the eyes. By this time, everyone in the chapel is listening carefully. "You don't bless us. God blesses His people. You are just a vessel. Besides, a Kohen is a descendant of Aaron the High Priest, a descendant of Simon the High Priest, and a descendant of Matityahu HaMacabee, from the family of the Chashmona'im. Blessing us has nothing to do with you or the level of your religious observance! You were born a Kohen and that is all that is required of you right now."

The young rabbi's emphatic response and the eyes bearing down upon him leave Avigdor with little choice but to do what he is asked. As he leaves his pew and makes his way forward to the front of the sanctuary, he remembers his father doing the priestly blessing. This was, for his father, a highlight of his synagogue experience and a centerpiece of his religious connection. There is one other Kohen in the room making his way up to the front. Once they reach the front, they stand side by side. Avigdor cuts his eyes to his left to watch and mimic his every move. He removes his shoes and throws his Tallit over his head. So does Avigdor. He faces the ark and Avigdor follows. Together, they recite the words, "Blessed are you God who has commanded us to bless your people with love."

For the first time in his life, Avigdor feels a resonance with his God. The language offers him a venue of expression that he never imagined he has. He spreads his fingers the way his father had taught him to, in five sets of two. He holds his arms up while he turns around to face those in the chapel. The leader of the service chants the words, "Be blessed," and the

Kohanim repeat the words.

"God Protect you." As Avigdor says these words, he prays for Lior.

"May God's countenance shine upon you." As he says these words, Avigdor thinks of his daughter and son-in-law.

"May God grant you peace." Avigdor wonders about his life of war and the many who have died at his side as well as the countless people he has killed for the sake of freedom, peace and security.

How could this be? Why the pain and suffering? Are we not all members of the same human family? I am a Kohen. I preach peace today, yet all I have known is war.

Immediately following the prayer service, the young rabbi stands before the worshippers and asks that they join him in reciting a psalm for the safe return of Lior Ben Yehuda. The rabbi begins, "I lift up my eyes to the heavens. From where is my help?"

All those gathered repeat the same words with enthusiasm and conviction.

"My help is from Adonai, creator of heaven and earth." Again, the congregants recite the words with fervor.

Avigdor realizes they are not just doing this because he is there. They are doing this for Lior, for a soldier of the state. For a young soldier they don't even know personally. At that moment, Avigdor makes up his mind. *God of heaven and earth, be my witness. This will be my greatest battle. I will find Lior and bring him home.*

25

La'uf
Lior's Mind

Memory: **Bakum I**

The day before BA'K'UM, when new recruits are processed at the base, we are taken on a mandatory visit to *Giva't Hatachmoshet*, Ammunition Hill Memorial Museum. I guess it made sense. That was the site of one of the fiercest battles of the Six-Day War. The guide was actually very impressive. She was enthusiastic and knew her stuff. I'm not sure the guys would have paid attention though if she weren't so beautiful. She told us how the hill had to be taken because it connected Mount Scopus, where the Hadassah Hospital and Hebrew University were, and West Jerusalem. The Jordanians were in large underground bunkers with fortified gun emplacements covering each trench. General Uri Narkis, head of the Jerusalem command, refused to bomb the hill from the air because of the possibility that there would be civilian casualties. Instead, the

IDF took the hill from the bottom up. Many of our soldiers were killed taking that hill.

I guess they wanted to impress upon us that we don't kill civilians and we fight no matter the odds.

Memory: Bakum 2

It's like everything in the military is an acronym: Tzahal, RaSap, SaMal, RaMatKal, Tat Aluf, RaSaN, SaGaR and on and on and on.

Waiting in lines all day. Just going from one line to the next with hundreds of guys and girls. Russian, Ethiopian, Mizrachi, Dati, every shade of Israeli society was there. The best line was when the *jobnik*, the guy behind the desk, asked me for my bank account information and handed me 100 shekels in cash. "Your monthly stipend will be automatically deposited into your account. Good luck." Off to the next line.

They photographed my teeth; they took a biometric picture of my face, a full body scan, blood samples and urine samples. "Do you have AIDS? Do you take any medications? Do you have any mental ailments? Any sexually transmitted diseases?"

"If you die, who will receive your belongings?"

Shit. No one asked me, "If you get kidnapped, how do you plan on getting home?"

26

Chashmona Region
Summer 310 BCE

NEWS FROM JERUSALEM IS DISHEARTENING. Ever since Simon left, the corruption in Jerusalem, particularly in the Priestly Quarters, has reached unimaginable proportions. The influence of the Hellenists is growing. They have even managed to sway the spiritual and religious functions of the temple. There are rumors of bribes and kickbacks, abuse of power, and the worst thing of all is the wretched persecution of the weakest members of society. It is clear that priorities lie in the financial rather than the spiritual realm. Simon had worked so hard to clean house, to ensure that the temple finances are beyond repute. It has all eroded in less than a calendar year.

This is not easy news for a man who has retired in the height of his prime, who feels like he abandoned his life task and knows very well that he can help. He spends hours in prayer and meditation, in search of a solution for these problems and his own peace of mind. As painful as it is, he listens intently to the periodic reports, and does not shy away from verbalizing his opinions.

"It seems like our people are at war with one another," he announces in desperation to the delegation of sages who have come for a visit. He knows they are likely to repeat his words to others in the city, and so he always chooses to use the inclusive first-person pronouns—we, our—to imply his goal of uniting rather than dividing. In the face of the Hellenist option, it is essential to stress a common Jewish identity. The growing factions within the Jewish community must come together on points of essential identity.

One of the sages, Rabbi Yosseh, son of Yo'ezer, nods. "The Kohanim are lending their support to the despicable heathen tax collectors, and those who oppose them are accused of being robbers and thugs," he says.

"Taxes are many and high—the poor cannot afford to feed their families while those who have aligned themselves with the Greeks prosper and grow rich," Samuel, one of the young sages, mutters.

"It isn't just a financial problem," Rabbi Judah continues. "For the first time in the history of our people, Jew testifies against Jew in foreign courts of law. The very fact that foreign courts operate in our midst is damning enough—that our people take their disputes there is an outrage! We have outlasted other empires that sought to impose their codes of law. But I don't know of any point in our history where Jews have actually brought cases against other Jews into the courts of our oppressors. What has become of the Law of Moses and the word of God?"

"People steal from each other and close their doors to those in need. Have we become a godless people?" Rama the waggoneer yells from outside the courtyard while shaking his fist in frustration.

"Rabbi Judah. Wise men," Simon responds. "Let us chose our words, and our opportunities for criticism, carefully. One does not win a war of hearts and minds with bitter tones. In the meantime, do not despair. God created a world in which we can dwell. It is our task to create a sanctuary in which God can dwell. That sanctuary, the Torah tells us, is among the people. Moses the great prophet sang: 'God is my salvation. I will build for Him a sanctuary.' Jerusalem is in our hearts and in our souls. It is our sanctuary and salvation. But even when that wondrous city seems beyond repair, do not despair. God lives within each of us."

Even as Simon utters these words, he struggles to find the optimistic tone he seeks. He has never been much of an actor, but optimism requires that he maximize that limited skillset. Positivity is hard to summon.

Jerusalem, his beloved, has become a city of feuding mobs. Good Jews are turning away from the long tradition of their fathers and grandfathers, embracing even the most distasteful of Greek ways. It is too much for him to bear. His health is deteriorating, and it seems as though the only thing that is keeping him alive is raising Yochanan. His daughters have all married fine men, priests living in Jerusalem. They will get on with life without him. *But what about Yochanan?* Simon's spiritual redemption hinges on the boy's future. The challenge invigorates Simon, giving him the energy he needs to usher the sages off with words of encouragement, however hollow they feel to him.

As the sages leave, heartened by Simon's rhetoric, the former high priest slumps down upon the cushions on his carpeted floor. His back has bothered him for years. Malka believes it probably has something to do with all of the standing he'd done during his service in the temple. Simon believes his back pain has more to do with his constant fear that something catastrophic is about to happen. He often feels shortness of breath and his heart beats faster than normal. He feels a sense of weakness in his arms and knees. Sitting on benches or stools for too long sends a shooting pain down his left arm; at times, the pain is so severe that he drops whatever he happens to be holding. Lying on his back, with just a pillow under his neck, gives him some relief. The only other source of relief is a few glasses of wine, but it is too early in the day for that option.

Lying there, Simon thinks of the strange problem he faces. Rarely has a high priest willingly abandoned that most prestigious of posts. Even in the occasional instance in history when the high priest has done so, Simon knows of no other time when a priest has retired so far from Jerusalem. It makes little sense for the man charged with tending to a flock to move away from the heartbeat of the faith. He can't face more time in Jerusalem though. Not with Yochanan in his charge. It seems fitting, in some way, to have moved for his son. After all, Simon has long felt as if he is living two lives. One began at birth. The other began after his encounter with Alexander the Great. Simon likes to think that, on that day, when he'd faced down the great warrior and averted disaster, he was reborn.

Simon has never mentioned his encounter with Alexander the Great to Yochanan. Moving away served two of Simon's most pressing concerns. There is no way the boy can officiate in the temple. He is just not a Kohen by pedigree. Being far from Jerusalem means the boy will not be trained in temple service. Additionally, it is his way of keeping the boy from hearing about the legendary encounter from people on the streets of Jerusalem. For Simon, explaining that the great warrior kidnapped his mother meant being too close to the "fire of their truth." Yochanan does hear rumors of a miraculous salvation that involved his father. When he broaches the subject, Simon looks the other way and says, "Nonsense, people say nonsense." Being far away from the capital, he could avoid confronting the issue directly with the boy.

The memory has not been blurred by all of the years that have passed. In fact, those years have clarified a few things, even made the recollection more vivid. The existential calm Simon had felt as the gates of the city opened upon the most formidable army the world has ever seen, the memory of Alexander's gaze, the traces of confusion he'd seen flash over the great warrior's visage as he spoke to him of God, and the look of loss and hurt the most powerful man in the world had been unable to hide when Simon demanded the return of Yael. Simon can play all of it upon command inside his own head.

He revisits the memory with regularity, mainly because he is proud of it and because the vision relaxes his entire body. Since childhood, Simon has left encounters with other people frustrated that he'd not been as clear as he wanted to be, wishing he'd phrased something differently. That day outside the gates of Jerusalem, looking out over Alexander's army, was the one time in his life that Simon had said exactly what he wanted to say, had done exactly what the best version of his self would have done. His approach to the encounter could not have gone better. He said the right things and read his nemesis perfectly. The memory still exhilarates him. But that exhilaration is due less to hubris than to faith. If there ever was a moment of divine intervention, that encounter with Alexander was it. God was there with Simon, gave him the words he used, gave him the calm and courage required. He gave him… the priestly garments gave him a level of gravitas that bewildered the great general.

It was almost like, in that moment, Simon had been a vessel for something bigger. All he had to do was give his body over to the work of God. Now he truly understands the wonders of God's ways and how battles can be won with faith alone.

He wishes his life would continue to demand so little of him. As much as he wants to keep reliving the past, the demands of the present come calling. Simon finds no similar level of clarity in his new obligations. He looks up. *God, where are you?*

As disturbing as the news from Jerusalem is, Simon has to focus on the present and on his duty as a father, a mentor and a guide. His purpose is simple enough. He has to rectify the lie he lives by doing right by the child. Simon understands that his own destiny will be defined by the life Yochanan leads. If only he can figure out how to exert some control over the child! If ever a person as stubborn has walked the earth, Simon has not met him or her. Worse, Yochanan has an intelligence to match.

Despite his difficulties, Simon looks forward to his daily lessons with the boy. They study Mishna, Jewish Law, and the Torah. Afternoons are spent grappling with the natural sciences and mathematics, topics that Simon is passionate about. Yochanan takes in everything, though his ability to grasp complicated philosophical concepts shines above all else. Simon's favorite moments are when they just speak freely on a range of subjects. The boy is hungry for knowledge. Simon truly believes that his task as a teacher is similar to that of a midwife. If Simon is clumsy and unprepared, his ideas will be stillborn. If he is unable to get through to this boy, he knows that he will be leaving the world with a likely monster. On the other hand, if he succeeds as an educator and inspires this boy to achieve his potential, the world could potentially be transformed for the better. If indeed Simon succeeds, a new life with unbounded potential will be born.

Every once in a while, Yochanan interrupts their lessons with some version of the phrase, "Tell me about mother."

This demand comes in different forms, but Simon's answer is always the same. "Your mother is God and her touch is the Torah. As King Solomon taught, 'Listen, my son, to the teaching of your father and the Torah of your mother.'"

Simon believes that no answer he derives or constructs can match the wording he finds in the Torah. And he sincerely hopes that, by offering a loving alternative to a traditional mother, he can teach Yochanan to focus on what he has rather than dwell upon the tragedy life has sent his way. "Better to focus upon all the blessings the world so regularly bestows than think of that which we lack." Simon's words of wisdom work for a short time. They work better some days than others. But that sort of vague language leaves a huge hole in the boy, a hole that Yochanan feels an insatiable yearning to fill. He wants details.

He recognizes that Simon is trying to soothe him. He feels the affection of his father and of Malka, his father's wife. But alongside that affection, a deep sadness grows like a shadow in his heart. The longing for his birth mother is most acute when he is around women who show affection to their children. How Yochanan wishes he would have something that belonged to her, something he can touch. The closest thing he has is her parents, his grandparents. But he hardly has them anymore either. It has been months, maybe a year, since he last saw them.

His grandparents live in Jerusalem and the trip there is dangerous and burdensome. Even when he is with them, details are hard to come by. His grandfather still gets emotional when her name is mentioned. *Parents should not outlive their children*, his grandfather thinks, ignoring Yochanan's questions about what she'd been like as a teenager. Grandmother is hardly any better. She describes silly things like bathing her young daughter as an infant, or the cookies she was able to bake. He wants real details. *Was she mischievous as a teenager? What did she dream about?* He has just learned about the soul. He wants to know what stirred his mother's soul, but details are scant. His grandparents refuse to travel up from Jerusalem, so he has few opportunities to extract details from them. Of just a few things, Yochanan is sure. Her name was Yael. She was beautiful. She would have loved him very much. That's what people say. That is never enough.

He paints her picture in his mind's eye countless times. He imagines her to be dark-haired and gentle. *She must have had fair eyes, for Simon certainly does not, and where else could my color come from? What would her laugh have sounded like? Would she have sung to me as I fell asleep? Beautiful... that could mean so many things. Was her skin smooth? Did her smile sparkle in the Judean sun?*

"I want to know more!"

"Hush," Simon says. "Focus on your studies, my son. Our eyes are in front of us so that we can look ahead and leave the past behind."

"Leave the past behind?"

"Yes, son."

"Why? All you ever talk about is the traditions of our forefathers and the prayers and laws of men written years ago. And you ask me to leave the past behind? Why is that past more important than the one about which I am asking?"

"Back to work!"

Other than his frustration about the stonewalling, life in Chashmona is perfect for Yochanan. He loves the open space, the rolling hills, the orchards and the physical work. He loves long hikes and running through the town with the non-Kohen children, despite his father always reminding him of his special social status. Above all else, he especially loves working in the stable with the horses. He shovels manure for hours just to brush the great beasts and hear the snort of their nostrils. He is happy to do menial labor in the stables if it means a quick ride on a particular horse. "Horses are not to get in the way of your studies," Simon says. His father is extremely demanding when it comes to his intellectual development in the study of Torah. And because Yochanan loves and respects his father, he abides by those priorities. It isn't like Torah study is miserable either. Much of it is fascinating.

Yochanan has another Torah teacher besides his father who he loves to listen to, maybe even more so than his father, to Simon's great dismay.

Natan the Pious lives in a small hut in the outskirts of the village. Many villagers gather there in the evenings to listen to his wise words. His teachings enlighten people about the heavenly spheres and how God created the world by contracting God's infinite light, the *Or Ein Sof*, in order to create space in the universe for mankind and human free will.

"The finite could exist only if the infinite made room for it," Natan says.

This seems to resonate with Yochanan in ways that Simon's teachings of law and dogma do not. Yochanan is especially mesmerized when Natan the Pious discusses the physicality of God's glory and *Shechina*, God's presence. At one lecture, Natan the Pious read with great animation the biblical verses from Exodus 33:19-23. In these verses, God offers Moses, the great prophet, the opportunity to see the divine presence:

And the Lord said unto Moses, "I will make all My goodness pass before you, and I will proclaim before you the name of

the Lord. … See there is a place near Me. Station yourself on
the rock and as my Kavod passes by, I will put you in the cleft
of the rock and shield you with My hand until I have passed
by. Then I will take My hand away and you will see My back
but My face must not be seen."

Natan spoke with his eyes closed and his head covered by his *tallit*,
his shawl. He preached with a sense of urgency that sounded like a mixture
of whispering and screaming that came from a deep place in his belly. "God
can be seen. The *Kavod* is that delicate aspect of God's body which takes
shape for the prophet who is worthy. The *Kavod* sits on a celestial throne
surrounded by angels and chariots of fire, the firmament, the wheels and
spheres. This is what Moses, the great prophet, asked to see when he be-
seeched God, 'Show me your *Kavod*.'"

Natan the Pious always fills his lectures with powerful images and
promises of great glory through miracles. He speaks of radical things, of a
God unreluctant to exercise great power. Yochanan knows that his father
is not a fan of these teachings. They have a political dimension, and Simon
especially objects to Natan's politics. But it is difficult for Simon to simultaneously encourage the exercise of religious thought and to refuse his
son's request to visit one of the more popular religious thinkers in the area.
There is no doubting the nationalistic fervor Natan tries to engender.

"The gentile heathens," Natan preaches and repeats over and over
again, "are not true humans." He insists his listeners memorize these
words. They are not human because the Jewish soul originated in the realm
of *Sefirot*, the highest heavenly levels, while the heathen soul of the non-Jew
comes from the realm of impurity and evil. He refers to this realm as the
sitra-aha, or the evil side. "When the bible speaks of Adam being created
in the 'image of God,' the bible is not referring to the creation of the non-
Jew. Adam and Eve were created with a higher soul. Heathens were created
by the *sitra-aha* with a lower soul. In the Messianic era, the non-Jew will
serve the Jew."

"Why is it that the non-Jew rules over the Jewish nation?" Yochanan
asks. "The reason the non-Jew has the upper hand is so that the Jews can
redeem the few positive sparks they may have in this world."

"Eventually," Natan preaches, "the entire non-Jewish world will be stripped of the few divine traces they might have nourishing their existence, at which point they will collapse."

With fire in his eyes, Natan the pious quotes Isaiah the Prophet as saying:

Gentile Kings shall tend your children
Their queens shall serve you as nurses
They shall bow to you, face to the ground
And lick the dust of your feet.

"These are the words of Isaiah the Prophet of Israel, not my own!" he says. "Isaiah the Prophet does not lie!"

This sort of revolutionary thought attracts all sorts of listeners, but teenage boys in particular love such sermons. The politics animate Yochanan in ways that his discussions with Simon do not. For Simon, these teachings do not represent the Torah taught by the sages of Jerusalem. These are teachings of the masses, for the uneducated. They are meant to incite physical violence, which the Torah is clearly against.

Having been a teenager himself, though, Simon knows the appeal Natan has for his boy and for others. However, it does not keep him from being frustrated about it. Simon is a recognized sage, head of the most prestigious Torah academy in Jerusalem, the center of Torah study. He has been the Kohen Gadol, high priest, no less. And despite his power and status, he can do nothing about Natan the Pious.

How tragic is it that all Natan can do is incite anger and divisiveness! Draw out the worst inclinations of his listeners! The villagers, including my own son, lap it up. They prefer to hear the rants and tirades of this man's imagination. Ranting can be harmless. But the stuff Natan says is rooted in racism, unbridled nationalism and messianic aspirations. All have dangerous implications. His teachings promote unrestrained zeal and fervor.

No matter how hard Simon tries to reason with Yochanan, to stress to him that calm and rational dialogue are the right path, the boy always seems to be drawn to the altered state of imagination fostered in Natan's rants.

"Natan has divine powers, Father. God communicates truth through him."

"If that were so," Simon responds, "why isn't he in Jerusalem leading the people and legislating Jewish law on the Sanhedrin?"

"Because, as a result of long inaction from the Jewish people, Jerusalem has become a heathen city. It must be retaken by the true servants of God."

It seems like the boy has an answer for everything. Unfortunately, his answers frequently involve the need for an overthrow through violence.

"Yochanan, how can you possibly speak this way? You'd do well to select your words more carefully and to talk with less enthusiasm of such things. Now get back to your studies."

Using the temple coffers, Simon established schools throughout Jerusalem and other cities inhabited by Jews throughout Israel. "The more students, the better our future," was Simon's motto.

"From our earliest history," Simon taught, "our prophets and teachers believed in the ability to affect and ennoble human beings. Denial of this belief renders the entire Torah irrelevant. Torah law is not instruction, but guidance. It is not law that is accepted, but rather a challenge to make the world into what it ought to be. We have to have the courage and patience to work through that challenge."

His deference to the ancient texts often led to controversy. Simon once preached that the life of one's teacher should be more valuable to someone than the life of one's father. "He who teaches another person's child, it is as if he fathered the child."

"If your father is drowning," he taught, "and your teacher is drowning, and you can only save one of them, who do you save, father or teacher? The law is clear. Teacher takes precedence over father. He must."

"How predictable," a student objects, "rabbis hoarding power for themselves."

"Bringing children into this world," explained Simon, "is a strictly biological act. What differentiates humans from animals and true parents from fathers and mothers is the act of teaching. Teaching is divine and is the real act of creation. Teachers not only inform students but *form* them as well. From teaching springs the human personality, the ability to think, a sense of reverence and faith." Simon was consoling himself as much as he was trying to convince his students.

27

Jerusalem, Israel
September 2006

A VIGDOR COHEN SPEEDS ALONG THE highway toward Jerusalem in his 1999 Volvo sedan. The drive usually takes about one hour and fifty minutes. On this day, the traffic is sparser. He can make it in better time. Cohen heads toward the town of Arad and makes a left onto a dirt road that leads to an armored military base. This is one of the few places he feels completely welcome and always at home. He will have a coffee with young recruits before he heads further north to Jerusalem to see the prime minister.

He does not make an appointment with the prime minister's office. There is no need. When he shows up, no one dares refuse his efforts to see his old friend.

Ehud Olmert is the State of Israel's prime minister. His political career is plagued with scandal and controversy. While he was mayor of Jerusalem, prior to running for national office, he had the habit of rubbing elbows with rich Americans who offered financial gifts for favors. The media is obsessed with him, and some secret part of Ehud seems to relish the attention, however critical.

Olmert and Cohen know each other from their days in the Beitar Movement. There, they'd listened to speeches about Zionism, and there, in their youth, they both enthusiastically embraced the vision that Jews needed to establish a foothold in their biblical homeland to provide a safe harbor for Jewish people around the world.

They have each progressed in their respective careers and have maintained similar political views. But Olmert has a knack for couching his hawkish positions in language that resonates with even the most liberal listener. The same cannot be said for Cohen. When he discusses politics, his views always sound harsh. Even to his more conservative listeners, he sounds unsophisticated, brutish and to some, medieval. He wonders how his childhood friend Ehud will respond to his family crisis. The friends have never refused each other before. *Today will not be any different*, he thinks.

Before his meeting with the prime minister, Cohen wants to recharge his spirits in a place he knows supports him and among those he feels most comfortable. Despite the size and importance of the military base, there is little security. A pair of conscripts in dirty green military jumpsuits, armed with M16s and mirrors on poles, stop his car to examine its undercarriage. As they approach, Cohen is immediately recognized. The soldiers smile and wave him through without looking under his car.

Within 100 meters of the security check, as he slowly navigates the bumpy dirt road on his way to the refectory, four massive Merkava tanks blaze across the road. *Probably on a training exercise*, he surmises. Cohen purses his lips and whistles lustily. Whenever he sees the Merkava, he cannot help but wonder the damage he could have inflicted upon the enemy if he had been armed with a killing machine like that in 1973.

Able to smash through enemy lines at sixty kilometers per hour, the Merkava Mark IV is the most sophisticated weapon on the ground in the world. Merkava is Hebrew for chariot. The 65-ton Merkava is much more than a chariot. It is the IDF's premier battle tank. Its internal 60-mm mortar and dual smoke-grenade launchers can turn a four-man crew of young soldiers into a deadly force. Were an enemy to face a group of approaching Merkava tanks, they would feel no less daunted and powerless than if they were facing the hand of the Almighty himself.

Cohen knows that the Merkava's night-vision and thermal-imaging capability, its 1,200-horsepower air-cooled diesel engine, automat-ic-fire-suppression equipment, and advanced nuclear, biological, and chem-ical protection make it the most feared machine on the battlefield.

He shuts off his engine and stands alongside his vehicle to watch the exercises. Watching the Merkava Mark IV pummel through the southern rock and sand brings back the rush of battle on that fateful Yom Kippur day in October 1973. The war caught the entire country by surprise. He remembers quite well how he had been lounging around, still recovering from his wounds of the 1967 war when the call came in. The voice on the other side of the receiver crackled, "Code Gideon, be at your base in one hour."

The order was so surprising, he asked for it to be repeated, "Please confirm instructions."

"Your base. One hour."

When he arrived at his battalion, the nets were already taken off the tanks. The engines were roaring. Cohen remembers asking, "Where's the war?"

What a naïve question. My nation, my people, we're always at war. Always. If the first trip into the fire of battle hadn't taught him, this one did. This time, though, he didn't have to go to the battlefield. His body was not yet fully healed from the wounds and burns he suffered less than six years prior. His superiors all advised him, in very clear terms, to stay behind at the base and communicate with his fellow soldiers on the field. Cohen would not hear of such a thing.

Unlike most other commanders, Cohen manned his own tank on the battlefield. Fighting a battle from the sidelines was bullshit, as far as he was concerned. He had pulled together his crew of three men, gave them a brief pep talk about honor and patriotism, jumped into his British-made Centurion tank and headed northeast toward the artillery shelling.

It was October 6, 1973, the holiest day on the Jewish calendar, Yom Kippur. Battalion Oz 77, Cohen's battalion, advanced in close formation to the assigned area, the town of Kuneitra and its northern parts. Positioned on the Bustar Hills, Cohen saw the enemy forces for the first time. Clouds of dust churned upward in the sky. Cohen's trained eyes recognized the ominous sight of the aggressively approaching Syrian tanks, barely visible through the thick sand clusters surrounding them.

Cohen never liked to talk about what happened on the battlefield. Recollections are always blurry—they come and go in spurts. He remembers artillery shells landing on his battalion's positions. One could not help but be impressed by the accuracy of the Syrian tanks. By late afternoon, enemy tank columns were in firing range. As night fell on his troops, his tanks were at a serious disadvantage because they were not equipped with night vision and it would be impossible to hit enemy tanks in the dark. *Those damn Syrians, on the other hand, were equipped with the most advanced infrared system, which could illuminate the entire Israeli tank base.* The only piece of equipment his men had that could help them at night was infrared binoculars. They were so inefficient. Their adjustments and spotting were incremental. It was no surprise they barely held on.

That cursed night, they suffered heavy losses. The combat was brutal and frustrating. Under the cover of darkness, the Syrians had successfully crossed the border fence. The Israeli minefields along the border had no effect on the Syrian onslaught. Now that they'd crossed those fields, Cohen knew that they were not just loath to retreat but that they'd be scared to do so. Crossing the border was a victory for the Syrian troops. Any Syrian who would retreat at this point would certainly be executed back home.

Mount Hebron, the 9,000-foot towering mountain which was, up until then, the eyes of Israel, lay in enemy hands. From that lookout, Syrian observation officers could train their eyes on Israeli positions with great precision. Even the daytime would find Israel outmatched.

Cohen vividly remembers being ordered to retreat.

"Oz 77, retreat back to ground zero. Cohen, Avigdor Cohen, I repeat. You are commanded to retreat back to ground zero."

That was an order he could not follow. He was young, but he understood enough to know how precarious the situation was, not just for the soldiers fighting, but for the entire State of Israel. He consciously ignored the command. *What the fuck do they know?* He was confident. *If we hold them until morning, we can beat them.*

To this day, he has never regretted that decision. Neither have his countrymen.

With the first glow of daybreak, there were more than 500 Russian-made Syrian tanks clustered about a kilometer and a half to the east.

The Syrians began to move toward Israel with the intent of cutting the country in half and overtaking Haifa and Tel Aviv. If that happened, it would all be over. The dream of a Jewish state, the hope that the world might leave room for one safe space for the Jewish people, would be gone— all of it. The very thought enraged Cohen.

Billowing dust from the moving tanks blew out over the Israeli forces that were barely holding on to their positions. The enemy continued to press forward in a way that, even Cohen had to admit, was resolute and courageous. The enemy shot in all directions. They shot fast. "They were fucking fierce."

On that morning, as the day's light peaked over those green hills of the Golan, an inspired thought came to Cohen. It was as if a voice from above whispered in his ear and said, "You are a descendant of priests, a descendant of Judah the Maccabee. You have nothing to fear. Charge ahead!"

Thus began the most incredible offensive or *defensive* in the history of tank battles. The enemy outnumbered Israeli armor by at least fifteen to one. Cohen fired at them furiously as he charged into their midst. With each passing moment, he was conscious of his dwindling numbers and diminishing ammunition. Israeli tanks that had followed his lead burst into flames or came off their tracks. Somehow, Cohen and his tank continued. His superiors watched in disbelief as he came to a stop hundreds of meters into the Syrian front lines.

By midday, Cohen and his men were in the heart of hell. Aggression didn't just come from the ground. Russian-made Syrian MiGs, assisting the offensive, punished IDF battalions. Some of the MiGs flew so low, he could see the pilots' heads. The true heroes were the evacuation team members who worked with incredible courage to find fallen soldiers and, in many cases, carry them back from the lines to the medic tents, kilometers from the battleground.

The Israeli Air Force was ordered not to engage the enemy in the air. "Where the hell are our birds?" his men had asked him. He had no idea. It certainly felt like they'd been left out on an island, abandoned. He has always dreaded the thought that maybe it was because he'd disobeyed clear orders. The lack of reciprocal support from their jets wasn't just a tactical problem. Apart from the power the air force provided, it would have done a great deal to raise the morale of the fighting men. Thankfully, the Syrian pilots were not accurate. They made more noise than anything else.

By dawn, the Syrian tank offensive had pulled back. Syrian soldiers were retreating by foot. Cohen was well aware of the fact that military experts and warfare students had a hard time explaining his victory. Of the many theories—including stealth air attacks from the Israeli Air Force, the pandemonium created by Cohen, which resulted in Syrians shooting each other, or the incompetence of Syrian or Russian training—Avigdor Cohen preferred calling it a miracle. The miracle narrative has always served him well. Commentators began to liken Avigdor Cohen to heroes of biblical proportions. The association to Judah HaMacabee, the Lion of Judah who held back the Greek armies and saved the Judean state, was made by Nisan Chetrit, the editor of *Yedioth*, in his weekly column following the battle.

Cohen was never apologetic or humble about the association. Minimally, he viewed the famous historical warrior as an apt inspiration.

The Merkava tanks disappeared into the distance. Cohen awakes from his daydream and cranks his car back up. At the base, as usual, Cohen is greeted as a hero. The welcome is somewhat tempered by the fact that everyone knows Lior Samet, the abducted young soldier, is Cohen's grandson. He appreciates how his fellow warriors never make him feel like a victim.

Young commanders, soldiers and new recruits come by to salute and greet their national hero. He welcomes each of them, paying far more attention to the admiration in their voices. When he stops himself to think about it, which is rare, he recognizes the hubris in his character. He knows why he came here. He also knows he has no business here.

It's during moments of insight like this Cohen recognizes he is handicapped. He cannot let go of the past. He yearns to relive the victory parades, the attention and adoration. Military life is where he is most comfortable—this is his refuge. Maybe he just needs a bit of refuge so that he, the war hero, can summon the strength for this fight he is about to undertake. He finishes his coffee and heads back to his car.

28

Modi'in City
Chashmona Region
Winter 307 BCE

YOCHANAN IS A TOWERING 15-YEAR-OLD. His curly blond hair and bright blue eyes set him apart from the other boys in Chashmona. He has a boundless source of energy that leads to a spring in his step and a prankster mentality. He also has a way of leaning into conversations that makes the raconteur feel like Yochanan is fully invested in what they are saying. When he asks questions, and as he listens to the answers, he works his jaw and bites his lip. He tends to nod his head in agreement or lean back if something strikes him as disagreeable.

Everyone expects that a young boy as handsome as Yochanan, and as different in appearance, will be a braggart. Indeed, first impressions in the village peg Yochanan as a spoiled child of nobility. With each individual encounter, he redefines those perceptions. His receptivity to the words of his elders, his zeal for debates, his wry smile that appears at the end of some pun or joke, all ingratiate him with the villagers. His physical ability somehow creeps into everyone's conversation. He rarely loses a race with the local boys. He can lift objects that weigh twice as much as he does, and his thighs seem to grow thicker by the month.

One incident has cemented his status among the village workers. On one of his errands to the outer parts of the village, Yochanan noticed some local construction workers struggling to splice the top of a splintered log back together. They took a rope and looped it around the log while two men pulled from one side and three men pulled from the other side. The log jerked from side to side but the wood would not splice back together. As soon as they got the two sides fitted even partially together, and one man let loose to tie them securely, the logs would splay out again.

"Get on that side and pull," one of the men said.

"No. We've tried that already."

"Well, let's try it again!"

Yochanan watched quietly as several efforts failed.

"Mind if I give it a go?" Yochanan asked.

"Go to school, boy. Leave the labor to the laborers," one of the men snarled. To have been struggling with this problem all morning and have a teenage boy offer help offended all of them.

"Just give me the two ends of your rope."

The men just stared at the blond boy who was giving them orders.

"What do you think you are doing speaking to us this way? Who do you think you are?"

"Do you want it fixed or not?" asked Yochanan with an unusual degree of confidence.

The men continued staring.

"Either I do it myself my way or you can continue doing it your way. And your way does not seem to be working."

"This is a waste of time."

"Oh. We've wasted our whole damn morning. Let's let him try."

They all watched as Yochanan took the two ends of the rope and loosely tied them around the splintered section of the log. He then reached for a sturdy stick and placed it between the log and the tied rope. He began to turn the stick. He used the pressure of the rope to squeeze the splintered log together. The more he turned, the tighter the rope squeezed the log. Within a minute, the boy had successfully achieved what five men could not do all morning.

"The heavens are our witness!" the men all said. They pounded him on his shoulder and asked where he'd come up with such an idea.

"I read about it. It is one of the techniques that was used in the construction of the temple."

Yochanan's charisma and love for horses has become an affectionate joke in the village of Chashmona. His loud demeanor and spontaneous bursts of passionate rhetoric concern his teachers and religious leaders, but those same leaders and teachers cannot help but love his enthusiasm. His muscular build and good looks make him the most eligible young man and every young girl's fantasy. Fathers are endlessly preoccupied, for they all know that if Yochanan turns his attention toward their daughters, he would steal their hearts. Not that having such a son would be a bad thing.

Yochanan doesn't just attract the attention of worried Judean fathers and dreamy Judean girls, he also has the attention of the Greek residents. It is just the sort of thing that worries Simon and causes his sleepless nights. One particular resident takes notice. On the hillside, just outside the village, Antipater the Antivasilaeus, Regent of Judea who was appointed by Alexander the Great, has wondered about this Hellenistic-looking boy for some time. He views his task as governor not just as the keeper of the law, but also as the one responsible for indoctrinating the locals into Hellenistic culture. He cannot help but notice this boy, the son of the high priest, that does not at all look like a local. Upon inquiring with one of his servants, he learns that the boy's mother had apparently died during childbirth. *Huh,* Antipater thinks, *perhaps the priests from Jerusalem liked to marry slave girls from other parts of the world.*

Alongside the fortress where the Greek residents live, Antipater has built a temple for his patron god, Heracles, and an impressive gymnasium. In this new open-air structure, boys learn sciences, read poetry, compete in physical disciplines, wrestle and mingle. Young Macedonians flock from various parts of the empire to this region. Many are paid to live there as a way of bringing Greek culture to the area. Some seek adventure, others a fresh start, making northern Judea their residence. It is close enough to home to return if necessary, but far enough to escape a regrettable past.

For the young Judeans reared in the Law of Moses, the gymnasium is a place of abominations. The prominence of idols is the least of their concerns. The nudity and intimate physical contact between men is the most shocking. The gymnasium has no redeeming qualities. The Judeans regard it as an absolute affront to all that is sacred.

The Judean population clings passionately to its traditions. While the Hellenistic boys awake and begin their gymnastics, or readings of Homer's Trojan Horse, the morning routine for boys like Yochanan begins with a ritual bath followed by the silent recitation of the Eighteen Blessings. Unlike Jerusalem, Chashmona does not have a community of educated and self-motivated religious youth. When he arrives, Simon takes the education of Yochanan into his own hands. Because he feels like the young boy needs peers to challenge his opinions and spar with philosophically, he takes upon himself the education of his son's friends as well.

The curriculum is entirely of Simon's own devising. He stumbles into some successes, and is open to changing some of the topics based on the interest of his students. But on some matters of learning, Simon is inflexible and persistent. He is of the opinion that the Eighteen Blessings need to be structured and recited in a disciplined manner. This is why he teaches Yochanan and his students that, "As servants of the Almighty, we first present ourselves before God by praising the Almighty in submission as servants to the Lord, recognizing our shortcomings. Then we ask God to provide our daily needs, some of which include sustenance, health and redemption. After our supplications to God, we conclude with words of gratitude and appreciation."

The Eighteen Blessings catch on. Everyone outside of Jerusalem begins reciting Simon's morning prayer. In some parts, it becomes known as the *Amida*, or "standing," due to the fact it is recited while standing. In other circles, it is called the *Tefilah*, which means to "self-reflect" or "self-judge." Simon uses the latter terminology, because the idea of beginning one's day with introspection and reflection on one's relationship with God resonates deeply with him and the experience he has had as high priest. He is not only reflective about his faith, but also about his move away from the heart of it. Simon misses the daily sacrificial service of the temple. For him, the morning prayers are an imperfect substitute for his absence from Jerusalem. That is why he always prays toward Jerusalem. But facing in the right direction isn't enough. He also imagines the Holy of Holies in the temple. Luckily, he has spent enough time in that sacred space to remember it well.

Immediately following the Eighteen Blessings, the entire morning is devoted to the study of Torah, mathematics and natural sciences. Yochanan and his peers delve deeply into the story of Jacob and Esau of the Bible. Isaac had two sons, each representing opposite worldviews. Yochanan is always skeptical when Biblical figures are described as representing something other than themselves. Nevertheless, he always enjoys his father's teaching.

"Jacob is the embodiment of the people of Israel and Esau represents the people of Greece. Jacob dwells in his tent while Esau is a hunter dwelling in the field. The tent is the temple, the study hall, the inner world and all that is spiritual, while the hunter only cares about the physical, the outer world."

The students are mesmerized by Simon's passion. The teacher makes the natural parallel between the ancient rivalry and the modern divide between the Judeans and the Greeks.

"Jacob took what was rightfully his, the birthright, from Esau. He had to do it in a way that appears deceitful to the untrained student. But it was not deceitful. He was instructed by his mother to disguise himself as Esau by taking goatskin and placing it on his arms. When his blind father would feel the goatskin, he would be convinced this was Esau. Isaac felt the goatskin and declared: 'the hands are the hands of Esau, but the voice is the voice of Jacob.'"

Simon pauses and looks at his students. He holds up his hands silently. "Imagine some other set of hands before you. Would you listen to your ears or trust your eyes? To which of your senses would you entrust your decision? This, my young students, is the point of the entire story! The hands of Esau represent the Greek worldview. They live in the realm of the physical. They worship the body, thus their gymnasium and all the emphasis on physical exercise. This is why they worship the human form. My dear students, the Torah rejects Esau and rejects the worship of the physical. The Torah rejects the hunter and the warrior, all of which are represented by the hands of Esau."

He pauses to let his point sink in. It is an argument that directly conflicts with what they have been hearing from Natan the Pious.

He sees some empty gazes and feels as if his exegesis might have lost some listeners, so he makes it more explicit. "I know this is not what

Natan is teaching you. He is teaching violence. But here in the scriptures, we see the blessings of God are bestowed upon those who think and study, not those who fight and hunt. Up there," he gestures toward the gymnasium, "they are not talking about these things. They are wrestling and lifting weights. The heart of the Jewish people is in spiritual and intellectual discourse."

The students sit still. The immediate association between the gymnasium at the edge of town with idol worship and the Greek veneration of the physical body is precisely the response Simon sought to evoke. The association between Natan's teachings and Greek culture touches a sensitive nerve.

Most of the students sit and absorb. They would hardly think of questioning their teacher, nor debating with him something about which he feels so passionate. Yochanan is not like most students. He has a great deal of reverence for his father, but he does not fear him. He also knows that questions that are respectfully asked do not offend his father.

"What then, of the physical body that God created, Father. What use is it?"

"What do you mean, my son?"

"God made us physical beings, Father. What right do we have to reject the physical? Your interpretation, which places the intellect against the body, relegates the physical to secondary status."

"Am I asking that you reject the body?"

"You didn't phrase it that way, but you certainly want us to emphasize something other than the body."

"That is indeed true. I want you to train the mind, not the body."

"Yes. And perhaps the blessing that Jacob received after his trick does suggest that God's blessing goes to the person who uses his mind. But what of that blessing now? Jacob was rewarded for his thinking. We are subjugated for ours."

"Subjugated?"

"Yes. If we do not train the physical body, we will always be weak and subjected by our enemies. Is this what God wants of his chosen people?"

"I believe that God wants spiritual fulfillment for his people," Simon replies dryly. "And you presume that the Jewish people could overthrow the Greek empire by doing a bit more weight training?"

"Are we not heir to great warriors who fought for our religious and national freedom?"

For the first time, Simon loses his temper. He is too young to know firsthand, but he certainly heard many stories of the death and destruction heaped upon his ancestors by the Babylonians only two generations earlier. "Have the Jewish people enjoyed victories and champions in our history? Yes. Was King David a mighty military man? Of course, but that was then. The age of military might is, if not passed, certainly a distant hope, the longing for which will only cause problems. And what do you make of the scripture placed before you? Upon what sort of activity does God seem to approve?"

"But, Father, I have answered you with stories from those same scriptures. Sometimes the stories suggest contradictory things and we must lean upon our own understanding. What if we are to enact the path of King David rather than Jacob?"

Simon grew up among sages and scholars whose word was final. No one ever dared challenge the Biblical interpretation of the Torah Sages. And here he has offered his interpretation of one of the more famous stories, only to find his reading rebuffed by the emotions of a disrespectful boy.

"The Torah is our truth and our guide. I do not approve of this kind of inquiry. You are old enough to obey the teachings of our prophets with humility. As for your mentioning of military heroes, God fights our battles—not weapons or chariots, and certainly not men! Often those arrogant enough to believe themselves to be chosen find that belief invalidated in tragedy."

With that last statement, Simon storms out of the room. Yochanan sees that his fellow students share ambivalence about Yochanan questioning the master. He is the son of the revered teacher and former high priest. In some ways, he is like a prince. They too are interested in the debate that has been waged. What is the right response to these occupiers of the Jewish people's promised land?

"What is the right answer?" Hillel, a close friend of Yochanan and fellow student of Natan the Pious, asks. "Should we fight or bury ourselves in scriptures? Does anyone here really believe God is going to fight our wars?" Hillel regrets uttering those words.

Interpreting their silence and averted eyes as chastisement rather than respect, Hillel storms out of the room and mutters, "Don't look at me that way!"

Yochanan also darts out. He heads straight for the stables where he feels at home and among good company.

"Hello, shoveler of shit!" the stable foreman greets him playfully.

"Clytomedes, good to see you."

"And you."

Clytomedes, the stable foreman, is a nice Greek man who knows horses very well. He is a retired legionnaire of Alexander's army that conquered the Assyrian regions. Alexander rewarded him with land and coin for his loyal service.

"Have you come to work in the stables again?"

"No. I have gotten into an argument with my father. Just walking out this way to cool off."

"A buck-strong teenage boy arguing with his father? What a surprise!"

"I know," Yochanan smiles sheepishly. "First time for everything, I guess."

"Tale as old as time."

"I need something to keep my mind off of it. Can you tell me another story about the great one?"

"Sorry. I'm busy. I must get five horses ready for the evening rides. Come back later."

"I'll help you! I'll do all the work. You just tell me a story while I do your work. Please!"

"You will do all the work? OK. We have a deal."

As they make their way to a painted-brown stallion, haughty and ill-tempered, Clytomedes watches in mild surprise as Yochanan brushes and readies him with caution and skill. The boy has a way with these animals.

"Which story do you want to hear?"

"Tell me a new one."

"OK. Have I told you about the Persian conquests?"

"No. But I love anything that involves conquests…"

"After his father's death," Clytomedes begins.

"At the hands of traitors," Yochanan interrupts in an outburst.

"That's right, at the hands of traitors. Anyway, after his father's death, Alexander vowed to fulfill his father's dream and conquer the Persian Empire. His first victories took place in Granicus and Halicarnassus. They would have satisfied most. But Alexander was hardly like most men. Wait… not that way. Attach the harness like this, see?"

"Yes."

"So, where was I?"

"Alexander's first victories."

"Yes. OK. He didn't stop there though. Young Alexander wanted revenge for the invasion of Greece by Darius I and Xerces. It was autumn. Alexander came upon the Persian armies, led by Darius III, near the village of Issus. Fortune was kind to Alexander in the choice of ground. His army was much inferior in numbers than that of the Persians. It is said that the Persian army had 500,000 foot soldiers and 100,000 archers who could blacken the sky with their arrows. But, Alexander stretched his right wing in advance of the Persian army left-center where Darius was fighting."

Clytomedes draws circles in the sand to illustrate his point, and Yochanan briefly stops fiddling with the horse's saddle.

"Alexander's instinct proved oracular when the Persian left gave way very quickly. A gap opened and Alexander swung his cavalry around against the rear of Darius' army. The Persian armies fled like sheep at the hands of the great warrior. Alexander chased Darius by horse and killed the Persian general with one blow of his sword."

"I would not have fled so quickly," Yochanan mutters.

"That is easy to say. But you have never faced the hand of Alexander's left flank."

"It is true."

"And if you had, you might have been fighting against the fates. After all, this was foretold," Clytomedes continues.

"Foretold? What do you mean?"

"Have you heard of the fabulously wealthy King Midas?"

"Yes, the hand of Midas. Everything he touched turned to gold."

"Right. Well, before his death, he tied a knot and vowed that anyone who could untie the knot would rule the entire Anatolian region. And who do you think untied the knot? It was Alexander the Great, the fearless warrior who freed the knot by slashing it with his sword! The sword,

Alexander believed, is the key to ruling the world. And he used the sword to seize the power of the oracle. In the Greek world, very little carries more weight than an oracle."

"So, it was ordained?"

"Indeed."

"Here, I'll finish this one. Run along now and clean those stables on the western side."

As he wanders away to clean, Yochanan cannot be more inspired and pleased with the day's stories. As he shovels, he dreams of conquest and peace. He meditates upon the meaning of Alexander's success, one his father would very much have hated. Yochanan is convinced more than ever that the sword is the key to power and peace.

29

Jerusalem, Israel
September 2006

HUGE GREEN SIGNS IN HEBREW, Arabic and English line the highways. They are a reminder of just how inherently fragmented this little slice of land along the Mediterranean coast actually is. The English is especially telling. When Israel was born into existence in the 1930s and '40s, the citizens of this new country came from all over Europe, North Africa, and the United States. They were united by nothing but a common heritage, and they certainly didn't share the same tongue. English was the only international language that made sense at the time. Until, of course, Hebrew was reincarnated.

Cohen drives past rusted shells of armored vehicles and burned out Centurion tanks purposefully adorning the roads, all monuments and reminders of how this stretch of land was secured. The road to Jerusalem on which Cohen rides is paved in a 3,000-year-old history that dates back to biblical times. The city is literally on a hill, perched high atop the Judean Mountains. Highway 1 climbs and winds through the twisting and curving mountain gorge known as Sha'ar HaGai. Cohen, like most Israelis his age, still refers to it by its Arabic name, Bab al-Wad.

That particular section of Highway 1 is a museum unto itself, a relatively new one. That curving pass is perhaps the most significant military sight of that struggle. Had Jerusalem been cut off during the initial War of Independence in 1947, the spiritual center of the country, and all the people therein, would have starved to death. But brave men and women had kept that route moving. Throughout the short history of this nation, and the longer history of the people, the road leading to Jerusalem has always been forged in fire. Those flames keep burning no matter how hard the wind blows. But at what, or whose, cost?

You can revisit patriotic memories and honor history all you want on this route, but it is also a pain in the ass. This road is always a traffic jam; today is no exception. Cohen lowers the window of his Volvo in the hope of feeling a cool breeze. Throughout the two-hour car ride, he alternates between listening to the news and just enjoying the silence. He has plenty to occupy his thoughts. When Highway 1 changes suddenly from a four-lane thoroughfare into a broad modern boulevard called Sderot Ben-Gurion, the traffic clears up. From there, Cohen's progress improves. He travels up to Kiryat Ben-Gurion in Western Jerusalem, where the office of the prime minister is located.

Over the years, Cohen has become familiar enough with this compound that he can, after clearing security, navigate his way to the underground parking garage without looking too much like a guest. Cohen makes his way up the spiral staircase to the prime minister's wing and asks the young lady at the reception to please announce his presence. Cohen sits in the waiting area and leafs through a magazine.

Within two minutes, a young man comes out in a cheap, blue polyester suit, one size too big, probably to accommodate his weapon. He clears his throat. "General, sir."

"Yes."

"The prime minister wants you to know he is meeting with VaRaSh right now on Lior and will be with you as soon as the meeting is over."

"Any idea how long that will be, soldier?"

"None, sir. Can I get you a cup of coffee or some water while you wait?"

"No, thank you."

Cohen settles into his seat, confident that this meeting might take a while. *VaRaSh* is a Hebrew acronym for the Committee of Heads of the Services. That committee includes: the director general of Shabak, the internal security service; the commander of Aman, military intelligence; and the Chief of Israel's intelligence service.

Meeting about Lior? Good, it looks like I came at the right time. I knew I could count on old friends. I am sure Ehud will open every door for me to do what it takes to bring him home. Maya and Leon will be thrilled. Cohen needs to get a handle on his thoughts.

Two and a half hours later, the prime minister strides purposefully out of the dark mahogany door and into the waiting area, where he warmly greets Cohen.

"Hello, General. It's been too long!"

"Ehud, Mister Prime Minister, you know why I'm here. He's my grandson—I want him back!" he says.

"Of course! We are doing, and going to do, everything we can to bring him home safely."

"I need more from you right now. Give me clearance—let me take the lead."

"Avi, you know that is impossible. How could you possibly think you can come here and make such a request? This is not Beitar. We are doing everything in our power to bring him home."

"I'm not convinced."

"Are you reading the newspapers? Within forty-eight hours of Lior's abduction, we arrested over 100 people in Khan Yunis while searching for your grandson. Two days after his abduction, we flew four F-16s over Assad's Palace in Latakia. Avi, I am doing what I need to do!"

"I read the fucking papers," Cohen says as he loses his temper, "and I know as well as anyone that the two operations in response to my grandson's abduction served you very well politically, but they did not bring my grandson home."

Avigdor regrets yelling. He composes himself.

"Ehud, I understand. I can't be involved, but please tell me you are going to do everything in your power, *everything*, to get him back." Cohen knows the prime minister understands his unstated request by the way he looks back at him.

"You know as well as I do," the prime minister replies, "this is a complicated situation. And it of course depends on how much we have to give up. Lior is a soldier, and I think he, above anyone else, would want to be treated like a soldier."

"I know what that is code for, Ehud. I don't want my grandson to face the same fate of those who are still rotting in God knows where, or have faced the executioner's knife because of how we treat our soldiers."

"If anyone knows the consequences of negotiating with terrorists, Avigdor, it is you."

"Ehud, we have known each other for fifty years. Imagine if this was your grandson. What would you do?"

"I would do what you are doing."

"Then you agree?"

"I didn't say that. Because, I think if you were in my shoes you would do exactly what I'm doing. I know you well enough to know that."

Cohen ignores the logic of this argument and the implications that he is in any way displaying hypocrisy.

"Do we know where he is? Can we send in a commando unit? I will lead it myself. Give me something, Ehud, Please."

From the moment he says these words, Cohen regrets pleading. It is clear from the way that Ehud recoils at being told what to do militarily, that this is overwhelming him a bit. Cohen is a retired general and a war hero, but he is speaking, after all, with the leader of the country.

"Listen, my good friend," Olmert takes Cohen's arm gently in his hand, "this is a diplomatic matter and we are addressing it as such. Avi, you know there will be no negotiating with terrorists. But we will get him home."

"What is it they want?"

"You know the answer to that question—don't make this harder than it is. Go home and be with Maya and the family. They need you now. Let us do what we need to do."

Cohen looks into the prime minister's eyes and sees impatience and distance. It doesn't feel good. The prime minister is a tall man, which, at the moment, makes Cohen feel especially small. For the first time in his life, he feels a sense of panic. He will not be getting any relief or help here. That much is crystal clear.

So he doesn't say a word. Instead, he responds to that old but omnipresent training from the military—don't question, obey the orders. He has lived his life according to that notion and does not abandon it when standing face-to-face with the prime minister. Cohen walks backward a few steps, turns around, and heads down the spiral staircase.

As he reaches the last step, he hears his name. Cohen turns around and notices Moti Rachmani moving in his direction with Yehudith a step behind him.

"General!"

"Shalom, First Sergeant Moti Rachmani." The formal enunciation of his name is meant to be in both jest and a great deal of warmth.

The man who approaches Cohen is a few years older than the general and was a superb commander and military hero himself. He had been planning to leave the army when the Yom Kippur War broke out. Once in that war, he was all the way in. During the war, he was among the first Israeli soldiers to cross the Suez Canal in a reconnaissance unit. Other components of his career were shrouded in a bit more mystery. Rachmani was a member of the elite Sayeret Matkal unit when he was recruited by Ariel Sharon to join the infamous and secretive Rimon Unit.

That group of tough soldiers is credited for annihilating terrorism in Gaza by capturing terrorists, taking them to dark places and killing them in cold blood. Of course, the Rimon Unit did not officially exist. But rumors that insist otherwise abound. Rimon's mission was to use risky and highly unconventional methods to do things that the general members of the army could not be expected to do. Rachmani's reputation as a killer was immortalized by a journalist who once said that every morning he would go to the field and use one hand for peeing and the other for shooting empty cans of soda. His views were simple: "There are enemies, bad Arabs who want to kill us, so we have to kill them first."

Rachmani's fame reached a whole new level when, in 1971, he came face-to-face with a grenade-wielding terrorist near a bus stop in Jerusalem. When this would-be assassin pulled the pin in the hope of killing innocent civilians, he happened to do so with Rachmani standing nearby. Instead of scrambling for cover, Rachmani jumped the man, ripped the grenade from his hand and threw it into a non-populated area. As if that wasn't enough heroism, he then quickly and bloodlessly killed the terrorist with his bare hands.

Defender. Protector. Executioner. That is how the media portrayed him.

Cohen and Rachmani share more than a background in military heroism. They share a deeper common past as well, one that surely galvanizes the bravery they so publically display. They are both children of Holocaust survivors whose families were wiped out by Nazi hatred. Rachmani was born Haberman on a train in the outskirts of Ukraine. He immigrated to Israel in 1945 with his parents. Things were hardly easy. He'd grown up in poverty in the poor neighborhood of Lod, some fifteen miles from Tel Aviv. He excelled scholastically early on and was sent to a state-sponsored private high school. There, he met Avigdor Cohen and others who would make up the governing elite of the military and the state. As young adults, they'd spent many an evening together over wine, telling stories of youth and war. After Rachmani entered politics, the social contact ended abruptly.

The two greet each other outside of the prime minister's office with a fierce hug of brotherly affection. When they break apart, they stand together silently. Then Rachmani introduces Yehudith.

"Yehudith, this is the famous—no the infamous—Brigadier General Cohen."

"I'm so honored to meet you, sir. I've heard so much about you."

"Thank you."

"I'm not surprised to see you here, Avi," Rachmani says.

Yehudit looks a bit surprised at that comment.

"How are Maya and the family holding out?"

"It's very difficult. We are hanging on to hope."

Suddenly for Yehudith, the entire abduction takes on new meaning. Her mind races, *Of course, this is the grandfather.* In a single moment, the entire drama becomes so personal and real. Seeing Lior's grandfather, hearing the name of an abducted soldier's mother. The pain pierces her heart.

"Moti, I want to do what it takes to bring Lior home," Cohen says emphatically. Rachmani looks at Yehudith as he determines what he can say. *Now is not the time for empty promises. This is not a man who will hear them.*

"Listen, Avi, I'm sure you spoke with the prime minister. He is going to do everything in his power to bring your grandson home."

"Yes. I spoke with him," Cohen answers dismissively.

Rachmani looks at the ground, glances at Yehudith and sucks in his breath.

"Avi, I'm not going to bullshit you. There are no easy answers here. Every fucking time our state has been faced with this kind of situation, we have failed. We have failed our citizens and our soldiers."

Cohen's body goes limp with the confirmation of what he has been thinking. *Failure just can't happen this time. Not with Lior.*

"And the media isn't going to help things," Yehudith mutters.

"The news reported that he didn't even fire one shot at the terrorists. My grandson didn't even fight back. Can you even imagine?"

"Ignore the news. They'll say anything."

"They are certainly not our best and brightest, those scavengers," Yehudith interjects and Rachmani agrees.

"Moti, what do I do? I can lead a commando unit into Gaza myself. I'll bring him home. Just tell me where he is."

Yehudith's eyes swell. For someone whose entire profession revolves around speaking, she is completely speechless. She cannot believe what she is hearing.

There is more silence between the grown men.

"Avi, I believe there is something you can do. Call me in three hours, here is my direct number. Come see me at Aman tonight. I will make sure you have the clearance." Yehudith could not look more surprised at what she was hearing, while Avi's palms begin to sweat as he takes the card that Moti had just written a number on. "There actually might be something you can do." Moti looked Avi square in the eyes, a ranking officer advising a soldier: "Avi, three hours for us at Aman means three hours, not two-and-a-half and not four. Call me in three hours."

"Yehudith let's go."

Avi just stood there.

30

Jerusalem, Israel
September 2006

AVI COHEN IS HAVING A hard time gauging his feelings. He stares at the card that was just handed to him as he takes measured steps out of the prime minister's compound. He feels angry with his old friend, the prime minister. And yet he feels a sense gratitude at the fortuitous meeting with Rachmani and the possibility that there is indeed something he or they can do. Rachmani is not a man of gab—he means what he says.

Avi also feels a sense of sadness with the incessant danger Israel faces. He has made a lifetime investment in a persona and an ideology he is beginning to reconsider. When the media wants a provocative quote to derail peace talks or to rile up the left, they know they can call on him, particularly on the topic of negotiations with unworthy negotiating partners.

As he trudges out of the prime minister's office, he realizes how impulsive this entire trip to Jerusalem has been. He feels the human dimension of this craziness more vividly than ever before. He has always known that soldiers have mothers and fathers, grandparents and families, but he never realized how limited his capacity for empathy has truly been. Avi is angry with himself.

Shit! Three hours. Where to now?

Cohen's cell phone rings just as he reaches for the keys in his coat pocket. He looks at the screen of his brand-new Blackberry. Maya is calling. There are three missed calls from her. His phone was on silent and he hadn't even noticed it buzzing.

"What did the prime minister say? Is he alive? When will they bring him home?"

She sounds hysterical. His heart breaks once again hearing his daughter's pain. "He is alive. We know that. The prime minister spent over an hour with me and he promised me he will do everything in his power to bring Lior home."

"What does that mean?"

"I can't go into many specifics. But I can tell you that they are working diligently on it. He promised he'd pull out all the stops for me and for our family. Maya, I need you to relax. I have a few meetings this afternoon. I will see you tonight."

Avi is broken. He cannot help but lie to his daughter. As the words leave his lips, he realizes how much he has been lying to himself. When he'd walked out of the house that morning, his daughter and her husband, not to mention his ex-wife, ushered him out with hopeful eyes; they were counting on his *protectsia,* slang in Israel for connections. His connections in the upper levels of government are the envy of all who know him, and yet, when he needs them most, they have failed him.

This is bullshit. I can't count on Olmert. That much I now know. What did Rachmani mean when he said there might be something I can do? Call me in three hours. Avi looks at his watch. It is 10:30 a.m. *I saw Rachmani ten minutes ago. Three hours is 1:20 p.m.*

He drives out of the parking lot. *I have two hours and fifty minutes.* He heads to a place he hopes will provide some comfort and maybe some answers. It is a place that has provided relief to its visitors for centuries. He makes a right onto Yitzhak Rabin, another right onto Betzalel, a left on King George Street and a right onto the famed Jaffa Street. That will take him right to the Old City of Jerusalem. He decides to make an unannounced appointment with an Ancient Wall.

His midsize sedan speeds along the eastern wall of the Old City, past the Zion Gate and into the parking lot at the Dung Gate situated on the southeastern tip of the Old City. It is the only entrance that leads to the Western Wall through the Jewish Quarters. Cohen cannot stand the Arab presence in the old city of Jerusalem. He remembers well the jubilation when he heard the news on the transistor radio from his hospital bed in 1967. "The old city of Jerusalem is ours," they said. He was lying facedown, staring at the floor, healing from his burn wounds. Despite the heavy pain-killers, he could hear his parents crying with joy. The entire hospital ward shook with victorious screams. He knew then that their finest soldiers had given their lives in the fight for this sacred ground. Despite the excruciating pain throughout his body every time he moved and spoke, he too screamed with joy. Nothing would mitigate his jubilation.

Avi often credited the unification of Jerusalem, the reports of how the paratroopers liberated the Western Wall, and the sound of the Shofar on the radio for inspiring him not to give up in that hospital room. Jerusalem was back under Jewish auspices, and he would heal and make the pilgrimage himself.

Years later, here he is, still forced to dodge certain parts of his people's victory. Over the years, after counterattacks and non-violent encroachments, the Old City has once again assumed its diverse divisions of Arab, Armenian, Jewish, and a few Ethiopian Christians. Jerusalem has reverted to a city of three Sabbaths. On Sunday, one can hear the ceaseless sound of Church bells; Friday, the sounds of the Muezzins can be heard throughout the Old City with thousands of faithful marching to the Mosque. And, of course, on Saturday the silence of the Jewish day of rest can be felt.

Even the most secular of Israelis have a soft spot for the Old City of Jerusalem. The city has been inhabited in some capacity by Jews for well over 3,000 years. The stones, which come in more shades of khaki and brown and yellow and red than ought to exist, whisper with echoes the of crusaders, Muslim invaders, and aspiring Romans who wanted desperately to please their Caesar. For Cohen, this enormous accumulation of historical rubble holds an unexplainable appeal. Seeing the magnificent stones, put in place by Herod the Great, make him wonder how the hell they were once moved. They also connect him, somehow, with those long past dead military figures.

What the Jews call the Temple Mount, the Muslims call *Haram al Sharif*, which means "noble sanctuary." In the Bible, the site is called

Moriah or Mount Moriah. The greatest builder of Jerusalem was Herod, the Roman-appointed King of the Jews. Christians know Herod for his appearance in the Gospel of Matthew, which describes him as the "Murderer of Innocents." The historical authenticity of that story is debated, that much Cohen knows. He cannot believe Herod would kill babies; he wasn't the Pharaoh of the Old Testament.

One thing he does know about Herod is that he sought grandeur and achieved historical greatness. To accommodate the growth of Jerusalem, Herod simply made the mountain bigger. He built a massive retaining wall around Mt. Moriah and filled it with stone and cement, creating a huge artificial plateau with the center slightly raised. The Second Temple stood at the highest point of the plateau. The First Temple was destroyed by the Babylonians, and was rebuilt into one of the great wonders of the ancient world. It has been said that those who did not see the temple Herod built in Jerusalem did not know beauty.

Herod's expansion proved so sturdy that nothing over the last 2,000 years affected it. Nothing could move that foundation—not wars, earthquakes, natural elements or man. But the groups that controlled the earth have shifted over time. Jewish sovereignty ended violently in the summer of 68 CE at the hands of Roman armies. After more than 1,000 years of Jewish autonomy in Jerusalem, the Romans attacked from the north. For weeks, the butchery and violence raged on in the narrow stone streets across Jerusalem. On the ninth day of the month of Av, the Roman legionnaires broke onto the Temple Mount and torched it to the ground. Everything but the stones burned away.

Less than seventy-five years after the destruction of the temple, the Rabbinic Sage Akiva and his disciples led a revolt against Rome. Simon Bar Kochba was declared *Messiah* of the insurgents. Having had enough of the Jewish resistance, the Romans systematically wiped out the entire remaining Jewish population in Judea. For 300 years, the Romans pillaged, killed and raped them. Somewhere between 800,000 to 1 million Jews were killed or sold into slavery. The slave markets were said to have skyrocketed throughout the Roman Empire and the cost of a slave tanked because of the infusion of Jewish slaves. Even the name Judea was erased by the Roman Emperor Hadrian, who'd ordered that, "From now on, Judea will be called Palestine."

In the early '80s, Cohen was part of a small entourage that included the president of the State of Israel and the prime minister, who were flown by military helicopter to a remote spot in the Judean Desert for an unusual state funeral. Archaeologists believed that the bones they dug up were the remains of Jewish rebels who fought the Romans in 130 CE. The funeral service, small but televised throughout Israel, offered the prime minister the platform to orate on how these remains "represent the courageous spirit of our 'glorious brothers' whose legacy lives on today." The sounds of drums and guns, fired by the military guard of honor, filled the room as the remains, carried by brigadier generals, were wrapped in Israeli flags and laid to rest. The Chief Rabbi of Israel recited the prayer for Jewish Martyrs and the Kaddish.

Cohen's politics have always been an aggressive response to that vulgar mentality of ancient Rome. Anyone could systematically attempt to rid a place of its people. The legacy of persecution ran deep. Hadrian's systematic attempt to wipe Jewish history off the face of the earth echoed throughout the world for the next 2,000 years. The Roman holocaust following Bar Kochva's revolt was outdone by Hitler's Holocaust in the 20th century. The Inquisition found popes burning Jews at the stake for refusing to convert. During plagues, Jews were blamed for poisoning wells.

And so, God's chosen people moved from one exile to another, and even when settled, they lived like second-class citizens in countries that never fully accepted them. Jews survived centuries of daily violence in Christian and Muslim lands, by looking inward spiritually, remembering the glorious past and always having faith in an even better future. In exile, Jews never responded with violence. The Holocaust changed all of that. That event stood as the starkest warning: If this people did not defend itself, it would be forever lost.

"Never Again" became the motto of the generation that established the new Jewish State. Never again would Jews go to the gas chambers as sheep. Cohen had been honored once at Masada, one of the more popular destinations in Israel. There, in the middle of the Judean Desert, on top of a steep plateau, a group of Jews had decided to wait out the Roman occupation. The Jews just kept to themselves, figuring that they'd be left alone out in the middle of nowhere, bothering no one. Instead, the Romans sought them out and sieged their forts. They built a massive three-kilometer ramp up to the top of the plateau. Instead of being taken as slaves, all of the Jewish inhabitants committed mass suicide. The refrain "never again" reverberates on visits to Masada as well. Never again will Jews wait for someone to knock on their door.

Cohen walks through the narrow ancient streets of Jerusalem, up the stone stairs, to the security checkpoint. There is a long line of people, young and old, Hasidic, Sephardic, Ashkenazi, South Americans, Swedes. This wall has drawn them from all over the world.

As he walks past the line and into another checkpoint line, he notices the young men checking camera bags and manning metal detectors. They appear to be Lior's age. Their olive green uniforms hang baggily on their growing frames. Cohen makes his way through the small walkway that overlooks the Western Wall Plaza.

At the Western Wall, it is believed that God answers the cry of every suffering soul. Legend has it that this wall is not only spiritually unique, but has remained intact over a period of 3,000 years because it was built by the poor and destitute. King Solomon had each of the four walls around the temple built by a different class of people. The Eastern Wall was built by the wealthy, the Northern Wall by the statesmen, the Southern Wall by the priests and clergy, and the Western Wall by the poor. The merit of the simple people who sacrificed themselves to build the wall earned the "Kotel," Hebrew for the Western Wall, its legacy.

Cohen places a yarmulke on his head. He descends the decline and walks straight to the towering wall. He looks to his left and right to see Evangelical Christians, who've adopted the wall in some way as their own sacred place. People come from all over seeking answers and consolation. A young religious Jewish man with fringes hanging on the sides of his pants and scrappy beard comes over to Cohen and asks if he wants to wear *Tefillin*, little black boxes placed on the forehead and arm. Growing up, his father never practiced that sort of thing.

"No, thank you," he waves the invitation away.

As vulnerable as he feels, he will not let his condition change him. He has come to this wall looking for something, but he will not abandon his principles. *I cannot abandon reason, and yet reason has abandoned me.*

He has done the most reasonable of things today, or so he thought. He called upon an old friend with whom he always agreed, who he thought would do anything for him. That friend had treated him just like any crazed parent, dismissing his pleas as imprudent and emotional. *What next?*

This part of Jerusalem felt more Jewish than any other spot in the world. Under his wedding canopy, like every good Jew, Cohen repeated the words after the officiating rabbi:

"If I forget thee, Jerusalem, let me forget my right hand. If I do not remember thee, let my tongue cling to the roof of my mouth, if I prefer not Jerusalem above my greatest joy."

Even in this happiest of occasions, a wedding, the rabbi explained, until Jerusalem is united and our Holy Temple rebuilt, no joy, not even the joy of the wedding canopy, is complete. He did his part in protecting this country, in ensuring its existence for future generations. Cohen loved the many stories of the priests who led their people both spiritually and militarily. A Kohen himself, Cohen has always wondered what it was that Simon the High Priest did or said that turned Alexander the legendary warrior away.

He had gone into the Prime Minister's office today and realized that he would do just about anything to save Lior.

Cohen places his head against the wall and tries to remember the prayers he'd been taught when he was young. He wants some sort of powerful words or incantations in this moment. Nothing comes to him. And so, the most revered military hero in Israel's short modern history, a man who has never met an enemy he would not eviscerate, leans against the oldest wall in the history of the Jews and cries.

31

La'uf
Lior's Mind

Memory: From Bakum to Basic Training

"I am not your friend! I will not be your friend! We will never be friends! I am your *Mefaked*, commander. I am going to teach you how to be a soldier."

Shit, those were the first words I heard at B'aCh, the training base. We were not allowed to speak on the bus ride up north to the base. If anyone spoke, we were told, the bus would stop and you would have to do push-ups.

It sounds so crazy right now. He gave us 45 seconds to retrieve our bags, throw them in a corner and stand in line. That's when the *Mefaked* delivered his brilliant speech about not being friends.

Being yelled at all the time is just something you get used to. They're nice guys, I guess... it's what they have to do.

32

Tel Aviv, Israel
September 2006

I T'S 1:30 P.M. COHEN DIALS the number on the card. An operator picks up. "To whom may I direct your call?"

"Moti Rachmani, Please."

The line goes silent for a moment, and then a strange tone is followed by, "Shalom, Avi. Can you get to Old Jaffo by 4 p.m.?"

"Yes, of Course."

"Good. Go to Abulafia Bakery on Yefet Street, past the clock tower. There your escort will bring you to our meeting. Avi, your security clearance code is 'Operation Dina.' You read that?"

"Operation Dina."

"OK, see you later."

The speed and efficiency with which the conversation happened surprises Cohen. The address is in Old Jaffo, right outside Tel Aviv. Cohen is not so familiar with this part of Tel Aviv. He does not want to take any chances. He heads out from Jerusalem immediately. It is a good thing because the mid-afternoon traffic out of Jerusalem toward Tel Aviv is completely unpredictable. An accident on Route 1 and a soccer game at TAU

Sports Complex significantly delay his arrival.

He finally gets to his destination thirty minutes early. The place is crowded with people, young and old, buying pita bread and muffins. It isn't long before a young man in his mid-30s comes over to Cohen and says hello.

He doesn't look much like a Shabak ranking officer. The only hint of the young man's status is his uncanny ability to appear casual, so much so that Cohen wonders whether he has ever met this man before. That such a person is sitting out of uniform in a public place is hardly surprising. There is something about Israel—the sunlight, the strange demographics and social order, the ongoing religious tensions, the love/hate relationships that average Israelis have with one another—that lends itself to a citizenry with a dramatically altered image. You often do not see what you think you have perceived.

The young man is tall and handsome; he has a length that suggests sinewy strength. He smiles comfortably. "Hello, Avigdor."

Cohen nods back. "Hello."

"My name is Yoram."

While discipline within the ranks of the IDF is lax, first names are not the norm in the military. Cohen assumes the secret service has its own culture. Cohen does not bat an eyelash. "Are we going to sit?"

"No. We are actually leaving right now," the young man replies. He places a few shekels on the counter, takes his muffin and leads Cohen down the street to a blue Honda Pilot.

They drive back into Tel Aviv along the Mediterranean coast past a series of upscale hotels. Cohen looks toward the Hilton Hotel on his left, when the young man makes an abrupt sharp right turn. "Are we not going to Aman Headquarters?" Cohen asks.

"No, Moti wants to see you at ISA, Israel Security Agency."

Cohen has no idea where this agency is located. Most people in Israel don't. Certainly, quite a few of the more jumpy Hilton guests would be shocked if they knew that their hotel was next to the Israeli agency responsible for anti-terrorism activities and all eavesdropping operations.

When they pull up to the gate, a woman in a generic security guard uniform motions for them to roll down their windows. "Were you given a security code?"

Yoram remains silent. He looks straight ahead.

"Yes." Cohen is uncertain. "Operation Dina."

"Thank you. You can pull forward." She nods toward an empty parking space.

Cohen's escort is stoic as he passes the guard.

"One of yours, I'm presuming?" Cohen asks.

"Sir, I really can't…" tails the answer into innuendo and silence.

When he makes his way into the non-descript office building, Cohen notices that the walls are not less than five feet thick. The plainclothes secretary doesn't say much as they walk by, but as soon as they walk through the double doors, the security measures become much more overt. They go through three different stainless steel doors, each of which require a different identity check. The first is voice-activated, the second reads fingerprints, the third is a passkey.

"Where are we?" Cohen asks.

"That I cannot tell you," the officer replies. "This is an eavesdropping station operated by Aman."

"Makes more sense now."

Yoram leads Cohen up a staircase to an office overlooking a large room full of data miners staring at monitors connected to mainframes and servers. On a big wall opposite his vantage point is a list of numbers and letters scrolling across a screen. In the upper right quadrant of that live wall, instant messages in a dozen languages and Arabic dialects flash in various colors differentiated by urgency.

One officer near the room's center scrolls through a series of photographs. Occasionally, he focuses on one and uses his mouse to insert a bright red arrow at things he believes look malicious or suspicious. When he sees the extent of this operation, Cohen feels his hopes of finding Lior lift.

As the door opens, Rachmani signals Cohen to sit and Yoram leaves the room.

"You see that young female officer in the cubicle in the far left side of the room?" Rachmani points from behind a glass wall. "Her name is Ofra Lalush." She has deep, dark eyes, short hair and looks like the kind of woman who does Pilates after yoga every morning.

"Ofra knows terrorism and the horrors of its violence all too well,"

Rachmani goes on. "She was enjoying a Danish and iced coffee with her father at Café Hillel on a sunny September morning in 2003 when a suicide bomber was apprehended by a security guard. The guard refused to let this suspicious man enter the premises, and so he detonated the explosives strapped around his body and killed eight innocent civilians. The guard who'd stopped the bomber was of course killed, though had he not stopped the bomber at the entrance, the casualty count would have been much higher. Thankfully, Ofra was in the back of the café protected by a large concrete pillar. Her father was not as lucky and suffered serious brain damage from shrapnel and flying debris. He cannot speak, feed himself, or walk without assistance. After her recovery, she devoted her university studies and career to defeating terrorism by brawn or by brain. She is a human database on terror cells. She could—if you had the clearance—rattle off the names of leaders, places of training and operation, and most likely Western targets for each of those cells. We like to think that Ofra here knows more about terrorism than the terrorists themselves.

"To her right is Gabi Louzon. Gabi does not have any heartwarming backstory, or at least he hasn't told us one.

"Gabi is one of the finest street-surveillance artists Aman has ever produced. He can anonymously blend into any neighborhood, from the ritziest hotel lobbies to the seediest back alleyways. He can assume the identity of life's downtrodden or the bourgeoisie while following highly trained officers or hardened terrorists. All this while gathering intelligence without arousing a flicker of suspicion.

"All of what you see in there, the technology and manpower, all of it is a project-specific data team. That entire group is on Lior's case, General," Rachmani says.

"Good, it is impressive. But have you found anything yet?"

"Of course. It isn't everything we want to know yet, but it is a damn good start."

"I presume you are going to tell me about it, otherwise you wouldn't have brought me."

"Listen closely, Avi. Lior is being guarded very carefully. The people who kidnapped him don't make mistakes. If you want to bring Lior home, you need to act now." Rachmani looks Cohen right in the eyes. "I'm about to go rogue here for a second. Are you willing to hear me out? The prime minister will not like what I'm about to tell you, and I know you two are old running mates."

"I'm willing to hear you out, yes." Cohen gets nervous about where this is going. He never truly trusted these elite spy agency folks.

"The universal wisdom is and has always been to starve stories like these. It has always been believed that the enemy is looking for international attention. The more publicity they get, the harder they can bargain."

"Right."

"Many experts will tell you that, for that reason, Lior is not in danger. They want him alive and well to use as a negotiating pawn. Here is the paradox. Our government, our prime minister, has staked our existence on two principles: 1) We don't negotiate with terrorists. 2) We will not give this story any media attention."

"I know those two truths well," Cohen interjects.

"So," Rachmani continues, "I'd argue that, while Lior isn't in short-term danger, the long-term reality is that he may very well die in some unknown Gazan basement. The long term, that is the killer."

"What do you mean, exactly?"

"What I mean is that Israel has tried this strategy for years and it has failed. That strategy works in South America or Pakistan. It does not work with Hamas and Hezbollah. You know as well as I do that we still have five soldiers in enemy hands. They are all probably dead by now. Worst of all, they aren't just dead. They are forgotten by everyone but their mothers and fathers."

"And grandfathers."

"Stay on point. Think about the way our system works. The military leadership changes over every three to four years. Lior's friends will be in the workforce in two years, out of the military and ready to think about something else. Our government will change over in three years."

"Right."

"With each year that this turnover happens, Lior drifts further and further from the national consciousness."

"Agreed."

"So, what I am telling you right now is contrary to our government's present policy. My advice is to get in front of every camera you can. Speak to every media outlet," Rachmani says. "The prime minister is going to

hate this and resent you. Hamas is not in it for financial gain. This is strictly political. Take the political game to them and to our government. Avi,
turn this into an international humanitarian cause. This is the 21st fucking
century!"

Avigdor sits silently, contemplating the idea.

Rachmani continues, "The prime minister is going to shit bricks.
And here's the other catch, Avi: You need him to shit, like, ten bricks. You
need to call him out. Hamas and Hezbollah, those terrorist bastards, don't
care about international media coverage. They couldn't care less about U.N.
resolutions. But the prime minister, he very well may want to be reelected
to change some policies. His staff may start to feel the heat and wonder if
exceptions must be made. You are just the person to apply it. Avi, do you
understand what I am telling you?"

"I do. And this much… I can do."

33

Modi'in City
Chashmona Region
Spring 307 BCE

THE WIND KICKS UP GENTLY from the west and carries with it the faint sound of a bird's song. Dust rises and settles in the distant plains with each strong gust of air. The tranquility and serenity of the setting belies the dynamic between father and son. Looking out over the yellow-orange basin from the comforts of their courtyard, Yochanan and Simon go at it once again.

"Why don't we kick them out of our land?" protests Yochanan. "They do not belong here. God, creator of heaven and earth, promised this land to our people. It is ours."

"It is Elijah the Prophet who will deliver us from the hands of the heathens, not you and not anyone else," Simon responds.

"No, Father! Let us take up arms and fight for our nation and for our land. We have nothing to fear. You could lead us. Like the priests of old."

For Simon, Jewish law dictates life. He cannot think of a stronger argument than proving his point based on the law. He refuses to lose his temper this time, and in a calm and measured voice he says, "Carrying weapons, as you know, is forbidden on Shabbat—is that not so?"

"Yes," concedes the boy.

"Do you know why it is forbidden to carry a weapon on Shabbat? Because weapons are a disgrace to those who bear them!" He raises his voice. "We are the people of the book, of the soul and of the mind. Not of war and not of weapons. I will hear no more of such talk."

Even while he states these words so emphatically, Simon is not convinced anyone really believes them. Yochanan does not feel beholden to the way Simon and the sages interpret the law.

That night, after the discussion between Yochanan and Simon, Natan the Pious holds a lecture packed with people. He begins his meditative monologue by asking a question.

"Why does the Torah begin with the creation of the world?"

These opening rhetorical questions are not meant to prompt verbal responses. They are a technique employed by skilled speakers who know that, if they can get their listeners thinking, their message will settle more deeply into their consciousness.

Natan continues, "Is not the Torah a book of laws? Do we really understand how God, master of the universe, created the world? Of course not. So why begin with the creation of the world? Listen closely, my beloved students. The Torah begins with creation so that no one can ever question the right of the Jewish people to the land of Israel. The One who created the entire earth is the One who gave this piece of land to Abraham, Isaac, Jacob and their descendants.

"God exhorted his people to expel all foreigners from his land, lest they lead you astray! It is the Torah that says these words, not I." Natan pauses, he looks down at the text in front of him and reads the words: "You must doom them to utter destruction, grant them no terms and give them no quarter. You shall not intermarry with them. Do not give your daughters to their sons or take their daughters for your sons." Natan gets louder. "These are the words of our Torah. How dare we ignore them?"

Yochanan feels enraged as he thinks of the gymnasium, not two parsings away. He wonders about the history of his people, and how ashamed those great founders of Judaism would be about the passivity of the populace in the face of such naked attacks on their faith.

Natan is a master orator who knows how to employ words and

inflections to create visual images that elicit signs of agreement. The young men who gather to hear him talk nod their barely whiskered faces and elbow one another to demonstrate their agreement.

"Yes, weapons are forbidden on the Sabbath," Natan says, recounting a line of reasoning he once heard from Simon's camp, "but they are permitted during the six days between Sabbaths—are they not?"

"Yes! They are allowed!"

"How, then, can violence from those weapons be fundamentally against the teachings of our faith? Did David not slay Goliath with a stone and slingshot? Did Solomon not wield a sword?"

"Aye!" the crowd responds.

"If these heathen Greeks are to live in our midst, in our land, the land rightfully given to us by God, creator of the heavens and the earth, they must follow the biblically mandated laws and pay taxes to the Judean state."

Natan makes these arguments in full knowledge that they will strike the Greek occupiers as absurd, that they could potentially prompt retaliatory action.

"We will not live in submission in our own land! By doing so, we commit the most abominable sin—the desecration of God's name!"

As he leaves Natan's lecture, Yochanan thinks of all the personal slights he's felt from the Greeks around town. Taking the need to resist as a given, he contemplates the best way to proceed.

Diadochi, the eldest son of Antipater the regent, on more than one occasion has challenged Yochanan to a wrestling match in the gymnasium. This, of course, is out of the question. Never would Yochanan willingly participate in such a thing. He believes he needs to model a revulsion with Greek traditions to demonstrate to his peers that they should as well. Other Judean teenagers are less oppositional.

The Greek youth make their presence known in the village bazaar and marketplace. The Judean boys and girls are mesmerized by Greek fashion and culture. In the face of all the Jewish law, the lack of corresponding rules strikes many young Jews as a welcome change. Greek influence sneaks its way into the Jewish household, and there is very little that can be done to stop it. A good percentage of Jewish youth study at the gymnasium, dress like Greeks and speak like Greeks. Of course, they only eat permitted foods and observe the laws of modesty. But the hold of the old ways on the young is slipping.

Had the Greeks just minded their own business, Natan's words might have rang a bit more hollow. Rare is the young person willing to give his life, or take up arms, to defeat amiable visitors. The Greeks behave like hosts and not guests. Bad hosts at that. Particular incidents spark outrage.

On the eve of the Sabbath, Diadochi and his friends accost Rivka, a young girl from the village. Despite her mother's warnings, she went out alone to run errands before the holy day. On her way from the grocer, as she carries the night's ingredients, she finds herself in a lonely alley. When she sees a few Greek boys ahead of her, she turns to go down another route. But that path is blocked as well. Before she can understand where they are coming from, she is surrounded. The boys spit on her and kick her. Diadochi mockingly says to her, "Next time, we will bring you to the gymnasium and use your lovely body for exercise." Thankfully, the girl does not get hurt. More than anything, they frighten her. She returns home crying.

The news travels fast, and the already tense Jewish populace learn of this assault quickly. When the news reaches Simon, he is relieved the girl was not raped. He doesn't verbalize it, but he has a daily reminder that such things are possible at the hands of the Greeks.

When he explains that perspective to his son, Yochanan cannot see Simon's silver lining. He is enraged that such an assault would go unpunished. The morning after the incident, on the Sabbath day, he let it be known that he is going to the gymnasium to confront Diadochi. A handful of Jewish boys follow, vowing to defend their friend if trouble arises, but secretly wondering if they would have the courage to do so.

The entrance to the gymnasium is a tall arch etched with an image of Aphrodite. The large structure contains open spaces. From the entrance, Yochanan can see the bathhouse. Alongside the perimeter of the gymnasium, older men gather at a series of covered porticos.

Yochanan is greeted by one of the *gymnastai*, coaches, and they invite him in. The gymnastai are always happy to see Judean locals enter the gymnasium. They view their jobs as cultural influencers as much as athletic coaches. They recruit the stronger and fitter boys daily and creatively. Every gymnastai in the area has taken a particular interest in Yochanan.

"I am here to challenge Diadochi," Yochanan announces. He thinks that this might be perceived as aggressive, and is slightly surprised when a gymnastai responds.

"Lovely." The red lipstick amplifies his smile. "Follow me," he says as he leads them across the open field of the gymnasium.

Neither Yochanan nor any of his peers have set foot in this place before. They try to hide their surprise at the numerous activities and competitions going on. People wrestle in each corner. The old men sit, sip and take notes on some of the matches.

"Someone is here for me, Gymnastai?" comes a voice from behind one of the columns.

"Yes, Diadochi."

Out from behind the gleaming white pillar steps a well-built, slender 18-year-old. His overindulged upbringing makes him arrogant and loathsome, but his training has sharpened his biceps and calf muscles, on full, impressive display in the skimpy Greek outfit,. Most boys would be daunted by the prospect of going against him. Not Yochanan.

A crowd gathers in anticipation of this match. Yochanan cracks the knuckles on his hand as Diadochi hands his robe to some compatriot and saunters out to the sandy pit.

"I have been challenged and I am here to fight," says Yochanan. The crowd laughed.

"You have been challenged?" the gymnastai asks. "You showed up here unannounced. Who has challenged you?"

"An affront to the honor of a Jewish woman is a personal affront to me as well. These boys," he motions to Diadochi and his friends, "they know why I am here. I demand a fight."

Diadochi rolls his shoulders and prances on his toes. "Then you will have a fight."

The gymnastai asks Yochanan, "Do you know the rules of wrestling, young man?"

Yochanan does not nod. He does not acknowledge the question in any way. He just walks up to Diadochi, grabs him by his hair and spins him around. He puts one hand around his neck as Diadochi grasps desperately behind him to regain his footing. Before anyone can respond to this breach of wrestling protocol, Yochanan puts his other arm around the torso of his opponent and lifts Diadochi over his head. He holds him there for a second, as if to torture him with the prospect of what is coming. Then he launches Diadochi a meter through the air and to the ground.

Pfftccckkk.

The sound echoes in the Gymnasium. Those who hear it, and those who watch as Diadochi rolls over to reveal a shoulder pulled out of its socket, know what has happened.

"Ahh!" Diadochi grimaces in pain.

"Bad form…" a referee calls out.

"That isn't permitted…." Diadochi screams in a pathetic voice.

Yochanan, who at this point is being restrained by his Judean friends, snarls, "Bad form? I don't give a shit about your traditions. I will kill you the next time you touch anyone from our village."

Yochanan continues in a loud and aggressive tone: "Is there anyone else who wants to challenge me to a wrestling match?"

With those words, Yochanan and the Judean boys leave the gymnasium. He walks the steps down and can hardly think for the buzzing in his own ears. The other Judean boys chatter childishly.

"That was amazing."

"You showed them."

"That'll do it…"

That will not do it, Yochanan knows. *That will most certainly not do it.* Unless, that is, by do it one means that his actions will incite a full-out war, because they might just do that. He might have just set off the Jewish people's struggle for independence. *How was I to know that Diadochi would be such a terrible fighter? It was too easy.*

When Simon hears of the event, he is both furious and terrified. He knows that his power and influence only runs so far in the Greek community. How can he protect Yochanan when the boy insists on seeking out trouble?

The boy is only trouble. What will I do with him? He doesn't pray anymore, he doesn't take his studies seriously, and now he threatens to kill the son of the Antipater.

A combination of fortuitous events averts Yochanan's arrest and punishment. The incident happened in the gymnasium under the auspices of the coaches and administrators. They were responsible for the matters that occurred there. Any injuries or assaults that take place in the gymnasium are chalked up to education and cannot be prosecuted under Greek law.

That isn't the whole story. In addition to Simon being a well-respected man among the Greek nobility, further publicizing this incident will only embarrass Diadochi and his family.

Simon is furious with Yochanan. Despite his ability to visualize the face of the young Jewish girl who had been so scared that she urinated on herself from the taunting of Diadochi and his gang, Simon insists that what Yochanan did was wrong.

"Please, my son," Simon implores, "get back to your studies. My teachers always taught me that it is better to be the persecuted than the persecutor. This lesson is learned from the dove and the pigeon. No bird is more persecuted than the dove and pigeon, and it is no coincidence that no bird is more eligible for the alter before God than the dove and the pigeon. Just as Abraham went to the mountain to offer his son to God, we too must accept God's commands and act accordingly."

From Yochanan's perspective, the advice starts poorly and worsens. The wedge that has been growing between Yochanan and Simon grows more decisive with each word. For Yochanan, being likened to a dove is the ultimate indignity. Not to mention the association with Abraham. *It sounds like Simon would offer up his own son if he thought there was a slight chance it would please some distant deity.*

"You misunderstand my fundamental nature, Father."

"How so?"

"Never, Father, never will I be a sacrifice on an altar. Never. If I must go down, I will go down fighting for God's honor."

34

Tel Aviv, Israel
September 2006

I T FINALLY SINKS IN. COHEN understands what Rachmani is saying.
The terrorists who kidnapped his grandson could not care less one way
or the other. Israel starving the story of media attention is bullshit. Media
is not what they are after. That strategy might work in other parts of the
world—the Middle East is another animal. For them, this is a battle on
behalf of Allah, and Allah has time on his hands. They're playing the long
game. Cohen knows enough history to understand that the indoctrinated
militants fighting the terror war of Hamas and Islam are not in this for a
better quality of life for themselves. For them, it's a war that started 1,400
years ago and may well be fought for another 1,400 years. What's the life of
the enemy of Allah worth?

Keep the story alive. Keep it in the media and play their game. If I un-
derstood Rachmani correctly, that will not only keep Lior alive but also make
this an international humanitarian cause that will pressure the Israeli gov-
ernment to negotiate his release. No prime minister of Israel wants the blood
of an Israeli soldier on his hands! The one promise that the Israeli military
makes to each and every one of its soldiers is that they will do everything in
their power to bring anyone who wears the IDF uniform home. The pressure

has to be placed on our elected officials. The burden is on us and not them.

Avi has a small apartment in Tel Aviv that he uses on occasion just to sleep. He keeps it as a gift to give to the first of his grandchildren who marry. *It can be Lior,* he thinks. As he leaves Rachmani's office, his mind races. He will convert his Tel Aviv apartment into his personal command center. No. Better yet, "The War Room."

He wastes no time. He calls Shula, his secretary of seventeen years at the Beth Halochem, the center for military veterans.

"*Ken*," says the annoyed voice at the other end of the receiver.

"Shula, this is…"

Before Cohen can finish his sentence, Shula begins, "I am so sorry. I heard the horrible news about your grandson. Avi, what can I do for you and Maya?"

"Shula, please meet me at my flat in Tel Aviv in half an hour. Bring your laptop. I am going to need your help." He makes mental lists in his mind. This is the time to call in a lifetime of favors.

Avigdor speeds into the heart of Tel Aviv's business district and stops at Mahsanei Hashmal Appliance Warehouse. He flags down a young salesperson talking on his cell phone and heavily chomping down on gum. The salesperson pretends not to notice, holds out his five fingers together and moves them in an up and down motion, which in Israel is a signal for patience. Patience is not what Avi is capable of exercising at this moment. "I need three flat-screen televisions delivered immediately to this address," he says.

The young man does a double take and speaks into his phone, "Sababa, Achi," and hangs up. "Three flat-screens, yes, which size? And which model?" Avi just points at a television that seems adequate and asks for three of them to be shipped immediately to his apartment.

He hands his credit card to the young man. "Have them sent over immediately." The young man senses the urgency. He promises the delivery will happen before the day's end.

Avi dials Bentzi, a fifteen-year veteran at HOT Telecommunications, Israel's premier cable company, and calls in the first favor. "Bentzi—*dachuf*, its urgent. I need a crew at my flat in Tel Aviv. I need to hook up three televisions to cable."

"What's going on, Avi?"

"The boy that was taken is my grandson. He is Maya's son. Bentzi, I need your help now!"

"Holy shit, Avi, we are on our way." There is camaraderie among men who fought together. Avi expects nothing less from Bentzi and from the countless others he calls upon.

By the time Avi reaches the flat on the corner of Ben Yehuda and Gordon, Shula is already waiting by the door with her laptop and a brief-case full of papers. Before Avi can open the door, Shula takes charge. "We need to make a list…" is the last thing Avi hears as he enters the dark apartment and is overwhelmed by a sense of loneliness and fear. The task at hand is overwhelming.

"Avi, let's make a plan, tell me what has to be done," Shula says.

"Shula, I don't know where to begin." Avi looks deep into her eyes. "I just met with Rachmani, head of Aman. He told me the only hope Lior has of ever coming home is by keeping this story alive. Making sure it's in the press and on world news every single day. We have to make sure the conscience of our people is tested every day that Lior is in captivity. Every citizen of this country, every Jew and non-Jew with a moral compass, has to know who Lior Samet is and where he is!"

"But Avi, isn't that exactly what Hamas wants? Isn't that playing their game? They want publicity more than anything else. Avi, this doesn't make any sense."

"I know this goes against everything we have been made to believe—Shula, don't fight me on this. That is what he told me, and I know he is right."

Avi steps away, looks out the window, turns back around and says, "One thing we know for sure is that our government has consistently failed in bringing home kidnapped soldiers. Lior's case is going to be different."

Every training, and every battle that Cohen has known was based on the promise that Israel's military is different. "We care about each and every soldier" and "No man is ever left behind in enemy territory" were imprinted in the subconscious of every IDF soldier.

"We don't pick the kind of war we will fight next. I didn't pick this battle, but I sure as hell will not lose it. Shula, we have our work cut out."

Shula is a single mother of three, all of whom served in the IDF. Her middle son, Yoni, lives in Amsterdam peddling souvenirs. Her daughter lives in Tel Aviv, also divorced, with two kids. Her youngest son is studying computer science at a technical school in Be'er Sheva. Shula always considers herself a sensitive person despite her rough demeanor and impatient personality. She lights a cigarette, plugs in her laptop and places it on the small wood table against the wall in the living room. As her computer is booting up, a middle-aged man walks through the open door with a big box and announces, "I have two more on the way up." Avi says. As the delivery man walks out the door, another man with equipment on hand asks for Avigdor Cohen.

Shula points to Avi and the young man says, "Bentzi sent me to install cable—am I in the right place?"

In the span of moments, the room awoke. "Yes, yes," Avi responds. "We want to hook up three different television sets in this room." Shula looks around, first in amazement, then for a place to put out her cigarette.

"While we work at the table or on the couch, we can see what's going on in the news at all times," Avi says.

"Who do we know in the media? Wait, Barry's cousin is a reporter for Yediot," Shula adds. Barry is her ex-husband. The minute she utters those words, she becomes sick to her stomach at the thought of calling Barry for the telephone number. Every interaction with her ex turns into a misunderstanding and a yelling match. It never occurred to Shula that her husband of more than twenty years would betray her. She had heard and read about husbands and wives constantly committing adultery. In fact, it was her favorite topic when she overheard her parents and their friends while growing up. It was the most popular topic of gossip among her friends. But for some reason, when she got married to Barry, she was steadfastly convinced that her own marriage would be spared. It wasn't.

Recently, they have fought over the man their divorced daughter is dating. Barry drives a taxi in Tel Aviv and socializes with lowlives. As far as Shula is concerned, he is not able to discriminate between an appropriate man from a loser for their daughter.

"I'll call Barry and get the name of his journalist friend," she says.

"OK," Avi says. "Shula, let's make a list. Let's plan this correctly."

"Avi, the news reported this afternoon that kids at Dimona High School launched a Free Lior campaign. Maybe we should reach out to those kids?"

35

Modi'in City
Chashmona Region
Fall 306 BCE

THE OPPORTUNITY TO CELEBRATE PASSOVER in Jerusalem has not presented itself since their move to Chashmona. It has been eight years, and Simon is determined to make the pilgrimage to the Holy city this year.

"I don't know how much longer I have to live," he tells Malka, his wife. "I miss Jerusalem. For years, I exhorted people to come to Jerusalem for the holiday—how could I possibly not make the effort?"

She comes up with all sorts of reasons why he shouldn't go: "Your health is compromised. Your sight is weakening. I'm just not sure you can make the journey. The roads are treacherous and I hear the accommodations along the way are less than desirable. But all of those things are minor. I am most worried about the size of the crowds and our safety."

Simon disputes each of those reasons in the order they were posed: "Better to die on the road to Jerusalem than here. I don't need to see any further than the horse in front of me. The roads are fine. We will be perfectly safe. I am no longer the desirable assassination target I once was. We are going. The boy needs to see his grandparents, and this will be the right opportunity to announce his engagement."

"Have you told him yet of this engagement?"

"Why do I need to hurry to tell him? He will do as he is told."

"He very rarely does what he is told, Simon. And, in this instance, I think discussing the plans with him is reasonable. You had a long conversation with your own father about our match before the broader public knew of it." A smile comes across Malka's face. "At least you had enough time to familiarize yourself with the painful idea!"

"Nothing about marrying you has been painful, my love." Simon smiles warmly and kisses her on the cheek.

Her ability to make him laugh as she gets her point across, or at least to draw a smile, is consistent and endearing. Malka is by all standards a saintly woman. Despite Simon's sudden marriage to Yael years earlier, which was as outrageous as it was out of character, she had adopted the boy as her own after the death of his mother. If anyone suspects anything, it has to be Malka. If anyone believes it is *impossible* for Simon to have fathered the child that quickly, it is certainly she. And yet, her devotion to Simon never wanes. Even while his attention is completely devoted to the well-being of the boy at the expense of their two daughters, she never complains. No one sacrificed more than Malka, not even Simon. He gave up his influence but preserved his status. Malka moved an entire family to a village. In Jerusalem, she enjoyed every luxury that made life easier and more efficient, servants trained to work for someone like her, and a network of family and friends. In Chashmona, Malka has next to nothing. She now cooks many of their meals, something she hasn't done since the earliest years of their marriage. She has no female family members to confide in. There are no events to attend to break up the monotony of the day.

It would be easier if she still had the girls, or their children, to distract her. But the daughters are married with children of their own and they now live back in Jerusalem. Yochanan rarely turns to her for conversation or help with tasks. Though she worries about the long journey at their older age, she relishes the notion of returning to Jerusalem for the holidays. Malka is not completely sure why she is playing devil's advocate and not seizing the opportunity to spend the festive holiday in Jerusalem.

On numerous occasions over the years, she has pleaded with Simon to come along with her, but he always refused. "Who will teach the boy if I go?"

"Don't you want to see your daughters, Simon?"

"Of course I want to see them."

"Well, it would be hard for me to convince them of that, seeing as you have refused to visit for a couple of years now. You must live your affections, dear, not just talk about them."

Rarely does Malka get her way with Simon. This time, she is more than happy to let Simon convince her that going to Jerusalem for Passover is a good idea.

"If this is what you want, then we will go."

Simon reaches across the wood table and takes Malka's hand. "Thank you, dear. I know this will be a sacrifice for you."

She grasps it joyfully. "Thank you. We will make the most of it." She smiles as she looks at him for a moment. Then she lowers her eyes in a gesture of modesty. "We will make this the most beautiful holiday."

The thought of celebrating Passover in the capital brings back memories for Simon, some not so pleasant. This festival in particular brought a huge number of pilgrims who came from all over Israel. Some even journeyed for months from overseas. As a young man on track to a promising career, Simon was appointed by the Great Assembly to oversee improvements of the roads, squares, and ritual baths in preparation for the influx of people. The city had plenty of reason to roll out the red carpet and welcome visitors. The time was a boon to local merchants, as the visitors spent money on food, lodging, and entertainment. When he was initially given the task, Simon failed to anticipate the complex nature of the responsibility. The weather and economic factors would prove frustrating over the preceding months.

Passover is always in the spring season. While the calendar is lunar, the holiday seasons are kept consistent by adding a thirteenth month seven times every nineteen years. The spring season meant roads damaged by winter rains. Graveyards had to be clearly marked so that pilgrims would not defile themselves before entering Jerusalem. The ritual baths had to be cleaned, and bathhouses inspected. In addition, the marketplaces, town squares and bazaars had to be auctioned out to vendors and local dealers.

Every decision had a consequence. Families and clans vied for the opportunity to make money. They wanted construction contracts, maintenance contracts and management agreements. Others wanted premium space to sell their wares. The expectation was to give preference to local vendors, and it was Simon's job to vet out the scammers. Simon did his best to hand out those spots fairly and honestly, though it was difficult.

The minute it was announced that young Simon was appointed by the Jerusalem board of governors to oversee preparations for the Passover pilgrimage, people began to stalk him. He had to hire a bodyguard for fear of being assaulted. Some came with bribes, others with threats. The most vicious were the members of the clay-oven unions. Ovens were necessary throughout the city to bake *matzah*, the traditional unleavened bread necessary for the Passover holiday, and to appropriately roast the Paschal lamb. Per the biblical mandate, the Pascal lamb had to be roasted and eaten on the same night. Nothing could be left over. This law, when combined with the number of people, caused some logistical headaches and demanded adequate planning. Months in advance, the oven union staked their positions throughout the city. No one dared interfere with their work. Sizable amounts of money would be made or lost during the weeks immediately prior to Passover and through the seven-day holiday.

Local merchants weren't the only beneficiaries. The priestly coffers were amply filled by the annual tax, called the half-shekel, that was paid for every man 20 years and older. This money was used for temple upkeep and maintenance.

The year he was in charge, everything went off without a hitch. A couple of angry vendors appeared at his doorstep, but even the most hostile of those were appeased by Simon's cool and logical responses to their protestations. While Simon received many accolades for his administrative skills, accounting abilities and negotiating talents, he vowed to never accept the assignment again. He wanted a job that didn't require twenty-four-hour protection from armed soldiers.

With those distant memories in mind, during the weeks leading up to Passover, Simon anticipates that all of Israel will converge on Jerusalem to bring their Pascal offering to the Holy Temple. He wants to make sure all the necessary accommodations are made in advance, so he sends Tobi to Jerusalem two weeks prior to make sure everything is set. He gives Tobi a half-shekel per household member and enough coin to reserve accommodations and time for usage of the oven.

"Try to get us rooms near our old place, or near the girls. Tobi, be safe on the road," Simon says.

"It will be done."

Simon and Malka are not the only ones eagerly anticipating the trip. Yochanan also wants to return to Jerusalem. It has been a number of years since he saw his mother's parents. They are the only real connection he has to the mother he never knew. He loves Malka and even calls her mother, but there are no secrets in the Priestly Quarters when it comes to genealogy. Pedigree is of the utmost significance when it comes to the priesthood. Ever since he was a child, he knew that Malka was his adopted mother, and that Yael, his biological mother, had died at his birth. Similarly, he'd always understood that Malka's parents are not his grandparents. Rachel and Samuel are his grandparents.

Yochanan has another reason for wanting to get to Jerusalem. He wants to get acquainted with the temple service. As Simon is a former high priest, he feels he is in line for a position in the temple. People usually start those sorts of jobs in their teen years. He could spend years in the lower positions before working his way up.

So, the time has come for him to meet the powerbrokers of the Jewish people. He wants to influence the political and religious future of the Jewish State, and Jerusalem is the center of the empire.

Ever since the incident with Diadochi, Yochanan has dedicated himself to enlisting a group of young men and women committed to defending the land of Israel, even if it means by force. Their spiritual mentor is Natan the Pious. They name their crew of enlisted men and women *the Maccabee*, a Hebrew version of the word "hammer" in Aramaic. The group meets in secrecy and each member maintains a vow of clandestineness. Yochanan has absolute faith in their dedication to the mission. Over a short period of time, the Maccabee grows in numbers and in influence. Their symbol is an embroidered star of David with a hammer at the center. They train in swordsmanship and hand-to-hand combat, and theorize about military strategy, often using the Bible as their guide. Their secret password and greeting is an acronym of the word Maccabee derived from a biblical verse: *Mi Kamocha Ba'Elim Adonai*, "Who is like You among the heavenly powers, Adonai?"

Yochanan is eager to introduce his following to the national leaders in Jerusalem. He is certain Simon's connections in the Priestly Quarters and in the Sanhedrin will embrace him and afford him the necessary opportunities he needs to prove himself. While Yochanan feels guilty, he does not share his plans with Simon. He believes it is a necessary secret for the safety and future of the Jewish nation. Simon will only try to stop him, and Yochanan is convinced Simon is wrong on this. Something needs to be done.

Yochanan has never envisioned his future being in Chashmona. He hopes to marry Hanah and move to Jerusalem, intern with the Kohanim and work his way up to power. His dream, which he only shares with Hanah, is to throw the Greeks out of the state, peacefully or forcefully. There can be nothing less than an autonomous state for the Jewish people.

Yochanan first noticed Hanah at one of Rabbi Natan's lectures. Not many women and girls attend, but Hanah is a regular. The few women who do attend sit in the back to the left, behind a hanging linen cloth. Hanah has none of that. She always sits in front of the linen cloth. On one occasion, Rabbi Natan asked her to move. In response, she lifted the linen cloth and hung it to the side. If Natan was going to demand she move, she was going to move the corresponding impediment to full participation in the meetings.

At first, Yochanan is offended by her boldness and even questions Rabbi Natan about the wisdom of allowing her to attend his lectures. Natan may want more propriety, but when faced with kicking out women or letting them push the boundaries, he airs on the side of tolerance.

"Torah and the word of God does not discriminate," he answers Yochanan's protestations. "Go and speak with her. Find out what moves her soul before you pass judgment." That advice seems like a great idea to Yochanan.

Hanah is beautiful but not delicate. She is taller than her peers but shorter than Yochanan. Her modest dress does not hide her curves, though she certainly does not flaunt them. Her sun-bronzed skin is a gentle olive color that perfectly accentuates the flecks of green in her eyes. During a rare bit of daydreaming in Natan's lectures, Yochanan has even taken notice of her lips. There is nothing extravagant about them, really, except for the way she purses them when she is thinking deeply. When Natan speaks aggressively of the Greek influence in Israel, she furrows her brow and puckers those lips. To Yochanan, it is an irresistible habit. Her hair, which he only catches glimpses of, is brown and curly.

Hanah's best quality in Yochanan's eyes is that she does not trifle with nonsense. She doesn't trudge around with a false modesty, trying ever so subtly to get the attention of boys. She does not laugh a bit too long or loudly to gain an audience. She simply completes her tasks and goes about her work with a steady dedication. Having grown up on a farm, she doesn't fear work. She doesn't have the tender hands of a spoiled brat. Yochanan likes the fact that this is a woman who can fend for herself.

Not that he cares, but Yochanan knows what the protests to their marriage will be. Simon wants someone high class for his son. The middle-class daughter of an uneducated dairy farmer is not what he has in mind. She is a bit old to be single. If Yochanan were to profess his affections, others might worry, "Why isn't she already married?"

Hanah is older than Yochanan, but their chronological years are blurred by his size. She is nearly 18, and she is ready to marry. Yochanan keeps this quiet for now, but he is not worried about the ensuing struggle. He plans on telling Simon and Malka sometime in the near future that he will chose a wife for himself.

36

La'uf
Lior's Mind

Memory: Dead Cat.

I wasn't sure if they were talking about me. They were definitely talking to me. The assholes that slept through their *shmira*, guard duty, and left me out there in the freezing cold for a second shift. It is forbidden to leave your post if you are not replaced. When I confronted the bully, he called me a "dead cat." I later found out he was referring to my new green *kumta*, beret. It was called a dead cat because it was stiff like a dead cat. I had no idea. It took me some time to figure out that guys purposefully abuse their beret, and even shave it, so that it becomes flexible and looks used. I wish I would have known. That's why I was a target for the bullies in the army. I really hated them.

37

Gaza City, Gaza Strip
December 2006

T HE DOOR OPENS AT THE same time as usual. What happens next is entirely different. Three masked men follow Faisal, each carrying an AK-47. One holds his like he is expecting a confrontation with this un-armed Israeli soldier. The other two sling their guns over their shoulders. They carry video equipment in their hands. To Lior's infinite surprise, they even have lights and tripods on which to secure them. They waste no time setting up.

"Soldier," Faisal says in an unfamiliar tense tone, "take off your clothing and sit here."

Lior does as he is told. Faisal then walks three or four steps to the chair where Lior now sits. It is then that Lior notices the beard trimmer Faisal carries in his left hand.

"Sit still," Faisal orders as he gently grabs Lior's head. He starts in the back, running the trimmer from the nape of Lior's neck up to the top of his head. Then, Faisal moves on to the sideburns. He finishes with the top. The entire haircut takes less than two minutes. Faisal pulls out an electric shaver. Not that Lior has much facial hair. Puberty came on late for the rest of his body—on his face, it seems to have never appeared. With a few strokes of the electric shaver, Lior's face is completely hair free.

"OK. Now get up," Faisal says as he turns off the hum of the shaver. "Aida!" he then shouts to the door.

At his command, the cleaning woman bustles into the room with a broom and dustpan. She sweeps the hair clippings. She takes them out of the room and comes back with a pair of hangers carrying Lior's freshly laundered IDF uniform. Meanwhile, the other soldiers are running cords from the camera to the lights.

"Put this on immediately." Faisal takes the uniform from Aida and hands it to Lior.

The soldier does as he is told. Afterward, Lior stands awkwardly in the starched uniform, unsure of what to do next. The cameramen finalize things and Faisal watches them. One of the men with the guns turns toward Faisal and says something in Arabic that Lior doesn't follow. Faisal nods and turns. "Listen carefully, soldier. We are going to videotape you and send it to your government. I want you to write a message and read it slowly and carefully. Introduce yourself and state your Israeli identification number, and the names of your parents and siblings. I will need you to state that you expect the government of Ehud Olmert to fully comply with the terms of the deal set forth by the negotiators who represent your interests and who wish you a safe return home."

Lior stands frozen, at a loss for words.

"Do you understand?"

"Yes, of course. I need a pen and some paper."

"Oh…" Faisal nods and purses his lips. He looks around the room as if he expected this sparsely supplied place to have such things on hand. He, of course, finds nothing.

Faisal catches Lior's eye and the Israeli soldier thinks he notices a flicker of apprehension therein. Then Faisal turns to ask the masked men, in Arabic, if they happen to have a pen and paper. They look at each other through their masks, and one raises his hands in confusion.

The cameraman, who has been doing most of the barking, turns to the man closest to the door and orders him out of the room. He runs out, presumably in search of a pen and paper. Faisal takes a deep breath and tries to pretend that everything is going as planned.

"We need you to state a memory," he says to Lior, "that only you would know and that would be recognized by someone close to you. We want to leave no doubt you are the one speaking."

One of the masked men taps Faisal on the shoulder and leans into his ear to speak a few words to him. Faisal nods in agreement, turns to Lior and says, "Add the fact that the Mujahedeen of the al-Qassam Brigades are treating you very well."

Lior quietly recites the things he is supposed to say in his mind. The pen and paper are taking a bit longer than expected. He holds out his fingers and goes through the major components:

Soldier information.

A personal story.

That you are treated well.

As Lior counts, Faisal nervously moves the only chair in the room, which Lior is going to sit in, from one corner to the other. At this moment of stress and anxiety, Lior longs for the Faisal who had spoken with him over the last three days, the one who was dogmatic but at least considerate. He isn't going to get that Faisal today. One of the masked men yells impatiently to the other remaining masked man. At that, the second one leaves the room, presumably to look for the guy looking for pen and paper.

Lior thinks to himself that, if his life were not at stake, this would feel a bit cartoonish. The guns are real enough though. It is no fantasyland, unorganized as these kidnappers are.

Faisal turns to Lior to tell him what he has ascertained already. "We are waiting for a pen and paper."

Another ten minutes go by and the third masked man carrying an AK-47 storms out of the room in exasperation and mumbles, "Elif air ab tizak." It is just Lior and Faisal, and Lior lets out a slight guffaw. He doesn't know a ton of Arabic, but he knows numbers and slang. And he knows that what he has just heard means, "A thousand dicks up your ass."

Faisal turns and smiles softly at Lior. But he is anxious as well.

Within minutes, the three masked men return yelling at one another. They hand Faisal a pen and paper. Faisal turns to Lior. "Here is a pen and paper. Now write your speech."

Lior sits and thinks for a second about the right way to start. Writing had never been his forte in school.

"Hurry up!" Faisal says impatiently.

"Faisal, I need time."

"You can't have it—these men are impatient."

Lior begins to write, *My name is Lior Samet. I am the son of Maya and Leon Samet, and the brother of Noa. My Israeli Identification number is 400097638. Today is…*

"Faisal, what's the date?"

"It's the fourteenth day of December, 2006."

Lior is jarred by the passage of time. He counts on his fingers. *July. August. September. October. November. December. That's six. More than six months has elapsed since my abduction.*

"Read to me what you have already written," Faisal barks.

Lior reads his brief start.

"Hurry up. Add your home address and name the village you live in."

"OK."

"When you state the date, I want you to say that you are holding today's edition of the newspaper, *Felesteen*, and hold it up to the camera so that the date can be seen by your government."

"Where is the paper?" Lior asks innocently.

Faisal rolls his eyes, turns to the masked men in disbelief and asks, "Who has today's El Phalestine newspaper?"

Each of the men look at one another—all three at a loss for words. Two of them even shrug their shoulders.

Faisal turns to the man closest to the door and, in a forced calm voice, asks him to fetch a newspaper.

"Kol Khara!" *Eat shit,* the man says as he snaps and walks out the door.

Once Lior has written all of the practical details required of him, Faisal gives him more orders. "Lior, I want you to write something like 'My government will do what it can to expedite my release.'"

Before Lior can finish writing that sentence, Faisal yells at him. "Read to me what you wrote."

Lior reads it in Hebrew, and Faisal translates for the others.

"No, you idiot!" one of the masked men interrupts the interpretation. "He should tell them how much he longs to get home and how every day he reads the newspapers in order to get information about what his government is doing to secure his release—write that."

Faisal nods and gives Lior these orders. He then adds, "Make sure you send your regards to your family and tell them you miss them. Your mother is surely worried."

"Read it now."

Lior reads what he has, Faisal translating all the while. When he finishes, it is clear from the discussions between the group that he isn't finished.

"The memory," Faisal says to him. "You still need a memory that will prove that you are the real speaker."

"I can't think of anything," Lior protests.

"Just think of something small. Something your parents or siblings would know, but that no one else would recognize."

One of the masked men bumps Faisal on the shoulder and says, "Also, tell them that we provide you with newspapers and radio information and you are desperately waiting to hear news about your release."

"But that is a lie, Faisal. I don't read the newspaper or listen to the radio!"

"Silence," Faisal yells. "Do as we say!"

He then leans in and says quietly, "Don't worry, I will bring newspapers. But it is important that they know that what they say and do will be heard by you."

One of the soldiers angrily makes the motion of writing to Lior, which he interprets as a demand that he should finish up.

"This takes time—it's not something I can do right now while you stand here," Lior protests.

"We are not going anywhere," Faisal says. "Write!"

After plenty of starts and stops, a few more interruptions and suggestions from Faisal's masked friends, and after the El Phalestine newspaper finally appears, the final draft reads:

> I am Lior, son of Maya and Leon Samet, brother of Noa, and I live in the city of Dimona. My identification number is 400097638.
>
> Today is Monday, December 14, 2006. As you can see, I am

holding today's edition of the newspaper, Palestine, December 14, 2006, published in Gaza.

I read newspapers on a regular basis in search of information about my case. I hope to find information indicating that my release and return home is imminent. I have been waiting and hoping for the day on which I will be released.

I hope that the current government, led by Ehud Olmert won't waste this opportunity to reach a deal, and as a result, I will finally be able to realize my dream of uniting with my loved ones.

I want to send my regards to my family and to tell them that I love them and miss them very much. To my mother, I want to say that I am healthy, and I pray for the day that I will see you again.

Abba and Noa, do you remember when you came to visit me on my day off during Pesach last year? We went to Latrun. We saw the exhibits and laughed at the familiar faces on the photographs on the walls. We then had lunch at Mitbach Rama in Kibbutz Moshav Nataf. We met up with Ima in Tel Aviv and poked fun at her for her aversion to visiting Latrun.

I want to tell you that I feel well, in terms of health, and the Mujahedeen of the Izz ad-Din al-Qassam Brigades, are treating me wonderfully. Thank you very much, and goodbye.

As he reads that final draft one final time for the approval of his captors, Lior is actually pleased with the writing. He knows that government and military experts, as well as his parents, friends, and relatives, will see this message.

"OK. Sit there," one of the masked men orders him.

All of a sudden, Lior becomes conscious of what he will look like on video. He isn't sure what makes him more nervous—the fact that his life depends on this speech or that camera that is filming him. He never, ever, makes speeches in front of other people. In fact, in the first year of high school, he'd refused to take part in a speech assignment. He'd taken a low grade and requested that he only have to read before the teacher. Lior prefers to be a spectator. He never places himself in the limelight. He is just as happy not being noticed, which made getting Moran's attention all the harder.

"OK. You ready?" Faisal asks.

"I guess," Lior replies as the lights come on.

"Action!"

38

La'uf
Lior's Mind

Memory: Guns

I didn't trust half the guys in my platoon with their guns. You basically sign your life over to that gun. You go everywhere with it, including the bathroom. If you lose it, you end up in prison. The IDF accepts no excuses for a missing weapon. And you're not even given a choice.

I never felt comfortable holding it. It's so cumbersome and bulky.

It was my sixth birthday party. I remember opening my birthday presents: books, toy trucks, a train set and games. Saba brought me a toy rifle. I could not have been more excited. It was the only gift I ran off to play with. Saba promised to show me his real guns one day. I could not wait. Even Noa was jealous.

Everything changed that night. "Leon, this is the

reality we are living," my mother yelled behind the closed door of her bedroom. Ima and Abba never yelled at each other.

"It's not the reality we have to perpetuate by raising our children with guns. I will not have your father influence my only son with his barbaric, ignorant, militaristic, violent views." Father's voice shook the entire house. I never heard him so angry. Ima cried.

The toy gun broke that night. My bedroom door accidently slammed close on the gun and shattered it to pieces. Saba never replaced it and neither did my parents.

Deep down, I always hated guns.

I could have reached for my weapon and shot. I didn't. I don't regret it.

39

Tel Aviv, Israel
December 2006

A VIGDOR COHEN IS FUMING. HE views, like everyone else, the video of Lior on prime-time television. "Why the fuck did I not know about this?" If there is something Avigdor hates more than anything else, it's not being kept in the loop. He found out that Maya and Leon were given a heads-up by the military that a video of Lior was delivered to major international networks by the German mediator in exchange for the release of twenty female prisoners. "Why am I the last one to hear about this?" Cohen yells out. The only one listening is Shula. Her heart hurts for Avi. He has done so much to keep the story alive. Sending out press releases to hundreds of reporters a day. Appearing in as many radio and televisions shows as will have him. Challenging the government to do more. He tirelessly spends every minute of every day reaching out to heads of governments, international religious organizations, and celebrities of every major country in the hope that keeping Lior on people's minds will keep him alive.

"Shula, call this number and ask for Moti Rachmani."

"The number doesn't exist, Avi—it's dead."

"Let me try." Avi dials the number Rachmani gave him. "It is a dead number. Shit."

"Please call Yehudith Goldwasser at the prime minister's office. Tell her I need to speak with Moti Rachmani. She will understand."

Within the hour, Avi's cell phone rings.

"Avi, this is Moti. You want to talk with me?"

"Moti, thank you for calling. The video, what does it tell us? Where is he? Does it offer any clues?"

"Listen to me, Avi. What you are doing is keeping your grandson alive. The last thing you want is Israel Security Services to send in commandos. It's a miracle we have no idea where he is. The minute we do it will mean the death of your grandson. You have to keep doing what you are doing and pray that Lior's captors don't make any mistakes. The government is caving in. I have to go."

"He's fucking right," Avi whispers to himself.

Modi'in City
Chashmona Region
Spring 306 BCE

WHAT WOULD NORMALLY BE A one-day journey is going to be broken up into two days. Malka insists that Simon not travel the entire distance in one sitting.

"He is not fit for such a journey. I will not have it."

The trip will include an overnight stay at an inn about halfway between Chashmona and Jerusalem. Finding an appropriate place to stay is no easy task. Inns on the thoroughfares of Judea have a reputation for attracting an unsavory clientele. The priests and rabbis often admonish those who visit the inns and partake in drinking and prostitution. Even though the overwhelming majority of travel lodgings are run by people who have little or no regard for the laws of Moses, Tobi finds an appropriate rest stop for Simon. This accommodation is about ninety stadions west of Jerusalem. It is run by a reputable Levite family and their children. They only serve kosher food and wine prepared by Jews. Modestly clad women or men serve the guests.

Provisions have to be purchased, prepared and packed. The women will need appropriate attire for a series of celebrations and holiday festiv-ities with family, friends and old acquaintances. Malka cannot present herself in Jerusalem like she has been doing in Chashmona over the last few years. Jerusalem is the capital. There she will mingle with the wives of dignitaries, scholars, priests and governors. She cannot remember the last time she permitted herself to be vain. She pulls out from under her mat-tress a flat bronze plate that she brought with her from Jerusalem. She can barely recognize the reflection she sees in it. Her face seems more wrinkled.

There was a time when her skin, the color of cinnamon, was soft like the belly of a baby. How the boys and men ravaged her with their eyes until, of course, she was spoken-for by Simon the Priest. She went from being a little, unknown girl from the Priestly Quarters to the wife of the honorable High Priest, Head of the Great Assembly, adjudicator and scholar Simon the Righteous. There was a time when he was the most powerful man in Judea. A part of her would have given up all the fame for a simple life.

"No sense in thinking about these things. Life moves forward, not backward," she says to herself. In the corner of the bedroom, she eyes the wooden chest that has not been opened in years. Malka carefully removes its cover and enjoys the texture and colors that spring out at her. She selects her favorite chiton, made of the finest Egyptian linen. As is expected of the garments of rabbi's wives, it has long sleeves. It fastens along the arms and belts at the waist into graceful folds. She also collects some of her jewelry—to accentuate the dress, not the person, she rationalizes. None of it is made of silver or gold, but it is beautiful nonetheless. The hairpin garnished with a carved flower completes her wardrobe needs for their holiday.

There will be plenty of kosher wine for Passover in Jerusalem. What they won't have is Chashmona's special brew of Passover date beer. Barley beer is forbidden on the Passover holiday because it is brewed from one of the five forbidden grains. The date beer on the other hand is completely permitted and will be a wonderful addition to the holiday festivities. The beer is brewed out in the date groves, far from the city and far from any product that might disqualify it for Passover use. During the date harvest, all available hands are sent to the fields to pit the dates. After the dates are pitted, they are crushed under stone cylinders, and then mixed with water and naturally fermented into an exquisite brew.

"One barrel or two?" Malka asks.

"Whatever you think, dear," Simon responds unenthusiastically.

Simon doesn't bother himself with any of the domestic preparation for the trip. He prepares by writing letters to the council of priests, to the head of the Sanhedrin, and to his personal friends, announcing his upcoming visit to Jerusalem. "It will be a short trip," he writes. "I look forward to seeing friends and acquaintances. Let me know if you will need my services and if I can deliver a study session." He also writes a note to Yael's parents—Yochanan's grandparents—announcing their arrival and hinting at the need to marry off their grandson.

If all goes as planned, the family expects to be in Jerusalem on the tenth day of Nissan, giving them ample time to prepare the Paschal lamb and assign those who will partake. Unlike every other temple sacrifice, the Paschal lamb must be completely eaten by those who present it.

Per the temple rules, worshippers have to furnish their own wood for the altar sacrifices. The Hellenist tax collectors do not make this an easy task. It is forbidden to use wood for purposes other than heat, construction or furniture. There is a heavy tax on all wood used for sacrificial purposes and often it is not allowed into Jerusalem by the Greek authorities. Yochanan suggests they build a chair and table of wood. "We will pass it through the tax collectors and gatekeepers as necessary home furnishing. Once inside Jerusalem, we can dismember them and use the wood for the altar." Simon isn't thrilled with the idea but he feels there is no choice.

Simon and Malka, per Tobi's advice, place coins in various hidden locations in their garments, bags, under the carriage and even below the testicles of the horse that will be pulling them. The coins will be used for supplies, road tax collectors and bribes.

The only thing left to do, which Simon dreads, is to inform Yochanan, that upon their arrival in Jerusalem, he will be engaged to marry the daughter of Rabbi Oshia, a distinguished scholar and leader. Yochanan was promised to her since he was a child.

Yochanan is 16 years old. Simon often says, "God blasts the bones of any man who remains unmarried after the age of 16. The finest students in the academy are the ones who marry at 16 because their minds are not overtaken by sinful thoughts."

41

Gaza City, Gaza Strip
December 2006

INSTANT CELEBRITY IS A STRANGE thing. To go from an anonymous member of the world to a character who merits a great deal of global attention can play tricks on the mind. It gives wings to hopes and future aspirations. When the broader universe takes note of you, it can lead you to think you are worth noting. Though he is famous largely through proxy, and though Lior is the one on video, it is Faisal's small bluebird room that is displayed on televisions all around the globe. It is his humble single bed, and his "guest," streamed endlessly on CNN, Al Jazeera, BBC and all of the local affiliates. His instructions and efforts led to the successful production of this film. As the news anchors speak in grave tones and attempt to deduce clues from a video devoid of them, Faisal is beyond pleased.

He feels certain his superiors will take note of his success and recognize his efforts by giving him some real responsibility in the fight for freedom. He has been involved in the cause for almost twenty years and his tasks have remained relatively minor. His boyish looks abandon him in every passing year; those thirty-seven years are beginning to show in the crinkles of his eyes and the specks of gray above his ears. His superiors have overlooked him on countless occasions. Surely, with his handling of Lior and the successful video, those who make the big decisions will learn his name.

These hopes rise in Faisal's heart every single time he sees the video on a new station. But those years that have given him signs of age have also given him a bit of caution. He knows enough to know that things don't always go as one hopes. He has tasted the bitter pill of disappointment frequently enough to fear it. The beginning of this experience is a case in point.

When he was assigned the secret mission of caring for the prisoner, Faisal originally thought that the task would bring him honor. It has brought nothing of the kind. Instead, Faisal endures almost daily mockery from his wife and her relatives. They watch him depart every day, hearing him explain that he has to go care for a prisoner. But they have no idea of the magnitude of that prisoner. Since they are in-laws, and since Faisal's in-laws often seem specifically engineered to be bigger pains in the ass than should be possible, Faisal goes quickly from hopeful that they would finally shut the hell up to dreading each new encounter with them.

His brother in-law has spent the past months spreading rumors that Faisal's twenty-plus years of dedication to the movement has earned him the title of private waiter to some unknown person. His mother-in-law openly laments that her daughter has married someone without prospects for advancement. "Why not a plumber or stone-mason?" is her chorus. His father-in-law takes great umbrage from his wife about nearly everything, yet he expresses no sympathy toward Faisal as he withstands her words. In fact, he often looks sideways at him with a mixture of disdain and silence, electing to ignore his daughter's choice in spouse as much as possible. Faisal longs for the day that he will earn the recognition he so deserves. He yearns to be useful to the cause he cares about so deeply. But above all else, he longs for a level of success that might enable him to tell his in-laws, once and for all, to go screw themselves.

That day will have to wait for a while longer. Everything surrounding Lior is couched in secrecy. Faisal cannot reveal to anyone about Lior—not even his own wife. That sort of thing is strictly forbidden. "Women are weak and not to be trusted with matters of great import," is a refrain he often hears in meetings with superiors and peers alike. But in matters such as these, the fewer people that know, the better. If anyone finds out that Faisal has any association with Lior Samet, his fate is death. That death would not be pleasant. It would be protracted and publicized and exemplified. Worse, his relatives will live their lives in shame, believing he cooperated with the Israeli military, conveniently confirming all their misconceptions.

There are moments when he doubts his own capacity. Faisal has no idea who he works for or who his real superiors are. Different couriers deliver messages. If you ask too many questions, you are suspected of working for the enemy. It is a world shrouded in mystery and fear; the currency of relationships is doubt and threats. All he and those like him have to motivate them is their belief and hope that they are doing God's work. They will surely see rewards for their efforts in the afterlife. But this world demands quiet. Faisal knows he is an important part of the resistance and freedom movement. He only wishes others would know as well.

Now that the video of his prisoner is all over the news, and even though his immediate family cannot know, Faisal hopes someone higher up in the ranks will include him in the grand mission of deliverance. He doesn't need to speak out about his role so much as he needs to know what that role will look like a year from now, three years out. Each time that bluebird wall pops up on Al Jazeera and BBC, Faisal gains confidence that those needs will be realized soon enough. He just needs to make sure he doesn't blow anything for the time being.

He turns off the television and walks up the stairs to see his guest with a lift in his step and grin on his bearded face. "Faisal!" Lior greets him as the door opens.

Lior is excited to see that he is without the other armed guards this morning.

"Congratulations, my dear guest!" Faisal replies kindly. "You and I have become an international sensation. People will be asking you for your autograph. I promised you a gift for writing so eloquently of your status. Let no one say that Faisal does not keep his word. Here it is."

Faisal unwraps a brand-new transistor radio and plugs it into one of the outlets in the room.

"A radio!" Lior greets the sight of this gift with excitement. He knows that he has just been given a metaphoric window into the world, a mental escape from the concrete confines of this tiny room.

"Pick a station. You will have perfect reception."

Lior fiddles with the dials. He is so grateful to Faisal for the gift. But it is certainly not a gift he knows how to operate. The knobs are foreign to Lior. The only radios he had ever really used were in the dashboard of his parents' car. He'd sometimes talked them into letting him turn the channel to '70s rock, especially when the news was slow. But those radios were digital. You just had to seek the right number with arrows. This radio has knobs, and Lior has to squint to read the little orange line as it moves in a circle between the numbers. He briefly passes a clear signal, then returns to it. All of a sudden, he hears Hebrew spoken as clear as day. It is the first time he has heard his native tongue—other than Faisal's pigeon efforts at it—in six months. His eyes swell as he listens to the DJ introduce the next song and describe some event that evening at a Tel Aviv club.

"Faisal, thank you. I don't know what to say other than thank you. I'm shocked. This is amazing."

"I am glad you are happy with it. I am pleased with how our video did yesterday. When a host is pleased, he should look to please his guest! Na?"

"Faisal, this music station is good. But how do I get a news station? Kol Israel? Israel news?"

"Easy enough, my guest." Faisal lifts the radio up so he can see the dial. "That station is Reshet Bet 95.5 FM—we listen to this station all the time. Very thorough. Here it is," he says as his fingers turn the knob ever so slightly, adjusting it to get the clearest signal possible.

As soon as the Hebrew words crackle audibly through the static, Lior hears the announcer like he is sitting next to him. "In the big story of today, and in the biggest change in this case in months, Al Jazeera and other news stations have been playing a video of the abducted soldier, Sergeant Cpl. Lior Samet."

The ringing in his ears begins as the first name is finished, and it becomes a fierce buzzing as that surname—Samet—echoes over the airwaves.

They are talking about me? I'm not a sergeant. Why would they call me sergeant?

The radio anchor continues, "The young man looks pale but seems to be in general good health. The video was authenticated by Israeli intelligence. They will not comment further on the matter, but it is believed that they are not able to trace anything in the video to any particular place. Ehud Olmert's government has been criticized for not doing enough to secure the release of Sergeant Cpl. Lior Samet. The prime minister's office responded to the video's release by insisting that Mahmoud Abbas take personal responsibility for the safe return of Sergeant Cpl. Lior Samet. Abbas has been under increasing scrutiny as this issue continues to ignite public outrage thanks to the ceaseless efforts of Brigadier General Avigdor Cohen, the young soldier's grandfather."

As a beer commercial blares out of the speaker, Lior turns the radio down and stares up into the blue corner of his room. He needs to think quietly. The more that he demands of himself to process what he has just heard, the more his mind sinks into a disorienting abyss. *I wonder what my parents are thinking. My mother must be so tormented. Do they actually miss me? Does the government really care? Aren't there more important things for them to think about? Does Moran even know I am missing?* He thinks of Noa, and his father, and his grandfather who everyone fears.

"Is this for real, Faisal?"

"Is what for real?"

"Is all of that happening? Have you seen it on TV?"

"It is indeed happening."

"Faisal, what's the point of all this? My parents must be sick with worry. Why can't you all just let me go?"

Faisal sits quietly for what feels like hours. He looks at the floor with his hands clasped together and his shoulders slumped over. Lior can tell that he is thinking of how to answer his question. Frustrated with the time it takes Faisal to respond, Lior blurts out, "Why am I being held against my will? Faisal, please, why are you doing this? You know this is wrong."

Faisal's silence snaps at this last statement. He has yearned for so long for someone on the other side of the coin, one of the parties responsible, to listen to his story. He has waited to unleash all of the heartache that burdens on his soul and so frequently darkens his mood. Close to twenty years of frustration and anger and bitterness spill from his lips in his snarled response, "Don't you dare blame me! How dare you ask me why am I doing this? I should ask you: Why did you do it? Why did you kill my father?"

"Huh?" Lior asks in confusion.

"You heard me. Well, not you personally, but your terrorist Zionist army killed my father. The callous government, whose uniform you wear, killed him for nothing—for no reason."

Lior sees tears well up in the corners of Faisal's eyes as he speaks, and thinks of his own dad. "What are you talking about? What happened to your father?"

"My father," Faisal inhales deeply to slow his emotions, "was a man who sought peace. He believed in peace. He provided abundantly for his family… my mother, my brothers and sister, his parents and his six brothers and sisters. He was a businessman. When I was just a teenager, he was flying from Lebanon to Cairo on a Libyan Airliner."

Faisal pauses and rubs his palms together, cracks his fingers. He then looks up from his downward posture and glares into Lior's eyes. "Do you understand what I am saying? Let me be clear. It was a commercial airliner full of innocent civilians, men, women and children. My apolitical father was one of them, my father who would throw me up in the air, who always smelled faintly of cigarettes and olives, and who cackled playfully at my mother. Your brave IDF pilots shot down that airplane for absolutely no reason."

"When? Why?"

"You weren't even born, Lior. It happened a long time ago. It was in the month of February at 10:30 a.m. He died along with all 115 passengers and twenty crew members, all of them civilians. *Rahamahon Allah Jamee'an*. May they rest in peace."

"I'm sorry, Faisal. But, I don't know what that has to do…"

"My father was a good man. His name was Mansour Ali Hamad. He loved peace and dreamed of a peaceful coexistence with our *Yahud* neighbors—and your terrorist Zionist army killed him. That is what this has to do with you. You are a member of that army. And we are the organizations and nations we… I don't want to talk about this anymore… but I want to make sure that you understand."

Lior stutters trying to summon a response. He wasn't even born until years after the Israeli Air Force downed the Libyan flight. Now that Faisal has reminded him, he remembers hearing vaguely about it in some class or on TV. But he has no idea why it happened or under what circumstances.

Surely, there are two sides to this story. But he feels intellectually unarmed in front of Faisal.

"I just don't know what to say, Faisal. I am so sorry for your loss, for what happened."

"Have you ever lost a family member, Lior?"

"No."

"It is a pain unlike any other."

"Faisal, I never meant to blame you. I'm just… confused, and I don't know how to handle any of this. And I don't really get why this is happening."

Faisal straightens up a bit and even flashes something of a wry smile. "I shouldn't bother you with these things. You didn't fly the jet or fire the warheads!"

"I wouldn't know the first thing about flying a jet."

"I don't know what got into me. You are different than the other soldiers I have met. You don't belong in that army of animals and pigs. I heard you did not fire even one bullet. Is this true?"

Faisal may have meant this as a compliment. He may have been looking for common ground. Instead he has settled on a dark and private shame that Lior has hoped was his and his alone.

How does Faisal know? Who else knows? Does my grandfather? His commanders? Moran?

"No, you are right. I did not," he says.

"Cheer up, Lior! I will see you tomorrow, my dear guest. Enjoy the gift."

As the door shuts, Lior is swamped in emotions. *What the hell was all that about, some plane crash? How in the world does that have anything to do with this kidnapping? How can Faisal conflate that event and this one? How might that vague and distant past justify these actions?* The other thought that plays over and over in his head is one of self-pity and regret: *I did not fire one bullet! Not one fucking bullet.*

La'uf
Lior's Mind

Memory: Birthday

My *Mem Mem*, platoon commander, gave me an extra break in honor of my birthday. So much time is wasted. I've known from an early age that dreaming is much better than real life. There was plenty of time for daydreaming in the army. It seemed like we were endlessly standing in lines, in formation, on guard duty— shit, that was nuts. And we were always being timed. Everything had to be on time. If the *Mefaked* said two minutes, he meant two minutes. We spent hours and hours on guard duty. Sometimes, it's a border or a no- man's land; other times, it's a city with store fronts, tire shops, electricians and men sitting around sipping black coffee.

43

Tel Aviv/Dimona, Israel
January 2007

W ITHIN MINUTES OF LIOR'S VIDEO being posted on YouTube, it goes viral. The video of Lior holding up a newspaper and making a statement has over 1 million views in the first twenty-four hours. This is exactly what Avigdor Cohen needs to generate worldwide awareness of Lior's plight and the humanitarian crisis associated with his abduction. Cohen is convinced Rachmani is right. Lior's abduction is not about Hamas. In other parts of the world, innocent people are abducted and ransomed in order to fund terror or other illicit activity. The policy of the West has traditionally been not to entertain any negotiations with those who promote such activities. Lior's abduction is different. Hamas does not need funding or media attention. Lior's abduction is about the Israeli government. The only thing that will bring him home is putting pressure on the government that is responsible for Lior's well-being.

In response to the video of Lior, Shula contacts every single news station, reporter and anchor she can find in Israel and invites them to a rally. The rally will take place in Dimona, Lior's hometown. The rally will be outside the high school Lior graduated. Brigadier General Avigdor Cohen, the mayor of Dimona, and numerous celebrities and sympathetic politicians will lead the rally.

"CNN promises to be there, as does BBC, FOX, and Skyway. All the Israeli channels and papers will be represented. Al Jazeera is not committing," Shula barks while staring at her computer screen.

The complexity of the issue does not escape Cohen. He has been warned. The government is calling this "an abduction." Lior was not taken on the battlefield. He was kidnapped in his own country while serving on guard duty. This language precludes the possibility of a prisoner exchange: If he is not a prisoner of war, how can he be exchanged for another prisoner? However, calling him a prisoner of war will condone, in some twisted way, the entire kidnapping. If every uniformed soldier is always at war, then they are always fair targets. The matter is further complicated by the politics surrounding these issues. Liberals want to bring Lior home but despise the fact that the young men are in uniform while the conservative-minded want a more militaristic state and refuse to negotiate with the enemy. Cohen's cause is an orphaned cause.

"I want Maya, Leon and Noa to stand right next to me at the rally."

"Avi, you know that's not happening. Maya believes this is wrong. The government officials have completely brainwashed her into believing that no press is the best strategy."

"I'll handle Maya and the family."

Despite his words, Avi knows that Maya, in her distraught state of mind, doesn't fully trust him. The thought crushes him. It makes him feel so alone on this strange battlefield. His mind plays horrible games on him. He cannot bear the possibility that Maya might think he is doing this for personal gain. He has had to bear the brunt of the media: "Cohen seeks the limelight at the expense of his grandson."

A part of him has to believe that his daughter could never buy in to such an idea. What he does know is that, as much as he tries to explain the logic of what he is doing to Maya and Leon, they will not listen.

Why is it that all they see is my failed past?

"Shula, they accuse me of running after publicity. God is my witness—I wish someone else would champion this cause. If only I could find someone else who is willing to take on our government, and the entire West, on how to deal with these terrorists. I would gladly step aside."

He has Shula get Maya on the phone. "Maya, how are you holding out? Anything new today?"

"Shalom, Abba. No, all is the same."

"Listen, my dear, we have created a degree of momentum in calling out our government to act more aggressively. You know we are planning a rally in Dimona. Bitton will be there as well as other elected officials. Maya," Cohen pauses, "I want you, Leon and Noa by my side."

"Abba, please, don't do this to us. We are torn. We have been given strict and precise instructions to never, ever speak to the media. It will hurt Lior and can endanger him. It's still too early. The government and military are promising me that they are doing everything in their power to bring Lior home. Making our government our enemy does not make sense to us. Abba, I want Lior to come home alive. Please don't make this harder than it already is."

Cohen is dumbstruck. *How dare she suggest that I am jeopardizing Lior's life. If anything happens to Lior, it's the terrorists who killed him. God forbid*, he doesn't even want to entertain that thought. "Maya, my dear, I'm doing the right thing. We need to keep this story alive… I know this to be true based on highly classified information."

"Please, Abba, no more. The answer is no. Leon and I will not be at the rally. we cannot support what you are doing. I have to go." Maya hangs up.

Avi wants to scream. If the wall in front of him was not solid cinderblock, he would have punched it with all his force. He is frustrated, but he has made up his mind. He is intent on going through with the rally and blaming the Israeli government for not doing enough to bring Lior home.

Avi calls his daughter again. "Please listen to what I have to say, Maya, and then tell me you disagree," he pleads. "The government can do more—they can bring Lior home now. We live in a democracy. The government has to act on behalf of the people. If we don't pressure them, they just assume the people don't care."

"Abba, that is ridiculous! Hamas does not care about your rally or what the people want. They want blood. Why is that so hard to understand? Abba I pray your rallies don't…" she doesn't finish her thought.

Avi knows what she was about to say. "Maya, you are right. They want blood, but our government needs to know that we expect them to bring Lior home precisely because Hamas wants blood and nothing else." Unsure if his words make any sense, Avi feels desperate.

"Father, Leon and I do not want to make our own government our enemy. We need all the allies we can get. We need them now more than ever—please don't turn them against us! Abba, do you hear me?"

Avi's heart is broken. The only way he could possibly convince Maya and Leon right now is to tell them about his conversation with Rachmani. He knows he is doing the right thing, but he cannot reveal his source. Rachmani would never trust him again, and worse, the whole thing could backfire. "I understand, Maya, I understand." Avi waits for Maya to hang up first.

The drama is too much. "There is just one goal right now and that is to bring my grandson home. Shula, let's go. No one is to know of this argument between me and my daughter. Is that clear? Let's go to the mayor's office as scheduled."

Dimona Mayor Benny Bitton, is in his mid-50s. He is a career politician who unapologetically uses his clout for personal gain. Getting in front of a national, if not international, audience is an opportunity Bitton will not pass up. For him, the issue is simple: Wanting to bring Lior home cannot be wrong, especially in front of the media.

As Avi and his entourage drive up to the *iriya*, city hall, the mayor formally greets him with a big smile and an even bigger hug. "I appreciate your support. Benny, we need to be forceful—Lior is as much your grandson as he is mine," Avigdor says.

"I could not agree with you enough. Where are Maya, Leon and the rest of the family?"

"Benny, right now she is not up to it. Let's leave it at that."

Dimona High School is three blocks from the *iriya*. About 100 people gather there marching together, a sea of reporters following them.

Dimona has been preparing itself for the spotlight. The rally is called for noon—the plan is that Cohen and the mayor will arrive at the school at 12:20 p.m. He can hear the noise from blocks away. There must be about 4,000 people at the rally. Thanks to the efforts of Moshiko and his friends, the entire city was informed. Thousands of flyers and posters are plastered all over the city. Local papers ran free ads announcing the rally in support of Lior. Business and cultural leaders join Cohen on the stage alongside the mayor. Shula cannot believe her eyes. "They really do care!"

Hundreds of signs are being waved, some read: "Bring Lior Home," others say, "Ehud Olmert, Do The Right Thing." Kids are wearing T-shirts with a picture of Lior. This kind of activism is a first for Dimona.

Benny Bitton is the first to the podium and starts leading the crowd in a chant of "Bring Lior home!" while shaking his fist in the air.

"Lior Samet is a beloved son of Dimona, and this city urges the government of Ehud Olmert to do everything in its power to bring our son home, now!" The crowd goes crazy. "Our soldiers come first, not politics," the mayor continues. "We will not be silenced until Olmert takes this issue to heart!" Bitton doesn't want to give up the podium. The crowd is in a frenzy.

Avi Cohen comes to the podium. He is wearing civilian clothes. He raises his hand, asking the crowd for silence. "I stand here as a grandfather, not only of Lior, but of all the young men and women who serve our country. Lior is alive, but we do not know his physical or mental condition. I call upon the government of Israel to do what it takes to bring Lior home now." As Cohen stares down at the two pages of prepared remarks, he realizes this is not the place for a formal speech. The mayor understood this better than he did. Avi Cohen lifts his right fist up in the air and says, *Am Yisrael Chai*," the nation of Israel lives.

The crowd spontaneously starts singing "Am Yisrael Chai."

"We will not allow Lior's abduction to go unnoticed. We will not remain silent while Lior remains in solitary confinement. We call upon the government of Ehud Olmert to do what it takes to bring Lior home."

The crowd is completely charged. Am Israel Chai turns into a chant of "Bring Lior Home." Cohen cannot believe the effect he has had on the crowd. There is hope. People do care.

44

La'uf
Lior's Mind

Memory: Alone Time

There was no alone time in the army. Two toilets, six showers and five sinks for fifty guys meant that there was always someone waiting for you to hurry up. Even *T'aSh*, the one free hour a day, was bullshit. That was the only time given to shave, shower, shit, brush your boots, organize your bag, make your bed and get rid of whatever was stinking up your personal area.

Memory: The Worst Part of the Army

Being noticed was not a good thing. Better to remain under the radar as much as possible. The last thing I wanted to do was make myself the center of attention.

I won't miss the running, the fucking running in

the sand, in the mud, in the rain. If we weren't running, someone was yelling at us to do push-ups. The
punishments didn't stop. They're always yelling. Yelling. Fucking yelling. "Is this hard? Are you going to call
your Ima? Are you a man? Are you a soldier? Is this a
playground?"

Bastards.

45

Dimona, Israel
February 2007

THE DIMONA RALLY WAS A huge success.

"This is not about geo-politics, or gender politics, or the usual social politics," writes Yedioth Ahronoth. "This is about a young man, a soldier, abducted and being held against his will and against international law."

"The people have been empowered," writes a popular columnist for a liberal newspaper, "and now the debate begins."

The combination of the grassroots swell of support for Lior and the release of the video by Hamas throws the drama of Lior's abduction into a spontaneous national and international spotlight. For the average Israeli, the horrific images of the two reservists who, in 2000, accidently took a wrong turn into the town of Ramala and were abducted and brutally dismembered, all while onlookers cheered, are relatively fresh.

"Had the kidnappers wanted Lior dead, they would have done so by now," people are saying. They speculate that "something is keeping Lior alive." Many theorize that "Lior is being held as a pawn for negotiations." Experts agree that the longer the government waits, the greater the chances that Lior's fate will be the same as every other captured soldier in the history of Israel.

According to Yedioth Aharonoth, 79 percent of the Israeli people support some sort of negotiation with Hamas, even if it involves an exchange for prisoners. Almagor, an Israeli organization that represents victims of terror, jumps right into the debate and accuses Cohen of betraying the state and its people. "Any form of negotiation with terrorists is a victory for our sworn enemy, Hamas."

Statistics begin to float: "Terrorists freed in previous prisoner exchanges have cost the lives of 180 Israelis. There is no reason," the skeptics argue, "that prisoners exchanged for a kidnapped victim would be any different."

The debate finds a platform in the print media, television, radio and on the Internet. While the varying sides express their views, appeals are made by the international community to allow the Red Cross access to Lior, but Hamas refuses.

"I will not remain silent. I will not be silenced. Soldiers need to be brought home at all costs." Radio and television talk show hosts love booking the brigadier general, the hero grandfather in front of the camera. The cynics accuse the media of blowing the story out of proportion for ratings and giving Cohen a platform to betray his country. When the attacks are personal, Cohen is affected. Cohen's enemies and political nemeses shamelessly accuse him of using his grandson's abduction as a means of reclaiming the public eye—unable to let go of his glory days. Those remarks hurt, but he can live with the enemies. The questions and doubts that are raised by those closest to him sting the most. Especially when they come from Maya and Leon. They also cause him to question his entire endeavor.

"Forget the fact that it's your grandson," Shula urges. "This is the right fight. You put the government on notice—it is up to them to respond. Your priority right now is to convince the government and the people, not Maya and Leon. They are heartbroken and can't think straight."

"No one knows how Hamas is going to react to the attention and social media frenzy. I only pray I am not going to get him killed," Avi says.

"Avi, if they wanted him dead, he would have been killed already! The debate is clear and it's not about you!"

The urgency is not only palpable but is contagious.

Many begin to wonder why the families of other abducted soldiers never took to the streets.

Shula cannot keep up with the telephone calls, emails, faxes and impromptu visits by reporters. Business leaders provide financial support, community volunteers spread the word, celebrities mention Lior's name in public.

Late-night talk show hosts are vying for exclusives with Avi Cohen. He takes a gamble and turns down some prominent stations in the hope that he can give an exclusive interview with Yair Lapid of Channels 2 and 3. Known for his liberal tendencies, Lapid is the highest-rated talk show host in Israel. He has a reputation for being a no-nonsense interviewer. Cohen understands that Lapid will want to be the first. His gamble pays off. Lapid's producer calls Shula to schedule a live interview. Politically, Cohen and Lapid have nothing in common. Avi hopes that, when it comes to Lior's abduction, they might find mutual ground.

The television networks and the print media do a great job publicizing the forthcoming interview. It will be on Friday night in the Neve Ilan Studio, right outside of Jerusalem. Avi has rehearsed his sound bites. He plans to get in front of the country and demand the government of Ehud Olmert bring his grandson home.

The day of the interview arrives. Cohen and Shula do not gauge the traffic correctly and arrive with little time to prepare. The general is whisked to the guest reception room and briefed on the wireless microphone to ignore the cameras. "Pretend you are in Yair's living room," a young woman in tight black leather pants and a fitted white shirt with an earpiece tells him with a smile. "I wish I had more time to prepare you. Mr. Lapid is a fanatic about punctuality." Shula paces the room, wondering if she can have a smoke.

The show begins. Yair Lapid greets Brigadier General Avi Cohen with the usual pomp of television extravagance and extends his hand in a warm gesture on stage. They walk together and face the camera as a live audience claps. They sit at a glass table in front of each other. It is just the two of them.

"Welcome, Brigadier General," Lapid begins as silence glides across the room. "Why are your daughter and son-in-law, Lior's parents, not here?" Avi is taken aback by the lack of small talk. He did not expect this question.

Lapid remains still. Cohen breaks the silence. "This is about Lior…" he stammers. "Lior's parents aren't ready to go public…" his voice picks up. "Yair, the truth of the matter is that our government's policy has always been to keep these matters out of the media and the press. They have convinced—no, they have bullied—my family into believing that remaining silent is the best for Lior. I don't buy it. It has not worked in the past, and I don't believe it will work here. This story has to be kept alive. Whoever is holding my grandson, if you are listening—he is innocent, let him go."

Lapid shows no compassion. "But what do you say to those who claim you are doing this for attention?" Cohen's face turns beet red. Shula panics, wondering if he will blow up on national television.

"I came on your show to voice awareness to the Israeli public and to the international community that my grandson was abducted by terrorists," Cohen says, his voice controlled but upset. "He is innocent and we want him back. I'm not on trial here."

"Yes, I understand," Lapid says. Shula prays that Cohen will not lose his temper. Less than five minutes into the interview and Lapid has successfully gotten under Cohen's skin.

Lapid's producer signals "enough" from the sidelines. Lapid pulls back. "Tell us about Lior. What kind of kid is he?" Again, Cohen is completely surprised by the question. That very moment between processing the questions and giving an answer has an eternal quality. Cohen realizes just how little he knows his grandson. "He is a nice boy. He would not harm a soul."

"Is he military-hero material like his grandfather?" Lapid smirks. Cohen keeps his cool, knowing that Lapid is baiting him. He will not give him what he wants in front of the public. "I don't know what 'military-hero material' means, Yair. Lior is serving his country with courage and with pride. He deserves that our government do everything in its power to bring him home." Lapid announces a commercial break and the cameras turn off.

Lapid doesn't even acknowledge Avigdor Cohen sitting next to him. He has himself touched-up with makeup, drinks some water and reviews his notes while Cohen sits in his chair uncomfortably.

"Welcome back to our show. We are here with recipient of the Medal of Valor, Brigadier General Avigdor Cohen. His grandson, Lior Samet, was kidnapped by Hamas and was seen alive and in relatively good health in a video, asking for the release of all the freedom fighters held in Israeli prisons," Lapid says just after the cameras come back to life. "Brigadier General, I want to read to you a letter to the editor that appeared in yesterday's *Yediyoth Achronot*, written by Ze'ev Rapp, the father of 15-year-old Helena Rapp who was murdered by Fuad Muhammad Abdulhari Amrin:

"'Those who support a prisoner exchange such as Brigadier General Avigdor Cohen don't understand the grief they are causing us. The memory of our loved ones cries from beneath the earth for revenge. Blood is pouring from our heart and soul. We are sorry for the kidnapping of Lior Samet, but we reject these bleeding-heart ideas.'"

Lapid asks, "How do you respond not only to this grieving father and mother but also to all those victims whose murderers could be released in exchange for your grandson?"

Cohen takes a deep breath. "Lior does not look good in the video. He is suffering, as are his parents, relatives and friends. Our state has a moral obligation to save his life and bring him home. As Jews, we have the sacred obligation of *Pidyon Shevuyim*, redeeming those held against their will. Hamas has not allowed the Red Cross to visit Lior. The only assurance of his well-being comes from terrorists. The IDF has an unwritten contract with every one of its soldiers: You fight the war and we will do everything in our power to bring you home. If we don't, countless soldiers will retreat. That, to me, is a much greater danger than former terrorists being released or the fear that they might commit crimes once out of prison."

Again, Cohen can breathe. He believes the interview is going well. Lapid thanks Cohen and introduces Professor Daniel Bar-Tal, renown editorialist and lecturer on political psychology. Cohen is taken by surprise. He has never heard of this professor and had no clue he was going to be on the show with him. Professor Bar-Tal has a distinguished look. He is tall and has a full head of salt-and-pepper hair.

"Professor Bar-Tal, welcome back to our show. It is always a pleasure to have you." The live audience is electrified by the professor's presence. "Please give us your perspective before we open the phone lines to our audience tonight. Some feel a deal with Hamas is the only recourse, while others claim a swap would be the greatest victory Israel could hand terrorism since its inception."

The professor nods, removes his glasses and says, "Yair, here we see the fundamental dilemma between our society's responsibility to the individual and our concern of the collective. This issue has tragically pinned victim against victim. Lior Samet has been violently kidnapped in a way that our society does not consider to be a normative means of struggle. This is why one side says he should be returned at any price, while the families of those killed by those very terrorists are also victims. They say no price should be paid to murderers. This is truly a dilemma. Neither side is right and neither side is wrong."

"Can we have your opinion on this matter, professor?" Lapid eggs.

"My opinion?" Bar-Tal asks. Lapid is silent. Cohen has no clue what to expect. "Well, my opinion is that the state of Israel has a responsibility to create a safe environment for its citizens and protect their well-being." The professor continues, "Therefore, given the opportunity to save one of its own, I cannot see how it could possibly refuse. To take into account hypothetical future attacks does not make sense to me. We must weigh the pros and cons that are presently quantifiable."

He continues, "Permit me to go on. If the opportunity presents itself to negotiate the release of Lior Samet without suffering one fatality, we must seize that opportunity and bring him home. If indeed the release of former terrorists poses a threat, we have to increase our security protocols. We should not determine the fate of this young man held against his will on possible or unforeseeable dangers. We should focus solely on the present circumstances." The professor takes a deep breath and says, "I do hope I answered your question."

"There it is, ladies and gentlemen. Our expert has spoken. Brigadier General, we thank you for being on our show. Professor, it's always a pleasure. Next, after the break, we have fashion star and entrepreneur Gila Kafash, from Rishon."

Dimona, Israel
June 2007
One Year Anniversary of Lior's Kidnapping

L EON SAMET FINALLY GETS TO bed. Maya is fast asleep. His mind is racing. He is not completely convinced that his father-in-law is wrong. If nothing else, Avi Cohen's crusade to keep Lior's story alive while testing the moral conscience of the citizens of Israel is stirring the government to make an issue of Lior's abduction. It has become clear that Hamas is keeping Lior alive because they believe a prisoner swap may happen. Ironically, the media, while serving Hamas, is keeping Lior alive. Despite Ehud Olmert's public hard-nosed position, the average Israeli does not agree with his policy.

Olmert's challenger Benjamin Netanyahu, the leader of the Likud Party, makes bringing Lior home the centerpiece of his election campaign. Despite his hawkish political tendencies, he is relentless about bringing the boy home. As a war hero and the brother of legendary IDF officer Yoni Netanyahu, who died while leading the liberation of abducted Israeli civilians in Entebbe, Uganda, in 1976, Benjamin Netanyahu's promise of bringing Lior home resonates in a way that sounds sincere.

Leon and Maya's life is on hold. People are in and out of their house every evening. Conversations range from local soccer results to national politics. That afternoon, Nina, a well-meaning and kind neighbor, mentions that she knows the Baumel family and if they want to, she will gladly introduce the Samets to them. Maya and Leon have no idea who Nina is talking about. In fact, none of the people in the home that evening have any idea who the Baumels are.

"Who are the Baumels?" Leon finally asks.

"Zachariah Baumel, along with Tzvi Feldman and Yehuda Katz, have been missing since their abduction in 1982," Nina answers. "They were kidnapped on the Lebanon border and have not been heard from since. The Baumels have been very courageous over the years and still believe their son is alive and will be brought home."

"Brought home by whom?" Maya asks.

"Our government, I assume," Nina responds.

The room turns silent. Nina realizes that what she had hoped would be a kind gesture turns out to be a disaster. Maya is mortified. "Since 1982," her words linger. People start staring at the floor. "Times are different now." The conversation is quickly changed.

"Maya," Leon whispers, "Maya are you awake?"

"*Ken*, yes, what is it?"

"Maya, have you ever heard of Nissim Toledano or Ilan Saadon?"

"No, why do you ask?"

"How about Nachshon Wachsman?"

"No, I have no idea who these people are."

"I did an Internet search right before I went to bed. They have all been kidnapped by terrorists in the last twenty-five years, and we never heard of them. I am willing to bet our government promised their families, like they have promised us, that they will bring their children home. I am certain they were told to silence the story—keep it out of the press, let the professionals handle the situation. Now these boys are lost to oblivion. Who knows if they are still alive? The Israeli government does not negotiate with terrorists. Their story has an end—they never came home and won't come home. What's worse is that they remain forgotten," Leon says. "Maya, your father is right. We cannot remain silent."

Maya sits up. "What are you saying, Leon?"

"Your father is right. For the first fucking time in his life, he is right. It looks like Netanyahu will be forming the next coalition government. We have to hold him to his promise that he will bring Lior home. What is your father's number?"

"Leon, it's 2 a.m."

"What's your father's telephone number?"

47

Journey to Jerusalem
Passover 306 BCE

T HE JERUSALEM *BATEI DIN*, JEWISH courts, meet on the second
and fifth day of every week to coincide with market days. On these
days, scholars and their students listen to litigants' arguments. Laws are
adjudicated on each case and then explained to the students. Simon plans
his arrival to be on the fourth day of the week so as to not create a conflict
between his arrival and the work of the scholars and priests.

The journey is pleasant; the weather could not be more accommodating. Simon and his family's expected arrival at the inn of Melekh Levi'im
was appropriately prepared. Two horsemen are dispatched to escort the
family into the estate. They enter a large room with woven mats on the
floor and torches strung on the walls that not only illuminate the space, but
also add an ambiance of royalty. The family washes and eats. As the sun
begins to set, the women go to their rooms while the men gather for evening prayers. Simon is asked to lead the service, but he defers to Yochanan.

After the evening service, Melekh introduces himself to Simon and
to Yochanan. "Welcome, prince of Israel, you honor us by staying in our
humble residence," he says as he kisses the high priest's hand. Yochanan is

shocked. He never saw this in Chashmona.

He turns to Tobi. "Will everyone in Jerusalem be kissing father's hand?"

"No, not at all. Unfortunately, the *Am ha'aretz* do not often see great scholars or high priests. They know how to show respect." He raises his eyebrow as he makes the comment. The *Am ha'aretz* are the uneducated, those who work with their hands or work the land.

Melekh whispers, "May I have a few words with our Master?"

"Of course, come sit next to me and my son. How can I thank you for the kind reception you have shown me and my family?"

"This is nothing. All my possessions are yours. Enjoy, your excellency."

"What is on your mind, my dear friend?"

Yochanan is fascinated by what this *Am ha'aretz* could possibly want to share with his father.

"The situation in our eternal and sacred capital is bad and getting worse, my prince." His words do not sound like those of an *Am ha'aretz*. Melekh Leviim is articulate and precise.

"What do you mean? Speak," Simon says.

"I wish I could be reporting better news. The news that reaches me on a weekly basis is frightening, I…"

"Speak, what are you talking about?" Simon is agitated.

"Leadership is bought. The priesthood goes to the highest bidder. Allegiances are made with the heathens. Hellenism, my master, is overtaking the Law of Moses. I apologize for reporting such news prior to your visit and on the eve of the sacred holiday of Pesach, *Haba Aleinu Beshalom*, that shall come upon us in peace." Simon is silent. Yochanan is intrigued.

"What evidence do you have of this?" Yochanan wants to know. Melekh Leviim does not even acknowledge the young man's explosive question.

Simon lowers his head, reaches out and touches Yochanan's arm, signaling him to calm down.

"Has my brother been corrupted?" Simon asks. "How about the Sanhedrin?"

Melekh stands up.

"You will be there tomorrow, my excellency. I am sure you will enjoy a wonderful holiday. May it be joyous and leaven free!"

With that, he hurriedly walks away. He turns around one more time and says, "Goodnight, and may your sleep be restful."

Simon has heard rumors. However, he had no idea of the extent of the corruption in Jerusalem. He feels faint.

"Father, are you OK?" Yochanan asks.

"Master, you don't look well," Tobi says.

Hearing this kind of news from an *Am ha'aretz* is especially disturbing. *Why didn't he answer my question about my brother?*

Simon feels short of breath. "Tobi, I'm feeling chest pains once again. I can't move my left arm. Help me up. Take me to my room."

48

Jerusalem
Passover 306 BCE

THE ROADS LEADING INTO JERUSALEM are congested, lined with people, vendors, pawners and shops. The noise is deafening and the odors of both humans and animals crowd together in the narrow streets. Yochanan is both shocked and mesmerized. This is so different from life in Chashmona.

The most oppressive scene is the slave market right outside of the entrance gates to Jerusalem. The slaves for sale stand on platforms in various forms of undress and with numbers around their necks. They stare out into the lustful crowds with vacant eyes. "Father, are these slaves Jewish?" Simon is as surprised as the rest of the travelers with him. When he governed Jerusalem, such slave markets were forbidden in public spaces and were limited to non-Israelite slaves. Any sort of transaction that involved humans had to take place under a roof in an enclosed setting away from bystanders and children.

"No, of course not. I pray that those for sale are not Jewish," Simon responds. Jewish slaves are bought and sold in a court of law under the auspices of the Bet Din. The circumstances in which a Jewish man or woman will be sold into slavery are so unusual that it almost never occurs—despite the fact that there is an entire body of biblical and rabbinic laws that dictate such possibilities. Simon still feels faint from the night before, and the sight of Jerusalem looking so different makes his heartbeat quicken.

His arrival is immediately announced. As his caravan passes inspection at *Sha'ar HaYovel*, the Jubilee gate, a delegation of official escorts surrounds him. Only Malka remains under the veil of the caravan. Simon and Yochanan sit behind the driver on cushioned seats while Tobi sits alongside the charioteer. A young man wearing a scholar's turban identifies himself as Pinchas.

"It is with great honor that we welcome you, *Morenu ve-abeinu*, our master and our teacher. Can we offer your excellency and those travelling with you some drinks, or some fruits?"

"No. Please take me to the *bet midrash*, immediately."

"Simon, please drop us off at my sister's home first and then go about doing your business!" Malka interjects.

"Very well. We will first make a stop at the courtyard of Akiba and Ruhama Kohanim OhebTzedek."

The narrow stone streets are bustling with activity in preparation for the holiday. Malka's sister lives in a modest residence with an open courtyard. The escorts clear the way so that it takes a fraction of the time to get there. The encounter between the sisters is very emotional. Simon is impatient as they unload the wagon.

"Pinchas, please take me to the bet midrash immediately," Simon repeats.

"But, your excellency, the midrash is closed. We are in the midst of Passover preparations. Scholars and students are between sessions."

"Where is Antignos and where are the scholars?" Simon is shaking.

"I will do my best to find them, my master."

Malka interjects, "You will go nowhere. You do not look well at all."

"Tobi," Simon says, animated and upset, "bring me the head of the Sanhedrin right now."

"Yes, master."

Simon is again short of breath. Yochanan is so disturbed by the ordeal, he does not recognize how poorly Simon feels. Malka is frustrated that her first visit with her sister is marred by Simon's discontent.

"What is bothering him?" she asks Yochanan.

"I don't think he is feeling well."

Antignos arrives. "My teacher, welcome back to Jerusalem. Why the urgency? I dropped everything I was doing." Simon regains his composure. He is assisted up and walks with Antignos to a corner of the courtyard away from the women, servants and children. Yochanan follows right behind, not wanting to miss a word of what will transpire between the two leaders. Tobi trails behind, annoyed with Yochanan's intrusion.

"What are the slave markets doing in the public squares?" Simon skips all the small talk.

"They are outside the city gates, Simon."

"They are in public. We have passed laws against the public display of slave auctions."

"Simon," Antignos begins, "The *Bene Tzadok* have overruled the law. They legislate in Jerusalem now."

"Who?"

"*Bene Tzadok*, the *Tzedukim*. Jerusalem, for the time being, is under their control."

"How could that be? I left just six years ago."

"Eight years, your excellency," Antignos says. "They have money and power. They bribe the Greek governor, tax collectors and customs officers. They ruled that, if slavery is permitted by the biblical Law of God and Moses, then the high priest or the Sanhedrin do not have the authority to abolish it or even diminish its role in our economy. They bribe their way into positions of power. They even succeeded to secure one seat on the Sanhedrin."

"How about the temple service? How about my brother, Yonathan?"

"They show him great respect, but he is powerless. This Pesach holiday, the temple service will be run by the Bene Tzadok."

"Father, let us overtake them by force. Oust them. They have no business here in Jerusalem," Yochanan bursts out.

The adults do not respond. Simon breaks the silence, "We don't do our business with violence. I need to rest."

Antignos and his two pupils quietly leave the room. At the doorway, Antignos turns around. Yochanan lifts his eyes and locks them with Antignos. The head of the Sanhedrin stomps out.

49

Jerusalem
Passover 306 BCE

THE CITY OF STONE IS feverishly bustling in anticipation of the most celebrated holiday in the Jewish calendar. Thousands of Jewish nationals from all corners of the ancient world converge on Jerusalem to celebrate the biblical holiday. Some come from as far away as Babylon, Persia and Rome. Countless caravans, carrying hundreds of pilgrims, line the roads leading up to the holy city.

The temple feels like a city within the city. It is an organization that employs more than 800 men and women. It fuels the entire economy of Jerusalem's 100,000 citizens in a relatively organized fashion. Temple representatives who are posted at every gate and junction collect the half-shekel from each male 20 years and older. Families are encouraged to offer the half-shekel on behalf of every member of the family as a positive omen for wealth.

Individual families begin their preparations for Passover thirty days prior to the holiday. They purge their homes, courtyards, and storage houses of all Hametz, leavened food products made of grain that have been combined with water and left to stand for longer than eighteen minutes.

One cannot eat, own or even see Hametz.

"For seven days, Hametz is an abomination. If a mouse can get to that spot, it has to be cleaned, lest a crumb of bread be found." Yochanan instructs the priestly staff.

Women shop and clean while men do what they can to fund the expenses associated with the holiday.

Shamashim, the temple ushers, who are exclusively of the Kohen or Levite families, go from neighborhood to neighborhood within Jerusalem and in the surrounding villages making sure that at least twenty individuals are assigned to one lamb. In some circumstances, up to 100 individuals will share one lamb for the Paschal sacrifice. Per the biblical command, every individual has to be assigned to a lamb, which has to be slaughtered at the Temple Mount courtyard and eaten at home at the festive Pesach Seder.

Yochanan is fascinated. He is eager to get involved with temple service, but he spends his time caring for Simon who seems to weaken every day. For some reason, the Shamashim treat Yochanan like an outsider, whispering to one another as they stare at him.

The family plans to spend the Passover Seder with Malka's sister and her children, and with Yochanan's grandparents and one of their daughters and her family.

As the sun sets on the night of the thirteenth of Nissan, Yochanan accompanies Simon to the Mikveh. The place is littered with men ritually immersing themselves in preparation for their visit to the temple courtyard. There they will slaughter their male yearling kid fattened for this purpose in order to fulfill the commandment: "Your lamb shall be without blemish, a yearling male from sheep or from goat. And all the assembled congregation of the Israelites shall slaughter it at twilight."

Simon and Yochanan get an early start the next morning. The communal slaughter of the Paschal lamb takes place in three shifts. The courtyard doors will open at the first half of the morning with the sound of the shofar. The first shift consists of priests, Levites, scholars and dignitaries. Rows of priests will line up with curved-bottomed silver basins. The priests are not allowed to place the basin down, lest the blood congeal. Once filled with blood, the basin is passed from priest to priest until the closest one to the altar dashes the blood onto the foot of the *Mizbe'ach*, the altar. All this is taking place while the Levite choir sings the hymns of Hallel, accompanied by the most exquisite musical instruments. After the lamb is slaughtered, the carcass is taken out of the courtyard and flayed by an expert butcher. The sacrificial portions are removed, placed on a tray and burned on the altar by the attending priest. The edible portion is packed and taken home to be roasted.

Simon dips some hyssop sprigs into the blood of the slaughtered lamb. Later, as he walks into his host's home, he outlines the doorway with the blood and says, "May the Lord of Lords, keeper of Israel, protect our home from all that is evil." Yochanan has never seen this but immediately recognizes the act as a commemoration of the Israelites in Egypt, who were spared the plague of the first born by placing blood on their doorposts.

It isn't long before all of Jerusalem begins to take on that gamey, foul smell of roasted lamb.

Simon teaches: "If one is on the way to slaughter his Paschal lamb or circumcise his son or perform any other biblically ordained commandment, and he remembers that there is Hametz left at home—if he can go back and remove it, he should do so. If not, he annuls it in his heart. This only applies when traveling for a mitzvah." Simon sprinkles his every moment with the law of Israel he so much loves.

50

La'uf
Lior's Mind

Memory: Being a Soldier

There are a lot of smart guys in the army. Some of the smartest are often the ones you least expect to be smart. It's funny how popular wisdom about health just doesn't apply in the army. It's the guys who smoke a pack a day who are the guys who can run better and longer than everyone else.

You also have the guys who are always looking for a fight. They joke about killing Arabs for target practice. Of course, they don't. But I hated when they talked so cavalierly about death. Shit, I remember when we found a dead body behind our school, beside a dumpster. Everyone said it was a gang killing. Who really knows. The body was black and blue, face down and scary as hell. I couldn't eat or sleep for days.

None are dumber than the tourists who love to

take pictures with soldiers. They call us heroes for doing nothing at all.

51

Gaza City, Gaza Strip
June 2010

L IOR TAKES A GOOD LOOK at himself in the mirror. He sees a slightly distorted image of a young man, a bit washed-out, but a more mature version of the person he used to be. Eitan, the school jokester, once told him that his face was just a bit off-center. In the almost imperceptible bulges and scratches of glass, this doesn't seem impossible. *Like the rest of me*, he thinks.

It has been two and a half years. Thirty months spent apart from his family, his platoon, his friends, his teachers, his bedroom, his life. *Shit, it's been two and a half years—is that a measure of time or distance?*

Looking into the mirror is like looking into the wrong end of a telescope. Spying on someone who has become small and faraway. There he is, Lior, living the life he is supposed to. Then who is this, living here inside this tiny room, a ghost? A stunt double? A computer animation? Suddenly exhausted, he turns away from the mirror and lies back down on the bed.

How strange. Just last night, he told Faisal how disconnected he felt from his life back home. He does feel homesick, maybe not enough. Still, even longing and frustration creep in. Is it for his old life or for the life he's not living? After all this time, it's as if he's longing for a place he's only dreamed. His mother's special barley soup, his father's dumb jokes, the soft, mahogany hair of the girl he had a crush on—all part of another country, another galaxy.

Though he has spent hours trying, he can't remember the layout of his school or the streets near his home. Is this amnesia? Dementia? Is he losing his mind?

The radio is his lifeline. He is so grateful to Faisal for providing him with this connection to the world, even if that world is no longer his. He's never been sorry that he cooperated in the making of the video that led to this reward. It's worth more to him than any object he has ever owned.

The people, the voices in the box, are his constant companions—news, chatter, commercials, music. They are, by turns, informative, melodic, gentle, obnoxious, comforting, surprising. As a child, Lior remembers looking under the dashboard of his father's car to see where the tiny people and musical instruments were kept. Even now that he understands the workings of a transistor radio, the process is still magical. Radio waves, like the waves of a distant sea, roll in, washing over him, reviving him, transporting him.

This ordeal will end soon; he knows this. For now, he lies on his bed, listening to a song he has heard many times before. Lior drifts, his fingers still holding the radio for comfort, maintaining his tenuous connection. In some ways, he is still little Lior, the small boy clutching his blanket for safety as he surrenders to sleep.

Lior is finally going home. He's not sure if he's going down the right street—it looks different than he remembers. Looking for something familiar, he sees the neighbor's house at the corner, the one with the brass mailbox with the big black N. Now he knows he's turning onto the right block, but as he turns, he feels his heart harden like a brick. His house is no longer there.

In its place is a large building, maybe a government building or a school. His school? Confused, on the verge of terror, he climbs the outer stairway and opens the heavy door. Inside, there is a reception desk, behind which stands a man as old as his grandfather. Is it the school janitor? Is it the man from the kiosk? Lior tries to remember how to be brave.

"I'm looking for Lior Samet," Lior says.

The old man nods without smiling and turns to look at a directory on an old computer screen. "Sorry. No one here by that name."

Lior becomes insistent. "Of course there is! I'm here. I'm Lior Samet!"

The man looks bewildered, then annoyed. "If you're Lior Samet, why the hell did you ask for him? What are you, crazy?"

Lior steps back, feeling himself about to cry. *Maybe I am crazy*, he thinks, unable to explain why he asked for himself. Fumbling for a reason, he says, "It's because I used to live here and I left something important behind."

As he says this, he realizes it's true. He's lost something valuable. "Nobody lives here," says the old man. "This is an office building, not an apartment house." Then, seeing Lior begin to cry, the old man softens. The old man is now his senior commander. "What did you lose, anyway? Maybe somebody turned it in."

Lior is really sobbing now because he can't remember what it is he lost. Certainly it was something important, but what? He starts running down the long hallway. A wallet? Keys? Credit card? Watch? The old man comes out from behind the desk and tries to console him. "Tell me what it is and I'll help you find it," he says. But Lior's brain hurts from trying to remember.

Wiping his eyes with his sleeve, he thanks the old man and opens the heavy door as he leaves. Suddenly, as the door closes behind him, he knows what he lost— his radio.

Lior awakens from the familiar dream sweaty and disoriented, thinking about his radio.

Nothing has been stranger to Lior than listening to those voices babble on and on about Cpl. Lior Samet. *Who are they talking about? How bizarre. The Lior from the radio is a fascinating person, someone to be respected and admired. He bears no resemblance to me. It is as if someone made up a superhero and mistakenly gave the superhero my name,* he thinks.

The first time Lior heard his name on the radio, it was both exhilarating and harrowing. Hearing the announcer refer to him as the "sole survivor of the attack," the attack that split his life down the middle, the attack that took his buddies—Shalti, Omri, Dudu—the attack that brought him to this half-life where he can hardly feel his own existence.

He already knew, of course, that Dadu was dead, but it was still shocking to hear the official announcement over the radio.

Lior remembers, as a boy, wanting to be blood brothers with his cousin, though neither of them were brave enough to prick their own flesh with the blade of a penknife. *Am I now brain brothers with Dudu?* This stray thought makes him giggle, though for over two years, thinking of that moment has made him wrench. *Is this what it means to toughen up? To become a man? Do you have to learn to laugh at what is gruesome?*

He learns a great many details of his capture from the radio. It is astonishing to think that he is the only survivor of the ordeal. He often wonders what it was like for his buddies, lying dead in the desert as the vehicle drove off with Lior in its trunk. He wonders what it is like for them now. *Is death really nothingness? No colors, no sound, no thought? If they could think, would they wish they were with me? No,* he guesses, *probably not.*

Lior has studied this room so carefully: a bed, a nightstand, a boarded-up window, a tiny bathroom. Everything he needs is here. He has heard many lectures on the possibility of being captured by the enemy and the things they do to their prisoners. He's not sure who abducted him, but it seems like they're not into beatings, or verbal abuse, or psychological torture. The blue ceiling makes him feel a bit less trapped. Faisal explained to him that blue is for good luck.

Lior can't say he's been treated kindly. Faisal has his moments. But there's been no cruelty either. Maybe it's this absence of caring that makes him feel so lethargic.

There is nothing to fight and nothing to pull toward. There is nowhere to go and nowhere to return to.

He wonders if this is what being dead is like.

He gets it. Lior knows why he has survived. It's not luck. It's not some special talent. He is a bargaining chip in a war he really doesn't understand. He is Brigadier General Avigdor Cohen's grandson. That's why he is still newsworthy. That's why he is walking the earth, if you can call a three-by five-meter room, "the earth." That's why he gets to sleep in a bed, eat figs and hummus, piss in a clean toilet. His grandfather, a man he's never really understood, is the reason for his survival.

Lior is not sure if he's grateful or annoyed. *Shit, disappearing is great. Going back home would also feel great.* He is glad to be alive, glad that there is at least a possibility that he will go home, be free, live like a regular guy.

The radio keeps talking about his grandfather, the rallies he leads, the interviews he gives, and the pressure he is putting on the government to release his grandson.

It's funny, Saba never really cared to understand me.

Lior knows without it ever being stated that in his grandfather's eyes, he is not tough enough to succeed, not brave enough to be admired. "Enough already with the music," his grandfather would say, "enough with the deep thoughts! Learn to be a man!"

Lior always treated his grandfather with respect. Even though he hated the boring military stories, he would listen because it seemed like everyone else was fascinated. *Saba's title was also a source of comedy. Saba took it so seriously! It represented his military might and stature, the outward appearance of straight-backed morality. Who knows what was hiding behind those colorful bars? Saba wasn't corrupt or a fake. But others were—I'm certain about that. To me, Saba is Saba. To the rest of the world, he is Brigadier*

General Avigdor Cohen.

Lior and his friends used to discuss this all the time. Knights in armor, and men in tanks, are like turtles in their seemingly impenetrable shells. Underneath, they're just slugs. This is no excuse for not firing even one bullet. There were some, like him, among his friends, who didn't want to go into the military, but of course it was inevitable.

Lior has never liked fighting, not even wrestling. His mother called him a sensitive boy, seeming a little disappointed as she did so.

"He's just not a tough guy," said his father. "No danger of Lior becoming a gangster." Underneath the teasing, Lior could always hear a tinge of embarrassment.

And now, his parents are being tough. Radio reports say they are camped out in front of the prime minister's residence, protesting their son's captivity. It is astonishing to Lior that they are doing something so public, so proactive. He remembers them once telling him that "real change takes place in the background," reminding him not to be a braggart, not to try to grab attention (like someone they knew very well). And look at them now! The radio announcers report on his parents daily as if they are rock stars.

The Free Lior cause is exploding. *Imagine, Kobi Peretz dedicating a song to me*, he muses. For two and a half years, the airwaves are filled with Lior's name. If only he could replay some of the radio announcements. He especially loved the one about the concert.

> **The deafening applause of 51,000 people filled the stadium in Ramat Gan as Kobi Peretz sang his most popular song, Shema Israel. He dedicated the tune to Lior Samet, the young Israeli soldier and grandson of Brigadier General Cohen, who is still being held somewhere in Gaza, presumably in solitary confinement. As the noted entertainment reviewer Shaul Ashkenazy said, "Peretz's lyrics concerning freedom will now forever resonate with a new intensity."**

> **Not to be outdone, Gad Elbaz, like Kobi Peretz, also dedicated a song to Lior Samet, during his recent concert in Caesarea. Other famous entertainers who have taken up Lior's cause include Rita, David D'or and Yael Naim.**

Strange very strange. Lior is not sure if he should be proud, embarrassed, ashamed or alienated. *What have I accomplished for Kobi Peretz to be dedicating a song to me? Does being victimized make you a hero? If only they knew about the vomiting and the crying, how I begged not to suffer.*

Throughout the period of Lior's captivity, he has often wondered if he is real to the people who speak about him on the radio or whether he is just a symbol. It's like nothing they say has anything to do with the real Lior Samet.

Lior loves listening to sports. He was never much of a sports fan, but in many ways they are more interesting. At least they're real. To distract himself from utter boredom, Lior sometimes plays a game himself, albeit without teammates. He balls his socks and throws them into the wastebasket from various places in the room. At times, he does this with his left hand. At times, with his eyes closed. These special shots, of course, gain more points than the ordinary ones.

He wishes he could attend an actual game, watch the action, be fully engaged in something outside himself. Yet the radio brings some excitement too. Hearing the plays, feeling the tension. The shouts of the crowds in the background draw him in, let him escape for a moment. Sometimes he shouts along with the other fans, feeling his voice join the exuberance.

It would be torture, he thinks, *to live with absolutely no human connection*. The old lady who comes in from time to time to clean the place has never said a word to him. Not one word. Once or twice, he's heard her clear her throat or sneeze. For all he knows, she may be entirely without language. *Since her face is always covered, I might doubt she has a nose*, he thinks with a chuckle, *if not for her sneezes.*

She has, on more than one occasion, left her cellphone in his reach while working. Lior never tried to take the cell phone. *What's the use?* he thinks. *Who would I call? What would I tell them? What if the call was discovered and they took away my radio?* He shudders at the thought. *Maybe they're testing me?*

The cellphone is like the plank of wood nailed over his window that he has never tried to pry away, a make-believe doorway into an unreachable world. Though he hears cars out on the street below, sometimes a whistle or a siren, he isn't really interested in anything or anyone outside. *What good would it be to see the people he occasionally hears, those enemies with loud, alarming voices? Who would I call out to? Who would even consider coming to my aid?*

As far as Lior is concerned, he's made a fair exchange. His captors give him figs, juice, fava beans, a lamp, clean underwear, the means to wash himself and, most importantly, a working radio. In turn, he doesn't give them any trouble. And if he does, Faisal will bear the brunt of it. It's a better deal than some diplomats are able to negotiate.

Faisal is OK. Not a bad guy. It's a strange kind of friendship. At the beginning, Lior was not convinced that Faisal believed everything he said. He pretends to be happy, but his eyes reveal sadness. In a peculiar way, Lior and Faisal have grown fond of each other. At least Lior believes so. *Maybe I'll maintain a friendship with Faisal when all this is over. That's a strange thought.*

Lior thinks it's funny how both he and Faisal ended up in this room. A kind of hell on earth for both of them but with no torture or suffering. The real suffering is outside the walls of this room. The room with no exit! *This would make a great book—I have to tell Faisal about this next time we see each other. We can call the book "Tea Time in Hell."* This idea makes Lior smile. Something about the plot rings familiar, but Lior can't seem to put his finger on it.

"What is all this commotion about you, my dear friend?" Faisal asks with a smirk. "Have you heard the latest news? Turn it up. Louder."

In the meantime, the family of abducted soldier, Sgt. Lior Samet, continues to camp out in protest in front of the prime minister's residence, reaffirming their determination to remain in their tent until Lior is freed. When asked by a reporter why they don't go home, his father responded, "Without Lior, it is not home." Their tent site is often busy with well-wishers who stop by and politicians who continue to turn meeting the sequestered couple into photo ops...

It has also been announced that the Samets will have an audience with Pope Benedict in January to discuss their son's plight as a keystone to the possibility of peace in the Middle East...

My parents talking to Pope Benedict? Lior is astonished. They've never shown the slightest interest in the Catholic Church. As a matter of fact, when Lior once voiced a desire to travel to Italy, his mother had said facetiously, "So, you'll stop by the Vatican to meet the pope?"

"Did you hear, Faisal? My parents are meeting with the pope."

"Ah!" Faisal says. "They should say some nice things about me, the person who treats you so well and teaches you so much. Why is no one noticing the important work I do? This is disgraceful. My own people don't notice."

On more than one occasion, Faisal and Lior listened together to the crazy broadcasts about Lior's captivity and the various efforts being made to keep him in the public eye. More often, they listen to soccer matches. To both of them, the soccer matches make more sense.

The broadcasts about Lior, his abduction, his family's and friends' efforts to gain his release and the periodic statements from the Israeli government are all referred to by Lior as the "battlefield." It's been a number of months since Lior began keeping a log of the high points on the battlefield. The soldiers include his family, famous people and all kinds of strangers. *I guess they haven't forgotten me.*

A rally calling for the immediate release of Lior Samet had over 2,000 students at the playing field of Maimonides High School in Tel Aviv. Students from all over the region...

Today, on Lior Samet's third anniversary in captivity, the top trending tweet on Twitter was "Free Lior Now"...

Next Saturday, in tribute to the brave, young soldier, the Israeli Philharmonic will dedicate the proceeds of their evening performance to the cause of Lior Samet's release. The concert has been sold out since the first day tickets were sold...

A demonstration at the maximum-security prison in Neve Tirzav prevented Arab families from meeting with their incarcerated family members. This demonstration, intended

to pressure Palestinian leaders to allow the Red Cross access to evaluate Lior's health and living conditions, was not entirely without incident. The few tussles that broke out on the prison grounds, however, were quickly subdued by police and prison guards...

"Lights Off for Lior," a campaign, that began at the Western Wall last September, is becoming a worldwide enterprise. In Rome last week, after the Samets' audience with Pope Benedict, the Coliseum turned off its lights to express solidarity with the cause. This week, two Swiss cathedrals have followed suit...

Lior Samet has officially become an international phenomenon as the "True Freedom Flotilla" circled the Statue of Liberty today, passing directly by the United Nations to protest the do-nothing response of world leaders to Lior Samet's ongoing captivity...

It's like an out-of-body experience, Lior thinks. *Like those people who are clinically dead, floating up over their bodies, watching themselves on the operating table. Only for me, I stay here on the operating table and the other people float over me, carrying the other Lior around, parading him, praising him, referring to him as a model patriot.*

Lior is not sure he completely understands the circumstances, but this is how he sees it: His grandfather is behind a lot of this commotion. Lior remembers lessons from a social studies class:

"We do not negotiate with terrorists!"

"We do not give the enemy a platform for their demagoguery!"

Though Lior had to memorize these words for an exam, he can't remember whose words they were. *Is it possible that my grandfather, already a famous general at the time, was the person being quoted? No. I would have remembered that.*

Now the news reports state that Brigadier General Avigdor Cohen is questioning Israel's long-standing policy that is endorsed by both the UK and the United States. "It is time to take action," he has said repeatedly, "we are wasting time and lives."

No one, including Lior, is surprised by his grandfather's bravery in speaking his mind. One might criticize the old man's values, but Lior knows his grandfather is afraid of no one. Nonetheless, the brigadier general's words are startling. For a man who has based his entire life on the safety and security of the nation of Israel to suggest negotiations with the enemy! Many have interpreted this as a sign of weakness, or at least fear that Hamas will perceive it as such.

> Brigadier General Avigdor Cohen, the grandfather of Lior Samet, has taken an outspoken stance on his grandson's ongoing captivity and has been increasingly critical of Israeli leadership. Cohen told reporters today that he expects the prime minister to commit to doing everything in his power to bring young Lior home. Accused of placing his family above the community and the country, Brigadier General Cohen was quoted in Maariv yesterday as saying:
>
>> They are all my grandchildren. Every enlisted soldier is my grandchild! It is time for the prime minister and all Israeli officials to consider each and every enlisted soldier as their child, their grandchild. We can no longer leave any of our children behind enemy lines.
>
> While Cohen insists that Lior's case is a human rights issue, not a familial one, some high-ranking officials have stated that this is clearly an instance of emotional priorities and that the brigadier general has lost his commitment to maintaining a stable, secure nation now that his loved ones are at risk.
>
> Others, in and outside of the government, maintain that Cohen is using this issue to garner media attention and increase his political power base.

Lior's life has been dispensed in radio sound bites. As he listens, he tries to figure out what's happening to him. It's like deciphering a code. Two dots, three dashes, a commercial, four more dots... but for the last few days, the radio news reports have become more coherent. They seem to be telling him something important about the Lior he really is, the Lior on this end of the backward telescope.

In the months since Netanyahu won the election, the tone of the radio announcements has changed. Especially since the March for Freedom, almost biblical in proportions with 10,000 people marching from Tel Aviv to Jerusalem, demanding Lior's release. His grandfather and his parents led the procession. *Imagine,* Lior thinks, *all those people, all those tired feet, all those cars unable to get through, only the marchers free to move forward.*

Maybe if the radio announcers gave a summary of my actual daily routine, they would infuse their broadcasts with a bit of reality:

It has been reported that this morning Lior Samet woke up at 7:35 a.m., rubbed his eyes, and proceeded to enter the bathroom to urinate. After having a breakfast consisting of dates, cucumbers and a pita, he was observed lifting and polishing his radio. The reasons for this action remain unknown. At 8:25, Lior re-entered the bathroom, presumably to move his bowels, although this has not yet been confirmed. After a brief rest of eleven minutes and thirty-five seconds, the prisoner performed seventy-five jumping jacks, then went back into the bathroom, apparently to wash up. He was then observed donning white, slightly frayed underpants, a pair of khaki pants and a blue T-shirt. For the next three hours and thirty-six minutes, the subject listened to several radio broadcasts: a news update, some popular music, and a soccer game complete with post-game analysis. During much of this listening time, Samet engaged in a childish game involving throwing his balled-up socks into a waste basket...

Yes, Lior thinks, *that would be more like it. What would the public make of that? Would they turn on me as a pretender or pity me? Would they still want to free me?* He feels pathetic, mildly disgusted with his own apathy.

After what seems like a short sleep, Lior awakens abruptly. Just another morning and yet something feels different, almost smells different. He's more alert than he's been in a very long time, expectant. This sensation is unfamiliar. Apart from meals and visits from Faisal, he can't remember expecting anything since the first few months of his captivity.

The morning news broadcast rouses him out of his reverie:

> **In the face of relentless international pressure and the urgent goading of Brigadier General Cohen, Israel's newly elected officials have vowed to negotiate the release of Lior Samet. As a first step in the process, proof that Samet is still alive must be provided by Hamas in the form of a current videotape.**

> **During the two and a half years of Samet's captivity, only one videotape has been viewed and no visits by the International Red Cross have been permitted.**

> **"Certainly," the prime minister said at yesterday's press conference, "the time has come to verify this brave soldier's life and health before any further productive discourse can take place."**

Another video? Lior thinks. *This possibility lends an air of credibility. Maybe something really is going to happen, even though, God knows, the last video didn't change anything.* Lior smiles, remembering the ineptitude of the videographers. *They might as well have been street cleaners for all they seemed to know about the craft. I had friends in high school who would have done a more professional job.* Still, the very fact that another video is being demanded bodes well. And since the last video, there have been countless demonstrations, not to mention that unbelievable March for Freedom...

As preparations are being made for a videotape of Lior Samet, it seems that negotiations with Hamas are underway. Although details of high-level discussions are being kept secret, government sources report that in exchange for Samet, an Israeli sergeant held hostage for over two and a half years, Hamas wants the release of as many as 1,000 Palestinian and Arab-Israeli prisoners. In addition, they are asking for the release of a Ukrainian prisoner and two Jordanian terrorists. This potential deal, so heavily weighted in Hamas's favor, would mean the release of great numbers of terrorists serving life sentences for heinous crimes against innocent civilians. While the opposition to such a compromise is vigorous and intense, with some labeling the impending deal as "a bloodbath bargain" on numerous occasions, there is evidence that negotiations are nonetheless continuing to move forward...

Strange as it seems, for once, a splash in the external world seems to be having a ripple effect, extending all the way to Lior's little room. Inside Lior, there is a stirring sensation, a feeling of motion about to be generated. The sensation is almost physical yet involuntary, like an itch or the beginning of an erection, the tremor of the tiniest earthquake in a faraway country. Yet he feels it in his own body.

Later in the day, Lior describes this sensation to Faisal. Faisal understands. He himself has been feeling something similar. He confesses to Lior that he has been contacted by a superior, one of the many strangers who directs his life from afar. Another video will be made soon, of this much he is certain. He doesn't know when. He awaits further instructions.

After all this time, Lior knows better than to get excited or even hopeful. Is it possible that the new government is really committing itself to bringing him home alive? This has never happened before in the nation's history. Will he, Lior Samet, be the first? He feels himself blush. He wonders how he has become so significant. *What a crazy world!* he thinks. *You enlist to fight battles that are pointless and you become the point.*

"What a pain in the ass, not to know who's giving you orders," Faisal complains, "like being a goddamned puppet!" Faisal's right about being a puppet, Lior agrees. They're both puppets. No autonomy. No real selves. Just pawns on a chessboard moved constantly by different hands. Even though Lior has been captured, the puppeteers can still put him back on the board and move him around. Or at least they can talk about it. Faisal, though he hasn't been captured, is never moved. What difference does it make anyway? It's not as if these two are kings or knights or even rooks. It's not as if it matters who wins.

Still, beyond the constant irritation and inertia, Lior feels the tug of coming action. This puppet is about to be on stage again, about to move his arms and legs, about to speak like a real boy. Although of course his words will be scripted.

Now that he feels certain another video will be made, Lior feels self-conscious. After all, it's been so long since anyone except Faisal actually looked at him. How will the world react to his appearance? What will his parents think? His grandfather? That girl... Moran? All those people who have been fighting so fervently for his release? Will they recognize him for what he really is—a boy in a man's body? A coward masquerading as a hero?

Or have they all been brainwashed? When the video is broadcast, will there be one person, one person who has not been told how important Lior is supposed to be? Will that one person see the truth—that Lior is nobody, that Lior is naked?

52

Jerusalem
Passover 306 BCE

THE PASSOVER FESTIVITIES WILL NOT be diminished by the politics in Jerusalem. The average pilgrim has no idea what is taking place among the governing elite of the sages, priests and Greeks. Passover is a time to celebrate with family and pray to the God of Israel for a year of health and prosperity. Proximity to the temple is universally recognized as a good omen. People really don't care which priestly family leads the service or how the biblical ritual is interpreted. The common worshipper wants to know that his or her family will be safe and that they will have enough to eat in the forthcoming year.

Shamashim distribute leaflets to the people on how to celebrate the mandated Passover meal and how to fulfill the biblical commandment to retell the story of the Exodus. Simon is given a copy. On the top of the leaflet are the words *Pesach Symposia* (in Greek) / *Haggadah* (in Hebrew). The leaflets recommend household heads encourage the young to ask questions in the Socratic tradition so that the story will be told to an attentive audience. Various parts of the meal are given symbolic meaning to solicit participation and interest from a youth that feels disenfranchised from religion. The leaflet reads:

> Green vegetables represent the spring season, while the bitter herbs are a reminder of the slavery and suffering of our ancestors.
>
> Include all your children in the discussion, even the simple son, or the wicked son, and especially the one who doesn't know how to ask questions.
>
> Drink four glasses of wine, each representing a different aspect of our ancestors' redemption, and drink the wine while reclining, resembling a free man in a free society.

While this doesn't resemble the way Simon has been observing the festive Passover meal, he does not protest.

"Very nice, a sign of the times. People need structure to commemorate such an important event," he whispers to Yochanan and those around him. "But why the Greek language?" He is especially disturbed by the last word on the page, *EfiKomos*, which means "after the meal." The law mandates that the last food consumed be the Paschal lamb.

"Saying it in Hebrew would suffice, no?" Simon asks.

"The young generation is raised with the Greek language, your excellency. This is what they understand," one of the Shamashim replies.

"I understand, I understand," Simon waves his arm.

The children and all the guests at Simon's table have a copy of the leaflet. This is quite a testament to the Shamashim who distributed them.

The brothers-in-law urge Simon to welcome the new traditions. "They are more inclusive and entertaining. The entire family will enjoy the ritual more, as will all the guests."

"There is much we can learn from the Hellenists," says Malka's nephew. "They know how to enjoy a good meal with everyone taking part—why not introduce some of their ways into our homes? It's harmless, really. We will observe the ritual and we will make everyone feel included!"

Malka nods. "As long as Simon will have the opportunity to recite the blessing over the wine, as well as the blessings over the Matzah and the Marror," she says, "and he will read the verses of the Exodus in Hebrew, then you can do what you like."

Everyone is in agreement. The guests arrive dressed in their finest clothes. The tables are set with ample cushions for the adult men and women to sit comfortably. Children sit around their own table and on their parents' laps. The food is exquisite, the wine plentiful and the date beer a huge success. The evening is filled with song and dance, the recitation of prayers and blessings. The biblical verses are not only read but also amplified with creative interpretations. The Greek words and translations sprinkled throughout the evening are a bit jarring to Simon and Yochanan, but they do not let that spoil their night. Children are given the opportunity to ask questions, while the adults discuss ancient texts as well as contemporary politics. The general consensus is that the Passover Seder is beautiful but too long.

"Three crowns," Simon begins, "were given to the Jewish people. The Crown of Torah, the Crown of Priesthood and the Crown of Royalty. And the crown of a good name exceeds them all."

"You yourself wear all of those crowns," Malka's brother, Rachamim, announces.

"My days are numbered," Simon says. Simon's voice is faint but audible to all who are present.

Malka looks at Simon with troubled eyes. "Hush. Don't talk that way."

"They are. I know it, and that is fine. I will not return to Chashmona," he says. Everyone begins to clap. "We need you here, Simon," someone shouts from the back of the room, "Jerusalem needs you now more than ever."

"I thank the almighty for the many blessings this lifetime has brought. None are more precious to me than my family," Simon continues. "I am honored to have served my God and my people. Like Nechemiah the Prophet, I can only pray that I be judged favorably in the courts of heaven and in the courts of history on this earth."

"Please, Yochanan, my son. Take me to my room. I need to sleep now." Yochanan immediately stands up, holds Simon's right arm and walks along his side.

They have barely exited the dining hall when Simon begins speaking in an urgent voice, "My son, your legacy will be my defense-witness in the

Lord's courtroom in heaven, a courtroom where I will soon be on trial. I will be judged for the choices I have made. Now, listen to me carefully." Simon is out of breath. His desire to speak his mind makes him restless.

"I know you want to marry Hanah of Chashmona. I approve. I canceled all plans of your engagement to the daughter of Oshia the Sage. It was a bad idea to begin with. Immediately after the festival, return to Modi'in, marry Hanah and settle there."

"No, Father, I will stay here with you."

"You will do as I say and return to Modi'in. Jerusalem is not for you. Listen carefully—I know I am dying. It is not my days but my hours that are numbered."

"Why do you speak this way, Father?"

"I was in the temple yesterday. The *Bet Hamikdash* is my second home. I have been a welcome guest in the Lord's presence for over forty years. Yesterday, for the first time, I did not feel welcome. I saw darkness and I experienced death. My entire life, the sanctuary has been a place of light, beauty, comfort and life. Yesterday, it was the angel of death that greeted me."

"Father, it is the wine that speaks tonight."

"No! I know what I say. You must listen to my every word. Your destiny is to restore order to our people and protect the laws of Moses and the honor of our God. Promise me, Yochanan, you will not stay in Jerusalem."

"But, Father..."

"Promise me now!"

"I promise."

"Take this, Yochanan. It belonged to your mother and it was left with me after she died." Simon places the silver eagle in his son's hand. Simon thinks of the young midwife and how she trembled with fear when she gave him the charm. The little silver idol remained a constant reminder throughout Simon's life that everything is not as it appears. Simon looks into his son's eyes, and his mind goes to Alexander the mighty warrior who was denied the dignity of death on the battlefield. Instead, messengers reported that he died at a young age, weakened and frail from fever, at the hands of God. The high priest's promise and blessing to the warrior was in vain—it never materialized. The great warrior barely made it to the shores of Egypt.

Simon reaches for Yochanan's hand and he thinks of Yael, the beautiful young girl he saved from the jaws of the enemy. How she was taken, violated by barbarians, but died while giving birth to the object of her greatest love. Simon harnesses the little strength that remains in his body. "Yochanan, you are my son by virtue of the most powerful forces in this world. You are my son."

"Yes, Father, of course." Yochanan takes the silver eagle and stares at it, perplexed. "Father, let me take you to your room. You need to rest."

That night, Simon dies in his sleep.

Some say it was a coincidence while others say it was divine, but the night that Simon passed away, the westernmost lamp of the temple that is always lit was blown out by an unexpected wind. It remained unlit for several days...

53

Jerusalem
City Square
306 BCE

YOCHANAN IS COMPLETELY DISTRAUGHT. HE cannot stop staring at the still body wrapped in a clean, pure white cloth. *He was once a towering figure,* Yochanan thinks, *who is now reduced to a lifeless, wilted sack.* While alive, Simon's long legs made him look clumsy, and yet he never stumbled. He carried himself with dignity and poise. *What happened,* Yochanan wonders, *to Father's sweet smile? It always found its way through his thick white facial hairs. What happened to his warm eyes?*

Thousands of people gather to pay their respects. People clamor at the square leading to the entrance of the Western Gates to be close to the podium and the lifeless body. The corpse lies on a slab of stone. Gamliel HaKohen, the eldest living priest whose reverence was earned by his age as well as his piety, is helped to the podium. The enormous crowd is silent. The fragile Gamliel HaKohen speaks in a hushed voice right next to a stout middle-aged man who belts out the sage's words from the Book of Psalms.

Protect me, O God, for I seek refuge in You.

I say to the Lord, You are my Lord, my protector, there is none above You.

I bless the Lord who has guided me, my conscience admonishes me at night.

I am ever mindful of the Lord's presence.

He is at my right hand, I shall never be shaken.

So my heart rejoices, my whole being exults, and my body rests secure.

For You will not abandon me to Sheol or let Your faithful one see the pit.

You will teach me the path of life.

In Your presence is perfect joy.

Wailers are commissioned for the funeral. They can be heard off to the side, bawling, weeping and crying in their high-pitched voices. *How odd*, Yochanan thinks, *why are we paying them to cry? This is the saddest day of my life.*

Gamliel is helped off the pedestal and Antignos emerges from the crowd to speak.

"Our glory has departed," he begins, "and the sun that warmed our very lives and illuminated our path has set, and we shiver in the cold and in the dark." Antignos is not known for his poetic abilities, but his words flow in rhythmical syntax. "We basked in all that glory... in his glory. The man, the prophet of our day—Messiah of the divine. We praise him and our words seem small. Praise of him signals our very existence. For him, no monument of bronze nor marble can pair with the heavenly fire he has enshrined in the hearts of his people.

"He graced the Lord's home, our Bet HaMikdash, with honor, represented us before the God of God's, creator of heaven and earth. If not for his piety, stature and wisdom, we would be naught.

"He was as comfortable with dignitaries and sages as he was with the lowly commoner. He celebrated with those in joy and suffered with the aggrieved. To praise such a man, we are not worthy. Words fail us at a time like this.

"He is the last of our links to the glorious past—to those who lived among the Prophets of Israel. Look at us. We are here in such large numbers, thanks to him. He unified us in his lifetime, and he unifies us in his death. He was our guide and our protector. He faced down the Lion of Greece and spared our lives. We owe it to him to live up to what he had hoped for his people.

"He had his share of suffering, but his tender face never lost its smile and he never spoke a harsh word to anyone. Generations from now will look back on this time and recognize that there once was a glory and it is no more. We did not recognize it as it walked in our midst. At the moment, we are in the dark and in the cold. In ages to come, we will be given undeserved merit for having lived along his side, for having some worth of being born in his generation.

"We have always known him as Simon the High Priest. From here on, he will be remembered as Shimon HaTzadik, Simon the Righteous."

The crowd is motionless. They attentively soak in every one of the sage's words. Yochanan is in a daze. Malka kneels alongside the corpse, looks over at Yochanan and places her hand on his. It has been years since he has last had any physical contact with Malka. Yochanan welcomes the touch. It feels comforting despite its ephemerality.

Suddenly, two bearded men lift him to his feet. One of the men whispers in Yochanan's ear, "In accordance with the Law of Moses, you will now tear your garment as an act of public grief."

The other man begins reciting the words, "Blessed is the Lord, God, whose decree is just." Yochanan grabs the collar of his tunic with both hands and, as he tears his clothing, he looks toward the sky and a guttural painful howl emerges from his vocal chords. The onlookers start bawling. The pallbearers reach for the bier and lift the body on their shoulders. The crowd systematically begins to position itself behind and alongside the bier, opening a direct path toward the western gate of Jerusalem.

Antignos recalls the last time Simon walked out this gate with the destiny of the entire Jewish people on his shoulders. *Simon never boasted about his encounter with the powerful general, Alexander the Great. He never even spoke of it. Whatever transpired on that summer morning goes to the grave with him*, he thinks.

The wailers wail, the Levites recite the appropriate psalms, and thousands escort Simon to his final resting place. Meanwhile, foreign soldiers in Greek armor line the top of the walls around the city and position themselves strategically to ensure the city's safety.

Gaza City, Gaza Strip
July 2010

A S NIGHT FALLS OVER GAZA, the air reeks of gunpowder from the repeated gunfire celebrating the release of the remaining 497 prisoners. Tens of thousands gather in Gaza City's central square to welcome home their prisoners. For Israel, the men being released are terrorists whose murderous campaigns are responsible for hundreds of Israeli lives. While the Palestinians of Gaza celebrate their victory, Israel's somber response does not detract from the overwhelming support for the release of Lior Samet.

Pandemonium breaks out as the first busses carrying freed prisoners arrives in Katiba Square. Faisal watches the celebration from a distant rooftop. He prohibits his wife and children from attending the celebration, but they go anyway. "Are you with us or are you with the terrorist Zionist state?" his brother-in-law asks in a demeaning manner.

Faisal can hear the fireworks being set off as huge speakers blast patriotic Hamas songs. He can see the prisoners getting off the bus as crowds wave green Hamas flags and yellow Fatah party flags. Once off the bus, the men are led into the mosque on the southern side of the square. From his vantage point, Faisal can see the masked armed Hamas security guards on rooftops overlooking the crowds and the sky.

Faisal understands enough about local politics to recognize that this prisoner swap is a success for Hamas and will significantly weaken the more moderate Fatah and its leader, Mahmoud Abbas. He will never dare speak publically about the promises broken by Hamas or the party's reputation for corruption, let alone its reign of terror on its people. He knows that, if the opportunity presents itself, he will vote for Fatah to govern Gaza.

Inside the mosque, the head of the Popular Resistance Committee, Hamas's militant group leader, Abu Mujahid, vows to capture more Israeli prisoners and release the more than 4,000 other freedom fighters in Israeli prisons. "We are going to cleanse all Israeli prisons of our men and women."

Faisal can hear the Sheikh's voice on the loudspeakers: "My brothers and sisters, your families here in Palestinian territories and around the world are looking at you. We are happy for your release. Your efforts have not been in vain. You have sacrificed and fought and paid a heavy price, but you will see the results of our struggle—an independent State of Palestine with Jerusalem as its capital." The ecstatic crowd cheers and chants while gunshots of jubilation blast the night sky.

In Israel, all kinds of information and misinformation trickle through the media. People are glued to their televisions and computers. Reporters are questioning people on the streets of Tel Aviv:

"What do you think of Netanyahu's bold decision to exchange one soldier for over 1,000 terrorists?"

Her name is Ella, and she responds right into the camera, "Bringing our soldiers home alive should be our government's highest priority." Every television station and radio station in Israel is reporting the events of Lior's release live. Some report that the exchange is being held up because two female Palestinian prisoners refuse to be deported to Gaza.

Leon waits at Tel Nof Airbase, while Maya, Avigdor and immediate family listen to reports from their home in Dimona. "Lior has been handed over to the Egyptians through the Rafah crossing but will not be released to the Israelis until all the Palestinian prisoners are freed," the anchorman reports. The moment-to-moment reporting only amplifies the sense of suspense and anticipation.

Lior knows he is a pawn. Being moved from place to place. He says nothing at all. He feels sick on the helicopter ride to Tel Nof. The attending military doctor diagnoses him as suffering from malnutrition and seasonal affective disorder due to a lack of sunlight over an extended period of time. The doctor is heard on the radio suggesting that everything should go as planned. Lior is deemed fit enough not to have to go straight to the hospital. His frailty magnifies an irony that is not lost in the media: "The quiet, bookish Lior Samet was the one seized. He never wanted to bother anyone, not even a fly. The boy who sought peace and tranquility has been at the center of political and ethical debates throughout the world."

It all happened quite fast. The entire flight to Tel Nof, Lior tries to put the pieces together. Remembering the details feels very important right now.

It was like Faisal was more surprised than Lior. Four masked men charged into the room with Faisal trailing behind them. He was yelling something about his not having received orders directly from his superiors. "You are coming with us," one of the men shouted.

That morning, Lior woke up feeling faint. It could have been because of the food, but it was probably because of the news from the night before. He had heard repeatedly: "**The release of Sgt. Lior Samet is imminent.**"

Are they talking about me? Lior kept wondering. *Release to whom? Where will I be taken?* A part of him understood that the media was obviously speaking about him, and yet, he wondered whether the person they were speaking about on the radio may actually be someone else, or maybe just entertainment, or possibly people trying to make news.

When the men entered the room, it was an invasion of his space. They immediately put a black cloth bag over Lior's head and escorted him down the stairs into what seemed to be a large vehicle. In what must have been a pathetic scene, Lior turned to the back of the room. "Faisal, are you coming with me?" He didn't fully understand why he asked that question.

He remembers thinking, *Are they taking me to my death or am I really going home?* That thought caused an all too familiar feeling. He tried to stay calm and collected. He repeated to himself: *Take a deep breath. Think about something positive. What was the last conversation I had with Faisal? Shit, what will happen to Faisal? I hope they don't hurt him. Why am I so upset?*

The car ride was short.

He was escorted by what seemed like a lot of people. The black sack that covered his head was removed. He found himself in a locker room. He was told to sit down. It all seemed so surreal. An elderly man wearing a kaftan and turban unpacked a comb, scissors and a shaver. After the grooming, Lior was then given a white towel and soap and told to shower. He moved cautiously because armed men carefully watched his every move. He was given a dress shirt. It looked more like a cowboy shirt from an old American Western movie. It had a multi-colored collar with a plaid design. The pair of slacks were not much better. He looked at the clothing, thinking that he would never have chosen this for himself.

It seemed like everyone around him was speaking in loud and stressed tones. Again he was put into the back of an SUV. The drive felt horribly long, but at least he did not have the sack over his head. The evening air was dry. He could see a dirt road ahead and lights in the distance. "Get out," yelled the masked man next to him. Another spoke loudly into a cell phone. They moved quickly.

Before he knew it, he was being spoken to in a gentle voice: "How are you, Lior? You are on your way home." These words hung in the evening air.

"Where are am I?" were the first words Lior uttered.

"In Egypt," a nice lady answered, "for now. We need to ask you a few questions. Please, follow us."

The bright lights, camera and armed men made Lior feel very uncomfortable. Completely exposed. He had not felt this uncomfortable since eighth grade when he was caught peeking into the girls' locker room and had to get a note signed by his mother that he had done so. He did the best he could answering the woman's questions. Lior later found out that the entire episode was broadcasted live worldwide. He remembers being there but does not remember even one question.

Lior tries so hard to recall the events leading up to his interview with the Egyptian anchorwoman, but most of it is a blur. By the time he is handed over to Israeli authorities, it is pitch-black outside. He has a hard time breathing and feels nauseated.

He is happy to see Israelis in uniforms with weapons. The Israelis are cautious but courteous. He is quickly taken to a trailer and asked whether he is ready to see his family or if maybe he needs time alone. "Please take me home."

He is asked to undress in front of a whole lot of people. Someone hands him a freshly pressed IDF uniform, but then takes it back and hands him another uniform. "This one is too big. Here, try this one."

Right before he walks out the door of the trailer, a man in a beige IDF uniform walks in and announces, "Lior, you are on your way home." The kind man asks Lior a few questions: "What is your full name? What is your rank? What is your father's first name? What is your mother's first name? How many siblings do you have? What is her name? What city do you live in? What street do you live on? Do you remember the national anthem? Can you please sing it for me? What time is it?"

Lior is stumped. "I have no idea what time it is."

The nice man hands Lior a watch and says, "Welcome home, young man." Lior is surprised. The interrogation ends. He looks at the watch. It is 10 p.m. Time has been lost. It's been more than four years. There is no watch that measures days, weeks, months and years. He puts it on his wrist as he is escorted out the makeshift trailer rooms.

He can see his father from a distance. They walk toward each other, the roar of the helicopter engine tuning everything else out. He is focused on his father when the prime minister and a bunch of other important people extend their hands to greet him. The little energy left in him remains fixated on his father's grin. They finally embrace while heading to the helicopter. Lior is exhausted. *I want to get home*, he thinks.

Takeoff is quick. The flight does not feel long. The helicopter flies low through the city square of Dimona so that Lior can see the thousands of people waving the Israeli flag, singing and dancing on the streets. Leon leans over to Lior and says, "They are all here for you." Lior cannot hear a thing.

He is escorted from the helicopter into a white car. He sits with his father in the back seat. He hears sirens. "We will be home in a few moments," Leon says. The motorcade weaves through hordes of people. If not for the countless people who line the streets of the motorcade, Lior might be able to recognize the neighborhood. People of all ages wave flags and shower white flowers upon the convoy. The faces of people cheering and singing seem absurd.

The car finally stops in front of his home. As he steps out of the car, he hears his name being chanted while bodyguards lead him right into the house. His sister and grandparents are impatiently waiting outside the front door. He knows that his mother is waiting for him inside as she always has. Lior stops and kisses Noa and his grandmother, then hugs his grandfather, Brigadier General Avigdor Cohen. He steps into the home and whispers, "Ima." He immediately falls into his mother's arms and, for the first time in as long as he can remember, he begins to cry.

"What have they done to you?" She asks.

Who is she talking about? Lior wonders.

Outside the home, Leon addresses the crowd. "I want to thank the Israeli government and the prime minister of Israel, as well as all the local and national activists who did not forget Lior. I want to especially thank my father-in-law, Avigdor Cohen, for his tireless and courageous efforts in bringing Lior home." He continues, "Lior, while happy to be home, is unable to be with large crowds of people. It's been a long time since he has communicated with people. It will be a long process of rehabilitation before he can get on with his life as normal. Today, we come to the end of a long journey. Today, we have gone through a second birth of our son, Lior. I want the people of our country to know that, even for us, this deal is not easy. I cried with many of the bereaved families with whom I have met over the last few months. Maya and I understand the price they are paying for Lior's freedom. I hope all of you, especially the media, will understand and let us get on with our lives."

"What was the first thing you told your Lior?" a reporter shouts from the crowd.

"I didn't say much—I just hugged him and welcomed him home."

Reporters try to question Leon. He quickly turns around and enters his home. The crowd does not disperse. A reporter looking for a newsworthy quote stops a woman on the street. "Excuse me, what is your name?"

"Gila Drori."

"Do you know Lior Samet?"

"Yes, of course, he was my student in the high school."

"What can you tell me about Lior?"

"He was always a quiet and shy boy. He focused on his studies mainly."

"When was the last time you saw him?"

"A few months before his abduction. I saw him hitchhiking home from his base. I believe it was during Hanukkah."

Moshiko and Moran decide to watch the unfolding events from her father's flat-screen television. They worked so hard on the campaign and feel like they should enjoy their success privately.

For the first time since the start of the "Bring Lior Home" campaign, Moran realizes what it means to release 1,000 terrorists. She had passionately debated countless people, unable to see anything but the position that Lior had to be brought home no matter the price. *What if it was a terrorist who killed a member of my family that was being released? Would I celebrate or mourn tonight?* Moran thinks.

She found the prime minister's words comforting. He acknowledged how difficult a decision it was to make the exchange. "Here in the State of Israel, we do not celebrate murderers and turn them into heroes. For us, life is sacred. All of Israel is tonight united in happiness and pain."

Those last words make Moran cry. She looks at Moshiko and says, "It all feels so strange."

55

Modi'in City
Chashmona Region
301 BCE

THE MIDWIVES SPRING INTO ACTION, remove the young lady's clothes and lay her down on the dried weed-filled mattress. Her eyes clench shut as she dreads the onset of the next contraction. She tries to concentrate on the psalms the young girls are chanting in the back of the room. "Make this stop, please," she screams.

Suddenly, the overwhelming urge to push overtakes her. She bears down.

"It will be over very soon," one midwife says in the most soothing way possible. "You are young and healthy. The baby is in an ideal position. Everything will be fine."

"It's a boy," the elderly nurse says, "a big boy, my dear. May the Lord of Israel heal your wounds and bless this child." She places the child on Hanah's breast.

The good news has yet to reach Yochanan while he sits with the young zealots of the Maccabee forces, the sages and leaders who have arrived from Jerusalem and all over Judea.

"The Hellenists target the rich and the noble. Our people are bribed when they are not being threatened. The Hellenists have only disdain for the Law of Moses and for our religious beliefs. They speak of freedom but do not practice it." Yoav is emphatic while speaking.

Gamliel, a young activist and dedicated follower of Yochanan, asks to speak. "Our people have no backbone. The richer they are, the faster they fall prey to the hedonistic ways."

"Yochanan," Rabbi Yehuda from Jerusalem interjects, "they place more value on lowered taxes than they place on preserving the sanctity of the temple. Power is bartered for cheap. The priesthood is given over to the most assimilated of the descendants of Aaron HaKohen."

"Your excellency, may the Lord be my witness, and may the Almighty forgive the report I bring to you," Shabtai, a young zealot from Judea, says. "Just last new moon, the high priest attended a match at the gymnasium in Jerusalem—on the Sabbath! God protect us."

"On the Sabbath?" Yochanan questions with disdain and anger in his voice. His mind is spinning from the news.

"Yes, your excellency, on the Sabbath."

"The Lord have mercy on us," is muttered by one after another.

"This is a battle that we have not prepared ourselves to fight. If only the enemy would attack us physically, then we would know how to respond. Instead they assault us where we are weakest."

As those words linger, a young messenger from the Talmud Academy comes running in. "The Lord, God of Israel, has granted you and your wife a third healthy son, Yochanan, High Priest of Chashmona. May the child be blessed and his parents as well."

Yochanan looks up in disbelief. He stands up, raises his fists in the air and in his bellicose voice calls out, *Hodu l'adonai ki tov. Ki le'Olam chasdo.* Bless the Lord for His goodness. His kindness is everlasting."

Yochanan saddles his horse in one jump and races to Hanah's side. As he rides into town, Simon, his eldest son who just turned 6, calls out, "Father, it's a boy. Another boy in our family." He latches on to his father's leg as he rides by and hangs in midair as Yochanan heads to the birthing home.

Once there, Yochanan looks tenderly into Hannah's eyes. "I did not know I could love you more than I did yesterday. But I do. Tell me, how do you feel?"

"You do not care to ask about your son?" Hannah asks as the mid-wife runs a cloth over her sweat-drenched face.

"My son will be fine. He is strong and healthy. Right now I care only about you." His tender words are uttered in contrast to his rough and clumsy demeanor.

Eight days later, Yochanan holds up a sharpened blade with which he will remove the foreskin of his newborn son. He looks over at Malka. She is aged and frail. She chose to come back to Chashmona and live her last days in the north. Yochanan never asked her why.

He thinks of his birth mother, the mother he never knew. Clyto-medes, the stable foreman, swears on all the gods of Greece that the silver eagle around Yochanan's neck was worn by Alexander the Great himself. The thought intrigues Yochanan and always brings a smile to his face.

He thinks of the many lessons he learned from Simon, his father, and the many teachings they disagreed upon. He loved his father, but Natan the Pious is his teacher. Yochanan regrets his father never bequesting the high priesthood of Jerusalem. He has to let go. The priesthood is something he will never assume. They call him the High Priest of Chashmona, but the temple is in Jerusalem. He welcomes the title, but he understands deep down that the silver eagle and the Maccabee forces represent a completely different world than the priestly garments represent today.

Yochanan closes his eyes and he prays for the men he is training for a future battle—a battle that he is certain is destined, yet whose time and place is unknown. Yochanan knows that the battle will have to be pro-voked by the enemy; it is just a matter of time.

He opens his eyes, lifts the blade and says, "This morning, I initiate my son into the covenant of Abraham, our forefather. Like Abraham, our forefather, who was prepared to sacrifice his only son for the sake of heaven, I too bring this blade upon my son as an act of sacrifice to the One, creator of heaven and earth. Through this blood, I vow to protect and defend our freedom, the freedom of our people, our law and our land."

Tears begin to swell Yochanan's already heavy beard. "I apologize to you, my newborn son. I bring you into a world that will know war. Be our redeemer and savior. I bless you and name you Matityahu, son of Yochan-an, Kohen Gadol of Chashmona."

56

Dimona, Israel
November 2010

C ANDLES FLICKER IN THE BRIGHTLY lit home.
"Lior, please honor us with the lighting of the Hanukkah candles," Leon, after consulting with Maya, announces. Lior accepts. He does not relish being the center of attention, but declining his father's request seems wrong. Lior reaches over the table, picks up the lit candle and lights all eight remaining candles of the Hanukkah menorah.

The family and guests all join together and sings the words: "*She'asah nisim la'avoteinu bayamim hahem ba'zeman hazeh.*" And the Lord did miracles to our forefather in the days past and today.

For a moment, Lior experiences déjà vu. The last four years seem like a troubling dream. He looks around the room and thinks, *At least one thing has changed since my "leave-of-absence." Mother has always insisted that Hanukkah be a private time for our family. This year, mother invited everybody. Even Moran and her fiancée, Moshiko, made it on the invite list.*

Lior actually mustered the courage to say hello to Moran, or maybe she said hello to him first. It was awkward. While they were in high school, she did everything in her power to avoid him, and now he is an international

311

celebrity, if a reluctant celebrity. *If she only knew,* Lior thinks, *how many countless hours I thought of her—the many memories of her tender face and her light brown hair. She campaigned for my release and kept my spirit animated throughout my captivity.* He, of course, will never reveal this to her.

"Hi, Lior."

"Hi, Moran."

"Thank you."

"No, thank you!"

"Congratulations."

"Congratulations to you!"

"I really like your parents and grandparents. I especially got to know Noa, and she is so sweet."

"Yes."

"Good Luck."

"Sababa." That was their conversation.

Benny Bitton, the eager mayor of Dimona, is frustrated that more media is not covering this event. He likes the company, but media would make it worth his time. *How quickly the media forgets,* he thinks. *The country was obsessed with this kid for four years. Now that he's home, no one gives a shit.*

"So what's next for you, Lior?" a well-wisher asks.

"I… I don't know," is about all he can suggest right now.

The room is buzzing with the news of the arrest of Shmuel Markowitz, the man who defaced the Yitzchak Rabin memorial in Tel Aviv with the words, "Free Yigal Amir." Yigal Amir, the extremist right-wing fanatic who murdered Yitzchak Rabin in cold blood for negotiating a peace agreement with Yasser Arafat, is in prison for life. Shmuel Markowitz's parents and three siblings were killed in the Sbarro restaurant suicide bombing in the heart of Jerusalem in 2001. As part of the Samet deal, two terrorists associated with the Sbarro massacre were released.

"He has no business equating Lior's release with Yigal Amir."

"Agreed, he is completely insensitive and inappropriate."

"Don't be so judgmental, the terrorists who murdered his family have just been released. That cannot feel good."

"Did you hear that Markowitz's only sibling, his sister, has vowed to release her brother from prison, relinquish her Israeli passport and move to the Netherlands?"

Leon and Maya are relieved the ordeal is over. While the phone calls continue, they are different. Now people want to meet Lior. News stations are trying to get exclusive interviews. Maya knows this attention is not for her son. Leon wishes his son would be more articulate and more interested in public life. "Lior should use the notoriety."

Leon becomes explosive when he thinks of the exploitative and insensitive interview by the state-owned Egyptian TV network. He later found out that, immediately following Lior's release at the hands of Hamas brokers, the Egyptians made an interview part of the release deal.

"Those bastards humiliated my son." There are times when the "bastards" are the Israeli negotiators and there are times when the "bastards" are the Egyptians. It depends who Leon is talking to. "Lior appeared so uncomfortable on television. He was being asked questions with armed Hamas militants standing alongside the camera. He was terrified. He could barely get the words out of his mouth. How could they be so callous, those Israeli negotiators who knew about the interview but did not intervene? It was a circus."

The Israeli press called the interview "amateurish, propagandistic and opportunistic." Avigdor Cohen called it downright cruel.

Lior made light of the whole "interview affair."

"I was distracted during the entire interview because she was the first woman I saw in a few years," he liked to say to those who asked.

"Leon why don't you go into politics and fix the damn system?" One of his friends suggests.

"Don't do it," another voice advises. "Politics is like a big whale, you get swallowed up in it and never come out."

"You have zero experience and no clue how to begin," another chimes in.

"You have to admit though, he is good, really good in front of the camera."

Maya wants nothing to do with it. "I will not have it at all. I want my old life back, and that means staying as far away from the spotlight as possible."

Lior is still processing all of this. Over the last four years, he has spent a great deal of time in his head and with his companion the transistor radio. He also felt as if he was just getting to know Faisal. It turns out it wasn't his real name—or at least that's what the Shin Bet debriefers have told him.

Not much has changed in four years in Dimona. Why has all of this happened to me? Why do we have to be at war?

Everyone in Israel, even the most liberal, were terribly offended when the Egyptian anchorwoman asked Lior if he would help release the more than 4,000 Palestinians in Israeli prisons. Lior actually took the question earnestly. *The last four years have given me an opportunity to think about a perspective that is disturbing. The only change I can make is to myself. That is what I will do,* he thinks.

"I am sorry to interrupt the festivity, but I have some business to address with you, young man," Mayor Bitton announces in a loud voice. The room is all-ears, which is exactly what Bitton wanted. "Tomorrow, we are unveiling the picture of you being greeted by the prime minister and your father at the Tel Nof Airbase. It will be displayed prominently in city hall."

Lior nods. "I'll be there." He remembers the moment very well. He felt faint but glad to be on Israeli territory and surrounded by men and women in Israeli uniform. He too was in uniform. They asked him to change on the plane. Even the second pair of khaki military pants were too big, but he was able to tighten the belt and move the excess waistline to the back. He could not be that creative with the green shirt. He put it on; it smelled fresh and felt clean. He proudly placed the dark gray Armored Brigade beret over his left shoulder. He wasn't part of the Armored Brigade, but he wasn't going to complain now. The gray beret actually stirred memories of growing up with books and images of Israeli tanks. His grandfather collected all images, magazines and books that had to do with the Israeli Armored Brigade. He often wondered why he himself did not join the brigade. His physical condition wasn't so great, and he certainly wasn't as motivated as some of the other guys. It was the right choice. He would never want to live in the shadow of his grandfather.

He remembers how, as soon as he stepped off the plane, he saw a broad-shouldered middle-aged man. "This is our prime minister, the honorable Benjamin Netanyahu." Lior immediately saluted the prime minister. Netanyahu stepped forward and gave him a big hug.

He looked at his father over the prime minister's shoulder. He is not sure why but he felt embarrassed. "Shalom, Abba!"

His father put out his arms and Lior just fell into them. "I missed you, my son."

"I missed you too."

Funny how he remembers that first encounter better than the first time he saw his mother. He actually had a chance to speak with her on the phone for a very short time just after he was handed over to the Israelis. Listening to her voice was like warm milk for the soul. All he had to say was, "Sababa, Ima, all is good. I'll see you soon," and she was comforted.

He could hear her crying over the phone. Between the deep breaths, she kept saying, "*Toda La'el*, Thank God." The first time he saw her, he was overwhelmed. He was flown to Dimona by helicopter and then driven in a big fancy car, a Range Rover. Hundreds, if not thousands, of people greeted him outside his home, waving Israeli flags and singing *Hevenu Shalom Aleichem*. It was strange—all the attention.

That's when he first saw his mother. It was like seeing her for the first time ever. He noticed things on her face and hands that he never knew were there. She was soft and gentle. He cried on her shoulder for a long time. Noa joined the hug and then—it seemed like life just went on.

Avigdor Cohen cannot help but second-guess himself. Would he have supported such a prisoner exchange had it been someone else's grandson? More than 1,000 terrorists were freed in order to bring his grandson home. Among them were the likes of Walid Abd al-Aziz, who was sentenced to thirty-six life sentences for his part in the Cafe Moment bombing in 2002 at the Hebrew University. Combined, these terrorists are responsible for the deaths of 569 Israelis.

Netanyahu said it best: "Today we are all united in joy and in pain." No words could better describe what Avigdor Cohen is feeling.

Hamas celebrated the deal as a victory and vowed "more abductions until all Israeli prisons are free of Palestinian freedom fighters." Other Arab nations congratulated Hamas on their victory. All of this enraged Cohen.

Soldiers are not abducted. The thought nauseates him. Cohen would never have allowed himself to be taken alive. *How outdated these thoughts are.*

Oren, who has recently found his religious calling, is animated as he preaches in a loud voice, "The few fought off the many and the weak overran the strong, while the righteous destroyed the wicked." Maya has invited him to the Hanukkah party despite his inability to set physical and social boundaries, not only because he is her sister-in-law's only son, but because he has called every week for the last four years asking about Lior's well-being while reporting on the countless Kabbalistic rabbis who were praying on her behalf. His eyes suggest he is talking to one or two people, but his voice is clearly directed at the entire room. He wears a large white knitted yarmulke that covers most of his buzz-cut head and has the word *NACHMAN* boldly crocheted on it. "Judah son of Matityahu the Maccabee was a great warrior! He single-handedly fought off the massive armies of the enemy. He saved the Jewish people from utter destruction. Rabbi Nachman writes that we all have that warrior spark within us that is charged by living life with utter joy!"

It is unclear if those listening to Oren are really interested or are actually egging him on as a comic relief between drinks and more relevant conversations. He is an easy target and a convenient example for everything that is wrong with religion.

"Why is every story in our history about us fighting wars?" asks one of the bystanders.

"No," responds Oren, "we don't fight our wars—God fights them for us." His message is amplified by his voice and swinging arms.

"So why did we need Judah the Maccabee? Why didn't God come down from heaven and fight the fight? Why bloody human hands?" another asks while rolling his eyes, smirking to the bystanders.

Oren's entire education of Jewish thought consists of a weekly ten-minute lecture by someone who calls himself a prophet. He also reads thin pamphlets full of exclamation marks presumably written by the Rabbi Nachman, and yet he has an answer for every question. "Rav Nachman says God fights our wars, but we have to show our trust in God by not being afraid. Fear is what cripples us. No fear. That is what Rav Nachman teaches. The entire world is one long, narrow bridge and we must not be afraid to cross that bridge."

"So why glorify the warrior? What do we know about Judah as a man?"

Brigadier General Avigdor Cohen listens to the conversation. He has always had a fascination for the Maccabee family of priests who fought off the oppressive Greek empire and returned autonomy to the State of Israel 2,200 years ago.

"What he did in battle is not who he was as a man and as a leader," he mutters to himself, then says in a louder voice, "that's not who he was."

Why he says anything at all baffles him. Cohen is very much to himself the entire evening.

He is standing alongside the shiny silver menorah, holding his Jack Daniel's on the rocks. The room turns silent. His words linger and all of a sudden, Oren's preaching seems irrelevant. Within seconds, people in the room start chanting "speech, speech!" The mantra moves across the room like a wave that begins with a ripple and ends up a tsunami. Something about the way he just stands there, alone, intrigues the crowd.

He surprised himself with how well he is handling the liquor. Usually it only takes about two drinks before he is standing on a table singing old kibbutz tunes. Tonight it will be others singing on tables. The celebration of Lior's release also marks the demise of Cohen's most passionate beliefs.

"War does not define a man," he says in a barely audible rasp as he looks at the flickering flames dancing on their oil-fueled wicks. "These flames represent hope in the face of the impossible," he says. "A tiny jug of oil," Cohen lifts his eyes, "that was supposed to last just one day, lasted eight days. Isn't that what the Hanukkah legend is about?"

Everyone who knows him knows that he often jokes that his fighting spirit is no doubt a trait in the DNA he carries from the warrior-priests of old. Tonight he wonders how odd it is that the Jewish people, heir to a peaceful tradition, are always thrown into battle.

Cohen isn't in a good place.

"War does not define the man or his family or his faith," he says. It is not so much that the faith upon which his world operates has been systematically rejected, but that, at a certain point, its entire foundation had simply collapsed. The world of politics and hierarchy that had once been thick with symbols and promises, cemented obligations, and redemptive aspirations is suddenly gone. What Cohen has lost, even if it is no longer tenable, is also no longer replaceable. This absolute collapse of every link with which he has engaged his world is deepened by the loneliness that has resulted from his break with the country, and with destiny.

"War is something that is flung upon us and fueled by our own twisted fantasy of that which is gallant and moral."

Cohen holds up his glass and all eyes across the room are upon him. He realizes that, over the last four years, very few people if any at all, really trusted him and his judgment. He always thought he projected confidence. Now he knows better. The right to project confidence, he now recognizes, has to be earned. *This is now so obvious. Why did it take me so long to get it?*

"Welcome home, Lior. I thank God you are safe. To me you are a true hero. Through this ordeal, and I speak only for myself, my entire world was turned upside down. What I believed to be true was actually a dream I created for myself and about myself. The possibility of losing you taught me the grit necessary to fight the real battles—the battles that are fought and won in the heart. You, Lior, not only brought all of us together, you did something remarkable, you united the entire Jewish people around the world who rallied on your behalf. You single-handedly brought much of humanity together, united for a cause that is—that is truly human. We are not about a land or a religion. We are first and foremost people. I'd like to believe that Judah Maccabee would have fought the way he did against tyranny and oppression to defend any and all people from the injustices perpetrated by those who only know hatred.

"There might have been a time when wars were won or lost. It hasn't been so in my lifetime. Wars are fought and fought again. Our enemies don't go away. As difficult as this is to comprehend and believe, this is our reality. We live in the 21st century and we are still fighting over land. It just doesn't make sense!

"My dear Maya, I know I haven't said it. I don't know why I haven't said it. Maybe I've been too busy saying the wrong things. I want you to know how very proud I am of you. You are my only child, and I could not have asked for a better gift in this world. Rachel, we did many great things together, but the best was bringing Maya into this world."

Avi continues. "There is nothing noble in war and certainly not in killing. The title I earned in this world was earned on the battlefield. I don't know what to make of that. The title I am most proud of is that of father and grandfather." Cohen's eyes start to well up.

Leon jumps in: "The title you earned on the battlefield, Avi, makes you father of this entire nation." Everybody begins clapping. Avi, though, doesn't have that warm feeling that comes from being flattered. His soul feels like it is hosting a storm.

The sound of the clapping snaps Lior out of his semi-conscious state of awareness. He doesn't finish the drink he has served himself. He is happy to have the attention diverted from him. He doesn't pay much attention to what his grandfather is saying, though he knows it is important and probably relevant. He just can't concentrate. It seems like life is on everyone's mind. He never gives much thought to living—it just happens. All of a sudden, people are asking him if he has a greater appreciation for life and freedom. He never really considered either of those ideas. He never feared death. He is afraid of pain but not death. Expiring is OK for him. Death is like—you're just not here anymore.

He never really considered freedom either. He doesn't want to even think about it.

He is actually feeling more anxious since his release than he has felt since his capture. *The military therapist said that's normal. She thinks I'm anxious because of the many expectations people have of me, now that I am a national hero.*

Lior thinks it is funny how billboards and buildings throughout Israel have his image hanging on them. Many are updated with a "Welcome Home" sign, while others still call for his return.

The military therapist and everyone else seems really interested in knowing what Lior plans on doing with his life now that he has returned home.

"I have no idea," he responds with a smirk on his face. The truth is that he has actually thought about it quite a bit. *I'll become a radio broadcaster—a disembodied voice that can't be confined.*

Author's Note

The encounter between Alexander the Great and Simon the Righteous is described in Josephus and the Talmud. Those sources were an inspiration for this novel.

Jewish law does not permit a Cohen or Priest to marry a woman who was held captive by the enemy for fear that she was raped. There are some sources, however, that permit a Cohen to marry such a woman if he does not consummate the marriage. The author meant no disrespect to the position of High Priest. This novel is fiction and meant to be thought provoking.

Acknowledgments

Finishing Sababa stirs me to reflect on life and to express a few words of gratitude. I am thankful to all who have helped navigate the many incarnations of my life over the last half-century. Those who are no more among the living their memory is a blessing. To the many friends, teachers, and students who remain steadfast anchors on this journey, I say – let us continue to make every moment count.

Some people standout for their involvement in this particular project and deserve special mention. Susan Astor is my mentor in writing a teacher in living. Her big heart is truly inspiring.

I am grateful to Joy Resmovitz for taking the time to read an early draft of this novel. Her insights and comments gave shape to the initial chaos. A special thank you to Dave Balson, editor at Berwick Court Publishing, for the time, attention and sharp editorial eye he gave this project.

I want to thank Nazy Moinian for believing in this project early on.

Saeed Amirian your trust and your friendship fuel the energy that allows us to do what we do. Joshua Setton there are no words that can express my deepest appreciation to you.

I am especially appreciative to Matt Balson, President of Berwick Court Publishing, for giving Sababa a shot and for expecting excellence.

Finally the gang that makes living a blessing: Amichai, Chana Gila and Zev, Yedidya and Miriam, Hananel, Shira, David, Eliyahu and Olivia thank you.

Afsaneh thank you for the fairytale.

CPSIA information can be obtained
at www.ICGtesting.com
Printed in the USA
BVOW01*1747271016
466120BV00002B/2/P